Reader Rev

'Absolutely bri
The characters felt lik
It felt like home. It will stay with me for a long time'

'Godfrey's writing is nothing short of beautiful'

'Funny, poignant and clever. Brilliant'

'Blew my mind. From the first page of this book,
right until the last page, I was completely obsessed'

'I loved every moment of the story.
The characters warmed my heart'

'Left a lump in my throat and a hole in my heart'

'A book I won't forget for a while'

'A beautiful and emotional debut that I know will
stay with me for a long time'

'A superb look at childhood, at growing up,
at starting to see the world around you'

INSTANT SUNDAY TIMES BESTSELLER

The List of Suspicious Things

'Fabulous. I loved Miv's spirit' *Prima*

'I can't believe this is a debut. Heavy themes handled with such tenderness and care, a moving, memorable tale of community, connection and curiosity. I loved it' **Emma Gannon**

'An extraordinary achievement' **Clare Pooley**

'Pretty sure this will be the book of 2024. Bring tissues' **Joanna Nadin**

'The characters completely burrowed into my heart. It's a warm, funny, huge-hearted book without any twee – it's truthful, carrying a sadness too' **Chloe Timms**

'An astonishing debut written with much talent and tenderness. It sings with humanity' **Amy Twigg**

'Brimming with what it means to be human, this is a book to be savoured and cherished. A book that should be required reading for current and future generations. A once-in-a-lifetime kind of book' **Awais Khan**

'Heartbreaking yet heartwarming, with compassionate characters you can't help but root for, *The List of Suspicious Things* is an unforgettable book on friendship and the power of human connection . . . A splendid debut' **Costanza Casati**

ABOUT THE AUTHOR

Jennie Godfrey was raised in West Yorkshire and her
debut novel, *The List of Suspicious Things*, is inspired by her
childhood there in the 1970s. Jennie is from a mill-working
family, but as the first of the generation born after the
mills closed, she went to university and built a career in
the corporate world. In 2020 she left and began to write.
She is now a writer and part-time Waterstones bookseller
and lives in the Somerset countryside.

The List of Suspicious Things

Jennie Godfrey

PENGUIN BOOKS

PENGUIN BOOKS

UK | USA | Canada | Ireland | Australia
India | New Zealand | South Africa

Penguin Books is part of the Penguin Random House group of companies
whose addresses can be found at global.penguinrandomhouse.com

Penguin Random House UK,
One Embassy Gardens, 8 Viaduct Gardens, London SW11 7BW

penguin.co.uk
global.penguinrandomhouse.com

First published by Hutchinson Heinemann 2024
Published in Penguin Books 2024

001

Copyright © Jennie Godfrey, 2024

Typeset in 13.10/15.52pt Garamond MT Std by Jouve (UK), Milton Keynes
Printed and bound in Great Britain by Clays Ltd, Elcograf S.p.A.

The authorised representative in the EEA is Penguin Random House Ireland,
Morrison Chambers, 32 Nassau Street, Dublin D02 YH68

A CIP catalogue record for this book is available from the British Library

ISBN: 978-1-804-94294-9

Penguin Random House is committed to a sustainable future
for our business, our readers and our planet. This book is made
from Forest Stewardship Council® certified paper.

In loving memory of David Godfrey

Author's Note

There is a whole generation of northerners whose childhoods were haunted by the murderer Peter Sutcliffe. One of my most vivid early memories is of the day that he was captured, when it became clear my dad knew him. I can still feel the shock of how close he got to my family.

This book is in tribute to the victims, survivors and those now adult children, of whom I am one. *The List of Suspicious Things* is my love letter to God's Own Country.

The List of Suspicious Things

The Wish

I

Miv

It would be easy to say that it all started with the murders, but actually it began when Margaret Thatcher became prime minister.

'A woman in charge of the country just isn't right. They're not made for it,' my Aunty Jean said, on the day the election results were announced. 'As if the last lot weren't bad enough. She's the beginning of the end for Yorkshire, an' I'll tell you why an' all.'

She was bustling about our small kitchen, vigorously rewiping surfaces I had already wiped. I was sat at the table, in my brown-and-orange school uniform, shelling peas into a colander on the chipped yellow Formica top, popping fresh ones into my mouth whenever she wasn't looking. I wanted to point out that, like Margaret Thatcher, Aunty Jean was also a woman, but Aunty Jean hated being interrupted mid-flow and it was just the two of us, meaning there was no escape from her opinions, of which there were many. So many, she began to list them.

'Number one,' she said, her wiry grey curls bobbing along as she shook her head, 'you take one look at that face, and you can see what power does to a woman: it hardens them. You can just tell she's no heart, can't you?' She took a wooden spoon off the draining board and wagged it at me for emphasis.

'Hmm,' I mumbled.

For a moment, I considered just nodding occasionally while secretly reading the book I had open, a corner tucked under the colander to keep it flat. But though Aunty Jean's hearing was less than sharp, her other senses were razor-like, and she would have smelled my inattention like a hunting dog.

'Number two. She's already taken milk away from poor children's mouths and jobs from the hands of hard-working men.'

I knew at least part of this was true. The rhyme 'Thatcher, Thatcher, milk snatcher' was still heard in our school, years after she had taken away the little bottles of disgusting lukewarm milk we used to have to drink daily there.

'Three. These bloody murders every five minutes. That's what Yorkshire's famous for now. Dead girls.'

She put the wooden spoon away and opened the door of our ancient fridge with its rusted corners, which creaked in protest. Immediately tutting about the lack of substance inside it, she pulled out the battered, spiral-bound notebook she carried everywhere with her, removed the equally battered pencil shoved in the top and licked the nub.

'Butter, milk, cheese.'

I could see her mouthing the words as she wrote them down, neatly listing them in the copperplate handwriting she was so proud of. Aunty Jean liked to tidy up the messiness of life, putting everything into order. I sometimes wondered if that was what she was trying to do to our family. She finished her list, closed the fridge and looked at me.

'Oh, and not just dead girls. *Those* types of women.'

I was bursting to ask about what types of women she meant, and whether they were the same type as Margaret Thatcher. I was always intrigued about the women Aunty Jean disapproved of – there were many – but I knew from experience that no comment was expected or desired, so I chose to say nothing and simply settled back into my chair, while Aunty Jean settled back into her opinions. I didn't need to ask which murders she was talking about though. Everyone in Yorkshire knew we had our very own bogeyman, one with a hammer and a hatred of women.

I had first heard about the Yorkshire Ripper two years before, when I was nearly ten years old. Me, Mum, Dad and Aunty Jean were all sat in our living room. It was not long after Aunty Jean had come to live with us, and I was rearranging myself around this new presence in the house, moulding myself into the new shape that was required of me. I was constantly trying to make myself smaller and quieter, but despite my best intentions, my personality kept jumping out anyway, like a jack-in-the-box.

The nine o'clock news was on the small black-and-white television, perched on a shelf. Mum, Dad and Aunty Jean were all perched on the settee looking up at it, as though they were at church, listening to a sermon. My hair was wet after its weekly wash, so I got to sit on the armchair usually reserved for Mum, whenever she came downstairs. It was next to the gas fire, the bars glowing brightly and warming my face when I turned towards it. The rest of the room was so cold you could see your own breath. My eyes were busy tracing the brown, orange and mustard swirls of our carpet – which looked like the patterns we drew on the Spirograph I had got last Christmas – when I became aware that something in the room had changed, as though all the oxygen had left it. It felt as if everyone had taken a breath and was holding it in, like we sometimes did at school, until we turned red and gave in, gasping and laughing.

I looked up to see that a solemn-faced policeman, laden with official decoration, had appeared on screen. I could see Dad looking at Mum intently, as though checking for signs of life. Finding nothing, he turned to Aunty Jean, his eyebrows waggling up and down in a way that would usually have made me giggle. But there was nothing funny about it. I couldn't understand what had just changed.

'*Today I can confirm that twenty-year-old Jean Jordan is the sixth victim of the Yorkshire Ripper. It was a brutal death. She was hit around the head with a blunt instrument and slashed repeatedly. The victim was another prostitute . . .'*

I sat up straight – this was a word I had not heard before. At the same time, Dad coughed, covering the sound of the television, and Aunty Jean got up to turn the channel over, but not before I managed to ask, 'What's a prostitute?'

Dad and Aunty Jean looked at each other again. Dad shifted in his seat; Aunty Jean froze. Mum continued to stare vacantly at the screen, a brief flicker of awareness the only sign that she was watching, a focus to her eyes which disappeared as quickly as it came. No one looked at me.

Eventually Dad piped up, 'Erm, it's, er, someone who helps the police.'

'Do you want a Horlicks before bed?' Aunty Jean asked, her voice as hard as granite as she left the room, motioning for me to follow. When I got back, something completely different was on the television and it was as though the conversation had never happened.

Since that day, the Ripper had floated around at the edges of my awareness. At school, kiss chase had morphed into 'Ripper chase', a much scarier game, involving the boys in my class wearing their shiny parkas buttoned only at the neck, so that when they ran their coats flew out around them like the wings on birds of prey. They swooped through the playground after the prettiest girls – my best friend Sharon among them – who scattered, screaming. But I didn't take much notice of his victims until a few weeks before the general election, when a nineteen-year-old building-society clerk from Halifax, Josephine Whitaker, was killed.

Dad had left the paper on the kitchen table while he had gone to the pub and I had picked it up to tidy it away. Aunty Jean hated mess. It was the pictures on the front page that I remember most: Josephine's wide-eyed, smiling face, framed by thick brunette hair, alongside photos of her partially covered body in the local park, where she had been stabbed twenty-one times with a screwdriver.

I had felt her death like she was someone I knew. Perhaps this was because of her age – she was young enough to still be called a 'girl' by the men on television – and not so many years older than me. Perhaps it was because of the way she was described, with words like 'innocent' and 'respectable'. She wasn't one of *those* types of women, as Aunty Jean had called them. I had stared at those pictures over and over, looking from one to the other, my heart thumping so hard I could feel it in my ears.

By the time Dad got home on the day of the election, it was past teatime, and I was sat at the kitchen table, itchy with hunger, waiting for him to wash his hands and join us. The familiar smell of musky sweat and Swarfega wafted into the kitchen as he joined me at the table and ruffled my hair, one of his rare signs of affection.

'It's nearly ready, Austin,' Aunty Jean said, nodding and putting a steaming mug of tea in front of him, and I wriggled in my seat in anticipation. 'Stop that, Miv,' she admonished, as she turned to me. 'You're like a lousy stocking.'

I stopped immediately and hung my head, biting my lip hard. Mum had used that expression about me all the time. The difference being that Mum had always said it with a smile.

'If you're stuck for summat to do, you can take this upstairs,' Aunty Jean said, handing me a tray with a bowl of soup on it, the smell of the thick, tomato richness expanding the hole in my tummy even further. I turned and looked through to the front room, realising that the battered armchair was empty. Today must've been a bad day.

I made my way up our narrow stairs, eyes on the tray and bowl, placing each foot down with exaggerated care, trying not to spill a drop. At the top, I laid the tray outside the closed bedroom door and lightly tapped, straining to hear if there was any movement, but there was only silence. I tiptoed back down and, just as my foot landed on the bottom step, I heard the almost whispered moan of the door opening and let my breath out in relief. At least she was eating. The day wasn't totally bad.

Back in the kitchen, Aunty Jean had removed her pinny and was wearing her customary cardigan, darned at the elbows and buttoned up to the neck. Apart from her opinions, Aunty Jean kept everything buttoned up, from her tight curls set under a hood in the hairdressers once a week, to her thick tan tights covering up any hint of flesh. She was now cutting into a large pie and putting it onto plates. Dad was immersed in the latest cricket news in the *Yorkshire Chronicle*, closing it once the food was placed in front of him. Then the three of us sat almost elbow to elbow round the circular table while we ate.

Before Aunty Jean came to stay, we used to eat our tea on trays on the settee with the telly on, where there was space for noise and occasional giggles. Even during the strikes that had left us with no electricity or heating a few years before, Mum had made it into a game. She pretended we were camping, and we ate by candlelight in our bobble hats and sang campfire songs. Even though we had to eat in the dark, life was all lightness then, not the drab greyness that had settled over us when Mum fell silent and Aunty Jean stepped in to fill the gap.

She cleared her throat and made the space even tighter by placing her notebook to the side of her plate and opening it up. She had made some more notes, neatly numbered, about why Margaret Thatcher was a *bad thing for the country, and in particular for Yorkshire*. The words were written as precisely on the page as they were spoken in person.

Dad silently ate his steak-and-kidney pie, his eyes intent on the food in front of him. He gave no sign that he was listening as she repeated the same points she had made to me earlier, and added some extras about how it was 'women getting ideas above their station' and something called 'immigration' that was to blame for Yorkshire 'going to the dogs'.

She sighed, her curls stiffly jiggling. 'I don't know, Austin. I sometimes think we might as well give up now and move Down South.'

I stopped, fork halfway to my mouth. Was she being serious? In our family, Down South represented a fate worse than death. 'We're Yorkshire through and through,' Aunty Jean used to say. 'We've the moors and the mills running through our veins as far back as the eye can see.'

I placed the mouthful of pie, dangling off the end of the fork, back onto my plate, appetite gone. Dad looked up. Before I'd even thought about it, the words came out of my mouth:

'We can't move away.'

The volume of the words surprised even me. They both turned in my direction.

'Is that right?' Dad said, an amused look on his face. There was no amusement in Aunty Jean's expression though.

'Tha'll do as tha's told,' she said, pointing at my plate as if to say, *and that includes eating your tea.*

'But EVERYTHING'S here,' I said, meaning my best and only friend, Sharon. I could feel the lump at the back of my throat and tried in vain to swallow it down. Crying was one of the many things Aunty Jean didn't approve of.

Dad put his knife and fork down and looked at Aunty Jean properly for the first time, instead of the steak-and-kidney pie. He picked up a piece of bread spread thickly with butter from the pile in the middle of the table and used it to mop up the gravy on his plate. 'Aye, you might be right,' he said, after a pause. 'A fresh start could be good for all of us. We should think about it.' He raised his eyes to the ceiling, and the sound of foot-steps pacing slowly up and down on the floorboards. I looked up too. When I looked back again, Aunty Jean was watching us both. I saw an emotion I couldn't quite name in her eyes, which she quickly tidied away with the plates.

It was then I knew that this was serious.

That night I lay awake in bed, the silent shadows of my desk, bookshelves and the heavy old walnut wardrobe illuminated by the moon peeping through a crack in the curtains. The eyes on the long-faded, too-young-for-me-now figures of the Wombles on my wallpaper looked like they were watching over me. The familiarity of the shapes made my throat ache again.

I gripped the sides of the bed, my hands rubbing against the stiff, scratchy blanket as my mind and stom-ach churned, roiling with the idea of leaving Yorkshire. I was reminded of the last time we had been to the Bonfire Night Feast in our town. Mum had decided I was old enough to go on the waltzers, and I had felt as though I might be flung off the edge of the world as we flew around. The only thing that had stopped me from screaming in terror was Mum's hand tightly holding on to mine. I could still conjure up the warm gingerbread smell of the parkin we had eaten, which clung to her skin. I knew that wouldn't happen again now. The last two years had taught me how much people could change. If I couldn't count on people, then I at least needed places and things to stay solid. We couldn't move away.

I turned to the one thing I could *always* count on. I had never found comfort in dolls or stuffed toys, so instead reached for a well-thumbed Enid Blyton book Mum had got me at a jumble sale. It was lying at the top of a pile by the side of the bed, its cover curled with age and the pages loose at the spine. It was one of the Famous Five stories. I was too old for them in public, but in private those books were like old friends. I loved the fact their adventures would always end with Aunt Fanny fussing over them, making sure they had plenty of sandwiches.

Reading the familiar words kept me occupied while I waited for my other daily comfort. Every night since the day Mum fell silent, Dad would come to my room to say goodnight. It was a poor replacement for when Mum used to come and sing me to sleep, stroking my hair as she did so. She never sang silly childish songs, only melodic, mournful songs by the Beatles, or the

Carpenters, made sweet by her beautiful voice. But as it was the only time I got to spend with Dad on my own, it had become a precious ritual, after which he would go downstairs and watch television with Aunty Jean, or 'pop out for a quick pint', which was happening more and more frequently. I put the book down when his head appeared around my door, ready to ambush him.

'Are we really going to move?' I asked.

He came in and perched on the end of my bed, playing with a loose thread from the crocheted blanket on top of me.

'Would it really be such a terrible thing?' he asked, a smile on his face. He nodded at the Famous Five book open on my lap. 'I thought you liked adventures.'

I looked up, surprised. This was a low blow, using books against me.

'What about the cricket?' I said. 'You can't follow the Yorkshire Cricket Club if you're not in Yorkshire.'

Cricket was the only common language Dad and I had. The complicated rules and language of the game ran through me like letters in a stick of seaside rock, thanks to Dad's obsession with the sport. It was family folklore that Mum and Dad had very nearly not had children because it might hamper him travelling all over the place to watch Yorkshire play. In the end, though, it hadn't been me that had got in the way of that. I was aware that I was somewhat mangling the rule about having to be born in Yorkshire to play for the team, but it didn't work anyway. Dad looked at his watch, as though his pint was expecting him at a certain time. 'Yorkshire's not what it was,' he murmured, getting up to go.

I felt the waltzers inside me start moving again.

'Because of the murders?'

'Yes, well, that's part of it,' he said, as he got to my bedroom door. 'But don't you be worrying about any of that.' He gave me a weak smile, switched off the big light and slowly closed the door.

I reached under the bed for my torch, switched it on and went back to my book. In just a few pages, my mind and body quietened as the words performed their hypnosis. I knew that my favourite character, Georgina – known as George for her tomboy looks and something called 'pluck' – would not be frightened about moving, or even about the Yorkshire Ripper. In fact, she would probably summon the rest of the Five to try and catch him.

What if someone caught him? I wondered, as I drifted off to sleep. *What if the murders were to stop? And we could stay? Then I would never have to leave Sharon and we could be best friends always.*

2

Austin

Austin closed the front door behind him, paused for a moment and let out a sigh. He slowly straightened his slumped shoulders and stooped body, like a miner emerging from underground. His house had become a place filled with need: the need for him to answer things, provide things, fix things. Yet the one thing he wanted to fix, he couldn't. Outside, he felt as though he could breathe again. He walked to the end of the road, playing 'Eeny, meeny, miny, moe' on the cracked grey paving slabs to the rhythm of his steps as he toyed with the choice of where to go this evening, deciding as he got to the junction that the Red Lion was the closest and most likely to be relatively quiet this early on, even though it was a Friday night. Most folks went to the pubs in town straight after work, not migrating further out until later. The most important thing was that there would be no expectations of him, except to buy a pint.

Reaching the pub, he pulled open the heavy black door. It was still light outside, the sun only just starting to set, but the deep-red carpets and flocked burgundy wallpaper made it look like night had already appeared, inside. He was right in his guess that it would be quiet. The regulars were there of course, perched on brown stools at the brown wooden bar, their brown-clothed bodies hunched over brown pints, a fug of smoke floating above them.

Austin ordered his pint and pointed at a pile of newspapers next to one of them. 'Aye, you can take 'em,' the man said, without looking up at him or removing his cigarette to speak. Austin rifled through the pile, looking for a local paper and the cricket news. The nationals were always filled with rubbish, and he knew they would be even more so that day. At least the front pages were not full of the Ripper for once. Instead, there was a different tone to the headlines, one of triumph and an optimism that Austin did not share. He flicked from one paper to the next, each one a love letter to the new prime minister: *Maggie All the Way, Maggie's Made It, You Can Help the PM Make Britain Really Great Again.*

'Drowning your sorrows, Austin?'

He was interrupted by Patrick, the short, stocky barman, who put his pint down in front of him. 'We're in real trouble now there's a woman in charge, eh?' he added, as though the news was amusing rather than devastating. Like his sister, Austin had no love for Thatcher, and based on her track record could only see further decline for the people of Yorkshire at her hands. He took a sip of his pint to avoid answering, but Pat moved on to a subject even less welcome.

'How's things at home?' he asked, his voice at least lowering so as not to be heard by the row of regulars.

'Aye, you know,' Austin answered in the equally vague way expected of him. Before Pat could say anything else, Austin took his pint and the local paper to the smallest table in the pub, a rickety wooden card table with a single chair in front of it. He tried to lose himself in its pages but found himself wondering what Marian – the Marian she was *before* – would think about Thatcher as prime minister. He could imagine her giving an impassioned speech about the rights of the workers, her cheeks rosy with feeling, until he could no longer hold off and would reach out to kiss her while she giggled and wriggled. '*Austin, I'm trying to be serious.*' He sighed, slowly letting the air out of his body like a punctured tyre.

There was no point in imagining these things, but Patrick's veiled question had made it impossible not to think about home again. How was he supposed to feel about his silent wife, opinionated sister and, most painful of all, his wide-eyed, neglected daughter? He swallowed down his rising guilt with a gulp of his pint.

He looked around the pub, determined to distract himself, and found himself staring at the only other person in there, except those crouched at the bar, who were more part of the furniture than actual customers. This man was huddled over his pint, and sat in the opposite corner to Austin, as if they were bookends. He looked up, perhaps sensing Austin's eyes on him, and

Austin immediately turned his gaze away, recognising the thick-set man with ice-cold eyes as Kevin Collier. This was a man you didn't stare at. Austin tried to keep himself to himself and avoided looking too hard at other people's private lives in return, but living with his sister meant that he couldn't avoid the rumours that were always swirling around a town the size of this one. According to Jean, Kevin ran with 'unsavoury charac-ters' and had a 'whole brood of boys' who would all end up 'going to the bad', and while many folks were considered unsavoury to his sister, he'd also seen Kevin have a go at someone with a snooker cue who had stared at him for too long, and knew that the amount of beer consumed would determine whether he saw eye contact as an act of aggression or not. Luckily it seemed it was early enough for Austin to get away with this momentary lapse in judgement.

'How do, Austin!'

He looked up and saw Gary Andrews, who had just come in. Austin began to fold the newspaper away and finish his pint.

'How do, Gary,' Austin mumbled, as he caught eyes with Pat, their eyes rolling in perfect unison.

There was more noise as Gary greeted everyone else in the pub by name, slapping the regulars on the back, one by one. His little troop followed behind him, nodding and laughing at his every word. Austin never understood why Gary had so many young men in his thrall. He could see why he made the girls giggle – by any measure he was a handsome lad – but to Austin's mind his brash, matey, 'man of the people' act was just that, an act. He suspected Pat felt the same.

'Can I get you another one?' Pat nodded to Austin's now empty glass, clearly delaying the moment he had to go and serve Gary and his mates. Austin looked at the clock. His wife would be in bed, his daughter likely with her nose in a book, and Jean would be pottering around the front room he'd made into a makeshift bedroom for her. The coast was clear. But he wasn't ready to go home yet.

3

Miv

The next Monday, like every day, before school I called for Sharon.

The way to Sharon's house was as familiar to me as the pages of my Famous Five books, and I zipped my anorak up against the bitterly cold rain and walked as fast as I could to hers. Last term at school, when we had learned about the First World War, I had become fascinated by the idea of men living in trenches. The terraced houses on the street where I lived made me think of the rows of battle-weary grey soldiers in my schoolbooks, wounded and bandaged from years of struggle and neglect. I passed street by identical street until they finally made way for the wider, leafier part of town where Sharon lived.

It made no real sense for me to call for her. To get to school we had to double back and walk the way I'd just come, but I liked going to Sharon's house. I liked the calm, neat street, and the promise of something my own home didn't offer. The difference wasn't just in the size of the houses or the spaces between them. It was in the little things, the heavily lined velvet curtains versus the see-through scratchy ones. The house name on a plaque versus the numbers on the door. The double-glazed, freshly painted windows versus the shabby wooden-framed ones. It was in the slow quietness of Sharon's street, broken only by the sound of rain, birds calling and the occasional car, versus the never-ending noise of kids playing in the road at all hours at mine, the dogs barking and the repetitive thump of a football against a wet wall.

Sharon was waiting for me at the end of her street, hood up, hiding her blonde curls, and we fell into an easy step beside each other. If I was tomboy George from the Famous Five, then Sharon was sweet-natured Anne. I was made of straight lines – like the stick figures I used to draw at school: short, straight, mousy-brown hair, a straight nose and a straight-up-and-down body. Sharon was all curves and waves: blonde hair in bobbles; a round button nose and pink polka-dot dresses. Even her writing looked like bubbles. I was always sure that to onlookers we made an odd pair. We picked up our conversation from the day before almost mid-sentence, as though it had never been interrupted.

The people we saw on our way to school were like the buildings we passed: predictable and unchanging. At eight-fifteen we chimed, 'Morning!' in perfect unison to Mrs Pearson, out walking her snappy Jack Russell. After her, we knew we would say hello and stop for a chat with the man in the corner shop, as he would be outside by now, arranging the daily newspaper stand. He would call us the 'Terrible Twosome' and we would laugh, as if it were the first time he had said it.

Just before we got there, Sharon nudged me hard in the ribs and muttered, 'Watch out!' under her breath. Following her gaze, I saw another familiar person, the only person we didn't say hello to on our journey and whose name we somehow knew was Brian, though we didn't use it. To us, he was just 'the man in the overalls'.

He was young, in his twenties, and not once had he ever made eye contact with us. He wore the same dark blue all-in-one smeared with grease, which extended to his face, and a knitted yellow bobble hat – its unexpected jauntiness jarring with the rest of him – and carried a plastic bag with a paper peeping out of the top.

We never knew whether he would appear or not, but when he did, we immediately crossed over the road to avoid him. At first, this was because Sharon suspected he smelled, though we never got close enough to discover if that was true. We had once viewed him as harmless, but recently our distaste at his scruffiness had hardened into something more disquieting. We sped up and passed him by on the opposite side of the road, Sharon gripping on to my arm and pulling me along with her, eager to get to the corner shop, and safety.

It would still be a while before we were seen as at risk from the Ripper by the adults in our lives. At present a serial murderer was routinely killing young women and we walked to school alone. These two facts existed in splendid isolation. But while the adults in our lives were unconcerned on our behalf, since the murder of Josephine Whitaker the constant cloud of the Ripper had loomed ominously over us. We began to look more closely at the men we passed. We would inspect their faces, instead of saying 'Ey up' in the usual Yorkshire way. The once friendly-seeming smiles now appeared to be purposeful leers with intentions we could only vaguely understand but which we knew weren't good.

After the shop, we wound our way round a series of shortcuts that took us through the dense foliage of snickets and wide-open fields, where it was possible to forget we were children in a bleak industrial town and instead imagine we were adventurers, discovering the countryside. The sign that we were nearing civilisation again was a large factory surrounded by barbed-wire fences and high windows that meant you couldn't see in. I always cringed as we passed it, with the discomfort of remembering one of the earliest 'adventures' I had led us both into.

The year before, a combination of the spy kit I had got for the previous Christmas, and my first James Bond film – *Goldfinger* – had helped me to realise that this factory was in fact a front for Russian spies. I had discussed this likelihood with Sharon, who happily agreed, as she did to all my ideas back then, and one day I suggested we should attempt to scale the fence and try to get in.

Sharon had rolled her eyes at me and just knocked on the door, claiming to the man who answered that we needed to go to the toilet and were desperate. It was my first glimpse of her ingenuity under pressure, and I was impressed. The man gave us directions to the loos, telling us to go straight there and back, but of course we took a diversion, just in case we could find anything interesting to back up my theory of espionage. We ended up peering around the door of a small office, where a man in a tan suit was sat at a battered brown desk, smoking, years of tobacco having browned the walls too.

'What you doing in here?' he'd said mildly, as though it were a common occurrence to see two eleven-year-old girls at the door of his office.

'Er. We were on our way to the toilets, we must've g—' Sharon started to say.

'What goes on here?' I'd demanded. I'd not yet learned to disguise my curiosity. The man had smiled at me from behind the desk, putting his cigarette out in the huge brown ashtray piled high with a mountain of crumpled orange-and-white butts.

'We make things. Wi' metal. Sheet metal.' He pointed to the sign above his head. *Schofields Sheet Metal*, it said. We beat a hasty retreat. There had been no Russians in there, just Kenneth Pearson, who lived on my street and said, 'Ey up' as we walked past him on the way out. This escapade hadn't exactly had the outcome I had wanted, and I'd hurried us past the building every day since, not wanting to be reminded of it.

When we rounded the corner for school, the way was usually signposted by the words *W—gs go home* in foot-high graffiti on the walls of a boarded-up mill, but that day they were obscured by a huge white poster. I stopped and stared. It was headed with the words *West Yorkshire Police* and almost covered the top half of the building. Underneath the heading, bold black letters read: *HELP US TO STOP THE RIPPER FROM KILLING AGAIN.*

I felt like it was talking directly to me.

Sharon carried on for a few more steps, still talking, before she noticed I was no longer with her and stopped too.

'What's up?' she asked.

'Do you think we know him?' I said, wondering. 'Do you think we see him every day and we have no idea it's him?'

Sharon stared at me, her nose wrinkling as though dismissing the idea. 'I don't want to think about it,' she said. 'Come on or we'll be late.'

But I couldn't stop thinking about it, and the daily siren call of the poster made me start to look for him everywhere, in every man I saw.

Our school trip soon after was to the North Yorkshire town of Knaresborough, near Harrogate. Aunty Jean called Knaresborough 'posh Yorkshire'. She spat the name out with the same disdain she normally reserved for the words *Down South*, but when I got up that morning, she had made me a packed lunch and left me detailed instructions of everything I needed to take with me for the day. Another list. The curly, neat writing, with *Don't Forget* double-underlined at the top of the faded yellow page torn out of her notebook, made me smile.

As we boarded the coach, its patchy orange paint job spotted with rust, everyone waited for Neil Callaghan and Richard Collier to get on first. They were the boys who had started 'Ripper chase' and were known for getting into fights. They had even been seen smoking. It was an automatic assumption that they would occupy the back seat. Richard, a tall, rangy boy with ice-cold blue eyes, blew a kiss in Sharon's direction as he passed us. Sharon pulled a face and rolled her eyes at him, but I could see the faint pink hue of a blush underneath her freckles. Even then she still looked pretty.

I couldn't remember exactly when it had started happening – that boys would react differently to Sharon – but I had become aware that she attracted a form of attention that I just didn't. In response, I pretended to look down my nose at the boys, and sometimes men, who stared at Sharon or swaggered in front of her. But sometimes, the knowledge that I was invisible to them would make my throat close.

'Move,' Richard said to a quiet boy named Ishtiaq, who was about to climb the stairs onto the coach. Ishtiaq stood to one side, without saying a word. Sharon and I got on next, wincing at the acrid smell of stale tobacco and bleach. We knew our place and took our seats in the middle of the coach, while at the front, the quieter students, including Ishtiaq, sat under the protection of our teachers, Mr Ware and Miss Stacey.

I sat silently on the way there, looking out of the window, concentrating hard to avoid being sick. Stephen Crowther, who was at the front, had already vomited into a bucket, much to the disgust of everyone seated around him, and while secretly hating that the boys in our class didn't seem to see me, I knew I didn't need *that* sort of attention.

Sharon chattered away excitedly to the girls sat behind us, the volume in the coach rising as Neil and Richard began play-fighting and others began to chant the rhyme that had been going around since the election. Drawing a stick figure on one hand, we would hold it up in the air and do the actions to the words:

'Here's Margaret Thatcher
Throw 'er in the air and catch 'er
Squishy Squashy Squishy Squashy
There's Margaret Thatcher.'

The chant finished with the triumphant holding-up of the scribbles on the other hand. Margaret Thatcher had been squashed into nothingness.

When the increase in volume reached the front of the coach, Mr Ware's head rose from behind his seat and silence descended. He peered at us, his dark eyes appearing to bore through every single person while he waited for a few moments in case we were in any doubt about his absolute power. Eventually he looked down at a piece of paper in front of him and said, 'Right, you lot. Old Mother Shipton was born in 1488 and was known as Knaresborough's prophetess. Anyone know what that word means?'

'No, Mr Ware,' we all dutifully chorused, except Stephen Crowther, who still had his head in the bucket.

'It means she could see into the future. She lived in the cave we are going to see and the whole town thought she was odd – a bit like we do you, Crowther,' he said, looking down at poor Stephen. 'Her "Petrifying Well" is supposedly enchanted, and some say that if you throw a copper into it, your wishes will come true.' The roll of his eyes and shake of his head told us what he thought of this piece of folklore.

I liked the sound of Old Mother Shipton and her well.

When we got to Knaresborough, it was warm and sunny, a stark contrast to the dark and cold of the well, and the cave, which smelled musty and damp. The slow, rhythmic drip of liquid from the ceiling echoed around the cavernous space, and the stone-like appearance of the toys, shoes, hats and kettles hanging from the cave entrance was the stuff of dark fairy tales. I thought that *petrifying* was a good word for the things hung in front of us.

'OK. Shush, everyone. Listen up,' said Miss Stacey. 'Get your coppers ready and think about what you want to wish for. Be very careful what you choose. Make sure it's something you won't mind coming true. Most importantly, remember you can't tell anyone what your wish is, or it won't.'

As I stood in front of the well, I considered several possibilities. I looked at Sharon, her freckled nose crinkling at the damp smell. Wishing for long blonde hair like hers was one option: my short brown boyish cut was a source of some shame to me. I also thought about wishing that we could go back in time, to before the day Mum changed. But I knew that the wishing well couldn't be *that* magical. I wondered about wishing we wouldn't move away Down South, so I'd never have to leave Sharon.

In the end, though, I made a wish that would ripple through the lives of everyone I knew, a wish that I would come to regret deeply.

As I threw my penny into the well, I wished that I would be the person to catch the Yorkshire Ripper.

Sharon and I wouldn't have been friends if it wasn't for her mum, Ruby. One Sunday at church she had come over to me and Dad. It was not long after the day Mum changed, so she didn't go to church any more, but Dad did. He still had faith. Or at least he still came to listen to me sing with the choir, which I did every Sunday. It was one of my favourite things to do, as it reminded me of Mum. Singing made me feel close to her. About a year later he stopped going too. Aunty Jean never went to church. 'Charity begins at home,' she would say.

It was after the morning service, when the vicar had prayed for the soul of Jean Jordan, the latest Ripper victim, the one who'd been on the news. No one had seemed worried then. The Ripper felt very far away from our small town. He prowled the big cities, his victims spoken about with whispered pity. They weren't people like us. We were safe in our church, cushioned by our righteousness.

We stood by the entrance, and I stared at the gravestones in front of me, crumbling and covered in moss. I wondered whether this was where the murdered women ended up. Whether they were allowed in the church graveyard, given that they were muttered about in whispers. I looked up to ask Dad the question, but he was in a murmured conversation with Ruby, so I waited. Eventually they noticed me, and Ruby leaned down to look at me straight on, a mist of Charlie perfume surrounding her. I blinked as she smiled and said, 'Would you like to come to ours for your tea one day? Give your mum and dad a break?'

I wasn't sure what was so exhausting about me that it required a break, but Ruby looked like Purdey from *The New Avengers*, her blonde pageboy haircut framing her smiling face, and I gravitated towards her and her sweet-smelling smile. In fact, everyone gravitated towards her, even my dad.

'Yes please, Mrs Parker,' I said, making no attempt to hide the eagerness in my voice.

That first time I went to the Parkers', I walked up the

drive feeling unsteady on my feet. I desperately wanted to hold on to my dad's hand, but at ten I knew I was too old for that. Sharon's house stood tall and alone, its wide sash windows and pristine white frames giving a glimpse into order and comfort. Ruby opened the door, and I could just see Sharon behind her, one cartoon-large blue eye and her curly blonde hair peeking out like half a golden halo. I was aware of Sharon already, of course; we went to the same school after all. But to me she was like a character in a fairy tale – a princess or a pixie – and I didn't belong in those kinds of stories. When she appeared in full, jumping out from behind her mum, she held her hand to me. I looked at it, confused, so she grabbed mine and pulled me inside and up to her bedroom, eager to show me her Holly Hobbie wallpaper and matching doll. We left Dad and Ruby chatting on the doorstep. I didn't even say goodbye.

Sharon had more teddies and dolls than I had ever owned, lined up along the entire length of her bed. It felt like some sort of rainbow-coloured surveillance unit, while I sat frozen on a small stool at her dressing table, not wanting to make any moves which might get me into trouble or have me removed. Despite my discomfort, I wanted to be there so desperately it was like a physical ache. I could feel my cheeks glowing, not just in response to their inanimate stares but also from the unfamiliar heat coming from the radiator.

I sat in silence. Waiting. I had already discovered by

then how much people would reveal when you stayed quiet. In no time at all I knew that Sharon liked guinea pigs and her favourite toy was her Holly Hobbie, named, somewhat unimaginatively in my opinion, Holly. 'You don't talk much, do you?' she said, her head on one side, as though I were a curiosity she couldn't quite make out.

'I'm just listening,' I replied.

By the time Ruby called us down for our tea, Sharon still knew nothing about me, but I could feel myself thawing in the face of her relentless warmth and chatter.

After we'd eaten our fish fingers, chips and peas – even the food at Sharon's was more brightly coloured than the greys and browns of home – I went to get down from the table.

'Where are you going? We've not had our pudding yet,' Sharon said.

Since the day Mum had changed, anything that might be considered a treat had faded quickly from our lives and I had forgotten about puddings. When Ruby placed bowls of jam roly-poly and custard in front of us, I felt myself almost jumping up and down out of my seat with every mouthful. I was humming with pleasure when I noticed Ruby's and Sharon's eyes glued on me, a softness in Ruby's face that somehow also looked like pain.

I would grow familiar with those looks from other children's mothers.

Just before Dad came to pick me up, Ruby wrapped up a slice of cake in a piece of kitchen roll, as though this were a birthday party. 'Here you go,' she said. 'You can have this for your pudding on another night.' She kissed me on the forehead and repeated this ritual every Thursday when I went for my tea, right up until everything happened.

So, you see, Sharon didn't really have a choice but to become my friend – but she was kind, so she did – and somehow we fitted together so that eventually you couldn't see the join; our friendship became like a seesaw. I had ideas, and Sharon made them happen. We provided balance for each other. I couldn't imagine my life without her.

And that was why I couldn't allow us to leave Yorkshire.

Once I'd made my wish, the Ripper began to invade my sleeping hours too. I was haunted by a recurring nightmare, where a faceless man would put me in the back of his dirty white van. Somehow, I knew he was taking me away and I banged on the doors as he drove off, but my efforts made no sound, and I knew that no one could hear me.

During waking hours, I devoured the news hungrily. What were the police missing? How might he be found? In the *Yorkshire Chronicle* one of the police officers on the case was interviewed and talked about the 'complexity of the investigation and the need for rigour, and structure', and while I wasn't sure what most of that meant, I clung to the words. They brought to mind

Aunty Jean and her lists, and her efforts to bring order to our lives.

The kernel of an idea formed.

I toyed with the idea of telling Sharon about my wish. I remembered Miss Stacey's threat about wishes not coming true if you told someone, but I knew I would need help if I was going to find the Ripper. In the end I decided it was safe, that telling Sharon was different from telling anyone else – it was like sharing things with a part of myself. So I broached the subject the next time I was at the Parkers' for my tea.

We were in Sharon's bedroom and I was on the bed, flicking through an old *Blue Jeans* magazine. The stuffed toys and Holly Hobbie wallpaper had been replaced recently by beige Anaglypta, along with the lip gloss and Blondie posters which Sharon had insisted on when she'd turned twelve, though I was pleased to see the Holly Hobbie doll on her pillow. Sharon was sat at the dressing table, pouting at her reflection and holding her blonde curls up on her head in a high ponytail, like the girl on the cover.

'I've had an idea,' I said. 'A really important one,' I added, to distinguish it from the sillier flights of fancy I had taken us both on. The Russian-spy factory had been the first, but it was the first of many. There had been a stint of pretending we were witches and putting spells on people we didn't like, followed by a short time of believing that one of our teachers was really a robot. I sometimes – and lately more so – worried that Sharon might not join me on these imaginative excursions. This time she looked at me in the mirror, an eyebrow cocked, while she picked up a can of Impulse body spray and covered herself in it, the sweet smell so overwhelming I started to cough.

'I'm not pretending to be aliens again,' she said.

I blushed through my near choke. I'd forgotten that one, which had taken hold after we had first seen *Star Wars*.

'No,' I said. 'This is about the Ripper. What if we decided to try and find him?'

'What on earth are you on about?' she said. 'How are *we* going to catch the Yorkshire Ripper, when the police haven't even managed to?'

I sighed. Her questioning my ideas was a recent and unwelcome element to our friendship. But it was a valid point. How would we catch him? We needed some sort of plan, a way of gathering clues and putting them into order.

I thought about what the policeman had said about structure, and then about Aunty Jean and her notebook, and the idea I had hardened like toffee. I knew exactly what we needed to do.

'We'll make a list,' I said. 'A list of the people and things we see that are suspicious. And then . . . And then we'll investigate them.'

'And why exactly would we do this?'

'Well, if we catch him we might get the reward the police are offering,' I said. 'Think of everything we could buy! All the books and lip glosses and sweets we could want.'

Sharon's reflection was now smiling at me.

'But even if we didn't, think about all the prostitutes we would save.'

Even though neither of us knew what prostitutes were, I thought that the idea of saving others would appeal to Sharon, who was the kindest person I knew.

'And everyone would know who I – I mean who *we* – were,' I said.

No more invisibility. No more pained looks from other people's mothers.

'Hmmm,' she said, 'I'll think about it.'

On the way into school the next day my suggestion about the Ripper hovered over us. I tried to talk about something else, to let Sharon bring it up, but as always he was everywhere. From the leaflets stuck to lamp posts to the headlines on the stand outside the corner shop, we couldn't have escaped the Ripper if we'd tried. It was making more and more sense to me that we try and catch him.

At the school gates, by some unspoken agreement we stopped for a moment and stood shoulder to shoulder while we watched a game of Ripper chase unfold on the playground in front of us. Richard Collier flew across the concrete, his face serious and his long legs taking the playground in strides. He was intent on the poor girl he was pursuing, his blue eyes fixed on her.

I first met Richard when we were at the same junior school. He had been much smaller than the other boys, but seemed older, his cheeks all hollowed out and his eyes looking like they knew things the rest of us didn't. He was shy – clinging to his mum every day as she came to drop him off – then sitting at the back of the group, curled in on himself until home time. We were both the first to read in our class and therefore given special privileges and allowed to sit and read our books without supervision – a fact I had been very proud of at the time, when it was still acceptable to be clever. We had often sat together in quiet harmony with each other. There was no evidence of that boy now. He was unrecognisable in the boy in front of me.

The girl he was chasing tripped over her own feet, her face stricken with terror as she picked herself up and ran on. I felt my heart pounding in my chest as I absorbed her fear, game or not. I wondered what the women pursued by the actual Ripper experienced. I shuddered, and felt Sharon's hand on my arm.

'OK,' she said. 'Let's do it. Let's try and catch him.'

I nodded and walked quickly ahead through the gates and into the throng so that she couldn't see the smile that was spreading across my face.

The Suspicious Things

I

Miv

Number One

We started our search for the Ripper on the day we broke up for the May half-term holiday. It coincided with another really warm day. The sun had brought out lines of washing across the back alleyways of the terraces, sheets billowing like cartoon ghosts as we wound our way to the corner shop, accompanied by the noise of women nattering over walls about the state of the nation and how everything used to be better. They sounded like Aunty Jean on repeat.

Sharon and I had sprinted home first to count our pocket money so we could buy the latest newspapers from the shop. Though he had briefly been replaced by Margaret Thatcher, the spectre of the Ripper continued to dominate the front pages. Even the spring sunshine seemed to be dimmed by his shadow.

When we pooled our funds, we discovered that we were rich. Between us, we had £4.50. Admittedly this was mostly Sharon's. She was given 20p a week, whereas I earned mine by doing jobs around the house, so the amount varied greatly according to my motivation. As well as the newspapers, we decided to buy a notebook like Aunty Jean's to write down our investigations in, and a 10p spice mix, to keep our strength up.

'It's the Terrible Twosome,' the shopkeeper said as we opened the door and the bell jingled. 'Where have you two been? My profits have taken a beating since you were last in.' He chuckled to himself, clearly pleased with his own joke. We dutifully laughed, and placed our orders, debating several times about the mix of sweets to buy while the shopkeeper stood, scoop in hand, ready to open the jars lined up in a kaleidoscope of colours behind him. Another customer walked in, and he smilingly raised his eyes.

'I hope you don't mind waiting for a moment while my two most important customers make their purchasing decisions.'

The man grunted and stood behind us, the newspaper he was about to buy tucked under his arm. 'Is that your car parked outside?' he said. 'You'd better keep an eye on it, there's some rough 'uns loitering.' He indicated up the street with his head, counting out the copper coins for his newspaper from one hand to the other as he did so.

We paid for our sweets and the spiral-bound notebook and left the shop. Mouths watering, we were stood on the kerb looking into our bags of sweets, trying to decide what to eat first, when the shopkeeper came outside, looking around as he made his way to his car.

We followed his gaze and could see three young men in the distance. From where we were, their almost shaved heads made them look bald, baby-like, reinforcing their youth.

'I bet it's Neil and Richard,' I whispered to Sharon, recognising the cocky set of their walk. But I don't think she was listening to me – she was staring at them with an expression I couldn't quite read. The shop-keeper locked his car, throwing the boys a wary glance before venturing back inside, and eventually we walked away, cramming flying saucers into our mouths. Suddenly I had a thought and grabbed on to Sharon's arm. 'What car was it?' I asked. 'Outside, I mean – the one the shopkeeper locked. Did you notice?'

She laughed at me, shaking my hand off. 'Why would I notice that?'

I swung round and went back to the light brown car, squinting as it gleamed in the sun. I opened the note-book with a dramatic flourish and wrote the registration down, reading out the model stamped in silver-coloured letters on the boot. 'It's a Ford Corsair,' I breathed, with no attempt to hide how smug I was at my knowledge of our case.

On a shelf in our pantry, along with bits of string, empty, washed-out plastic margarine tubs, and thin plastic bags stuffed into other thin plastic bags, Aunty Jean kept old copies of the local newspapers 'just in case'. I was never clear in case of what, but had since become grateful for her hoarding. After making my wish I had started sneaking copies up to my room, poring over them instead of the Famous Five, looking for clues that might help in our quest. There was no shortage of material.

According to the *Yorkshire Chronicle*, the Ripper's ninth victim, forty-year-old Vera Millward, had left her home to buy cigarettes at ten o'clock one evening. She had been found by workers arriving to do the gardens at the Manchester Royal Infirmary the next day. She had been attacked with a hammer and stabbed repeatedly. The police were able to identify the tyre tracks of the vehicle the Ripper had used as belonging to one of only eleven models of car, one of which was the Ford Corsair.

Sharon looked at me aghast and then back at the shop. 'You can't think he's the Ripper,' she said in a low voice. 'That's ridiculous, Miv.' She folded her arms and shifted her weight to one leg in indignation. 'He's the nicest grown-up we know.'

I took a moment to consider this. Sharon was right. I had never seen the shopkeeper in a bad mood, and he was the sort of grown-up who listened and talked to us as though we were grown-ups too. They were a rarity in our world, which still subscribed to the idea that children should be seen and not heard. I smiled as I thought about how, when there was no one else in the shop apart from us, he would turn up the tinny tape recorder on the shop counter and play pretend piano to Elton John, who he loved.

'He's not just a pop star, he's a true artist,' he used to say to us.

However, I put such sentimental thoughts aside, realising there was no place for them in our investigation. Instead, I continued to write in the notebook, listing the things we knew about him and reciting them to Sharon, who folded her arms and smiled while I did so, ever indulgent of my need to be right. For the first time, I understood why Aunty Jean made her lists. I seemed to stand taller and felt full of certainty and confidence as I wrote down my suspicions.

'One, he has dark hair. Two, he has a moustache. Three, he has dark eyes. Four, he's not from round our way. And five, he drives a Ford Corsair.'

There had been no mention of the Ripper having brown skin, but there were lots of references to his 'black' eyes and hair and his 'dark' stare, his 'bushy, dark' eyebrows and his 'swarthy' complexion in all the descriptions I had read of him. Most people I knew were peculiarly afraid of anyone with darker skin than their own. It was suspicious by itself. Sharon nudged me in the ribs and pointed to the sign above the door.

'Look. His name's Mr Bashir. I wonder why we never knew that?' she said. 'If we're going to do this properly, you'd better write it down.'

I followed her gaze; I'd never looked at the sign properly before, and as I stepped back and stared at the outside of the shop, I took it in fully for the first time. I mean, I'd always been observant, noticing the little things other people didn't, but I would need to be extra-vigilant if I was going to do this and do it right. Sat at the end of a terrace, the shop had been there since before we were born, part of a uniform grey landscape we never thought to look twice at.

Inside was where it mattered. Inside was a treasure trove of sweets, crisps and fizzy pop in an array of primary colours, with Mr Bashir in smiling residence behind the counter. The aroma in the shop was one of my favourites. A curious mix of sugary sweetness and warm, woody pipe tobacco that wrapped itself around you like a comfort blanket. I found it intoxicating.

When Mr Bashir had moved in, Aunty Jean had arrived home, bristling with concern that he might bring with him funny spices, and the neighbours had muttered ominously about someone 'foreign' having taken the job of someone born and bred in Yorkshire. Two months on and some of the residents of the surrounding streets still refused to go into the shop. They would instead trudge miles into town or wait for market day rather than trade with the man with brown skin.

However, by and large, most people had seemed to settle into an uneasy acceptance of Mr Bashir's presence. 'Needs must,' as Aunty Jean would sigh, and, after all, our neighbours had to get their milk and bread from somewhere. Thing is, while Sharon was right and he was one of the nicest adults we'd met, I also knew that Mr Bashir wasn't all that he seemed. That beneath the surface there was something else, something tightly coiled and controlled.

Only a few weeks before, when I'd been in the shop on my own, browsing the shelves and deciding how to spend the 10p I'd earned doing the washing-up, I'd overheard Kenneth Pearson from down the road, who worked at Schofields, talking to the local rag-and-bone man, Arthur, about 'all the P——s moving in' and how 'soon there'll be whole streets of 'em'.

I had stood, stock-still, not wanting to look to see if Mr Bashir had heard. I had felt the heat rising in my cheeks, even though it wasn't me who said it. There was something about that word and the way it was said, usually shouted by the worst children at school, or spat out by grown-ups, like a threat. Even Arthur had seemingly been struck dumb, the silence stretching out until it became almost unbearable. 'I didn't mean you, of course. You're different,' Kenneth had said, in an unnaturally loud voice, taking his things to the counter.

'I know exactly what you meant,' Mr Bashir said, each word crisp and impressively delivered. Kenneth seemed to take this as a sign that all was well, but I knew from Mr Bashir's voice that it wasn't. Adults were always doing this, in my experience, saying one thing and meaning another, the truth a blur in between. Living with Aunty Jean I had learned to translate the meaning that sat lurking underneath, and I could tell by the almost undetectable narrowing of his eyes and the set of his jaw that Mr Bashir was furious. After the two men left, I took the packet of crisps I had decided to buy up to the cash register.

'Why didn't you say anything?' I asked, putting my hand over my mouth after the words had escaped. I had not planned to say them, but Aunty Jean's words when I'd told her about being bullied at school once were ringing in my mind. 'Stick up for theeself,' she'd said, although I had been too afraid to, and instead had just faded into the background of school, becoming quieter and quieter until they left me alone. That was until I had Sharon. But Mr Bashir was an adult. I didn't want to think of adults being afraid.

Mr Bashir looked at me, his expression unreadable. 'Because I wouldn't have any customers left,' he said, through gritted teeth, his control somehow making the anger feel more dangerous. That moment came to mind as I thought about the possibility of Mr Bashir being the Ripper, alongside everything else we knew about him.

And so he was the first suspect to go on the list.

1. The Man in the Corner Shop

- He has dark hair
- He has a moustache
- He has dark eyes
- He's not from round our way
- He drives a Ford Corsair

2

Miv

'I've been thinking,' I said to Sharon, as we walked to the shop the next morning. It was another bright day and we'd both taken off the anoraks we'd been forced to put on by Aunty Jean and had tied them around our waists. It was another of Aunty Jean's 'just in case' instructions, this time just in case of rain, though there wasn't a cloud in the sky.

'We need to find out more about Mr Bashir,' I continued.

'Like what?' asked Sharon, twiddling her hair around her finger as we went along.

'Well, like is he married? And if not, then why not?' I said. An adult man being unmarried was almost unheard of in our world, and therefore suspicious on its own. 'And what he gets up to when he's not in the shop.'

I had decided it was unlikely that the Ripper would be married. I couldn't understand how anyone could manage to keep such crimes from a person they lived with. We were on top of each other in our house, and though no one ever talked about anything, we could all see and hear what was going on. In fact our whole street knew what was going on, if their pitying looks were anything to go by.

'But it's better if you do the asking,' I said, turning to Sharon and looking at her almost cherubic profile. She turned towards me, her forehead crinkling into a question which I answered with, 'People always like you,' leaving the 'more than me' unsaid.

When we got to the shop and were paying for our cans of dandelion and burdock, Sharon, continuing to play with her hair, her eyes wide and her voice clear and sing-song, asked Mr Bashir, 'Where did you come here from?' and I knew I'd made the right choice. I would have fumbled the question if I'd had the courage to ask it at all.

Mr Bashir laughed in response, a deep, knowing rumble. But then again, he laughed at almost anything. 'Bradford,' he said, to our obvious surprise, his face straightening to a more serious expression. He waited a beat while we stared at him, and I suddenly began to feel awkward, until he continued, 'But my family is from Pakistan – originally.' He broke into a smile and winked.

He pointed behind him at the door leading to the stockroom and living area of the house. Pinned on it were small square photographs of families, houses and landscapes alien to both of us. He pulled up the counter, allowing us through to get a closer look. I held back, but Sharon motioned to me to step through behind her. As we got nearer to Mr Bashir, I inhaled his tangy, warm skin, a smell peculiar to dads, and I wanted to stand as close to him as possible. Sharon pointed at each photo on the door in turn, asking, 'Who's this?' and 'Where's this?' while Mr Bashir answered every question in his soft, melodic voice. At one point he looked at me and, frowning, said, 'What's the matter? Cat got your tongue?'

Sharon jumped in before I could answer. 'Don't worry, Mr Bashir, she's only quiet because she's thinking.' Then she added in a conspiratorial whisper, 'Me mum says she thinks too much.'

I drew back from them both, initially puzzled at this observation, but then shrugged to myself, realising it was probably true. Mr Bashir looked at me, his own expression thoughtful. 'I see,' he said, nodding at me, and I found myself nodding back, feeling like he recognised something in me that I couldn't quite name.

At that very moment the door to the back of the house was wrenched open and a boy burst out, laughing as he did so, limbs everywhere, making the three of us jump. The second our presence was registered he stopped, stared and seemed to shrink back in on himself. Sharon and I stared back.

'Have you met my quiet, well-behaved son?' Mr Bashir asked, rolling his eyes. 'Ishtiaq.' Sharon and I both looked down and shook our heads, though of course we had. Tall and skinny with jet-black hair and eyes, Ishtiaq was in our year at school. His expression told me he recognised us too, but he said nothing.

'Back in there, you,' Mr Bashir said, his voice

affectionately scolding. 'I've told you it's dangerous running through the door like that.' The boy quietly disappeared back into the house, and with the spell of connection broken we headed off, taking our cans of dandelion and burdock with us.

Later, I wondered at the difference between the shy and silent Ishtiaq in our class and the boisterous, laughing boy I had seen in the shop. I wondered if he was just thoughtful, like me. As if reading my mind, Sharon commented on it too.

'I've never even seen him smile at school,' she said.

3

Omar

Omar Bashir watched the girls go, his face arranged into its customary smile. As the heavy door closed and the bell jangled, he turned back to the collage of faded pictures stuck to the back of it, both drawn to and repulsed by the photograph he loved and avoided in equal measure.

It was the obligatory portrait they had taken to send back home as proof of their success and prosperity to the family they had left behind. His hair was still black then – none of the salt which infused the pepper now – and he looked uncomfortable in front of the camera, though there was an expression of relief on his face as he stood there in his Bradford City Transport uniform.

Like every other young, fit man in his village, he'd come over to work in the mills. He had soon looked for an escape from the back-breaking, monotonous work and had landed himself one of the coveted jobs on the buses, mainly thanks to his learning the language so quickly, his love of words and books being of unexpected benefit in this new life. His relief was because this meant that Rizwana had been able to join him more quickly than he'd dared to hope. She was by his side in the photograph, her eyes on him, smiling and relaxed, in contrast to his awkward and stiff formality. She was resplendent in a turquoise salwar kameez.

As always, the grief was visceral, like a sharp kick to his gut, causing him to steady himself against the shop counter, bracing himself while the pain passed. He slowly stood up, shook his head and went into the back room to see Ishtiaq. On the door opening, Ishtiaq turned to look at him, his dark eyes so reminiscent of Rizwana's that Omar's vision blurred.

'You all right, Dad?' Ishtiaq asked, his voice quiet yet full of concern.

'Of course,' he replied, leaning forward to ruffle his son's hair over the back of the sofa.

Ishtiaq returned to whatever cartoon he was watching but Omar continued to gaze at him. Ishtiaq was so sensitive, Omar worried about him daily. He was often blindsided by the extent of his deep love for the boy and found it hard to balance the desire to protect him with the freedom he and Rizwana had always wanted him to have.

'Just be careful if you go out.'

Ishtiaq turned back round at the serious tone to his voice.

'There's some lads out there, short-haired, rough looking . . .'

Ishtiaq nodded, his expression resigned.

*

Back behind the counter the rest of the morning passed by busily with deliveries and customers, *Goodbye Yellow Brick Road* playing loudly on his tape recorder whenever the shop was empty. When they had first moved in, he'd been surprised at how routine the days were. It had been exactly what he needed: the soothing, hypnotic rhythm of the same people, at the same time, buying the same things had carried him through those initial days of loss.

As early afternoon was always quiet, he restocked the shelves and tidied up. His only regular customer during this time was Brian, a young man who lived two streets over with his mum, Valerie, who worked at the biscuit factory. She and her friends would have given the aunties back in Bradford a run for their money: they knew everything about the comings and goings of the town's inhabitants. Omar often wondered if Brian's silence was because he had never managed to get a word in edgeways at home, and his vocal cords had atrophied as a result.

He suspected Brian chose that time to come in because he knew the shop would be quiet. He'd sometimes see him stood outside, in his oily blue overalls and yellow bobble hat, watching the shop, presumably waiting for it to empty before he came in. Over time, he'd learned that Brian preferred not to make eye contact, so he prepared his order – a packet of ten Mayfair cigarettes and a copy of the *Yorkshire Chronicle* – and left it on the counter.

When the door jangled, signalling Brian's arrival, he did what he always did and turned the volume of the tape recorder down. He'd noticed early on that Brian winced at the noise when the music was loud, his shoulders rising as if trying to cover his ears. Omar concentrated on replacing things on the shelves, swallowing down his natural inclination to chat while Brian picked his order up and left the right amount in silver and coppers on the counter in exchange, the only indication of his having been there at all the sound of the door as he left.

Valerie had once come in to collect Brian's order, and, as she'd left, she'd gruffly thanked Omar for 'looking after my boy'. It was the first time she'd ever actually spoken to him beyond the exchange of money for goods, and it had signalled a new phase of acceptance of his place in the community, an acceptance he was often unsure about whether he wanted or not. She had since brought all her friends to the shop and she often stopped for conversation, always asking about Ishtiaq.

A few hours later, Ishtiaq's head appeared around the door to the house, his daily reminder that it was time to shut up shop and make their tea. When Rizwana had got sick, she had insisted, despite his protests, that he learn how to make their son's favourite dishes, not wanting to give up her secret recipes to the women who clucked around her. He quietly thanked her for this every day, knowing that the familiarity of the food gave the boy comfort.

He nodded and sent Ishtiaq out to bring the newspaper stand inside while he closed up. Within moments,
there was a strangled cry. Omar's mind went immediately to the short-haired boys, and he ran outside,
putting his hand over his mouth to cover up the shout
when he saw what was written on the walls of their
home. Ishtiaq's eyes were filled with angry tears. Omar
knew he was old enough now to hold on to these things,
to remember them and carry them with him. And these
things had been happening his whole life.

'This can't go on, Dad,' he said, the words of reproof
quietly spoken yet sharp, cutting so deeply that Omar
winced as if they were slicing through his skin.

'Son, it's not everyone,' he replied. 'It's just a few
ignorant people who shout louder than the rest. Things
have been getting better lately, haven't they?' He was
acutely aware that this was a desperate attempt to placate his son, or was it a desperate attempt to placate
himself? Suddenly he wasn't so sure, and his shoulders
slumped with an exhaustion that he had battled with
every day since Rizwana had died.

'You say that every time, Dad. And no, it's not getting better.' Ishtiaq was looking down at his shoes as he
said this, almost muttering.

It hadn't escaped Omar's notice that Ishtiaq often
came home with scrapes and bruises that he shrugged
off with the answer 'Dunno' when pressed about where
they were from. At one point Omar had done what Ishtiaq had resisted, and gone up to the school to discuss

his son's injuries directly. He'd found himself sat in a stuffy staffroom, opposite his son's teacher, after everyone else had gone home, inhaling the smell of stale cigarettes and coffee. His chair was lower than the teacher's and he briefly wondered if that was by design.

Mr Ware, a tall, imposing figure, appeared distracted and impatient to get rid of him. 'If Ishtiaq won't say what's happened to him, then I can't see what we're supposed to do about it. Who's to say it happened at school or even has anything to do with the school? I know it must be difficult to keep an eye on your son, given your . . . situation.'

The word *situation* was said with a distaste Omar almost found funny. His situation was that of a widowed father who had to work. Yes, it would be better if Ishtiaq had a mum who was alive and able to be with him, but it was hardly something to be ashamed of. Omar stared at the teacher, waiting for him to give him full eye contact before he said, 'I'd like you to explain what you mean by that.'

He'd enjoyed watching the teacher squirm; he got the sense the man was unused to being challenged in that way. But regardless, he'd left without a resolution. Unless Ishtiaq would say who had hurt him, there was nothing to be done. He was half angry and half proud that his son wouldn't give their names up. Ishtiaq told Omar, 'It'll only make it worse if you stick up for me. I'll deal with it, Dad,' any time Omar pushed, which he did frequently, trying multiple strategies, from kind and caring to anger and threats. His son was getting more like his mother every day. There was never any shifting Rizwana once she'd made up her mind.

'Dad.' He was brought back to the present moment. 'Maybe we shouldn't have come here.' The words were crisp and clear though quietly spoken, and Omar felt each one physically, almost putting his hands up to shield himself against them. He stared at his son. His quietness vibrated with emotion, the source of it so deep that it seemed to shake the entire shop.

'Son, you weren't born when we moved here,' Omar said, his voice as quiet as Ishtiaq's, 'so you won't know how hard it was back in Bradford, and how me and your mum used to feel like we would never fit in. And I don't know that we ever did, but somewhere along the line Bradford became home.' He found himself pausing, as a surge of memories flooded his senses: their little house in Bradford that Rizwana had made so beautiful, their pride in it, how happy they were when Ishtiaq was born.

'This place will become home too. It will,' he finished, trying to inject his wobbly voice with more conviction than he really felt.

Ishtiaq's face softened. 'OK, Dad,' he said, and though Omar knew he was being placated, that the conversation wasn't over, that it would probably never be, he suddenly felt exhausted. He put his hand on Ishtiaq's shoulder and led him inside.

Later that evening, after the boy had gone to bed,

Omar sat in the lumpy, frayed armchair next to the window, a delayed rage overtaking his body so fiercely that he began to shake. He imagined what he would do to the people who painted such things on walls and who hurt his son. It was a rage that often overtook him in the darkness of the evenings and was one of the many reasons he made sure he was always busy in the daytime. He couldn't afford to let it spill out then.

'Our son needs one parent to be around,' Rizwana had told him. 'What do you think happens when people like us get arrested in this country?' She'd extracted a promise that he would never physically fight back, for Ishtiaq's sake. He was a man of his word.

At the sound of a noise outside he sprang up, powered by anger and adrenaline, and peered around the side of the orange nylon curtains, through the faded beige nets, on alert for the short-haired boys. As he took in the dusky alleyway and the backs of the shabby, tiny houses, packed together in rows, he realised this could easily be Bradford. His head echoed with the voice of Rizwana's brother, Masood, when Omar had announced they were moving here, away from family and friends.

'You can't outrun grief, brother.'

But when the shop came up for rent, it had felt like a sign, and Omar had carried on anyway, despite Masood's warnings that 'it won't be like Bradford', meaning there wouldn't be so many brown faces here. But he'd wanted to start a new life, away from any reminders of Rizwana's last months and, in truth, away from her family – who had all followed her after she had come over – and their cloying closeness. He didn't want to be around people who grew up with her, looked like her, or used the same expressions.

So they'd moved to this town, where the unspoken segregation of streets meant that they were indeed the only brown faces. Had they moved to a street only half a mile away, they would have been submerged into a new, if smaller, community of friends, but that would have meant interference in their lives and he couldn't bear anyone telling him how to raise his son except her. They had her practicality to thank for the fact that after her diagnosis they'd had endless discussions about the approach he would take on everything, from language – he was to speak both Urdu and English with Ishtiaq – to marriage and possible careers for their son, and had landed on the same approach for them all: don't push him or he will resist. Omar didn't need anyone else's opinion.

Not long after she had passed, he had begun to get unsubtle hints about how he should get married again as soon as possible, and how he should be raising Ishtiaq. The arguments with Rizwana's family had continued until the day they'd left, but he'd held firm. Rizwana had wanted freedom and opportunity for their boy and had impressed on him his responsibility to make sure this happened.

'We are Muslims,' Masood had declared. 'We have a duty to take care of each other.'

'Yes,' Omar had argued, 'and I am taking care of my son. Doesn't that count?'

He wondered for a moment whether he had been entirely selfish. The person who would have told him honestly was no longer there.

4

Miv

'I've had an idea,' I said to Sharon when I went to call for her the next morning. 'A way we can find out more about Mr Bashir and whether he's the Ripper.'

'Go on,' she said, smiling, as she closed her front door and joined me on the pavement.

Eager to keep a superior air of mystery, I shook my head.

'You'll see. Just follow my lead when we get there.'

Sharon rolled her eyes but was still smiling as Mrs Pearson and her Jack Russell barrelled past us. Saying a cheery 'Hello!', we carried on to the shop. When we arrived, Mr Bashir was scrubbing the wall outside vigorously with a big bucket of water beside him, the soap-sodden water, tinged a dirty pink, running in rivulets through the cracks in the pavement. 'Morning, Mr Bashir,' we shouted in unison.

He turned and looked at us, nodded and smiled briefly, the smile nowhere near reaching his eyes, which seemed to shine with an unexpected anger. I felt Sharon stiffen beside me, but I was curious. He was very cross about something, and this was interesting to me, as the

Ripper was often said to be angry. He turned straight back to his task. I could just make out the outline of the letters *N* and *F*, surrounded by a circle in red spray-paint, this outline all that was left of whatever had been daubed across the wall. It was a symbol I saw often on walls and windows, and I had always assumed it was someone's initials. I had never seen Mr Bashir look so serious. Maybe he was cross about the graffiti, I reasoned. I could imagine Aunty Jean's response if it had been our house. *Young people today*, she would have said, with cold fury, *you don't know you're born*, as if somehow I'd been responsible for it, just by being young.

I looked around, and for the first time noticed curtains twitching as neighbours watched Mr Bashir. Valerie Lockwood – from the next street over – was talking quietly with the local rag-and-bone man, Arthur, both shaking their heads and nodding towards the shop. It felt like something more had happened than simple graffiti, but I couldn't work out what.

'Is Ishtiaq in?' I said a little nervously, not sure what reaction I was going to get.

Mr Bashir stopped and looked at us properly this time, wiping sweat from his face with a handkerchief he pulled from his pocket.

'He's in the back, watching something on the telly,' he said, then added: 'Can you get him to make me a cuppa while you're there?' His features softened as he said this and I nodded, feeling relieved that the Mr Bashir I knew was back again.

'Of course, Mr Bashir,' said Sharon solemnly, and I looked at her quickly. 'Can we do anything else to help?'

He shook his head, and we walked through to the back of the shop.

As we pushed open the door to the living area and stepped inside, I was surprised to see that the hallway looked like one you'd find in all the other houses on the street. I'm not sure what I'd expected, but it certainly wasn't the same swirly-carpeted, beige-walled Anaglypta that we had too. The only difference was a delicious, unfamiliar aroma that made my tummy rumble.

Ishtiaq was sat in the darkened living room, curtains drawn, deeply intent on the television. He didn't look up as we stood in the doorway. Sharon nudged me hard and nodded her head at him. 'Go on then,' she hissed, 'this was your idea.' She pushed me ahead of her and I stumbled into the room, righting myself just before I fell. He finally turned his head.

'Ey up, Ishtiaq,' I spluttered. He stared at us both, brow furrowed, taking us in.

'Hi?' he said. His voice had an uneasy question mark in it. 'What do you want?'

'We've, er, we've come to say hello,' I continued. 'And, um, to see if you wanted to laik out some time?' I felt flustered, and I could see Sharon's eyes widening in surprise as though this was the last thing she'd expected from me. My eyes drifted to the TV, and with relief I saw that he was watching cricket. This was my opportunity. 'Do you play?' I asked, indicating the screen.

Ishtiaq nodded, keeping his eyes firmly on me, narrowing them slightly, as if mistrusting my motivation for asking.

'I can,' I said, standing tall, as though that would somehow demonstrate my cricketing prowess. Ishtiaq's expression remained sceptical.

'Me dad says I learned to play as soon as I could walk,' I said proudly. 'He says cricket is in my blood.'

Ishtiaq's face finally broke into a smile. Whether he was relaxed or amused I couldn't tell.

'OK then, why don't we play?' Ishtiaq said. 'Tomorrow morning, in the park. One can bowl, one can bat and one can field.'

'All right,' I replied.

'We'll call for you in the morning then? When the shop opens?' I continued.

He nodded his head but looked quizzically at us again, as though he was still confused about our motives. We were just about to leave when Sharon turned back.

'Oh,' she said, 'your dad said can you make him a cup of tea, please?' Her voice sounded wobbly, as if she had not used it for a while and was out of practice, like when I hadn't sung for a bit. Ishtiaq smiled at her and nodded once more as she looked down at her feet.

'See you tomorrow then,' I said, puzzled at Sharon's sudden shyness.

'Prepare to be battered,' I heard him say quietly, as we left.

'What was all that about?' asked Sharon when we got out onto the street.

'I could say the same to you,' I said, but my eagerness to share my plan overtook my curiosity about what had come over Sharon.

'Now we've made friends with Ishtiaq, we can find out more about Mr Bashir, ask Ishtiaq where he goes and that. We can also find out what happened to Mrs Bashir,' I said, a note of triumph at my ingenuity creeping into my voice. 'Have you noticed that we've never ever seen her?' I nodded, knowingly.

'You're good at this,' she said with a chuckle and even a hint of surprise. I walked tall the rest of the way home, feeling Sharon's praise in every limb.

But on the way over to the Bashirs' the next morning, Sharon was unusually silent. It was early – I always got out of the house as soon as possible, even in the school holidays, or maybe especially in the school holidays – and the only sound on the streets other than our footsteps was birdsong and the gentle hum of the milk float making deliveries. Sharon's silence lasted so long, however, that I started to wonder if she had changed her mind about the day.

'You all right? You're dead quiet.'

'Yeah,' she said and went quiet again.

I waited, knowing that Sharon took a while to admit when all wasn't well.

'Me dad asked me what we did yesterday, so I told

him,' she continued. 'He wasn't happy about us laiking out with Ishtiaq.'

I didn't need to ask why.

Shazia Mir had been the first brown girl to join our junior-school class. She wore trousers under her uniform skirts and was the first person I'd seen with a nose ring. I'd wanted one immediately. I can't remember when the boys started holding their noses when they walked past her, or when everyone stopped sitting with her at dinnertime. I can remember when the chanting started though.

'Roses are red, violets are blue,
Shazia smells like an animal in a zoo.'

At first, I had joined in, never comfortable but wanting to be part of something. Until one day the chants were aimed at me:

'Roses are red, violets are blue,
Your mum's in a loony bin and you will be too.'

And I never joined in again. Even though it seemed like a long time ago, I always felt uncomfortable when I thought about Shazia, sitting alone every day in the corner of the playground, until one day she disappeared. No one ever told us why. Aunty Jean had said, 'I'm sure they're very nice, respectable people,' when talking about her family, 'but I hope they keep themselves to themselves.' Which seemed to sum up the feelings of most of the people in our neighbourhood.

Then a memory prickled at the outer edges of my mind, and I wondered whether Sharon's dad's feelings might go even further. Before Mum fell silent, before Mr Bashir came, and before Sharon and I were friends, something had happened in church.

In those days Mum used to sing in the grown-ups' choir, and Dad and I would sit and listen, Dad completely absorbed, me squirming uncomfortably in the wooden pews. That particular Sunday we happened to be sitting on the same row as Sharon's mum, Ruby, and her dad, Malcolm. They were merely nodding acquaintances then. The vicar said something about 'welcoming people of all backgrounds and creed to the town', and Malcolm said, 'Not bloody likely' so loudly everyone turned to stare at him.

'Do you want to do something else today instead?' I asked. 'I can always see Ishtiaq on my own and report back later.'

'No!' she said immediately, frowning. 'But if anyone asks, can we say it was just us laikin' out? Mum and Dad ended up shouting at each other and I don't want them to fall out over it. Dad's gone away again for a few nights, so he won't know. And anyway . . .' She didn't finish the thought, turning her face away from me.

'Are you crying?' I said, my words hesitant.

She shook her head slowly, keeping her face turned.

I knew that no one would ask what I had been doing, but said yes to her request anyway, feeling strangely unsettled by the thought of Sharon's parents arguing, as though the floor under my feet had become unstable or I had missed a step. They always seemed to be so content, and were my proof that happy families existed. They were my hope that my family might one day be the same.

As we drew nearer to the shop, Ishtiaq was already outside, seemingly anticipating our arrival. His hair was brushed neatly into a side parting and his outfit of jeans and a white T-shirt looked unusually smart. At school, he suffered from the double social hex of being both brown and clever, but today I realised for the first time that he was rather handsome. I looked down and saw he was also carrying a sports bag with wickets and bats. I raised an eyebrow; he was taking this seriously.

We were just about to leave when Mr Bashir's head appeared around the shop door. He was holding out a full carrier bag, one of the shop's candy-striped ones, which he waved in Ishtiaq's direction.

'Food,' he said, beaming.

'Thanks, Dad,' muttered Ishtiaq, grabbing the bag as if embarrassed.

As we made our way to the park, Sharon and Ishtiaq walked side by side on the pavement and I walked with one foot on the kerb and one on the road. Ishtiaq and I discussed our favourite cricket teams and who might win the Ashes next, while Sharon stayed quiet, having no real knowledge of the sport, but kept her eyes glued on Ishtiaq. Then I remembered what we were supposed to be doing. I had written a list of questions in the notebook which I had memorised.

'Is your dad always in the shop?' I asked. 'Every time we come in, we see him.'

'Aye, he is,' Ishtiaq said, his small smile appearing.

I made a mental note.

'I mean, what if he gets sick or something?' I asked, genuinely curious, and, before he could answer, continued, 'Do you have a mum?' at which Sharon nudged me, and I knew I had gone too far. A shadow crossed Ishtiaq's face.

'I did, but she died,' he said, his voice flat.

I was stunned and stopped in my tracks. I hadn't even considered this as a possibility.

'Oh. I'm sorry.' I knew that's what you were supposed to say, though I didn't quite understand what I was apologising for. Ishtiaq stopped too, his eyes narrowing.

'Why all the questions?' He was suspicious again.

'Just being nosey,' I said honestly. 'So it's just you two then? Does your dad ever leave you with anyone else? Babysitters, family, like?'

'No. We don't see our family much any more,' he said, and I watched as he closed down fully, like the shutters on the shop, disappearing into himself until he became the more familiar, quiet Ishtiaq.

'Well, you've got us now,' Sharon said gently, and briefly touched his arm. He looked straight at her and eventually spoke again, his voice so quiet now I had to strain to hear him.

'Since Mum died, we're always together. We call

ourselves the Dynamic Duo. Oh! And you're the Terrible Twosome.' He seemed to find this hilarious and laughed so infectiously that Sharon and I joined in, dissolving the tension.

I was not disappointed by this revelation of their constant togetherness. This surely meant that Mr Bashir was in the clear. If he was always in the shop or with his son, I couldn't see how he could be the Ripper, and actually I'd hoped he wasn't. I liked Mr Bashir. I caught Sharon's eye, and we smiled at each other; she was thinking the same thing as I was.

I stepped ahead of Sharon and Ishtiaq, leading the way to the park, and before long realised that they had fallen into conversation. I tried to tune in, but she had lowered her usually clear, melodic voice to match Ishtiaq's murmurs. She seemed to be finding it very easy to make him talk, and the quiet hum of their voices rippled through the air until we got to the park, where we laid out a cricket pitch using the wickets Ishtiaq had brought and our anoraks.

The 'park' was really a large stretch of grass which only loosely earned its title thanks to the wonky swings and rusted roundabout that occupied a small corner of the space. The edges were framed with piles of rubbish – crisp packets, cans and endless cigarette butts – but there was enough green and worn brown grass to play on. Located between my and Sharon's houses, we had played there ever since we became friends. We still favoured it over hanging around the shops or in bus shelters, which many of the other girls in our class now did, in the hope of bumping into boys. At least I thought that Sharon still felt the same way I did.

One match turned into a best of three and then a best of five. I ran, exhilarated, from one end of the park to the other, losing all my usual self-consciousness in the desire to win, glowing with pride when Ishtiaq said, 'You can actually play,' and at some point I realised that I was having fun. The realisation crept up on me, like it had tapped me on the shoulder, and I was surprised to see it there. Eventually, tired from running around, we sat down to eat our dinner on the checked blanket that we had brought. Mr Bashir had made a feast fit for the Famous Five from the shop – cheese sandwiches, cans of pop and more than one flavour of crisp – which Ishtiaq pulled out of his bag, along with a sleek-looking camera.

'I like to take pictures,' Ishtiaq said, the explanation somewhat unnecessary.

I took the camera and carefully inspected it. My only experience of cameras was Dad's Box Brownie and the cinefilm camera he used to take on holiday with us when we were a proper family. I wasn't allowed to touch them. When we got home from Filey or Scarborough, seaside towns on the North Yorkshire coast where we always went, he would insist we watched the silent films of us running in and out of the sea, even though we had just got back and could remember it quite clearly.

Ishtiaq's camera was a small, rectangular black box with a red button. It looked distinctly space age in comparison with Dad's. I asked Ishtiaq if I was allowed to take a picture, and he nodded, showing me how to hold it straight. I took one of Sharon and Ishtiaq, caught in a moment of laughter. Then I used the little window to follow two figures in the distance who were heading our way. Ishtiaq followed my line of sight, then sat up, suddenly alert, like an animal catching a scent.

Seeing him stiffen, I put the camera down.

The figures were closer now. It was Neil and Richard from our class. Out of our usual school setting they looked different. More adult. Both were wearing green nylon bomber jackets, with white T-shirts, rolled-up jeans and black monkey boots. They looked identical, like soldiers in uniform.

A sudden feeling of fear started coursing through my body, as though the sugar we had consumed had been directly injected into my limbs.

Ishtiaq began packing away the cricket kit, his movements jerky, tense. *But we know these boys, they won't hurt us*, I wanted to say, but found the words had formed a lump in my throat I couldn't dislodge.

'Where are you go——?' Sharon started to say, but was interrupted by Richard, who was now within speaking distance.

'What you been eating, Bashir? Curry? You can smell it from miles away,' he said, sneering.

'Nothing,' mumbled Ishtiaq, his gaze on the floor,

his expression closed. I found myself quietly observing what was happening, as if I wasn't really there. Was this what Ishtiaq felt like most of the time?

Richard turned his attention to me and Sharon, saying, 'What are you two doing playing with him? Haven't you got any friends?'

Sharon stood up. 'He *is* our friend,' she almost shouted as she picked up the blanket we'd been lying on and started to fold it, violently.

'Leave 'em. They're only girls,' Neil said, putting his hand on Richard's arm, but Richard shook it off.

'You shouldn't be playing together,' he said, his voice filled with a quiet menace. 'It's not appropriate. You should stick to your own kind.' He nodded at Ishtiaq.

I wondered where he had got the word *appropriate* from, then remembered the boy I'd known at junior school, curled up next to me with a book. I stared at Richard's face, trying to appeal to that boy with my eyes.

'Who says?'

I jolted in surprise that Ishtiaq had spoken. He had drawn himself up, as though he might match the boys' height, but instead highlighting his thin frame against theirs.

'Let's go,' said Sharon, making eye contact with Neil, who indicated with his head that we all needed to move on. We turned to go, and I briefly glanced behind me. Richard was staring at Sharon unblinking, while Neil held on to his arm, his knuckles white with the strain of holding him back. Sharon's face was a fiery red, but I realised with a start that this was no blush of embarrassed shyness. She was furious. We walked quickly across the park and Sharon turned to Ishtiaq. 'How much does that happen?' she asked.

'All the time,' said Ishtiaq, shrugging.

As we made our way home, the further away we were from Neil and Richard, the more we began to chatter about who played cricket best and who caught the most balls, as if releasing all the noise swallowed down in the boys' presence. I kept turning back, hoping not to see the sight of their black boots behind us.

Back at the shop, Mr Bashir had cold cans of cherry-ade waiting. I guzzled mine so quickly that I got the hiccups, which made Sharon giggle so much she snorted hers through her nose. Mr Bashir and Ishtiaq caught the wave and all four of us laughed uncontrollably until everything hurt.

When I got home that evening, the house was silent and the battered brown armchair where Mum sat when she came downstairs was empty, showing the grooves of her shape in the leather. The banging of a window somewhere alerted me to the fact that there was a cool breeze running through the house.

I found the back door open. Mum was sat outside in our tiny patch of garden, still in her nightie and shivering with cold, looking blankly into the distance. I stared at her sunken face. Before everything happened, what looked like straight lines on me would have been described in one of my books as 'refined features' on Mum. I knew she had been beautiful, in a fragile way, but now she just looked gaunt.

Her haunted eyes turned to meet mine and I approached her slowly, as you might step towards a wounded animal. I felt myself disappear inside myself again, the feeling reminding me of the one I had experienced in the park earlier. It was like being in a fairground hall of mirrors, as I watched a version of me say, 'Come on,' while encouraging her up with hands that weren't my hands, using the tone of voice she had once used whenever I was upset. Kind, but firm. This version of me washed up and made toast for us both, Mum chewing hers slowly, in tiny bites. I found myself saying, 'Good girl, good girl' to encourage her to finish it all, then I tucked her into bed before Dad and Aunty Jean got home from work, like she was my child, not the other way around.

I didn't come back to myself until later, when Dad appeared at my bedroom door to say goodnight. I was on the verge of telling him about everything – the incident at the park, coming home to find Mum outside – when I looked at his face and noticed the grey weariness in the lines around his eyes.

'Night, Dad,' I said instead.

'Night night.'

The weather broke the next day and the smell of spring rain filled the air. It was too wet to call for Sharon, so I decided to spend the morning curled up on the settee, reading, while Dad went to the delivery depot where he was a supervisor and Aunty Jean to the Unemployment Office where she worked. I was surprised to see Mum downstairs, given how she'd been the day before. She was sat silently in her armchair, her beige nightie and pale face blurring into each other, watching the television with the sound turned right down.

I was so rarely at home during daylight hours that I wondered whether this was what she did each day and if she got bored, though 'only boring people are bored', as Aunty Jean would say whenever I complained of boredom myself. I could only vaguely remember the house being full of the sound of her – the radio always playing while she sang along – even though it was just a couple of years ago. The thought of how lonely she must be made my eyes sting and my throat hurt. I wanted to reach out and touch her, but it was as if she had an invisible forcefield surrounding her, like someone on *Doctor Who*. I couldn't bear it. I felt itchy with the need to get away from the sadness.

As soon as the rain retreated to a light drizzle, I guiltily slipped on my cagoule and ran round to Sharon's, where she was sat eating apple and cheese with Ruby. Surrounding them on the table were sheets of drawing paper covered in felt-tip pen. As I looked more closely, I could see that the drawings were of the robes and jewellery of one of the women we'd seen in the photos on Mr Bashir's back door. Ruby left us to it, planting a kiss on both our foreheads as she picked up the plates and took them to the kitchen. I took a deep breath in to inhale her scent of baking and perfume.

'Shall we go and call for Ishtiaq?' asked Sharon.

I was puzzled for a moment. 'But we've crossed Mr Bashir off the list, haven't we? He's not the Ripper. He's always in the shop, Ishtiaq says. So why would we need to go and see him again?'

Sharon sighed. 'That wasn't what I meant. I meant shall we call for him just to laik out?'

'Oh,' I said, absorbing this turn of events. 'Why?'

Sharon's brow furrowed, but she was smiling as she said, 'Because yesterday was brilliant, because we laughed so much, because you love cricket and because he's nice. We are allowed to have fun, you know.'

Not for the first time I wondered whether Sharon had been given some secret to life that had not been bestowed on me. 'OK,' I said hesitantly. 'Can we go back to the list later though?'

She shook her head at me, still smiling. 'Yeeessssss,' she said in the manner of indulging a small child.

I pushed her. 'Oi, cheeky,' I said, and she shoved me back until we collapsed into giggles.

'Let's go and call for Ishtiaq then,' I said.

When we got to the shop there was a piece of paper sellotaped to the door. In shaky blue biro it read: *Closed for cleaning*.

We peered in the window to see Mr Bashir on his

hands and knees scrubbing the floor with a brush, his eyes unseeing and glazed. I knocked gently on the glass.

'Mr Bashir, can Ishtiaq come out to play?'

He got slowly to his feet and opened the door, the strains of 'Rocket Man' on the tape recorder accompanying him. It somehow sounded mournful and sad, matching his expression. 'Go down the ginnel at the side and you can go in the back,' he said, then immediately shut the door. We did as we were told, unsettled by Mr Bashir's abruptness. Sharon tapped on the back door and Ishtiaq answered.

'You laikin' out?' she asked.

As he stood in the door frame, the sun briefly appeared from behind a cloud, illuminating the streaks of tears already shed.

'What's going on, what's happened?' I blurted, unable to stop myself.

'Somebody threw a bottle of wee into the shop,' he muttered, looking down as though ashamed. 'It went everywhere.'

At first I thought I had misheard. But the sharp gasp from Sharon told me I had heard correctly. We both stood stock-still, staring at Ishtiaq in horror. It was as if the two of us had been turned to stone, like in some fairy story.

'Why would someone *do* that?' I asked, my voice breaking. 'Have you called the police?'

Ishtiaq looked at me, an opaque expression on his face. He shook his head. 'I'm not playing out today,' he said. With that he tried to close the door, but Sharon's foot shot out and blocked the way. He looked down at her bright white pump, then up at her, confused.

'Do you have any games? To play, like?' she said, as if the rest of the conversation hadn't taken place.

'I've got Operation,' he replied, sounding even more confused.

Sharon and I looked at each other. Operation was the most coveted game at school: a board in the shape of a man whose bones you had to remove with tweezers, and which buzzed if the bones touched the sides. 'Well then, let's play inside if you're not laikin' out,' said Sharon, as though this was the most logical suggestion. Ishtiaq looked down, and I held my breath for a moment, wondering if he would say no, when he opened the door properly and let us in.

While Ishtiaq hunted out the game from his bedroom and Sharon went to the toilet, I took a proper look around the living room for the first time. It was full of contradictions. The television sat on wooden packing boxes with the names of fruit and veg printed on the sides, and the brown settee was worn and threadbare at the seams, but piled high in a dark corner were Ishtiaq's cricket equipment and teetering towers of the very latest games and books, their primary colours shining out against the dull and dingy walls and floor. Perched on the top was my favourite game, KerPlunk, which I thought was funny, seeing as the game was all about balance and the entire lot looked like it would collapse if you removed just one of them. Taking the whole room in, I knew that Aunty Jean would declare, 'This place needs a woman's touch.'

Sharon kept up a steady stream of chatter as we set up the game and began playing, while I stayed silent, struck mute by my inability to express my horror at what had happened to the Bashirs. As I watched Ishtiaq slowly re-emerge, and join in the game, I realised I didn't need to say anything. Maybe just being here was enough. But I couldn't let it go. It wasn't until our second round of Operation – the first having been won by me, even though I suspected Sharon was trying to let Ishtiaq win – that I blurted out, 'I'm so sorry,' making Ishtiaq jump while trying to remove the patient's funny bone, and the board buzzed loudly.

'Why are you sorry? It wasn't you who did it.' He seemed cross that I'd brought it up, and I went to apologise once more when a tired voice spoke from the doorway.

'She means she's sorry it happened, don't you, love?'

I looked up to see Mr Bashir framed by the doorway, sweat gleaming on his forehead, cloth in hand. I nodded.

'Right, who wants a Sherbet Fountain?' he said, full of mock jollity, pulling from the pocket of his apron three yellow tubes with liquorice sticks poking out the top.

'Yes, please!' we chorused. Mr Bashir ruffled my hair when handing me mine and I inexplicably swallowed down a sob.

Later, we had just said goodbye to Ishtiaq and were walking down the ginnel to go home when he called us back.

'Do you want to laik out again tomorrow?' he said. 'Dad says you can if you want.'

'Yes,' said Sharon firmly, before I even had chance to take a breath.

'Yes,' I repeated. It seemed we were becoming friends now.

As we turned round to go again, I saw the dark shadow of a person disappearing at the other end of the ginnel, the sound of their boots echoing on the path. I wondered if someone had been watching us.

5

Miv

Numbers Two & Three

The next time I saw Ishtiaq I very nearly collided with him. I was walking down the main corridor at school on the first day back after half-term and I was overly intent on my book – I'd recently begun *Jane Eyre*. We both started and looked up at each other, eyes locking. There was a moment when it would have been possible to make a sign of recognition, but instead I carried on walking as if nothing had happened. A few moments later I looked down at my book again, only to notice that it was trembling in my hands. Why had I not said hello to him? Acknowledged our fledgling friendship?

I tried to focus on the words but found them impossible to make out as a sick, guilty feeling started to form in my tummy. I turned round, intending to call his name, but he'd disappeared into the classroom and the quiet corridor was starting to fill with noise as everyone made their way back inside after break. I contemplated running after him to explain. To say that I didn't know why I hadn't said hello. That I was sorry. But I didn't do any of those things. Instead, I looked around at the people immediately in front of me.

Three older, pretty girls were stood together, their heads almost touching, wearing the same pink lipstick and identical hairsprayed hairstyles. Nearby, there was another girl called Janice, who I knew vaguely, her socks wrinkled and her shoes scuffed. Like me, she mostly didn't exist for girls like them. She smelled like she needed a bath, and everyone called her Four Eyes because of her pale blue NHS glasses, held together in one corner by a plaster, but she aced every maths exam.

One of the girls looked up to see Janice watching them. Her eyes narrowed and I somehow knew that what was coming would be worse than being invisible. I wished Sharon was here. She knew how to defuse situations like this. She was pretty enough to have the ear of the popular girls, and weird enough to have a friend like me. Still with her eyes on Janice, the girl drew the rest of her gang to her, their heads bobbing like birds feasting on a worm. Their whispers about her fluttered in the air, then disappeared, the only trace of them now in Janice's tearful expression.

I continued to stand there, rooted to the spot, when four rowdy boys appeared, running up the corridor, bags swinging while the pretty girls squealed and flattened themselves against the wall. One of the boys roughly shoved Janice out of the way and the pretty girls sniggered as her skirt flew up, revealing grey knickers, the sort of grey that had once been white.

One of my most painful memories came surging back. One summer, when I was at infant school, before Sharon and I were friends, me, Mum and Dad were on holiday in Filey. We made friends with another family from our town who had a daughter the same age as me, Joanne. I worshipped her. She was almost posh, pronouncing all her words fully and not using Yorkshire words like *laik*, *snicket* and *bairn*, like the rest of us did. I thought of her as a princess. We spent that holiday making sandcastles and exploring the Coble Landing together.

When we went back to school after the holidays, I ran up to her, eagerly wanting to share my news from the rest of the break. She looked at me, nodded a hello and turned away to talk to the friend next to her. She never acknowledged me again. It was the first time I realised that I didn't quite have what it took to fit in. I just wasn't someone she could openly be friends with. I had felt it as hard as if she had pulled my hair or slapped me around the face and was relieved when she had gone to the local grammar school, not high school, like me.

As I moved to get out of the boys' way, I wondered where the rules had come from. The rules that said that pretty girls didn't laik out with poor girls or clever girls. The rules that said that boys and girls couldn't be friends, and certainly not white girls like me and Sharon and brown boys like Ishtiaq. I couldn't work out how I had absorbed these rules, and why I still abided by them. The corridor slowly emptied as I stood there, listening to the sounds of chatter and chairs scraping on wooden floors, then I made my way into my first lesson, seeking out my desk, next to Sharon. I took the sick, guilty feeling with me.

The usually cold classrooms at Bishopsfield High were filled with row after row of wooden desks, chipped and battered from years of use and names graffitied on with compasses. There was a main hall for assemblies with a wooden floor which smelled of antiseptic and sweat, and the playground was an unkempt field. There was a toilet block outside where our voices would echo and our bodies shiver when we had to use it. It reminded me of the school in *Jane Eyre*. Bishopsfield had been built in Victorian times, according to the history posters framed inside the school entrance. It looked as though nothing had changed since then, but I could imagine that it had once housed children very much posher than us.

It being the first day back after half-term, it felt like all thirty of our class were fidgeting, pulling at our uniform collars and wishing we were allowed to remove our jumpers. We were currently learning about the Industrial Revolution through the imagined stories of mill workers in the West Riding of Yorkshire. It was not enthralling stuff and we wanted to go home. A small scuffle broke out at the back of the room. Everyone turned round to see what was happening and I sighed inwardly. It was the usual suspects, Neil Callaghan and Richard Collier. The volume of chatter and discontent quickly increased.

'Right,' said Mr Ware, his voice containing a warning tone. 'Everybody stop. Hands on heads.' It took longer than usual for the wave of obedience to reach the back of the class, and eventually Mr Ware rose from behind his desk and stared down his nose sternly at us, his moustache bristling.

'Enough,' he said. The steely edge to his voice made even the rowdy troublemakers at the back stop what they were doing. 'You've just earned yourselves some extra homework. I want you to find a local story about the mills. It could be from your parents, it could be from the library, but I want a story, written up, with drawings, by the end of next week.'

While I was part of the collective groan that followed this announcement, I was secretly pleased. I loved homework. I also knew a bit about the mills as the women in my family had all worked in them. Aunty Jean now struggled with her hearing, dimmed by years of working on noisy mill floors from the age of fourteen. The most used word among the women in our family was *eh?* and Aunty Jean spoke in a permanent shout.

'If I hear another groan out of any of you, I'll give you something to groan about,' said Mr Ware, at which point a sulky silence descended and I attempted to focus on my work, distracted by the thought that had struck me as I stared at Mr Ware's cross face.

A recent newspaper article had focused on a photofit of the Ripper and described him as having a Jason King-like moustache. There had also been some speculation about the kind of man the police were looking for: he could be 'angry' with women, the newspaper had reported. The angriest man with a moustache I knew was Mr Ware.

While most of the teachers at Bishopsfield had been there forever, Mr Ware was a recent arrival. He had only been at the school for two years, having moved to our town from elsewhere. Just like with Mr Bashir, that very fact made him suspicious: he was not from 'round our way'. Not only that, but in that time he had built a fearsome reputation. Mr Ware was a six-foot-two, athletically built man who did not spare the rod.

As soon as he turned his back to write on the blackboard, I took the opportunity to get Sharon's attention and turned to her, eyes wide. I was met by the same expression. Clearly, she was having similar thoughts to me. When the lesson finished, we hurried out of the door and straight into the playground to find a spot out of earshot, under the shade of a large oak tree.

'Mr Ware!' I said, at the same time as Sharon said, 'The mills!'

We both froze, staring at each other.

'What did you say?'

'The mills,' she repeated breathlessly. 'They're the perfect place.'

We had decided that, as well as suspicious people, we needed to look for places where the Ripper might hide a body. My night-time research had uncovered that one of the Ripper's victims – Jayne MacDonald – had been discovered by children near an adventure play-ground. And another victim – Yvonne Pearson – had been found hidden on a stretch of wasteland in Brad-ford. A passer-by spotted her arm sticking out from under an old settee. He'd thought it was a tailor's dummy. If we could find those kinds of places, we might find him, we reasoned. Our town was littered with abandoned mill buildings – a relic of a once thriv-ing industry. Sharon was right – they were the perfect places to hide a body.

'What were you saying? About Mr Ware?' she said.

I had cut out the piece in the newspaper which described the Ripper as being angry with women and tucked it into the notebook, with our list. I got them both out of my bag and, as I did so, another article fluttered out and fell to the floor. It was about the four children of the Ripper's first victim, Wilma McCann. We read it together. Silently. As I read, I could feel my throat tightening, and coughed, trying to clear it, mor-tified as it emerged as a strangled sob. When I looked up, tears were also streaming down Sharon's face.

'Why are you crying?' Sharon asked, through a watery smile.

There was something about those left behind that made my tummy hurt. I wanted to say, *For the women who died and the people who loved them*, but the words seemed to be tied up in a jumbled knot in my head, so I just shrugged and she nodded back at me.

Then, I wrote *Mr Ware* and *The Mills* on the list.

2. Mr Ware

- He has a moustache
- He has dark hair
- He's always angry
- He's not from round our way

3. The Mills

- Dark and scary
- Great place to hide a body
- Are they haunted?

6

Mr Ware

Mike took his rage out on his cigarette, pulling hard and enjoying the searing feeling in his lungs, as if he was taking down all his anger and letting it swirl around his body, before blowing it out and infecting every corner of the room with it. He was sitting on his own, as usual, on one of the dark green fabric-covered chairs chosen specifically to hide the inevitable nicotine staining of a secondary-school staffroom. His colleagues, milling around him, chatting and drinking endless cups of tea, gave him a wide berth, his mood as visible as the smart suit and tie he wore every day to school, even though it wasn't necessary.

His fury had followed him from home that morning, like a vapour trail behind him. He had left the house with a slam of the door that had vibrated as far as his teeth, leaving his wife weeping in a heap on the hallway floor. He hadn't looked back, not wanting to feel any pity for her. The curtains of the house opposite had twitched as he climbed into his car, and he had left the driveway with a screech. He could imagine their neighbour, a woman of a certain age whose name he refused to learn, rushing over to find out what was going on as soon as he was out of sight. He knew how it looked. He knew how he looked. Like a mean, angry man, his wife a beautiful, helpless victim. Or so everyone thought.

He could see another teacher, Caroline Stacey, approaching him tentatively from his left side, looking anxious. Most people treated him this way. She was one of those 'young' teachers, wide-eyed and full of enthusiasm. She believed in every child and was loved by all of them too.

'What?' he said, his voice dripping with sarcasm. She jumped slightly, as though she had been caught doing something wrong.

'I just wanted to talk to you about one of your students, but if it's a bad time . . .'

She looked on the verge of tears, and in that moment he deflated. Despite her naivety, this was someone he liked. Someone funny and intelligent who had made him feel welcome when he moved to the school, unlike some of the others.

'Sorry, one of those mornings,' he responded with a weak attempt at a smile. 'Who is it you want to talk about?' He indicated for her to take a seat.

'You can probably guess,' she replied, giving a half-smile back and sitting down tentatively, as if ready to jump up again at any moment.

He rolled his eyes. 'Which one? Richard or Neil?'

'I suppose it's both of them. They're being really disruptive in class. I mean, more than usual.' She paused for a moment, looking at him. 'Of the two of them, Richard seems to be the one in charge though.'

Mike took another drag of his cigarette, less violently this time, pondering the thought. Neil was more upfront in his anger, confrontational, but Mike could handle that as he could recognise it in himself. There was no artifice to Neil. You knew what you were dealing with. But Richard, a quiet boy who could get straight A's if he applied himself, which he sometimes did? There was something more unsettling going on there.

Mike remembered the last time he had caught him smoking. He was used to even the hardest of kids quaking under his stare, but the boy had coolly held eye contact as he put his cigarette out on the floor and walked away. Mike put his own cigarette out. 'I think you're probably right.'

'Maybe there's something going on at home,' Caroline said, her voice growing stronger every time she spoke. Mike smiled wryly to himself. Here we go. But perhaps she was right about that too. Hadn't his father recently lost his job? Nothing new there around this town. But hadn't he also heard rumblings that Richard's dad, Kevin, wasn't someone you crossed? What if Kevin was like that with his own son? It wouldn't be the first time a father's rage had been focused on his sensitive, studious child.

'I was wondering whether, well, whether we should separate them – I mean in class,' she continued, the hesitancy back in her voice as she made the suggestion.

Was this the effect he had on his colleagues? Intimidate them so much he made them nervous to give an opinion? Was this what his wife had been talking about? For a moment he felt some sympathy for her, but it passed as quickly as it had come up, leaving only the embers of the rage he'd felt earlier. He knew if he carried on thinking about her, they would catch alight again, so he turned his attention back to Caroline, slowly nodding his agreement, to her evident surprise as she blushed and gave a small smile.

'You're right,' he said. 'They're bad for each other, and separating them might give Neil a chance to stand on his own two feet, step out of Richard's shadow. I don't know about Richard though. He's a worry . . . I'll talk to them.' Caroline's eyes widened for a moment. She'd clearly expected him to disagree, or maybe suggest more punitive measures.

'Thanks, Mike,' she said as the staffroom began to empty, everyone heading to their next lessons.

As he made his way down the corridor, he thought about his own son. How glad he was that he didn't go to a school like this one – ramshackle, overcrowded, mainly rough neighbourhoods equalling mainly rough children – even though he had chosen to work there, had wanted to help people less fortunate than he was. He used to feel ashamed of living in what his pupils would call a 'posh' area, but was now grateful they could afford a house there, thanks to his father, relieved that they could send Paul to a private school where his child wouldn't be at the mercy of boys like Neil and Richard. The thought made him shudder. He'd tried to toughen his son up but so far had failed and was instead left with a strained relationship with Paul and screaming rows with Hazel about him 'bullying' his own flesh and blood. She didn't understand that he was trying to prepare him for the world.

He wove through the crowds of kids, watching as they shuffled out of his way to leave a pathway for him to walk through, unencumbered, until he reached the door of his classroom where a student was crouched on the floor, placing presumably spilled books back into his bag. He knew who it was instantly.

'Come on, Crowther. Stop dilly-dallying, unless you want to be walked all over.' His voice echoed along the corridor to the sound of sniggers from the students around him.

'Yes, sir. Sorry, sir,' Stephen Crowther replied, his wobbly voice on the verge of breaking.

Stephen looked up at him, his pale skin and wide eyes filled with a need that made Mike want to shake the weakness and vulnerability out of him. He stepped over the boy, kicking the pile of books over, meaning Stephen had to start stuffing them back into his bag again while children streamed around him. The boy needed to learn to be less of a victim.

7
Miv

That evening, I sat cross-legged on my bed on top of the scratchy multicoloured blanket made up of crocheted squares sewn together by Aunty Jean. My torch in hand, I was surrounded by newspapers, with the notebook in my lap.

Each time I read about his method of attack – he would hit his victims on the back of the head with a hammer, then stab them repeatedly with a screwdriver – I paused and screwed my eyes tightly shut, as though if I couldn't see the words, it might not have happened. The images remained and I frequently noticed my hands shaking as I turned the pages.

I turned my thoughts to Mr Ware, and whether it was possible for him to commit such acts. I couldn't imagine it, but then considered the fact that the Ripper was out there, living his life without anyone thinking that he could be capable of it either. The police were clearly thinking the same way. On every page I read, they urged the public to be vigilant, and make sure they were on the lookout for this man, where we might least expect him to be. I decided our first step in being vigilant around Mr Ware was to change where we sat on the coach.

I was glad of the interruption of Dad coming to say goodnight. He'd taken a rare day off to watch the Yorkshire cricket team play at home against Lancashire, our 'arch enemies since the War of the Roses', according to Aunty Jean. The grudge match had run long into the balmy evening. His face was pink and his breath warm and yeasty as he kissed my forehead, the weary lines on his face softened.

'Was it good, Dad?' I said, keen to be distracted away from murder and the list for a moment. I lay back on my pillow, listening to Dad's story of the match, my mind drifting off to sleep with the slow hypnotic rhythm of his voice.

Our PE lessons took place at the local leisure centre, with its pool and outdoor athletics ground, none of which were available in our part of town, so required a coach ride with Mr Ware and an accompanying bus monitor. As we climbed on the coach ahead of our next lesson, instead of taking our usual seats in the middle, Sharon and I sat at the front, just behind Mr Ware and Mr Frazer, so that we could listen in. Ishtiaq was in the seat behind us.

'All right, Ish?' Sharon said, as we sat down. She spoke so loudly that everyone turned to look at us.

'Hiya,' he said, his voice quieter, his eyes skimming over me to look at her.

'Hiya,' I said too, determined to redeem myself in his eyes. He glanced at me, then looked back down at the book he had in front of him. I was crestfallen, but I couldn't blame him and so I tuned into the conversation in front to distract myself from my discomfort. I found it difficult to imagine teachers existing outside the realm of the classroom and was hoping for an unguarded insight into Mr Ware's personal life. Instead, Mr Frazer was talking about his class.

'The kids sang "Congratulations" – you know, the Cliff Richard song. It was so funny, but it was a really nice surprise, then they were all asking if they could come to the engagement party. I said I'd have to ask Miss Stacey and I'm hoping they forget.' I could clearly hear the smile in his voice even though I couldn't see it.

'You're planning on a long engagement?' asked Mr Ware, his voice more muffled as he was angled towards the window, not quite looking at Mr Frazer.

'Oh aye, we've not the money to get married yet. We're both staying at home to save.'

'Well, watch yourself.'

'What do you mean?'

Mr Ware turned to face him fully.

'I know it all feels wonderful now, but you need to know that it doesn't last forever, and you'd do well to make double sure you're doing the right thing – don't make the mistake I made and definitely don't rush to have kids.'

There was a long pause. Aside from the information

about Mr Ware, we were beside ourselves with excitement that Mr Frazer and Miss Stacey were engaged. Miss Stacey was a teacher who we adored and who I wanted to be. All our romantic strings were pulled by this news. The thought of them kissing and holding hands made me want to giggle.

We leaned in for more.

'I appreciate you're going through a difficult time,' Mr Frazer said, 'but would it kill you to be pleased for me, Mike?'

Mike. His name was Mike. I wrestled the notebook from my bag and wrote it down.

'Sorry, mate. Ignore me. I'm getting bitter and cynical in my old age. I'm really chuffed for you both . . .' His voice trailed off as he turned back towards the window. As they settled into silence, I wrote a note and showed Sharon.

It must be his wife he's on about?

'Doesn't mean anything,' she whispered, shrugging.

During the PE lesson Mr Ware seemed angrier than ever, and viciously so. It was a cuttingly cold day and my legs felt stiff and chapped. We were running relay races and he taunted me that my awkward run was slowing my team down. I was teetering on the verge of tears, but I wasn't the only one. He also shouted at Stephen Crowther, who was both skinny and small and who ran with his feet turned out over the uneven field, stumbling as he went.

'Get a move on, Crowther, you fairy.'

Stephen finished his run and cowered at the back of his team. Like me, I could see his eyes were filling with tears and he was desperately holding on to them so as not to let anyone see. In that moment I hated Mr Ware. Stephen was often a target for the bigger boys. He had once forgotten his PE kit and been forced to wear a netball skirt, which left him open to all manner of insults. This name-calling from a teacher also incensed Sharon.

'Now they'll all call him fairy,' she said. 'You know what, you're right, he *deserves* to be on the list.' Her usually soft, rounded features were momentarily hardened with fury, her blue eyes flashing. She used her anger to fuel her run and I watched her, ponytail bobbing as she took back the lead for our team with a focus and intensity I was unused to from her. It earned her Mr Ware's begrudging praise, which she ignored. On the way back to school on the coach she turned to me and said, 'He's a bully. We've got to find out more about him.'

I nodded, my brain already whirling with ideas about how we might do so. Something in the way he had spoken about his wife told me she would be the key. I spent the rest of the day in quiet distraction, hatching a plan.

When we arrived at school the next morning our attention was taken by the next item on the list. Neil and

Richard had broken into Healy Mill, a boarded-up building on a quiet street, and our ears pricked up. West Yorkshire was littered with these derelict buildings, misleading in their outward grandeur, reminders of a time when our town was a bustling hub.

'It was dead easy to get in, and it were massive inside,' Neil told his wide-eyed classmates as we gathered around him.

'Yeah,' Richard agreed, 'and it were dead spooky, like all cobwebby and that, spiders as big as your hand.' Ever the storyteller, he ran towards the girls, throwing his arms up in the air and shaking them, to which there were lots of squeals and running away. Sharon and I stood our ground.

'It were as though no one's been in there for a hundred years or something,' Neil continued. 'You could hardly breathe for dust, and there were all this machinery and stuff.'

Richard came back and added, in a deep voice, 'And then we heard it. The sound of footsteps.' He dropped the volume for melodramatic effect and Sharon rolled her eyes at me as if to say, *Here we go*. I swallowed down a giggle.

'You could hear the clip-clop of clogs on wooden floors, and the creaking of doors.' Neil took a deep breath then, and his face changed from the mock seriousness he had adopted to a genuinely solemn expression. 'When we went to go up the stairs though, honest to God, the weird thing was we saw the shape of a little boy in the shadows on the wall. And then we heard whistling. Like a proper tune.'

Neil's voice trailed off as Richard interrupted, 'And then an old man burst in and shouted, "I'll get you pesky kids, just see if I don't." We groaned and dispersed at his Scooby-Doo voice while Richard laughed at us all, but when I glanced behind me, I could see that Neil wasn't smiling. We walked back into class.

'Do you believe in ghosts?' Sharon asked, her voice serious.

I thought about it. I'd stopped believing in the fairies and pixies and goblins that I read about in books, but did I believe in ghosts?

'I'm not sure,' I said tentatively. I had enough to worry about in the real world. 'Why, do you?'

'I'm not sure either. But I felt like Neil might've been telling the truth about the little boy.'

I did too. Of course, rumours of this and other hauntings were used to scare us from any desire to explore these empty buildings, but warnings had the opposite effect on a certain kind of child.

When I went to call for Sharon the next morning, she was already waiting for me on the street corner. 'I've been thinking about Healy Mill,' she said, as if we were already mid-conversation. 'I asked me mum about it last night and she said it *is* haunted. By a little boy.' She looked at me closely then added, 'And I didn't

even tell her that they'd seen the shape of a little boy.'
A gleam entered her eyes as she paused to allow the
words to sink in.

'You mean?'

'Yep. We've got to investigate it.'

There was a triumph in her voice that made me want
to laugh with giddiness. I had always thought of Sharon
as being the well-behaved one of the two of us. The
fact that she was so keen to explore this next item on
the list made it feel even more exciting. We were growing even closer.

That night, the Ripper was replaced in my dreams by the
outline of a little boy, hiding around corners and in the
shadows. The nightmare jolted me awake and I looked
around the room, checking the angles and shapes for
any signs of the ghostly child. I found only the familiar outline of the Wombles, however. Unlike Sharon's,
my wallpaper had not kept up with my tastes and I was
stuck with my five-year-old choice. On finding no trace
of the supernatural I reached for my book and torch as
though for a comforter and settled back down to read
myself to sleep again.

Moments later, on registering the slow creak of a
door, I realised I'd actually been woken by someone
moving around downstairs.

Suddenly I was fully alert.

Given that the bathroom was next to Mum and

Dad's room, it couldn't be one of them getting up to use the loo or get a drink of water. Besides, Dad had told me that Mum took special tablets that made her sleep so deeply it would take an earthquake to wake her up. He'd told me that not long after Mum had changed. I had bounded into their room to play like I used to and couldn't rouse her. I'd left deflated.

It was unlikely to be Aunty Jean either. She slept downstairs, in the room at the front of the house, and I'd never once heard her stir after her door was closed. I sat up in bed and turned the torch off, sliding the switch slowly and carefully, ensuring I made no noise. I stayed motionless, as if playing musical statues, but all I could hear was the pulsing of blood around my body.

No more sound. I wondered if I'd misheard. Sharon would surely laugh at me for being a scaredy-cat when I told her about this tomorrow. I must have been more affected than I thought by the story of a ghostly little boy. But then, as I readied myself to curl back up and go to sleep, I was halted by the sound of footsteps in the hallway. I sat bolt upright again.

Before I'd even thought it through, I tiptoed to the top of the stairs, holding my breath. As I did so, I heard the whirring sound of the phone being dialled and Dad's quiet voice. I sat on the top stair, straining to listen to him talking in the darkness. I could only pick up odd words but then I heard clearly, 'I don't know what to do.'

My stomach slowly turned. Dad always knew what

to do. That's what everyone said. 'Ask your dad. He'll know.' I inched my way further down the stairs, pausing after every step to make sure I had not been detected. As soon as I could hear fully, I sat, clutching the banister.

'She's not doing very well. It's exhausting.' There was a pause. 'I don't know how long I can keep doing this.' There was another pause as he said, 'I just need a break.'

He was using his serious, grown-up voice. I didn't like it. The back of my throat started to close when I heard him say, 'We've been talking about whether a move might make a difference. Get us away from York-shire. But . . .' He sighed so loudly, I could hear it from my place on the stairs. 'That won't get us away from the murders on the telly every five minutes.'

Of course. It was about the move. And about me. Did Dad know about the list? How? Didn't he under-stand that I was doing this so we didn't *have* to move? I felt as though I had been punched in the stomach. I had once been told off for something minor at school and Mr Ware had looked down at me and said, 'Your mum and dad have got enough going on without you adding to their problems, young lady.' I hadn't known what he meant by that. I only knew that I felt like a disap-pointment. This felt like confirmation. My eyes stung with shame. I slowly stood, and made my way back upstairs, holding the tears in until I could safely sob in my room. I fervently promised myself not to be any more trouble, which definitely meant I had to keep the

List of Suspicious Things hidden until we caught the Ripper, no matter what.

My promise to behave lasted only until an opportunity to find out more about Mr and Mrs Ware presented itself. Ruby was holding a coffee morning in the church on Saturday for all the local mums. It was to raise funds for a toy library she'd set up, and she was making and selling cakes to order. She volunteered Sharon and me to help.

'Right, you two can man the cake stall,' she said, and we eagerly agreed. The list had given us a reason to want to be around other people instead of staying in our own little best-friends bubble. I mostly preferred it being just the two of us but had never asked Sharon whether she did. Ruby left us behind a large wooden trestle table, laden with home-made cakes and buns, the fresh-baked smell of them fighting with the musty odour of the church, which always smelled as though it had been locked up for a hundred years, even though it was used every day.

'You can do the talking,' I said to Sharon. 'You're better at it than me. I'll make notes.' I patted the notebook which sat, as always, in the front pocket of the dungarees Aunty Jean had made me. I had various pairs in odd colours and patterns, all made from left-over material bought from a man who sold it in the market.

As we stood behind our table in the draughty church

hall, I watched as people smiled at Sharon. She was dressed smartly, in a white frilly blouse – the kind I would get dirty in seconds – her hair in shiny blonde bunches. I looked down at my jumble sale T-shirt and dungarees, realising it was no wonder that people were impressed with her and tended not to notice me.

There were groups of women and children milling around and the volume in the hall had increased when a striking-looking woman glided in, accompanied by a sullen, gangly boy who was the spitting image of Mr Ware. I watched as the small groups of women nudged each other and voices became hushed. The atmosphere in the room changed, almost like it did when the Ripper was mentioned.

I studied the woman closely. Tall and willowy, with long golden hair in a middle parting, she was dressed in dark-blue jeans and was the picture of cool elegance. I thought of the blonde one from Abba and fell in love at that moment. She was everything I wanted to be and was not. She seemed flustered – albeit glamorously so – and surveyed the room a number of times before making her way to our table, the boy trailing behind her. I looked around for Sharon, but she had disappeared, so I found myself stutteringly asking if I could help.

'Hello, young lady,' she said, smiling. 'I'm looking for the one with "Hazel Ware" on it.'

She spoke without the flat, broad tones of the West Riding accent, which made her seem even more glamorous. I looked down at the rows of pre-ordered cakes for the one with her name sticker on it and, buoyed by her friendliness, dared to ask a question. 'Are you married to my teacher?'

She smiled and said, 'If your teacher is Mr Ware at Bishopsfield School, then yes, I am,' she said. 'And you are . . . ?'

'Miv,' I replied, and held out my hand to shake her elegant, manicured one.

'Miv,' she said, as she shook my hand, my name sounding exotic on her lips. 'What a lovely name.'

I stood taller. 'Pleased to meet you,' I said, having heard from somewhere that this is what polite people did. Hazel Ware definitely struck me as polite.

She took my hand. 'Pleased to meet you too.'

Locating her order, I handed it over, all the while desperately trying to think of another question that might keep her talking to me when another mum came over and I stepped back and listened in.

'Hazel . . . it's lovely to see you. I wasn't sure you'd come and I'm so glad you have.' She smiled at Hazel, but it looked frozen, fixed. Her head moved to the side, as though consoling someone after a death.

'So nice of you to pop over and say hello,' said Hazel. 'And of course I came.'

Her words sounded polite and her voice was as calm and melodic as it had been while speaking to me, but there was a steeliness not evident before. She turned to check on the boy, who was now slumped against a wall and appeared to be in another place altogether, his eyes downcast and his dark hair flopping over them. He looked to be older than us by a couple of years.

'How *are* things?' asked the woman, her voice syrupy, but with an edge I couldn't name.

'Things are fine, thank you so much for asking. Busy as ever.'

I was used to grown-ups having conversations that left the important things unsaid, they happened in my family all the time, but I couldn't quite work out what was going on here. Hazel nodded towards the boy. 'Speaking of busyness, I'm on my way to take Paul to an appointment, so I really should go.' She abruptly turned away from the woman and looked at me, her face softening. 'Thank you for your help. It was very nice to meet you, Miv.'

Hazel walked away without another word, much to the apparent shock on the face of the mum who had been speaking to her. She had definitely breached some unspoken Yorkshire rule by ending the conversation so suddenly, especially without giving enough away to be gossiped about. I swallowed the smile twitching to get out, for fear of further fuelling the outrage. The boy slowly unfurled himself off the wall, going to follow her, but just before he turned away his eyes caught mine and I could see the faint glimmer of a smile on his face too. Something inside me fizzed. I found myself standing even taller, heat rising through my body. Before I could analyse my reaction further, he was gone.

When she came back, I eagerly updated Sharon,

asking her to listen out for chatter about the Wares among any of the other mums. We struck gold shortly afterwards. The woman who had stopped to ask Hazel Ware how she was had moved on to a small group of other women, all drinking tea and looking more like the grown-up women I was used to. Knitted skirts, tan tights and hair that had been permed or set. We would see them in the hairdressers on the High Street, Aunty Jean among them, sat under the huge hoods that made them look like rows of Stormtroopers, protecting our town from invasion. Nothing like the exotic Hazel.

'I'm surprised she had the nerve to show her face,' said one.

'Aye, that's some brass neck she's got.'

'They'll be divorced before t'year's out.'

'Tart,' said one woman to murmurs of agreement, followed by shushes from the rest, noticing that there were children close.

'Well, it's true,' she insisted.

I became aware that I wasn't the only one eaves-dropping on this conversation. Ruby was stood nearby, watching the women intently. She was flushed, her eyes shining. There was something unsettling in her unblinking focus.

Divorce was a relatively new idea to Sharon and me. Nearly everyone we knew had parents who were married, and we had assumed, until recently, that every-one had a mum and a dad and that they were married to each other. One day at primary school during the

'News' section (where we wrote about and drew pictures of what we had done over the weekend), a boy in our class had written about going to see his dad in his new flat. We had all laughed at him, assuming he'd got it wrong. Our teacher had explained what divorce was, saying, 'Sometimes mums and dads don't get along any more, so they live separately.' She called them 'broken families'.

I had never thought that parents getting along was necessary in life. Since Mum had fallen silent, we had simply adjusted. Aunty Jean did the cooking, cleaning and telling me what to do, and Dad did the practical things. I just tried not to need a mum. I couldn't imagine things being so bad that living apart would be better. My family might be broken, but we had stuck it together with makeshift glue, at least for now. I wondered what had happened to make this an option for the Wares.

Curiously, what we'd heard did not cast our suspicious Mr Ware as the villain of the story. Instead, the fault seemed to lie with Mrs Ware. The question for Sharon and me was whether what she had done had caused him to be angry enough to want to exact revenge on all women. As I mulled this over, I suddenly remembered the word *tart* having been used. I knew I had heard this word in relation to the prostitutes the Ripper favoured. Was Hazel one of 'those women'? If so, then was it possible that we were really on to something?

'What do we do next?' asked Sharon.

'Let me think about it,' I said. 'And in the meantime, let's go to t'mill next Thursday when I come to yours for tea.' Sharon never came to my house for tea, and it was never discussed. Somehow, she knew that our house didn't have visitors, and was kind enough not to ask me why.

The coffee morning was now finished, and as we had helped Ruby to tidy up, the rest of the day was ours.

'Shall we go and call for Ishtiaq?'

Sharon's suggestion made my whole body clench. I still hadn't worked out a way to tell her about what had taken place in the school corridor, but maybe this might be my opportunity to make amends.

'OK,' I said, trying to inject some cheeriness into my voice to cover my hesitancy at facing him. I could feel every nerve jangling as we walked up to Mr Bashir's, and on arrival he chucked my chin, which made me feel even worse. 'It's the Terrible Twosome,' he said, to Sharon's loud giggle and my half-smile.

'Ishtiaq's in the back.'

Ishtiaq's eyes lit up at the sight of Sharon, then, as they rested on me, he nodded politely, as though we were new acquaintances. I winced. In the back room, the television was on and the small table set up with what I recognised as a chessboard. Seeing an opportunity, I said, 'Can you play?', which was met with an exaggerated eye-roll and an 'Of course.'

'Can you teach us?' I said, eagerly. Another James Bond film I was obsessed with was *From Russia with*

Love, in which one of the villains had been a chess grandmaster. The game still held a fascination for me, even if I'd let go of ideas of Yorkshire espionage factories.

'Oh, yes please,' Sharon added.

'Right,' said Ishtiaq, his voice serious and commanding, 'take a seat.'

Over the next hour, I watched, engrossed, while Ishtiaq walked us through each piece on the board and talked about their moves, playing a mock game against the two of us. It was the most I had ever heard him speak and I found him mesmerising. Sharon's silence said the same. There was something about the soft clarity of his voice and the intensity of his gaze that meant we had no choice but to listen and learn.

'Oh no.' Sharon looked at her watch after we had been playing for a while. 'I'm going to be late.' She jumped up. 'I promised I'd be home before five. You coming or staying?' she said to me.

I looked at Ishtiaq, who shrugged.

'I'll stay,' I said.

The spell of chess broken by Sharon's departure, we turned our heads to the television, which was still on in the background. It was *Grandstand*, and the cricket report had just started. By unspoken agreement, Ishtiaq strode to the television and turned the volume up, and we sat in companionable silence before I said, 'I'm sorry.'

To my surprise, Ishtiaq laughed out loud. 'Maybe at

some point we can laik out together and there will be nothing for you to apologise for.'

For some reason I found myself laughing too, the sound bubbling up in my throat until I was snorting and trying to catch my breath. Ishtiaq was the same, slapping his thighs with the force of each wave of giggles. We were so loud, eventually Mr Bashir peeked his head around the door, shaking his head and smiling at the state of us. The sight of him made us laugh even more. And I suppose that's when I knew Ishtiaq had forgiven me, and that he was a better person than I could ever be.

While we were eating our tea at Sharon's house that Thursday, Malcolm came home. He travelled for work and was often away, so he was a rare and treasured presence in both our lives. Whenever he did come home, he would loudly declare, 'Hi honey, I'm home' with a fake American accent that made us giggle as he opened the door. He kissed Ruby first, then held her so that her head was under his chin and took a deep breath in, as though inhaling her. I watched her squirm away from his grasp, half laughing, half cross. Then he whirled Sharon around and kissed her on the forehead saying, 'How's my favourite girl?'

He looked like the dads on American television shows we were sometimes allowed to watch when I was round there, clean-cut, smart and handsome. So, when he gave me a wink, ruffled my short hair and said, 'And how's my second favourite girl?' I blushed so hard I felt like I was on fire. I often felt as if Sharon, her house and family were like the Technicolor bit of *The Wizard of Oz* – vivid and bright, full of life. Whereas me and mine were the black-and-white part, faded and worn, drained of all colour.

When we finished our tea, we asked for permission to go back out. This wasn't something I was used to. I tended to come and go as I pleased – the preference in my house, meaning Aunty Jean's preference, was that I was out of the way.

'All right then, girls. Home before it gets dark, please. And make sure you take your coats,' said Ruby.

This gave us two hours.

What had begun as a sunny day had given way to a cooler, more breezy evening as we set off. We zipped our anoraks up, Sharon shivering as she pulled her hood over her ponytail. The way to Healy Mill took us through less familiar streets in the more industrial part of town, peppered with new grey factories and warehouses that looked even bleaker than the derelict buildings they had replaced. Nothing that the modern world had added to the landscape seemed to enhance it. The best bits about our town were the bits that had been there before the war. Before both wars, actually. Everything beautiful had been made long before I was born.

As we neared the mill, dark clouds were forming, and when we rounded Healy Lane it looked like a black-and-white photo of a Victorian street, with the mill looming ominously against the sky. All it needed was smoke billowing from the top to complete the impression of a Lowry painting, like the 'smoky tops' in the song about matchstalk men and matchstalk cats and dogs that Mum used to sing me to sleep with.

The building was large, four storeys high, with long, thin windows and faded stencilled lettering on the brick face: *Healy Mill Shoddy and Mungo Manufacturer.* I thought about what Aunty Jean would say whenever clouds were looming in our own lives: 'There'll be trouble at t'mill.' Maybe that was why the mills were associated with bad things in my mind?

'Right, let's see if we can find a way in,' I said loudly, attempting to cover up the wobble in my voice with volume. 'Shhhh,' said Sharon, putting her finger exaggeratedly to her lips and looking around us. We walked around the outside of the building. There was graffiti, along with *DANGER. DO NOT ENTER* signs and the sour smell of stale urine. The windows were boarded up, apart from one that had clearly been broken into at some point but was far too high for us to reach.

Eventually we found a ginnel down the side of the building, enabling us to get to the back, where we found a set of narrow black wrought-iron stairs, clinging to the outside like poison ivy. We stared up, and I spotted a fire exit on the first floor that was held slightly ajar by a thin piece of wood, which must have been where

Richard and Neil got in. I had planned our cover story and brought with us a box of chalk. Sharon got some out from the box and set to work drawing a game of hopscotch on the concrete path while I paced the perimeter, looking and listening for signs of life before we attempted to enter. If stopped, we would innocently claim to be looking for a big enough stone to use for our game. Grown-ups weren't to know we were too old for hopscotch. My experience was that grown-ups always thought I was too young for all the interesting things and too old for all the things that brought me comfort.

As soon as I was confident that there was no one around, I went back to Sharon.

'I think we're all right,' I said.

She looked up at the sky, which was closing in on us.

'Shall we go in together?'

She nodded and I realised she hadn't said a word since we'd arrived.

'Are you OK?' I asked.

She still didn't reply but led the way as we headed up the stairs to the first floor where the door was propped open, our shoes clattering on the iron. I got out my torch, opened the door and we stepped inside. The scene before us brought to mind a hymn we sang at school about 'dark satanic mills'. All around us was rusted old machinery covered in cobwebs like thin threads of clothing on a skeleton. I reached for Sharon's hand, my heart pulsing in my throat.

'Don't be scared,' I said, the quiver in my voice giving away my own terror.

'I'm NOT!' she hissed, snatching it back from me.

I turned the torch on her. How was she not as scared as me? But as I saw her pale, wide eyes reflecting the torchlight back, I realised that she was pretending just as much as I was. I reached my hand out again and she took it. We held on tight to each other.

So that we could get a sense of the space, I shone the torch like a spotlight around the cavernous walls and ceiling, where pipes and beams criss-crossed each other in neat rows. I pictured the equally neat rows of men and women working beneath them, on the now defunct and silent machinery. The rows of people in the mills had been replaced by rows of people in the Unemployment Office, where Aunty Jean now worked.

I had only ever seen Aunty Jean cry once. You couldn't even really call it crying; it was more like watching someone in a silent fight with an emotion that they quickly wrestled away. She had been talking about how her dad (my grandad) had never been the same after the mills closed. I found the fact that Aunty Jean had emotions uncomfortable.

'It's hard for Aunty Jean,' Mum had told me. 'She was here when our town was something to be proud of. Before it became so beaten down and ashamed of itself. It hurts much more to see it now when you've seen what it was.'

Every sound in the mill was amplified, from the

creaks of an old building with tired bones to the rhythmic *drip-drip-drip* of an unidentified liquid echoing off
the walls. I thought I could hear the scurrying of mice
or rats somewhere distant but shoved the thought away
as I shone my torch from side to side, like in TV police
shows.

Each step we took produced a corresponding groan
from the floor beneath us and I was caught between
using the torch to light the way ahead and pointing it to
the floor to make sure we weren't about to fall through.
All the warnings from grown-ups suddenly felt justified. I felt Sharon's grip on me tighten as a loud bang
came from downstairs. We stopped, breaths held, and
I turned the torch off. Then nothing. It must have been
the wind, I reasoned, but was reminded of the feeling
of being watched outside the corner shop. It was physical, like a nettle sting of awareness.

I switched the torch back on and we started to walk
again, light swinging across the floor like a lighthouse
beaming its warning as we looked for anything suspicious. I avoided looking at the flickers and shadows on
the walls in case pictures started to form in my mind.
We were looking for bodies, not ghosts. We tiptoed
forward, assessing the safety of each step before we
took it, stopping abruptly when a loud thump seemed
to shake the floor.

There was definitely someone or something in here
with us.

All the stories of hauntings flooded back. I'd been

planning how to deal with a real-life man with a hammer, but I hadn't thought about what we'd do if we came face to face with a ghost. I had to grit my teeth to stop them from chattering.

The thump had now become heavy footsteps. It didn't sound like a little boy, but then I heard the eerie sound of jaunty whistling. I don't know why we didn't run. Instead, we stood rooted to the floor, listening to the tune of 'You Are My Sunshine' echoing through the darkness. It was another song that Mum used to sing to me, made sinister by circumstance.

As the sound got closer, flickers of light started to appear from the other end of the building until what at first looked like a shadowy ghoul showed itself to be a man wearing a jacket with a badge on. This was no ghostly apparition. As he walked towards us, I could see his head shaking. I was still rooted to the spot.

'I'll do the talking,' whispered Sharon.

'We're really sorry, sir,' she said, looking down at her feet. I followed her lead and looked down at mine.

'What on earth are you two doing here? You must know it's not safe,' he said. 'Come on, spit it out!' he added as we stood there in silence.

'We were looking around because of a school project,' Sharon said, this time staring at him wide-eyed, the lie tripping from her tongue as if it were the most natural thing in the world.

'Is that right?' he said. 'Is that why I caught two young men about your age t'other week an' all?'

Neil and Richard, no doubt. We both nodded. He muttered something that sounded like 'Bloody teachers' and shone the torch in our faces. 'You two want to be learning what really happens in buildings like this, not the bloody fairy stories they tell you at school.'

We blinked in the glare of the torch and looked down at our feet again. I found myself wanting to giggle at the word *bloody*.

'A young lad lost his life in here, you know. Ask your teachers about that. Ask them about John Harris. He were strangled to death in this very room.'

Sharon and I looked at each other.

'Sometimes you can hear the sound of his clogs.'

At this I started. The clogs were what Neil and Richard said they'd heard. Maybe this was not a myth.

'Now. Do you promise me I won't find you here again or do I need to come and talk to your elders and betters?' he said, shining his torch in our faces again.

'No, sir,' we said in unison.

'Off you go then.'

Sharon went off home, but I wasn't ready for mine, my mind too alive with the drama of the day. So instead I went to Mr Bashir's, calming myself with a game of chess with Ishtiaq, so that when the time came to go home, I was ready to face the silence.

By the time I got there, Aunty Jean was long back from work, which meant the noise of her industrious bustle had replaced the quiet. I was surprised to see that Mum was up too, and was even out of her nightie, though the thick jumper and skirt she was wearing were both too big for her.

I wondered if she would react if I told her about the mill, and the song the man was whistling. I was almost tempted to sing it, to see if it might reach her somehow, wherever she was. But the thought of there being no reaction was almost too painful to consider, so I went straight to the kitchen instead, where the smell of sausages and batter gave away the fact that I had missed having toad-in-the-hole for tea.

I had taken one step on the linoleum floor when Aunty Jean swung round at me, spatula in hand, like a cowboy drawing his gun.

'Don't. Even. Think about it,' she said, and I realised that to my left, on the rickety yellow table, was a plate of leftovers. I was about to jump into a spirited defence that I hadn't even known they were there when we were both distracted by the door opening and closing and the sound of my dad's heavy tread hitting the floor, home from the pub presumably. He came straight to the kitchen too, following the scent like I had. He immediately picked up a sausage, much to my protestation and Aunty Jean's horror.

'Austin!' she said. 'You're w'arn at'bairn.'

As Aunty Jean said this to my dad with some frequency, I knew this was Yorkshire for 'you're worse than the child'. I always thought it unfair that I was the measuring point for bad things but resisted arguing about it because in that moment we almost felt like a family again.

After school on Friday, under the guise of our home-work we went to the library to see if we could find the story of John Harris. The library building in our town was another grand Victorian one. I often escaped into its walls, when the weather was too bad for laiking out or the atmosphere at home too oppressive. I found its silence comforting, not lonely. I had introduced Sharon to its joys and we would go together, treating it with a reverence normally held for church.

On this visit there was an unfamiliar person behind the desk, younger than the stern librarian we usually dealt with. She had her head down, stamping and piling up books with a pinched face and a furrowed brow. She looked up at our arrival, her pale, almost blue skin giving her a ghostly, supernatural appearance.

She took in Sharon, then me, and smiled. It com-pletely transformed her face. She looked like I imagined the pixies and elves in my Enid Blyton books would look, all small and delicate features with sparkly green eyes, like Audrey Hepburn. According to the badge she wore, her name was Mrs Andrews. I warmed to her immediately; she was like a child inhabiting a woman's body.

'How can I help you two young ladies?' she said.

I nudged Sharon, so that she would tell our prepared

story. Since the mill, we had agreed that I would do the thinking and she would do the talking.

'We're doing homework on the mills and we're looking for the story of John Harris and Healy Mill,' she said. 'Can you help us?'

Mrs Andrews' brow furrowed again, and she looked at us as if she wanted to ask more but instead led us to a section on local history. After some searching, she left us with a book open on a page headed 'Hang Palmer'.

'Come and ask me if you need help understanding anything,' she said as she went back to her desk. I could see her still watching us as we read.

HANG PALMER

In 1856 the infamous Dr William Palmer (a killer known as the Rugeley Poisoner) was hanged at Stafford prison. The case was dubbed the 'trial of the century', and more than 30,000 spectators came to watch his execution. The souvenirs, songs and stories that were created about his killings made their way to a small Yorkshire town and the ears of four young boys, one of whom was twelve-year-old John Harris.

The boys invented a game called 'Hang Palmer' and played it over and over in the mill building where they worked. During one of these games, John played 'Palmer' and was tied to a steam-operated crane. Elsewhere, the crane was set to work by another mill worker and John was strangled. He was rushed to hospital but died four days later. His three friends were charged with manslaughter.

They were later found not guilty, but the tragedy has produced endless ghost stories and warnings of playing around mill buildings and equipment.

The irony of such a tragedy happening to boys who were obsessed with a killer was not lost on me and I decided not to cross the mill off the list just yet. It felt as though our investigations there were not over.

8

Helen

Helen Andrews watched the girls as they pored over the local history book, their concentration so absolute they looked like little adults. She hoped that the story wouldn't be too scary for such young eyes; she didn't really know if it had been appropriate to let them read it. She was twenty-three and still felt like a child herself. She wondered how parents made decisions like that, how they decided what was right and wrong for their children. At the sound of a throat clearing, she turned away from the girls and faced the next person in the queue.

'Morning, Valerie,' she said to the woman in front of her.

'Morning, Helen,' Valerie Lockwood replied as she spilled the contents of her arms, which were filled with Second World War books, on to the desk. Helen knew from her recent training that there was a lending limit of five books, which she also knew that she would waive. Even though this was a new job, she understood without asking that these books would be for Valerie's son, Brian, who wouldn't come into the library if it was busy.

She'd no doubt he would be stood outside, smoking a cigarette and waiting for his mum, his yellow bobble hat pulled down low on his brow. She decided to count the books as being for two people. While she was stamping them, the girls came back up to the desk, leaving the book she had lent them on the side.

'Thanks, Mrs Andrews,' they chirruped.

The two women watched them leave until Valerie turned back to the desk, her head shaking.

'Poor little bairn,' she said as she looked at Miv, and even though this was the first time Helen had officially met Miv, she didn't need to ask why. Everyone knew about Miv's mum. 'And how are you, love?' Valerie asked. 'Is it going all right?' She nodded her head at the desk, indicating that she meant the job. Helen organised her face into her customary 'Everything's fine, thanks' expression and nodded. The spotlight of town gossip had swung her way in recent months, with the death of her own mum, and she was keen to make sure it didn't linger, even if that meant hiding her grief.

'It's good to see you out and about. You mind yoursen.'

Helen slowly exhaled as Valerie left.

Later, she got to spend time among the shelves, putting books away. This was her favourite part of the job. She would breathe in the musty smell from the rows of books and sometimes sneak a read or make a note of a book she'd like to borrow. She was deep into Stephen King's *Carrie* at the moment. Mrs Hurst, the chief librarian, had been visibly shocked on catching her reading it one breaktime.

'You just don't look like the type,' she'd said, shaking her head.

Helen was on the verge of laughingly asking, 'And what is the type?' when she remembered the town spotlight and just nodded and smiled. She deliberately chose books that dealt with the horrors of the world, and as there wasn't much opportunity for reading at home, she would use her breaks as her chance to step into a different life. Her colleagues wanted to believe the world was a safe and comfortable place, maybe as an antidote to the real world, or maybe because, to them, it was. But she knew it wasn't.

After her shift, she walked home with a feeling of unfamiliar lightness. It had taken some doing, persuading Gary that a job was a good idea. What had swung it in the end was the promise of some much-needed extra income to supplement his work as a plumber, that it was part-time – meaning she'd be home in time to make tea – and the fact that she was unlikely to meet any dashing young men at the local library.

She stopped in at the corner shop to indulge her sweet tooth as a reward for finishing her first week and found herself humming along with Kiki Dee to 'Don't Go Breaking My Heart' blaring from the tape recorder on the counter, and jumped, then laughed, as Omar's head appeared from behind it, singing the Elton John part. She picked up a packet of Toffos, then immediately put them down again as the tooth that was loose in the back twinged, and instead asked for a bag of rhubarb-and-custards.

'You're in a good mood today. It's lovely to see,' Omar observed, as she paid.

She looked up from counting out her money, checking his face for mockery, but all she saw was the softness in his eyes and his kind smile.

'Yes,' she found herself saying, 'I suppose I am in a good mood.' And as she spoke the words, she realised they were true.

'How's the new job?' Omar said, as though he knew that was the cause of it.

'Oh, Omar, I love it,' she said, her voice expanding with the joy she felt. 'It's just so nice to be, I don't know, useful! And everyone's so friendly, and I get to read books, and talk about books, and it's just so lovely to be out of the house and . . .' She stopped, fearing she'd said too much, but Omar's smile had simply got wider and he was nodding along with every word.

'I'm so pleased for you,' he said.

On the street outside, she stopped to close the fastening on her bag when she felt a prickle at the back of her neck and had the creeping, all-too-familiar sense that someone was watching her. Remembering the Ripper, and the fact that these days there were threats less close to home, she looked around, gripping her bag tightly just in case.

The street seemed to be empty, so she carried on

walking, now alert to her surroundings. She was used to being vigilant, and her body responded like a reflex, her senses expanding so she wouldn't miss a thing. At the sound of footsteps, she whirled around, only to see someone wearing black work boots disappear into the shop as the bell on the door went. That was all it was. Nerves jangling like the shop bell, she continued towards home. The closer she got, the more she folded back in on herself with each step.

9

Miv

The following week brought with it our monthly swimming lessons at the local baths, an activity I associated with intense dread. I hated the cold, smelly changing rooms and the embarrassment of tugging my swimming costume over my skinny ribs, of shivering so much my teeth chattered, while wondering why no one else seemed to mind.

I had tried to get out of swimming many times by forgetting my kit, slowly putting my hand up when Mr Ware would shout, 'Who's sitting out?' Eventually he had threatened to throw me in the pool naked if I didn't remember my kit, and the whole coach laughed. The humiliation only added to my dislike of him.

That week as I got changed, I found myself gulping for air even before I had got into the water. I comforted myself with the thought that this would be a way of keeping an eye on Mr Ware, who was quiet and appeared distracted that day, missing obvious opportunities to shout at us. Sharon, seeming to sense my anxiety, helped me with my locker and towel as I fumbled everything into my bag. We were the last two out of the changing room and squirming in the pre-pool cold shower – another part of swimming lessons I hated – when we heard a loud splash and a scream and ran out to the poolside and a chaotic scene.

Richard Collier was holding Stephen Crowther under the water. His eyes held the same cold intensity as they had when he was playing Ripper chase. I felt a knot of fear take hold. Amidst the noise, emphasised by the echo chamber of the pool, there was a quiet violence to Richard's expression. Neil Callaghan was cheering him on, holding on to Stephen's arms while Ishtiaq and two other boys were attempting to pull him off. All at once a sharp whistle pierced the air and Mr Ware was running down the side of the pool.

'Stop that now!'

Richard didn't move and it felt as though the room took a collective breath in.

Then he let go, putting his hands up in mock surrender.

'We were only messing, sir,' said Richard, his face suddenly relaxing into an almost mischievous smile, like this was merely a game.

We all expected Stephen to stand up, but he remained where he was, hair floating above him in the water. The room went into slow motion. Mr Ware jumped in and pulled his limp body out. As we watched on, horrified, he lay Stephen down and began giving him mouth-to-mouth. The whole class stood in rare total silence. I felt Sharon's hand slip into mine.

There was a splutter.

Then a cough.

Miss Stacey, who was on duty with Mr Ware that week, hurried us all back into the changing rooms, while the pool attendant ran to call 999.

I put my hand out and grabbed Ishtiaq's arm as he went to go past us.

'Are you all right?' I asked.

He nodded silently, looking at both me and Sharon, his face frozen with shock. Her free hand reached out to him and he took it, briefly.

As we left the side of the pool, I looked back at the scene to see Mr Ware leaning over Stephen. Tears were streaming down his face.

'I'm so sorry, I'm so sorry,' he repeated again and again, and I wondered what he was apologising for.

The bus back to school was subdued. We were never that quiet. Even Neil seemed cowed by what had almost happened, keeping his head down, though Richard sat straight in his seat, unbowed. Sharon silently seethed, her anger radiating heat like the red bars of the heater in our living room. Eventually she turned to me, her face glowing pink. 'I'm glad we're doing the list,' she said, forcefully. I couldn't see the connection and my face must have told her that. 'I can't stand it. Someone being hurt like that, someone who can't fight back. And those women . . .' Our eyes met. And I understood.

The next day at assembly the headmaster, Mr Asquith, made an announcement.

'As many of you know, there was an unfortunate incident at the pool yesterday. I am pleased to say that Stephen is recovering well and is back with us,' he said, as we all turned to look at Stephen, who was visibly shaking. I suspect he'd never been under that level of scrutiny in his life. 'Richard Collier and Neil Callaghan, however, have been suspended with immediate effect. An instructor will be giving a talk about pool safety at the next assembly to remind us of how dangerous deep water can be.'

There was no mention of Mr Ware, though he was absent and had been replaced by a supply teacher with no explanation. For once, we didn't take advantage of the situation, supply teachers normally being fresh meat for misbehaviour. Instead, everyone in class seemed to be going through the motions, operating under some sort of shell shock, and we were surprisingly well behaved, though that may have been due to Neil and Richard being absent too. Stephen was more popular than usual – the drama of the situation having increased his social standing – and at breaktime he stood surrounded in the playground.

'We'll never get to ask him about Mr Ware,' I sighed, frustrated. Seeing Mr Ware crying and saying sorry to Stephen made me wonder if he might have some useful information for us about what made Mr Ware tick, given we'd never imagined such a display of emotion possible.

'Yes, we will,' said Sharon and pushed our way to the

front of the crowd. Stephen's eyes lit up on seeing her and he turned towards us, ignoring everyone else. He told the story of what had happened with the air of someone who had practised delivering it many times, complete with dramatic flourishes. I asked him about Mr Ware crying.

'I don't remember that,' he said, brow furrowed. 'Did he really? He did come with me to the hospital.'

'What did he say?' Sharon and I spoke in unison.

'It were a bit weird actually,' said Stephen. 'He said he was really sorry for what had happened to me, sort of like it was his fault. And then he said he was sorry he'd called me bad names.' He paused as we took this in. I'd never heard of an adult apologising to a child in this way, especially someone like Mr Ware. 'Anyway, then he said that I should stand up to the likes of Neil Callaghan and Richard Collier.'

This was the most we had heard Stephen Crowther say in the three years we had shared a class with him. As we went to leave, he stopped us, holding on to Sharon's arm and adding, 'Me mum said that Mr Ware's getting a divorce because his wife left him to be with another man and that he's gone a bit do-lally, and that he's a lovely man who doesn't deserve it. She said he's moving away because he can't stand to be near her.' He barely paused for breath as he delivered this astonishing titbit of gossip, as though he'd memorised it word for word from his mum. His knowing nod at the end of it was one Aunty Jean would have been proud of.

We left Stephen to his crowd of admirers, stunned by his revelations, but not before I saw an almost imperceptible glance exchanged between Stephen and Sharon.

'What was that about?' I asked her as we walked away.

'Oh, it was nothing really,' said Sharon, gesturing with her hand as if waving the point away. 'I just helped him with his running after that last PE lesson – you know, when Mr Ware called him a fairy.'

When did she do that? When I was at choir? How did I not know?

It occurred to me then that, like our suspects, Sharon might have a secret life I knew nothing about. I wondered what else she did when I wasn't with her.

I also found my feelings about Hazel Ware were conflicted. I still thought she was wonderful but imagined what Aunty Jean would have to say about her behaviour. My feelings about Mr Ware were even more confusing. The description of him as a 'lovely man' and his remorse at his treatment of Stephen gave me doubts that he could be guilty of such horrible crimes as the Ripper murders. Should we cross Mr Ware off the list?

Before he left, he had marked our mill homework. Mine was my summary of the story of John Harris. The last note I got from him was written in my exercise book underneath that story and noted with concern my *continuing, possibly unhealthy interest in death*.

He wasn't wrong, but Mr Ware didn't understand that there was more to be afraid of from the living than the dead.

10

Mr Ware

'You got someone you're visiting?'

The man sitting next to Mike was taking long, slow drags from a cigarette while holding on to the drip attached to his arm. Mike suspected he wasn't as old as he looked. The ravages of illness, and probably the cigarettes, had added years to his face, but his eyes were those of a young man. The two of them sat on a wobbly wooden bench at the entrance to the hospital. Since the 'incident', Mike had found himself here every day, even though Stephen had long been discharged. He didn't know where else to go.

The first time, when he'd brought Stephen in, he had stayed until the boy's mum had arrived, then gone back to school where he and the head had met with Richard's and Neil's parents. The meeting had been deeply dispiriting. While Neil's parents had made him say sorry, they were full of excuses for the boy's behaviour, claiming that 'boys will be boys'. Richard, on the other hand, had made no apology, and Mike had seen at first hand why Kevin Collier had such a reputation. The man had not said a word, and just stared, unblinking, at the head, who had seemed to fumble and stutter in Kevin's presence. His wife did all the talking, and implied that the incident had been a 'misunderstanding'. The only sign of vulnerability that Mike had detected in the boy had been Richard's constant checking of his dad's expression every time he spoke, seeking his approval. It had made Mike shudder with familiarity.

Since then he had taken leave from school, got dressed each morning in his suit and tie, and come to the hospital, spending the day just sitting, watching, thinking. He wasn't about to explain that to this man though.

'Not exactly. I just came to visit someone. A pupil of mine,' he lied, turning to the man and smiling briefly.

'Oh, you're a teacher then? I'd better mind me p's and q's.' The man laughed, which sent a series of wracking coughs through his skeletal frame, and Mike nodded. 'Well, that's right nice of you,' the man said after he'd recovered. 'Coming to see a pupil. Can't imagine anyone I were taught by caring that much. Bastards.'

Mike nodded again, not sure what to say to this.

'Teachers in my day were more likely to land you in here than visit you,' the man carried on, shaking his head. 'Went home covered in bruises more than once. Maybe it's different now.' He threw his cigarette onto the floor, stubbing it out with the bottom of his slippers, heaved himself to his feet and slowly made his way back through the sliding front doors of the hospital, saving Mike from commenting.

He thought about what the man had said, glad he hadn't had to respond. What would he have said anyway?

I'm no different from the bullies who taught you?

I'm partially responsible for the boy coming here?

In the days following Stephen's assault, Mike had been haunted by a memory of his father. He could remember being in the cavernous hallway of his childhood home, the cold black-and-white chequered tiles under his feet. He was wearing the shorts and blazer of his prep school, his knees scuffed and his hair sticking up after he removed his cap. He couldn't recall why he'd been upset, only the looming presence of his father standing over him.

'Stop. Crying,' he'd commanded, with all the stern bearing of the military man he had been. Mike had slowly raised his eyes to him, tears still flowing.

'Only sissies cry,' his father had growled at him, which made the tears worse, and he'd made him stand in the corner of the room until he stopped.

Later, his mother had held him close while he'd told her what had happened.

'Try not to antagonise Daddy,' she'd said to him, stroking his hair.

According to his mother, it was the war that had changed his father, though Mike couldn't remember the man he was before that. He'd made a decision that day to never let himself become like him. He had resisted a military career to become a teacher in a state school, to his father's ongoing and deep disdain.

He could remember the fear that would rise in him whenever his father stepped into the room after that. And how the teacups would rattle in their saucers as his mother placed them on the table at breakfast time. About the tablets she began to take 'for her nerves', so many that she began to rattle too. And now? He wasn't sure when or how it had happened, but somehow, despite all his efforts, he was exactly like the man he'd sworn he'd never be.

When he arrived home that evening, he was just about to put his key in the door when he realised what he was doing and knocked on the door instead. He watched Hazel's reaction carefully as she opened it and winced as she flinched when he went to kiss her on the cheek.

'Come in,' she said, and he followed her to the kitchen, where she was preparing dinner. They'd agreed he would come round so they could talk while Paul was at choir or orchestra, or whatever else he did that Mike had taken no interest in.

'Good day?' he said, hoping he sounded casual. She turned towards him with a look of astonishment. Was it really that long since he'd asked?

'Erm. Yes. Thanks,' she said. 'You?' Her face was flushed from the warmth of the kitchen and she was make-up- and shoe-less, reminding him of the young woman he'd first met.

He gritted his teeth as he pulled out a dining chair from around the large table where they usually ate their meals in silence. 'Sit down,' he said gently, and pointed to the seat opposite. She took it, looking at him as if he had gone completely mad, which he supposed he might well have done.

'I. Well. I just wanted to say I'm sorry,' he said, aware that his words sounded stilted. 'For everything. I know I've not been easy to live with. For some time.'

Hazel stared at him for a few moments. 'OK,' she said, as though not sure if she was hearing him correctly.

'I just wondered if it's too late. For us, I mean?' He looked down at the table, not wanting to see her expression or read the answer in her eyes. Her hands moved from her lap to find his across the table and he held on to them, still unable to look up. He heard her breathing, ragged and unsteady.

'Mike. Thank you for saying this. For saying you're sorry.' Her voice cracked with emotion. 'It means more than you'll ever know.'

She inhaled sharply.

'But it is too late.'

11

Miv

Number Four

The summer holidays started in the best possible way, with a chippy tea on the day we broke up. I got home from school giddy with freedom, and Aunty Jean was waiting for me as I arrived. 'I'm too meithered to cook,' she said, before even saying hello, and got out the battered notebook. 'Right, let's make a list. What do we want to order?'

After a few bad days had turned into a few bad weeks, Mum had gone away for one of her 'breaks', so it was just me, Dad and Aunty Jean at home. I knew I *should* miss Mum, but I didn't. Whenever she went away it was like an invisible pressure valve had been released. I could breathe. Even Aunty Jean became her own version of light-hearted.

I did miss the person Mum had been before. Even though that person used to annoy me by always telling me what to do – *wash your face, brush your teeth, tidy your hair, close your mouth when you're eating* – that was OK, because mums were supposed to be like that and she had a way of saying things that felt light, melodic, like her singing. Now I just had Aunty Jean saying it, and that was different: heavy and tuneless.

When we got to the chippy, Mrs Pearson – her snappy Jack Russell tied to a post outside – and Valerie Lockwood – ordering for her and her son Brian, the man in the overalls – were in the queue. This meant that Aunty Jean had the opportunity to indulge in her favourite pastime: a very loud, very indiscreet conversation about people in our town. Aunty Jean's job at the Unemployment Office meant she knew more than most about the private affairs of others, but I suspect she would have found out the information anyway, she was so fond of gossip, and particularly fond of knowing more than anyone else.

'I hear the Blackburn brothers are in bother,' said Mrs Pearson.

Aunty Jean closed her eyes and shook her head, in disapproving sorrow. 'Aye. Claiming t'dole and selling scrap on the side. It's a sorry business,' she said.

'They've some brass neck,' Mrs Lockwood chipped in. 'When you think about all the honest folk trying to put food on t'table. Was it one of the Howdens who reported 'em?'

The Howdens were a wealthy family who owned the local scrapyard. They were Yorkshire royalty, which meant that they had money but were not very posh at all. Aunty Jean's mouth tightened, the Howdens being another thing that she disapproved of. The conversation was interrupted by the arrival of Mrs Pearson's cod and chips (with a battered sausage for the dog) and she left, Mrs Lockwood following behind shortly afterwards.

At the counter, we were served by the owner, who I always presumed was called Barry given that the shop was called Barry's Chippy.

'I've put in some scraps, for t'poor bairn,' he said, and nodded in my direction, as though I wasn't right there listening. My eyes began to smart, and I was sure it was the vinegary smell causing it. As I breathed in the aroma, I remembered how Mum and I would make chip butties together. She would slather white bread with margarine and ketchup, then I would sprinkle it with scraps before she added the chips. Like a delicious conveyor belt. Scraps were my favourite bit.

'I'm not sure that Marjorie should be ordering that dog a battered sausage,' Aunty Jean sniffed as we walked home. Although it was a warm evening, she clutched the top of her cardigan to express her disgust. 'Have you seen the size of it? Mind you, I'm not sure she should be ordering fish and chips for herself either.' In Aunty Jean's mind, the wider the waistband, the looser the morals. While I carried our dinner, wrapped in newspaper, the heat and vinegar seeping into my hands, trying to ignore the rumble in my tummy, she carried on talking about the Blackburn brothers, the Howdens and her disapproval at anyone who attempted to 'cheat the system'. She was as animated as when she talked about Margaret Thatcher, and as distracted as when she talked about how things 'used to be', so I let my mind wander on to the Ripper and the list.

Her views about the Howdens (rough) and the 'criminal element' (thugs) they attracted had sparked a thought about the suspicious nature of the scrapyard. An image of the wide expanse of broken-down cars and machinery came to mind. If Sharon and I investigated Howden's Scrapyard – another brilliant place to hide a body – and uncovered other wrongdoing in the meantime, there was a chance I might actually do something to win Aunty Jean's approval.

I had found the next item on the list.

I went round to Sharon's the next day to tell her about the scrapyard. She opened the door as I walked up the path and stood in the doorway almost dancing. 'Come on, come on . . .' she said, indicating that we should hurry upstairs.

Before I had the chance to tell her about Howden's, she sat at her dressing table and pressed 'play' on a small tape recorder. 'Dad let me have it so I could tape the Top 40, and I used it to tape this off the telly instead,' she said.

'Is it the Ripper tape?' I said, beside myself, as she shushed me. The machine crackled into life and played the words that we already knew by heart, as they had been playing repeatedly, everywhere we went. It was the voice of Wearside Jack – the man who said he was the Ripper and had sent a tape of his voice to Assistant

Chief Constable George Oldfield, the man in charge of the Ripper Squad.

'I'm Jack. I see you are still having no luck catching me. I have the greatest of respect for you, George, but Lord, you are no nearer to catching me now than you were four years ago when I started.'

The alien sound of his flat, north-eastern accent made the voice even scarier to us. After we listened there was silence. Sharon played it again.

'Do you think it's really him?' I said. 'Do you think it's *really* him we're listening to?'

Ever since the tape had first been played, people walked around looking like their ears were cocked in readiness to identify the voice. If it happened to be on the radio in Mr Bashir's shop, people would stop what they were doing, suspended in mid-action until it was finished. Every time Sharon and I came across someone who didn't have a Yorkshire accent – a rare occurrence – we would ask ourselves, *Is it him? Is it him?*

Even Aunty Jean had been silent while listening to the recording for the first time, while Dad had shaken his head sorrowfully, wondering out loud what the world was coming to, a rare expression of opinion about anything other than the cricket scores. I wondered if Mum had heard it, wherever she was, or if she was kept safe from the Ripper. I didn't even know if she knew who he was.

The emergence of the tape was accompanied by announcements in factories and workplaces that women were not to walk home alone. We were starting to realise that Yorkshire had changed forever in ways we couldn't fully comprehend, and that was underlined the day that Dad locked the back door before we went to bed. He'd had to hunt around in our kitchen drawers to find the key.

There was of course some relief that the accent wasn't a Yorkshire one, but it only strengthened the general distrust in our town of anyone not from round our way. The side-eyeing suspicion that the Ripper might be 'one of us' was gone, and we had all the excuses we never even knew we needed to hold strangers at arm's length, reluctant to let them in. 'I *knew* he wouldn't be a Yorkshireman,' Aunty Jean had said.

'Does that mean we can stay here? Does that mean we don't have to move?' I had immediately replied. But a look exchanged between Aunty Jean and Dad made me realise that there were conversations taking place that I knew nothing about.

I still hadn't told Sharon about the threat of moving, and as I sat there on her bed, listening to the tape, watching her face, full of life, I decided to save it for another day and told her about the scrapyard instead, reminding her that Jayne MacDonald's body had been found by children and that Yvonne Pearson's had been hidden among rubbish. As Sharon stared at me open-mouthed, I realised the horror behind my words. We agreed the scrapyard should be next on the list.

4. The Scrapyard

- Perfect place to hide a body
- No one there at night and easy to get into
- Known for 'attracting the criminal element' (according to Aunty Jean)

12

Austin

Austin always felt like he was in a bunker whenever he sat in the stuffy little Portakabin that stank of cigarette smoke and stale coffee. Everyone called it 'the Shed', but it was supposed to be an office where he and the other managers could do their paperwork while watching the vehicles coming and going, and more importantly the men. Les, his boss, had put it there deliberately to give it a prime view of the loading bay. Austin always had the radio on full volume when he was working in there, the quiet too reminiscent of home, though sometimes he had to turn it down, whenever a song came on that Marian used to sing. She was never not singing or humming before, and the sudden stop made the silence unbearable. He craved noise.

Just lately though – more often since Marian was back in hospital again – he had found himself staring aimlessly out of the large window in front of his desk, his paperwork ignored. He was caught in one of those moments, pen loosely in hand, when they came in, the clean lines of their uniforms a stark contrast to the dust and grime of the delivery depot and its workers. He got up and reached for the door handle on autopilot and, on opening it, noted the quiet that had descended. There was always a radio blaring, and people shouting, laughing, swearing at each other, but the sight of the two officials had silenced everyone.

'Can I help you?' Austin asked, surprised at the formality in his voice.

'Aye, can we come in for a minute?' the older of the two policemen responded, and Austin relaxed slightly at his casual tone. He indicated for the two of them to step into the Portakabin, while clearing files off the two spare chairs and moving the ashtrays and mugs from the desk, leaving a pattern of brown circles all over it. Closing the door, he could hear the hum of noise outside begin to build again, the air filled with the inevitable speculation about what the two were there for.

'I'm Sergeant Tanner,' the older one continued, taking a seat. 'And this is Constable Radcliffe.'

'Austin Senior.' He nodded at both the men, watching as Radcliffe sat down and placed a small tape recorder on the desk.

'We're here on behalf of the Ripper Squad,' Tanner said, and his eyes held Austin's for a moment, presumably to let the words sink in. Austin found himself holding his breath, feeling his heart pulse in his neck as he watched the two.

'You've heard about the tape?' Radcliffe said, not waiting for Austin's reply. 'Well, we're going round all

THE LIST OF SUSPICIOUS THINGS

the depots and factories and we're playing it for every-one to see if anyone recognises him.'

For reasons he could not explain, even to himself, Austin breathed a sigh of relief that they weren't here for him. 'Right, so do you want everyone in here at once or one by one?' he asked.

Tanner looked out at the bay, his head nodding as he counted the men out there. 'One by one,' he replied. 'And we might as well start with you.'

Austin felt his heart rate quicken again and he moved around in his seat, attempting to shake himself out of the tension he felt. 'Aye, that's no problem, fire away.'

The sound of the voice that crackled from the tape recorder was so familiar he almost started to recite the words, but focused instead on arranging his expression, wanting to somehow show these men he was listening without looking as if he was too eager or had anything to hide.

'So, do you recognise the voice?' Tanner asked, lean-ing forward, face intent.

'No,' Austin said firmly. He didn't. The two men nodded.

For the next two hours, Austin joined the rest of the loaders, picking up the slack while the men went one by one into the Shed and came out again. He noted their pale, serious expressions as they walked in, followed by the noisy relief from the others waiting outside when each man came out, with calls of 'Did they catch you then?' to break the discomfort.

153

'Good job Jim wasn't driving today,' he heard an unidentified voice say on the way to the break room to gales of laughter and shouts of 'Way ay, man' in imitation of Jim Jameson, their only Geordie lorry driver. Austin wondered how it might feel to be a man like Jim right now – under observation, joked about and perhaps even suspected of the worst crimes Yorkshire had ever seen.

Austin watched all the lads as they filed out: the loud, confident ones, like Andy and Geoff, always the first to rib the others and make crude jokes at every opportunity; the quiet, reserved ones, like Stanley and Peter, who you could sometimes forget were there; the family men and their boys, barely out of their teens, who also worked there, following in their fathers' footsteps. Were they all like him underneath? Did they all have stories to tell? Secrets you would never guess from looking at them? No one understood better than Austin the capacity some men had for compartmentalising a life in order to continue living it.

Was that what the Ripper did?

Did he look the people he loved in the face and lie to them?

Like Austin did.

13

Miv

The summer holidays were my favourite time of year. The only rule, even for Sharon, was to be home before dark, and by July we had already taken full advantage of our freedom, playing cricket with Ishtiaq most days, or all three of us picnicking with our books.

We waited until Wakes Week to investigate the scrap-yard. Wakes Week was the annual rolling shutdown of the mills and factories of the West Riding when workers were given a week's holiday and everywhere else closed too. Even though the mills were mostly boarded up, Wakes Week was still a Yorkshire tradition and even Mr Bashir had shut the shop for the week and taken Ishtiaq to see his family in Bradford. We knew that Howden's would also be closed and while the scrapyard gate would be locked and bolted, we were small enough to wriggle underneath it. This was our opportunity to take a look around.

I always called for Sharon first thing, so we had as much of the day together as possible. It was a bright but cool sunny day and we walked down to Howden's in jeans and T-shirts, our cardigans, which Ruby had made us bring, tied around our waists. Situated at the end of a narrow, untended lane banked by dark green bowing tree branches, Howden's Scrapyard was huge, and Aunty Jean called it an eyesore. Consisting of piles and piles of precariously balanced cars, parts of cars, tyres, piping, railings and metal of all descriptions, it was a dangerous playground for children and the perfect place to hide a body.

Sharon scrambled under the gate first, but as I went to follow her, she placed a warning hand on my leg. I stopped and looked at where she was pointing. Emerging from the Portakabin on the site, usually occupied by one of the Howden brothers, chain-smoking and drinking out of endless flasks of tea, was an unshaven man dressed in dark clothes and wearing a bobble hat. He was too far away for us to make him out fully, but there was something familiar about his gait as he walked over to a large plastic barrel, removed his hat and began washing his face.

While he did so, Sharon and I crawled over to a mountain of junk and hid behind it. I was quivering with excitement.

Next the man removed his dark blue donkey jacket. I nudged Sharon in the ribs, pointing at the jacket and nodding, wide-eyed. She shrugged at me, her brow furrowing into a question mark, and I shook my head as if to say, *Never mind.* To our horror he continued to undress piece by piece, washing as he went. Neither of us had seen a naked man before and we were torn between staring and hiding behind our hands at the sight of his white-and-pink blancmange-like chest. We crouched down and crawled out of earshot.

'Did you see, did you see?' I exclaimed, the whisper pushed out forcefully with my panicked breath.

'Shhhhh, keep it down. Yes, I saw,' she whispered.

'The donkey jacket?'

She looked confused once more. I took a deep breath and let it out in a shuddering sigh in an attempt to calm myself, then said, 'You remember when we read about what the Ripper looked like, and they said he wore a dark blue donkey jacket?'

As well as the victims he had killed, the Ripper had also attacked a number of women who had survived. One of them had described her attacker as wearing a jacket just like the one the man in front of us had removed. We stayed frozen in place until the sounds of water splashing stopped and the door of the Porta-kabin closed, and then we ran, scrambling back under the gate and not stopping until we reached the end of the lane. We looked at each other, half laughing, half with shock at the realisation of how real our search had just become.

'What do we do now?' Sharon panted.

'Hang on a minute,' I said, winded and fluctuating between fury at myself for running and relief that we had. We sat on the grass, catching our breath while I pondered what we had seen.

'How do you remember all these things?' Sharon said. 'Like the donkey jacket?'

'I don't know,' I said. I thought it was a strange question, as it had never occurred to 'try' and remember these things. I just noticed things and held on to them in my mind.

'Do you think he's a tramp?'

'I don't know, I couldn't see him clearly enough to be able to tell ... except ... do you think there was something about him that seemed familiar?' Sharon's eyes narrowed with the realisation that there was, and she nodded, confirming I was right. 'We've got to go back. We've got to get a closer look,' I said, with more courage than I felt.

Sharon shook her head. 'I don't think I can, I don't think it's a good idea. What if he ...' She trailed off at the sound of a vehicle driving down the lane from the scrapyard and we ran back into the surrounding trees, then lay flat on the ground, out of sight. Unable to see, we listened until the vehicle passed us. We didn't move until there was silence. Whoever it was had left. 'We've got to go back now,' I said, determined. 'There's no one else there.'

'But what if he comes back?'

'Well, why don't you keep watch while I look around? I promise we'll leave the second we see anyone else. What if it's our only chance?'

'OK,' Sharon shrugged.

We crawled under the gate again and headed straight for the Portakabin. It was locked, so I peered inside while Sharon kept watch. The interior was covered in stuff. Clothes were piled on the chair and underneath the desk was a sleeping bag and pillow, along with a camping stove and some discarded tins. Someone was clearly living there. Curiously, there was also a gilt-framed black-and-white photo of a bride and groom in pride of place on an upturned crate next to the make-shift bed; the old Hollywood look of the photograph stood out against the shabby interior of the Portakabin. I wrote it all down in my notebook.

As we wandered home, we were both unusually quiet. I was dreaming up theories about why a person would be living in the scrapyard. There could be no good reason. If in fact it was the Ripper, how might we prove it and safely catch him? Away from the scrapyard I was the brave heroine of the story.

I suspected Sharon was having more sensible thoughts, as when it came for us to go to our separate houses she looked down at her feet and said, 'I think we should tell a grown-up.'

I baulked at the idea.

'Can we wait a bit before we do? Please, Shaz. Please. I just want to think about whether we can work out who it is first. It might be nowt. He might be nobody.' I didn't think that was true and hoped she wouldn't see through the lie. 'I promise that if anything scary happens, we will. I promise.' I put my hands together in a praying position, my eyes beseeching her to give it more time.

'OK,' she murmured. 'I'll think about it.'

I sighed with relief.

Investigations were put on hold the next day, as Ruby, Sharon and I went swimming. It had taken some work from Sharon to persuade me to go with them to the local baths.

'None of our class will be there and there will be no Mr Ware shouting at us,' she'd said. 'And Mum will buy us hot chocolate afterwards.'

When Ruby dropped me off at home that evening, Dad was back from work already and stood quietly chatting with her while I bundled my things together and got out of the car. I watched them out of the corner of my eye, their faces solemn and their tone concerned. I hoped it wasn't about me again.

'Come over in the morning and we can make a plan about Howden's then,' I said to Sharon, my eyes still on Dad and Ruby.

We looked at each other as we heard Ruby say, 'It's not fair, Austin,' to my dad, a strangled emotion behind the words that neither of us could identify. Dad was staring intently at her. The intensity of her expression reminded me of when I'd seen her watching the other mums talking about Hazel Ware. I knew then that the conversation wasn't about me, so it must have been about Mum. The look on Dad's face was one I only saw in his unguarded moments, when I caught him looking at Mum, presumably searching for the woman she used to be. Sharon coughed and it broke the spell. They looked over at us, their faces rearranging themselves into smiles before Ruby took Sharon and then left.

The next morning Sharon came to call for me and we decided to walk down to Howden's again. As we set off down the road with Mr Bashir's shop on it, we heard a familiar cry:

'ANYRAAAAAAAAAAAAAAAAGNBONE!'
'ANYRAAAAAAAAAAAAAAAAGNBONE!'

I caught hold of Sharon's arm at the same time as I heard her gasp. We both knew exactly where we had seen the man in the scrapyard before. It was our local rag-and-bone man, Arthur, whose regular cry as he travelled the streets of our town collecting unwanted items was as familiar to us as birdsong.

Everyone knew Arthur. It felt like he had been in this town forever. I didn't know how old he was, nor did I know his surname. He was always just Arthur. Our parents remembered him being there when they were young too. When I'd once asked Aunty Jean about what a rag-and-bone man did, she said it was a 'noble' profession, even though I'd no idea what that meant. Mum had explained that he'd started out collecting old scraps of cloth, which he sold to the mills to make shoddy; then, when the mills closed, he began collecting unwanted household items and eventually scrap metal. Before Mum went silent, she used to come out whenever he was in the street, to give a sugar cube to his horse, and a kiss on the cheek to Arthur, making his ruddy face even redder. One of his main customers was Howden's.

He still used a horse and cart and was beloved by every child, including me and Sharon, as he allowed us to stroke and feed Mungo carrots from his bag. Arthur and Mungo were part of the fabric of our town – Aunty Jean called him 'a dyed-in-the-wool Yorkshireman' – he couldn't be the Ripper, could he? That definitely wasn't his voice on the tape. Unless he was putting the accent on?

Without any thinking or discussion, we went to see him, waiting patiently while he conducted his transactions with the people on the street. 'Hello, young ladies,' he said. 'And how are you this fine day?' He gestured to the blue sky. He always talked to us like this. Like he was from olden times, which actually he was. His accent was so broad that sometimes even we struggled to understand him. I wasn't sure I could imagine him talking like a Geordie, but you never knew.

'We're all right, thanks, Arthur,' Sharon said. 'It's the summer holidays,' she added, by way of explanation.

'Aye, I know, you've got t'weather for it,' he said, smiling down at us.

'We went to Howden's Scrapyard the other day,' I

blurted out. Sharon looked at me, shocked at my boldness. 'We saw you.'

Arthur's smile stayed in place, but his expression changed. There was a pause before he said, 'It's not safe to be laikin' out down there. It's dangerous.'

'Yes, but why are you staying there?'

'Ah . . .' Arthur paused, clearly thinking about how to answer this, then smiled indulgently. 'I decided I wanted a change of scenery,' he said. 'You know what thee say, a change is as good as a rest.' At that he turned away from us and prepared to go. 'Now say ta-ra to Mungo and I'll see you soon.'

As I watched him leave, I felt Sharon's hand grip my arm again. 'Look who it is,' she said in a low murmur, as though not wanting anyone to see that she was speaking, 'down the road.' I turned to look, and the man in the overalls was stood opposite Mr Bashir's, at first watching Mr Bashir's shop, then watching Arthur and Mungo, the yellow pom-pom on his hat bouncing like a tennis ball with the movement of his head. It was as if he couldn't decide which one to keep an eye on. Eventually Mungo won, and as Arthur led him over, the man in the overalls tentatively stroked the horse's nose. His face softened, and he looked almost childlike. I turned to Sharon.

'We're going back to Howden's first thing tomorrow,' I said. 'Even if it's just to rule Arthur out.' I wasn't ready to look properly at the man in the overalls yet.

That night I dreamed about being chased and caught

by a dark stranger in his van. The van transformed into Arthur's cart, and yet the shadowy figure of the man chasing me didn't have his face. Even my nightmares couldn't make a villain of him.

On arriving at Howden's the next morning, we walked down the lane with some trepidation, wondering if Arthur would be there, and if he was, what we would do then. I hovered between believing there was no way that Arthur could be a bad person and a growing awareness that behind every grown-up was a story I knew nothing about. Who was to say Arthur couldn't be a criminal? As we wriggled under the gate, the smell of bacon wafted from the yard and a small transistor radio sang out Abba's 'Waterloo'. Arthur was sat on a deckchair in front of a camping stove. My tummy growled loudly, and Sharon and I attempted to swallow our giggles but failed.

'Hello, you two. Fancy a bacon butty made by my own fair hand?' Arthur didn't sound surprised at our being there. Our scarcely hidden curiosity the day before had clearly given us away.

'Yes, please,' Sharon said, without hesitation.

I wasn't sure that we should be taking food from Arthur, in case he was a criminal, but the sight of soft white cobs and brown sauce was enough to convince me, and I nodded my head. Arthur methodically put together three bacon rolls.

'I've no more plates, so we'll have to make do,' he

said. He pulled over an old oil container, brought a rug out from the Portakabin and indicated for us to sit, before handing us our rolls. We sat and ate contentedly for a while, until, through a mouthful, Sharon asked him the same question we'd asked yesterday.

'So why are you staying here?'

Arthur took a deep breath. 'It's not forever. It's just while the yard is shut, and t'Howdens are on holiday. They've been having trouble with some young thugs breaking in and that,' he said.

Relief swept through me, like a soft wave.

'Oh, is that all?' I said. Sharon glared at me to shut up, clearly noticing he had more to say.

'Well, there is . . . it's just . . .' He stopped, looking up as if for strength from some unseen force. 'Did you ever meet me wife, Doreen?' We looked at him, surprised at the change of subject. We hadn't met his wife, but we knew of her as she was as familiar a sight as Arthur: a stout, silver-haired woman who always seemed to be cleaning the front step of their house with a scrubbing brush. Like Arthur himself, she was reminiscent of a time soon to be history. 'Well,' he said, 'she . . . she passed away.' His voice was so quiet we had to lean forward and stop munching on our breakfast to hear him. 'A few months since.' He slowly got up and disappeared inside the Portakabin. We sat silently.

He came back out, clutching the black-and-white photo I had seen of the bride and groom, and held it out for us to look at. The raven-haired beauty in the picture bore no resemblance to the Doreen I knew, but something about the proud, upright man stood next to her was unmistakably Arthur. 'When t'funeral was over, I went back t'house and it were like a place I didn't know any more. All t'bairns have left home and moved away or they've got their own families, so it's just me and it didn't feel right. I just, I mean, I didn't want to be there.'

'Why didn't you go and stay with someone else?' asked Sharon, eyes shining.

Arthur looked at her with mournful kindness. 'Oh, young lady, I don't want to be a bother to no one. I thought I'd come down here. I've the keys to the yard and the van so I can bring scrap down still, and I keep Mungo here. I decided I'd have a little camping holiday till you two rumbled me.' He smiled at us.

A loud sob made us both turn to Sharon.

'What's the matter?' I said, puzzled.

Arthur put his hand on my arm. 'Let her cry,' he said quietly.

The three of us sat wordlessly, apart from Sharon's crying. Arthur nodded along to the radio, and I finished my bacon sandwich. When Sharon's tears finally stopped, Arthur handed her a hanky from his pocket.

'Here. Blow your nose, flower.'

Sharon looked at him and sniffled, then blew her nose loudly.

'Me nana died, and I miss her so much,' she said

falteringly, her sobs threatening to start again. 'Even though it was ages ago now. I still miss her every day.'

As Arthur reached out and took her hand, I watched their shared grief, hoping I would never have to feel that way. Then I remembered Mum.

On the way home that day we were silent again until the time came to say goodbye.

'I . . . I didn't know about your nana,' I said, feeling sick. How had I not known?

Sharon sighed. 'I know. It happened when things went bad with your mum. Just before we were friends,' she said. I couldn't respond. We never talked about what had happened to Mum.

I wrestled with deeply uncomfortable feelings as I walked home. At church we were told to look out for others in everything we did and to 'be kind to our neighbours'. I really wanted to be a good person, and as I hadn't been aware of Sharon's sadness it made me wonder if I was. Was this why Mum and Dad needed their 'breaks' from me? Sharon just seemed to know how to care for other people instinctively. She did it with me, with Stephen Crowther, with Ishtiaq. I resolved to watch her more carefully and learn how to be a good person. She was the best person I knew.

For the rest of Wakes Week we would go and see Arthur almost daily. Our time with him bookended our days with more innocent things. We would share a cup of tea from his flask, and he would talk about Doreen and the children, and we would tell him about our day, minus our hunt for the Ripper. We discussed taking Ishtiaq down to meet him when he got back from Bradford, but we were still cautious about telling grown-ups we were friends with a brown boy.

One morning when we arrived, we were shocked to see Arthur's belongings strewn around the yard, with the Portakabin's door half pulled off its hinges. Arthur himself was sat on his deckchair, his eyes closed and skin grey. In his hands was the photograph of him and Doreen.

I put my hand out as if to stop Sharon from moving any closer.

We looked at each other.

'Is he dead?' Sharon whispered.

We tiptoed towards him, hearts in our throats, and were relieved to see him move, if only a fraction. 'Arthur?' I said, tentatively.

'Good morning,' he croaked, his eyes half opening.

'What's happened?' Sharon said, her voice high and wavering.

'Them young thugs,' he said. 'They came . . .' The words seemed to be stuck.

I looked around at the mess as he got up out of the deckchair slowly, wincing at each move. 'Are you all right?' I said, rushing towards him to take his arm.

'Aye, lass.' He brushed himself down. 'They didn't hurt me. They were just out to take advantage of an old man. Now, let's see if we can find the stove and get the hot water on, shall we?'

'Did they take owt?' I asked.

'Nowt much,' he said. 'Some piping and the like.'

'Did you recognise any of them?' said Sharon, her voice stronger and more determined now. But Arthur just shrugged and refused any further attempts to talk about what had happened, so we quietly helped him tidy everything up and he screwed the hinges of the door back on.

Sharon saw the newspaper stand outside the corner shop first.

'They're back!' she said, with the first proper smile in a day. We went straight in and ordered a 20p mix.

'It's for Arthur,' Sharon said to Mr Bashir. 'Do you know what sweets he likes?'

'Course I do,' said Mr Bashir, and pulled together a selection of mint humbugs, midget gems and liquorice. 'Old people sweets' Sharon and I called them.

'That's right kind of you two to spend your pocket money like that,' Mr Bashir said.

Before I could stop her, Sharon told Mr Bashir all about Arthur, the scrapyard and the attack. I wasn't sure Arthur would want anyone to know, but it also felt like sweet relief not to carry it on our own. Mr Bashir nodded as he listened intently.

'Ishtiaq's in the back,' Mr Bashir said, opening the counter up for us. 'He'll be pleased to see you.'

We went into the back room to find Ishtiaq reading a book so closely it was almost as though his head had disappeared into it. He didn't hear us enter, so I nudged Sharon and we both said, 'Ey up, Ishtiaq,' at full volume. The book fell from his hands as he jumped, but his face quickly spread into a wide grin.

'How was Bradford?' I asked.

Ishtiaq shrugged. 'Lots of aunties fussing over me,' he said, visibly squirming. 'I'm glad to be home.'

'We're glad you're home too,' Sharon said, her voice unusually low. I looked at her, to make sure she was all right, but her eyes were fixed on Ishtiaq.

'Operation, cards or chess?' I said, and we spent the rest of the afternoon playing 'Happy Families', shouting at each other so loudly that Mr Bashir had to come and tell us to shush.

'Not every customer wants to know who has won and lost every round,' he said, his smile giving away his delight in our fun.

14

Omar

Omar let the girls through to the house, then returned to the counter, their story about Arthur on his mind. His first thought was whether Arthur's attackers might be the same boys who had been troubling him. He was sure they were responsible for the damage to the shop, especially as one of them had walked past while he was cleaning off the graffiti and 'accidentally' bumped into him, knocking him and the bucket over, the soapy water sloshing across the pavement. He'd picked himself up and run after them, but they had youth and a head start on him and he'd had to stop, panting, watching their green jackets and turned-up jeans disappear into the distance.

As he began to unpack newly delivered tins of beans, placing them carefully on the shelves with the fronts all facing the same way, he wondered whether he should do something about Arthur. Like everyone else in the neighbouring streets, Arthur was a regular customer, but not one who stopped for conversation. Not someone who ignored him or avoided eye contact with him either though. He still got that, but Arthur struck him as 'old school' Yorkshire – keeping himself to himself and never complaining about his lot in life – and not the kind of man who easily asked for help. Particularly not from the likes of Omar.

Then it struck him sharply that he'd not seen him since Doreen had died and the can of beans he was holding dropped to the floor. How had he not noticed that? When he'd heard about Doreen's death his whole body had responded and he'd struggled not to physically crumble under the weight of his empathy. He and Rizwana had only been married for fifteen years and the loss had bored a hole inside him he wasn't sure would ever be healed. Arthur and Doreen had been married for thirty-five years.

The door to the shop opened and Mrs Spencer, the wife of the local vicar, strode in and began plucking things from the shelves with an impatient air.

'Afternoon, Mrs Spencer,' he said as he picked up the tin from the floor, using the moment to breathe deeply and pull himself back together.

'Afternoon,' she replied, without breaking her focus or looking over in his direction, one neatly manicured hand on the pearls she always wore around her neck. He considered whether, given who she was, he should tell her about Arthur. That Arthur might be more responsive to the concern and care of the local vicar's wife than of the local shopkeeper, it being her job to look out for the community.

'No fresh butter?' she said.

THE LIST OF SUSPICIOUS THINGS

'Ah, no, sorry. There's some marge in there though.'

He watched her grimace, took another look at her pointed face and narrowed eyes and decided against it. Mrs Spencer didn't exactly exude sympathy or softness. She was all sharp edges and judgement. He decided he would wait until Arthur's daughter came in and talk to her instead. Mrs Spencer moved over to the counter to pay, unloading an armful of items topped by a newspaper. Omar pointed at the headline as he rang the rest up on the till.

'He needs catching,' he said, indicating the main story: *Help Us Find This Man. Have You Heard the Tape?*

Mrs Spencer made a 'hmmph' sound. 'He's just another symbol of an increasingly godless country,' she said loudly, with the clarity of someone used to making pronouncements without challenge. She looked at Omar properly for the first time.

'No offence, of course.'

While she rummaged in her purse to pay, Omar exchanged the tin of beans she'd bought for the dented one that he'd dropped, then opened the door for her as she left – slamming it shut after her with satisfaction.

Later, while he was cooking tea for himself and Ishtiaq, he found himself making extra. So much so that he put a whole other portion into a piece of the Tupperware Rizwana had used constantly and that he would never get rid of. After tea, he instructed Ishtiaq not to answer the door, and drove down to Howden's, the Tupperware on the passenger seat with some foil-wrapped chapattis balanced on top. As he drove down the lane leading to the scrapyard one-handed, the other hand keeping the Tupperware upright, he pondered calling out to Arthur, to make sure he was OK. He parked up at the locked gate and peered into the darkness of the yard, lit only dimly by a solitary lightbulb in the Portakabin. He could just make out the shadow of Arthur moving around before the light was switched off. He left the Tupperware on the gatepost, flashed his headlights three times until the light in the Portakabin came back on, then drove away.

15

Miv

The day after the attack we went and helped Arthur pack his things up and move back into the house he and Doreen had shared. As a treat he allowed us to sit in the cart, and we went through the streets of the town waving at everyone as we passed, like the Queen. As we clattered past the market, with its bustling stalls set on cobblestones and the shouts of offers on fruit and veg, I saw a figure I recognised, her blonde hair glinting in the sun.

'Look, Shaz, it's Mrs Ware. Hazel.'

We both stared, mesmerised, as though she were a film star picking up a pound of tomatoes. I strained my neck to keep watching as we got further away, and saw that she was laughing at someone behind her, someone who was holding her hand. It wasn't Mr Ware. They looked like a golden couple, surrounded by a halo that marked them out as beautiful and different from everyone around them. Her: elegant, blonde. Him: tall, dark-haired, gruff-looking but handsome. I felt consumed by unidentifiable emotions as I watched them, a mixture of deep attraction and a jealousy that I would never be like her, I was too plain.

Trailing behind them was Paul Ware. He was looking at the floor, his fringe hiding his eyes. I wondered how he might feel about his mum holding hands with a man who wasn't his dad.

Sharon jumped from the cart as we arrived at Arthur's house, with its swooping net curtains in the windows, and said to the pale and quiet Arthur, 'If you give me the key, I'll open up.'

His face crumpled into a slow, sad smile. How did she know to go in first?

He swallowed. 'Thank you, flower.'

We still went to see Arthur regularly, on a Saturday afternoon, while he picked up the reins of his life and moved through his grief. We would find him, more often than not, in his back garden tending to the pigeons he now owned.

'Doreen would never let me get any. She thought they were mucky birds,' he said.

He was always telling us to be safe and mind ourselves, so we decided not to tell him about our search for the Ripper, though one day when we arrived Arthur was reading the paper on a stripy deckchair in the garden. I could see from the front page that the Ripper formed the main content. I nudged Sharon.

'What do you think about him then, Arthur?' I indicated the front page.

Arthur flapped the paper back over and looked at the story.

'He's not for you to worry about,' he said, his voice firm and expression closed.

'But why not?' I persisted. 'He's a "danger to all women and girls".' I pointed at the headline.

'Yes, but not t'likes of *you*.' He got up slowly from the chair he was sat on. 'Right, I'm going to put t'kettle on.'

With that, I took it that the subject was once more closed. No one ever seemed to want to talk to us about the Ripper.

16

Helen

Helen could have sworn she'd told Gary she was planning to see her dad that evening. She hadn't been round to his for ages, a fact that had been nagging at her for weeks, and now that Omar at the shop had told her this strange story about Howden's Scrapyard, she knew she needed to. She told herself she hadn't yet because she'd been so busy with her new job, but she knew there was more to it than that.

She was stood in the kitchen area of their small bedsit, putting foil over his dinner, when Gary arrived home from work.

'What you doing?' he asked, nodding at the plate on the table. 'Oh,' he said when she reminded him she was going to visit Dad, his voice and expression plaintive, like that of a small child.

She knew what was coming, that he wouldn't want her to go; she'd thought about this already. 'You can put it straight into the oven to warm up, you don't have to do anything,' she said, trying not to sound as if she was patronising him, which he'd told her she was guilty of before.

'It's not that,' he said, and she could see he was arranging his expression into his charming one, the one that everyone loved, that no one could say no to, particularly her. 'I just wanted to take you to the pub. The lads from work are going out for a pint and I just like to show my beautiful wife off.' He was closer to her now and nudged her shoulder gently, wheedling.

Despite herself, Helen found herself glowing at his praise. It was like a reflex action. She looked at the mournful expression in his eyes and laughed. 'All right then,' she said, not giving herself time to think about it. She could go and see her dad tomorrow.

Later, she was in the bathroom, applying what little make-up she had, rubbing some lipstick onto her pale cheeks, when the words 'Actually, it's been ages since we went out' escaped from her mouth before she had thought them through. Immediately she felt the air in the room thicken with tension, and knew she'd said the wrong thing. She froze, her hand poised between the sink and her face, but at that moment the strains of a song by Dr Hook, 'When You're in Love with a Beautiful Woman', began playing on the radio. Gary loved Dr Hook. The moment passed.

She emerged from the bathroom almost coquettishly, like a teenager going to her first disco. She'd made an effort, and was wearing a blouse she knew he liked: pale pink with lace around the collar, much fussier than she would normally wear. Gary smiled his approval.

'We make a good-looking pair,' he said with pride as he held out his arm for her to tuck hers into, all ready to go off to the pub together like they were a normal, loving couple.

It was late by the time they left and the Red Lion was busy as they made their way to the bar, weaving in and out of groups of people as though they were in a maze. Of course Gary knew everyone by name, and their progress was slowed by him stopping to talk to various men, clapping them on the back, winking at their wives and laughing uproariously at any given opportunity. Helen, trailing behind him, holding on to his hand, watched as his face and tone altered depending on who he was talking to, chameleon-like, the comments cruder and the voice louder when they reached the group of friends he worked with and their wives and girlfriends who were standing next to the bar.

'You've all met my lovely wife,' he said as he pulled her to him and flung his arm around her. Helen blushed and nodded at the sea of faces. The men she'd met before, but the women were new to her.

Gary leaned into the bar and loudly ordered a round of drinks from the barman, Pat. She knew he would offer again and again, buying round after round for his friends, basking in his image as a generous man, despite them being ill able to afford it. It made her cringe a little, but the lads worshipped him.

'Way ay, man,' Gary shouted at a man sat at the bar, slapping him so hard on the back that he spat out his

drink and began coughing. The lads laughed raucously –
at what, she didn't understand – and the man turned
his boyish face to Gary, smiling at him – humouring
him, Helen thought. While Pat refilled the man's pint,
Gary looked at her confused expression and said, 'Jim's
a Geordie. You know, like the Ripper,' as though that
made some sort of difference. She looked back at the
bar and noticed Pat and Jim raising their eyebrows
at each other. Pat saw her looking and Jim followed
his gaze. When they both smiled at her kindly, Helen
immediately felt embarrassed, detecting sympathy in
their expressions. Pat nodded and mouthed 'hello'. She
was surprised he remembered her; she didn't accom-
pany Gary to the pub that often. She was just about to
acknowledge him in return when she sensed that Gary
had also seen the exchange. She gave Pat the smallest of
smiles, hoping he would see it, and turned back to the
group, joining in the hero-worship of Gary as enthusiastically as she could, laughing at his stories and hanging
off his every word.

As they left the pub later, she went to slot her hand
in his. He took it and held on tight, so tight she realised
it was beginning to hurt, her fingers crushed.

'Gary?' she said, her voice gentle, questioning, not
wanting to let the fear show.

But the charming man of a moment ago was gone.

17
Miv

Number Five

'I can't laik out tomorrow,' Sharon said one August afternoon when we were parting for the day. 'We're going to the shops for school stuff – you know, new clothes and that,' she added, rolling her eyes dramatically for effect. It hadn't occurred to me until that moment how close we were to the end of the holidays.

As I walked home, kicking stones as I went, scuffing my already worn shoes even more, I looked down at my faded, frayed jeans. They were flapping around my ankles, quite clearly too short. How had I not noticed until that moment? When I got home, letting myself in using the key I kept on a ribbon around my neck, I ran upstairs and pulled my school uniform out of the wardrobe. I took my T-shirt and jeans off, put my school shirt on and stooped down to look at myself in the mirror above the dressing table.

As I had suspected, the shirt now gaped in the middle. I had chosen to ignore the lines of my once straight-up-and-down body growing more fluid, even after someone, Aunty Jean I assumed, had left a 'junior bra' on my bed a few weeks ago. I had stuffed it into my drawer without even trying it on, but realised I could ignore it no longer. I pulled my school shoes out from under the bed and put those on too, feeling the pinch at the toes before I kicked them off and slumped down on the bed.

At the sound of another key in the door I jumped up, put my T-shirt and jeans back on and went downstairs. Aunty Jean was already bustling around the kitchen. She'd put the kettle on and was pulling tins, a pan and a wooden spoon from drawers and cupboards. I stood in the doorway and watched her, trying to work out how to bring up the subject of my school uniform and shoes.

'What you lurking for?' Aunty Jean said, without looking at me.

I screwed my eyes up, as though hoping to avoid the impact of something heavy falling on my head. 'It's nearly time to go back to school and my, well, my stuff doesn't fit,' I said, readying myself for a tirade about 'when I were a lass', likely involving not wearing shoes, or having to wear clothes that were hand-me-downs from Edwardian times. Instead, I was met with a brief nod and a long silence.

'Leave it with me,' Aunty Jean said in a business-like tone, still without looking at me, and I could sense her discomfort as she stood there, straight as a pencil, until I left the room.

*

The longer Mum was away, the more conversation took place at the kitchen table.

'That driver I were telling you about, Jim Jameson, he came into the depot today,' Dad said that evening to Aunty Jean, in between mouthfuls of corned-beef hash. Even though she was sat to one side of me, I could tell that Jim Jameson did not pass muster – it was something about the set of her shoulder – but I was not sure why. I was always amazed by how much disapproval Aunty Jean managed to convey with the tiniest movements of her body and face. A raised eyebrow from Aunty Jean had the power to decimate an entire character.

'We gave him so much stick. One of the lads kept quoting the tape at him. I thought he was going to cry at one point.' As he took a mouthful of tea, I dared to ask a question.

'Who's Jim Jameson?'

'Oh. He's one of the lorry drivers at work.'

'Are you talking about the Ripper tape?' I asked, hesitating to say his name, hoping I wouldn't be shut down. Dad spluttered, then put his mug of tea down on the table and looked at me, concerned.

'What do you know about the Ripper tape, young lady?'

'Everybody knows about the Ripper tape,' I answered, confident in the knowledge that actually everyone did.

'Oh. Right.' He paused as though weighing up the truth of this statement and deciding I was probably right.

'As a matter of fact, yes, I am. Jim's from Newcastle, you see, so not only does he have the shame of being a Geordie, but he's also got this an' all.' Seeing my eyes widen, he laughed and added, 'Don't worry, love. He's not the Ripper. He's as much of a big girl's blouse as you.'

But the seed had been sown and would only come to grow over the following days.

Dad oversaw the loading and unloading of vehicles, and the men who worked there. He was proud of his job, which he'd got after years of unemployment and casual labour. He'd started as a loader himself, and still considered himself one of the lads, despite now holding the grand title of 'Supervisor'. He would always make sure people knew he'd 'started at the bottom and worked me way up'. I'd never been to his work, but after this conversation I began to think up reasons for going to visit him and catching a glimpse of Jim Jameson the Geordie – but thinking about his work caused images I didn't want to flash up in my brain. Images of that day. The day I tried never to think about. The day everything changed.

It was during the school holidays and Dad had gone to work as usual, despite the events of the night before – events I had only really heard from my bedroom, as I'd not been allowed out. 'Stay in your room, Miv,' Dad had shouted, when I'd opened the door a sliver, having heard Mum come home from the bingo. Halfway through the next day I had got home from laiking out and found Mum lying on the floor of the bathroom, a trail of vomit coming from her mouth. I'd tried to wake her up, but couldn't, my own stomach lurching like I was on the waltzers.

Luckily, the number for Dad's work was stuck on the wall next to the phone and I dialled it, saying to the person who answered, 'Can you tell my daddy to come home? My mummy is poorly.' There had been an ambulance and everything. Aunty Jean had come over to look after me while Dad went with Mum, then she'd never gone home.

That was the first time Mum went away for one of her 'breaks', a word which conjured up images of trips to Bridlington and Whitby, but which I somehow knew even then were very different. I hadn't heard Mum speak since. That was the day I realised that life could change overnight, that you had to keep an eye out for danger. Be vigilant.

While I finished my tea, I wondered what reason I could give to go to the depot and investigate Jim Jameson. I was just starting to clear away our plates when I noticed that Aunty Jean was wiggling her eyebrows and nodding at me, trying to get my attention. With a quick movement of her head, she indicated for me to leave the room and, though confused, I did, retreating only as far as the settee so that I could listen to what was being discussed without being seen.

'Can't you do it?' I heard Dad ask.

To which Aunty Jean answered, 'She needs at least

one parent to notice her existence. And I wasn't made to raise children.'

'What makes you think I was?'

'If you used your eyes to see what's going on inside your own home rather than concentrating on *other* stuff, you might notice these things,' Aunty Jean said, her voice so ice-cold that even I froze, though it wasn't directed at me.

'What do you mean by that?' Dad said, in a tone I didn't recognise.

'Don't think I haven't noticed where your attention is, Austin,' Aunty Jean replied.

My throat closed, putting a stopper on the multitude of feelings swirling around my body, none of which I was willing to look at. I tried to think about the Ripper and the list instead. On his way out to the pub, Dad passed by me on the sofa.

'Apparently we're going shopping at the weekend,' he said.

It was with a heavy heart that I got ready to go shopping that Saturday. It wasn't just that the trip was taking me away from what little of the summer holiday was left, it was the fact that it was blatantly clear from the sighing and eye-rolling while waiting for me that Dad was doing this under protest.

'Shall we walk or get the bus?' Dad said, to my surprise. I had thought he wanted to get the whole thing over with as soon as possible.

'Walk,' I said decisively, and we headed off in the direction of the shops.

We made our way down endlessly repeating rows of identical houses, the streets branching into each other, connected like the nerves and veins we studied in Biology lessons, our pace leisurely in the heat of the summer sun. At one point we headed down a cul-de-sac, at the end of which was a cut-through that led straight on to the High Street. It was a small ginnel amid a row of lock-ups and parking spaces. It was there that Dad stopped and stared at the small lorry parked up in the corner, out of the way.

'Hmmmm,' he said, 'that's interesting.'

I got the feeling he was talking to himself, but eager to keep on the right foot, I decided to be polite and show I was listening. 'What's interesting?'

'That's Jim Jameson's lorry,' he said. 'I thought he'd gone home for the weekend. Wonder what it's doing here.' He took a step closer and carried on. 'He were stopped and questioned on his rounds this week, apparently. I get the feeling that they think the Ripper might be a lorry driver.'

At this I was on high alert. 'The police, you mean?'

'Aye,' he said, distracted, then looked back at me as if remembering I was there.

Desperate for an opportunity to write down the registration number in my notebook, I said, 'Why don't you see if he's in there and if he's all right?'

'Aye, I will. You wait here.'

As he walked closer to the lorry, calling out 'hello' as he went, I hurriedly wrote the registration down. No one answered his call, and there appeared to be no one around so we carried on to the shops. Dad seemed distracted, but I was so buoyed by the discovery of the next item on the list that, after we had got my uniform, I settled for the first pair of deeply unattractive and practical shoes Dad suggested, much to his relief.

As soon as we got home, I went straight back out again to tell Sharon about Jim Jameson, his lorry and the police, and get her agreement to add him to the list. I decided to go via Mr Bashir's and stock up on the newspapers on the way, to see if there was any mention of the lorry-driver theory. The door of the shop was propped open, presumably to let what little breeze there was flow through, and I glanced inside, notebook in hand, smiling at the sound of Mr Bashir's out-of-tune 'Saturday Night's Alright for Fighting' ringing out from behind the shelves. I was just about to take a step inside when I stopped abruptly. 'Shaz?' Sharon had appeared from the back room and was making her way out. Her expression froze.

'Oh, hi, I just came over to . . .'

'Laik out with Ishtiaq?' I finished the sentence for her, seeing that she was stumbling over her words.

'Yes,' she mumbled, looking down at her shoes. I followed her eyes. She was wearing her best sandals, with the baby-blue straps, normally reserved for birthday parties and school discos. I picked up a newspaper and paid for it, then said to Sharon, 'See you tomorrow?' in a wavering voice that matched her own. Heading in the direction of home, I turned back only briefly to see Sharon watching me, Ishtiaq a step behind her, his face over her shoulder. I didn't even stop to tell her about Jim Jameson. I had always seen Sharon as a part of me, and suddenly aware of our separateness, I didn't like it.

Sharon was at the door first thing the next morning.

'I know it's a Sunday, and I'll see you at church,' she said, tripping over her words, 'but I wanted to come and explain.'

'It's nothing. You don't have to explain seeing Ishtiaq without me,' I said, feeling hot with shame about my reaction the day before. She didn't need to know how much I needed her.

'It's not nothing,' she said, forcefully. 'I did call for you, but no one was in, so I went to see Ishtiaq instead.' Her eyes sought mine.

I nodded slowly, acknowledging the possible truth of this and the confirmation that she didn't prefer him. I let myself breathe once more.

'Do you want to know what's next on the list?' I said, and took her arm as we walked to church together. Her nod was almost imperceptible, but I pressed on anyway, pulling out the notebook and telling her about Jim Jameson and his lorry, ignoring the uncomfortable sense from her silence that maybe her interest in the list was waning.

5. The Lorry Driver

- He's a Geordie
- He drives a lorry
- He's been stopped by the police
- Even my dad seems worried about him

18

Miv

'I told Jim Jameson we saw his truck,' Dad said over tea later that week, nodding at me. 'I said he might want to park it somewhere a bit quieter if he's intending to stay in it.'

I wasn't quite sure what had changed after my shopping trip with Dad, but something had. He'd started to talk to me more like I was a grown-up.

'You mean he's living in his lorry?' I asked, unable to hide my interest.

At this Aunty Jean spluttered. 'What on earth is he doing that for? I mean, I'm all in support of hard work, God knows there's little enough of that these days, but really?'

'I know, I know,' Dad said, shaking his head in puzzlement, 'I reckon the wife's kicked him out. He said it's a temporary situation, so I told him to park up on that lane near Wilberforce Street instead.'

At this my interest increased even more. Wilberforce Street was where Arthur lived.

*

What had started as a cool, bright day had developed into a searingly hot one as we headed to Wilberforce Street the following Saturday afternoon with our cardigans tied around our waists.

'Ooh, it's as hot as 1976,' I said in an impression of Aunty Jean that made Sharon laugh out loud and reply, 'There's warm and there's warm.' Every grown-up we knew referred to the summer of 1976 as the barometer of all hot weather and would discuss it endlessly. It was a running joke between us.

When we arrived at Arthur's he was out the back with his pigeons. As we walked down the path, we called out our hellos and he looked up and beamed.

'Well, well, well. Look who it is.'

Our visit continued in its usual companionable way. Arthur showed us the latest additions to his flower beds, we talked to the pigeons, and he told us about his children and grandchildren. He had two sons, both of whom 'lived away' – meaning outside of Yorkshire – and one recently married daughter who he very rarely saw.

'Thanks to that husband of hers. Waste of space,' he said, as he pointed to a wedding photo on a side table next to the kitchen door. It showed a tall, strikingly handsome man with a mane of curly hair stood beside a tiny woman, almost a girl, wearing a large floppy hat that almost covered her face. From the little I could see of it she looked vaguely familiar.

'Is that them?' I asked.

'Aye,' said Arthur, his expression pained.

When we left, promising to visit again soon, we planned to search the nearby streets for Jim Jameson's lorry and hopefully catch a glimpse of the man himself. Walking along the road, I'd just opened the notebook to check his registration number when Sharon said, 'Hi, miss.'

I looked up to see Mrs Andrews, the librarian.

'Hello, girls,' she said, smiling.

19

Helen

Helen's smile lingered as she passed the girls. Their serious expressions – Sharon looking around with intent, and Miv concentrating hard on a notebook – reminded her of herself at the same age: intense, bookish. She was glad they had each other. She'd been the only girl among brothers and had struggled to make friends at school, always being grateful whenever anyone took an interest in her, which turned out to be her downfall.

She took a deep breath as she approached the house, debating for a moment whether to knock on the door instead of using her key. It had been so long since she had been there that she felt like a visitor. She used the key in the end – knowing that if she didn't her dad would be upset and hurt. He was washing up in the kitchen, and as he turned round at the sound of her entering the house the expression of joy on his face made her feel sick with guilt. She had to concentrate hard to look casual, as though her popping around was an everyday occurrence.

In fact, she realised with a horrified start, the last time she had been here was after the funeral, where it had felt like the whole town and the next town over had crammed into her childhood home to pay their respects. There were people spilling from rooms, stood cheek to cheek in the garden and queuing up with their muddy shoes on the very doorstep that her mum had spent so much of her time scrubbing. Her dad had held court in the living room, telling anecdotes and acting the gracious host as ever, but the moment everyone had left, he'd sunk into the settee, the weight of his loss suddenly setting in. He'd seemed to shrink in size in that moment. The energetic, vital man she knew had looked old.

Then Gary had appeared at her elbow, eager to get home. She'd tried to impress on him that she needed to be there to help Dad clear up, but he'd insisted that it was time for her brothers to 'step up', as he called it, and that she couldn't be expected to do everything for her dad, not now she was married.

'Hi, Dad. Just thought I'd pop round, see how you are.'

She'd decided she would give him the chance to tell her what had happened in the scrapyard before she asked him about it.

'I'm not so bad. Nowt to write home about,' he said, turning back to the sink and putting the kettle on. 'Now, I'll make some tea. And what about some biscuits?'

He busied himself making the tea and Helen sat down on an armchair. She refused to sit on the settee, the space her mum had occupied still worn into its shape. She almost couldn't bear to look around the room and see the thick layer of dust that had accumulated on every ornament-covered surface. Instead, she looked at the photographs on the side, avoiding her wedding photo. She'd never particularly felt comfortable in that big floppy hat – had wanted to wear a more traditional veil – but Gary had convinced her that she would look good in it. He was good at that. Convincing people.

She remembered the day she'd first met him. They'd both gone to the local college, him to learn plumbing, her to do her A levels, and he'd been leaning against a wall, smoking, as she'd walked past him on the way to get her dinner. She'd thought he looked like James Dean, and when he'd put his cigarette out and caught up with her, walking in step with her and asking her every possible question about her life, she felt as if she was interesting and attractive in a way she'd never felt before. When she'd arrived in the canteen with him, all the girls had been beside themselves with jealousy.

She picked up an older photograph instead, wiping the veil of dust off it with her hand. She smiled, remembering the day it was taken, and traced her finger around the shape of the girl she'd been then. It was the end of her first year at grammar school, and she was in her navy-blue uniform, still too big for her, even after months of wear, so that she looked lost inside it. She wasn't sure she'd ever 'grown into it', as her mum had insisted she would, refusing to pay full price for a uniform that would only fit for one school year at best. Helen was proudly holding up a bright blue rosette that she'd won for being the top of the English class. She'd won one for maths too, but the blue one had been the one she was most beside herself to win. Her brothers had laughed at her, calling her a 'boffin', and her dad had told them off, clipping both of them round the ears.

She'd wanted to be a teacher then. That had seemed something that a girl like her could do. She coughed to cover up the sudden unexpected rush of feeling. Her ambitions, never huge to start with, had been whittled down until she couldn't hold on to them any more. Maybe the library might be a chance to build them up again.

She went to find her father and saw that he was stood in the kitchen, his shoulders rounded and his head bowed while he made the tea. He was getting smaller too.

'Dad. When were you going to tell me about Howden's? And the attack?'

He swung round to have another look at her, with a speed that contradicted his age, but his face, grey and shrunken, gave it away.

'Omar at the shop told me,' she continued, 'and before you say anything, he was concerned about you.'

'Ahhh,' he said, looking as if he'd just received the answer to a confusing problem. 'It'll be him that dropped the food off then.'

'He's not the only one worried.' She took in a deep breath. 'Gary says hello.' She tried not to wince, expecting a Gary-related outburst, but Arthur just grunted.

'And how are you, love?' he said.

His change of subject was so obvious she almost laughed but decided to let it go for a moment. 'I'm really good, Dad. The library is going well, and I'm ever so busy . . . you know how it is,' she said, hoping he would pick up that she was sorry she'd not been round much.

'Come and see the garden,' he said.

He took her on a tour of the latest planting in the immaculate garden and she found herself nodding and admiring on the outside while working her way through a thicket in her mind. She alternately wished that she and he could really talk – about grief, about the attack, about Gary – while knowing that they didn't because if they did, they might be faced with reality and the need to make changes.

When she went to leave, he took her hand in his and she felt herself tense as he touched the tender, bruised part of her wrist. She hoped he wouldn't notice her flinch.

'Come back soon, love. It's always nice to see you.'

She'd just been about to step out of the door when he called out again, with an urgency that made her turn round and look at him.

'Will you give us three rings when you get home, love, so I know you're back safely?'

'Dad, it's the middle of the day,' she said, smiling at him.

'I know, I know,' he said. 'But this man, he's getting more brazen, he doesn't care what time it is, nor who it is . . . I just want you to be safe.'

Helen could have wept at the irony, but instead she nodded.

'I will, Dad.'

She looked at her watch as she set off, breaking into a run on realising how long she'd been. Gary had gone with a friend to watch Leeds play at home, and while he wouldn't be home yet, she had a lot to do, including making sure that his tea was ready when he did come in. He wouldn't actually mind that she'd been to see her dad, she knew that really. It was just that he was concerned to make sure that she didn't give too much of herself. Especially now she was working too. Gary was just looking out for her, wasn't he? That's what he always said. And that was what she was going to choose to believe.

20

Miv

The second I spotted the battered lorry parked up, I almost squealed. Forcing myself not to, I gently nudged Sharon and pointed. She followed my gaze then turned back to me, laughing.

'What?' I asked, affronted.

'You. Pretending not to be excited when I know you are.'

I wanted to be indignant but couldn't help smiling too.

'Well, shall we go and have a look then?' she added, eyes rolling, and my smile spread further. Wilberforce Street was a familiar row of terraced houses, replicated street after street in our town. The only difference between them and ours was that the ones on Wilberforce Street had originally been built to house mill managers, meaning they were bigger and had proper gardens. The lane at the end of the street had once acted as a thoroughfare to another road which had long been flattened and rebuilt with more modern houses, houses that looked like identical grey boxes stacked in a row. The lane was now a dead end and had fallen into disrepair, overgrown with moss and weeds, and the houses at that end of the street were mainly unlived in – boarded-up and crumbling – meaning a relatively small lorry, which this was, could park there undisturbed.

As we approached, we could hear the sound of a radio playing David Soul's 'Don't Give Up on Us Baby' through the open window and we instinctively slowed. The person inside had seen us through the wing mirror, however, and the door of the cab opened. A short man with light brown hair and a round face appeared. He was almost goblin-like, with rosy round cheeks and a wide grin. Although his hair wasn't dark, he did have a moustache, I noted, and his hair colour could easily be changed.

'Can I help you?' The jerky yet melodic tones of the Geordie accent confirmed that this was indeed Jim Jameson. I had been thinking about how to handle this, and to Sharon's surprise, before she could say a word, I replied with confidence, 'You work with me dad, Austin, at the depot, don't you?'

He looked at us. His brow furrowed, but his expression was friendly.

'Aye, ah know Austin.'

'Well, we, er, we just wanted to check you were all right,' I said. I heard Sharon snort beside me, my acting not meeting her standards.

'Aye, I'm all right,' he said, his brow furrowing further.

'Right then.'

After a short, awkward pause we walked away. When

I turned back to check, Jim Jameson was watching us, a puzzled look still on his face.

'It's not him,' I said, my voice firm.

Sharon gave me a sidelong glance. 'And how can you be sure?'

'He's too . . . I don't know . . . normal?' I said.

Sharon stopped walking and turned to stare at me. 'But maybe the Ripper looks normal an' all. I mean, he must do, or surely they'd have caught him by now.'

I stopped too and thought about this for a moment, wondering whether she was right. Whether we would be able to tell, or whether he would appear to be just like us.

'It's not fair. It's not fair if you can't tell,' I said, surprised by the fury that welled up in me. I felt as though I wanted to stamp my feet and scream. 'How are we supposed to keep safe?'

Later that week Dad came home one evening while I was reading in my room and called me downstairs with a grave expression. 'Did you and Sharon go and see Jim Jameson?' he said, clearly knowing that we did.

'Well, we were walking that way and we saw him.' I was scrambling for a justification, trying to cover our tracks. 'Arthur lives on the same street.'

'Well, I don't want you going up there again.' His face remained unsmiling.

Though his tone brooked no argument, I couldn't stop myself asking, 'Why not?'

He sighed. 'Look, love, the police have been in again asking after him. I just, I think you should keep away.'

I was caught between disappointment at having my activity curtailed and the unexpected warm glow of feeling cared for. It was only later that it occurred to me that this might mean we were on to something.

On the news the tape was still being played repeatedly. I listened hard for any glimmer of recognition that this was Jim Jameson's voice. We hadn't talked to him for long enough for me to be sure, but the voice on the tape sounded flatter and lower than the man we had met. I wasn't even a hundred per cent sure the accent was the same.

I'd first learned about accents when we went on a school trip to the Peak District and stayed in a youth hostel. A group of girls from a different school mimicked our voices and called me Hovis. I thought that their impressions made us sound stupid and ugly, and that was how I learned I had a Yorkshire accent. Until that moment I had thought everyone talked like me. The realisation was shot through with shame. I wondered how Jim Jameson felt about his accent now that it would forever connect him with the Ripper.

Sharon's first comment on hearing about the conversation with my dad surprised me. 'So, when are we going back?'

Not for the first time I wondered whether Sharon's reputation for being the 'good' one of the two of us came from her wide blue eyes and innocent expression more than her actual behaviour.

On the way to Wilberforce Street the next day we bumped into Richard Collier, leaning against the street sign on the corner where Mr Bashir's was. We'd not seen him since the pool incident and his suspension from school. He was nudging the ribs of another familiar figure, taller, older, his yellow bobble hat perched askew on his head, eyes not meeting ours. Since when had the man in the overalls been hanging around with schoolboys?

Somehow Richard looked older in the man's company. His cheeks were even more hollowed out than usual, and his eyes had such dark shadows underneath that they looked almost bruised. It made him more striking, handsome, yet cruel. His eyes washed over me with a sneer as we walked past and on to Sharon, who I could sense was bristling beside me. He sniffed.

'Not going to see your P— boyfriend?' he spat, nodding towards the shop.

The man in the overalls stayed silent and expressionless.

I gripped on to Sharon's arm immediately, forcing her to keep walking, feeling her body vibrate with fury.

'Don't rise to it,' I said, keeping my voice low so they wouldn't hear me. 'There's no point.'

She stayed silent, steadying her breathing as we walked the rest of the way.

*

When we got to Wilberforce Street we were disappointed to find that the lorry wasn't there. We half-heartedly began to hunt around the lane for clues, but there was so much litter it was difficult to determine what should be of interest.

We were on the verge of giving up and heading to Arthur's when the lorry drove into the lane with Jim Jameson at the wheel. We stood and watched, blatantly staring as he parked up and swung down from the cab. His forehead was bandaged, his nose swollen and wonky, and he winced as he landed on the ground, his previously rosy cheeks now pale and grey.

'Are you all right?' Sharon asked.

My attention was caught by the words on the side of the lorry: *Ripper woz ere* was written in red spray-paint. An image of Mr Bashir cleaning red smears from the wall of his shop came to mind. And of the boys on the corner.

He grunted. 'What do you think?' he said, wincing again. As he looked more closely at us, his face crinkled into a small smile. 'Oh, it's you two.'

I took in his face, his sparkling and friendly eyes. Could a monster really look like this? In that moment I made a snap decision. 'Can we help? Can we get you anything?' I said as Sharon nudged me in the ribs. I wriggled away from her.

'No,' he said, his expression rueful. 'And you'd best not be hanging around either. I'm not sure your dad'd be best pleased.'

'Why not?'

His whole body seemed to sink then, and he looked tired and sad.

'The lads at work,' he said, 'they think I've done something. Something bad.' His eyes started to fill with tears, and I felt my own throat tighten. Men didn't cry. This was all wrong. He seemed to give himself a shake, and with a laugh that didn't seem to find anything funny he said, almost to himself, 'Irony is I couldn't hurt a bloody fly.' He disappeared into himself for a moment, then refocused on the two of us. 'Anyway, you two had better be off, I'll be all right.'

Reluctantly we left, wondering what had happened to cause his injuries.

I found out a few days later, when Dad arrived home with Jim Jameson in tow and asked Aunty Jean if she could add another place for tea. I tensed as she sniffed, but with a slight nod of the head she agreed to this intrusion. The bandage had now been removed from Jim's head, revealing a large cut and bruise. The swelling on his nose had gone down, but his eyes were blackened and sunken, giving him a skull-like appearance. He smiled at me and gave a little wink while Dad and Aunty Jean weren't looking. I hoped this meant he wouldn't reveal having seen us again. I was right to trust him. He didn't say a word.

Tea was a lively affair. We so rarely had anyone who wasn't a family member in the house, it was as though we became different people. It was like watching a family on the telly. Even Aunty Jean smiled and occasionally laughed, a sound that made me jump when I heard it, it felt so unfamiliar to me. Somehow Jim Jameson charmed her. He was full of chatty good humour, and this seemed to bring out the same in my dad. Aunty Jean pulled out all the stops and made chips, then surprised us all with crumble for afters.

'Go on, have some more,' she said, after serving Jim a dish piled high with pudding, the spoon poised and ready to give him more, while serving herself the merest morsel. 'Keep your strength up,' she continued, using a phrase she often repeated to my dad. I thought it was funny that it was men who were encouraged to be strong, when according to the papers it was women who were under threat. I served myself an extra portion of crumble when she wasn't looking.

I learned that Jim had two children, both boys. I also learned that he and his wife had separated, hence him living in the lorry, but he was hoping she might let him go home soon. I would come to learn that Jim Jameson could put a jolly frame around any picture, no matter how bleak. As Aunty Jean and I started to clear away the plates after tea, the conversation between Dad and Jim became quieter and more serious in tone.

'Can I just say again how sorry I am, Jim,' my dad said.

'Ahhh, don't you worry. It's over now and it's not like you encouraged it, man.'

'No, but I didn't stop it either. And I should've, the lads never should've . . .'

'Look, there's no harm done – well, apart from this,' Jim said, smiling and pointing at his nose.

'You're more forgiving than I'd be.'

'Aye, well, ah suppose I think meself lucky in the grand scheme of things, man.' Jim's voice wobbled slightly. 'I mean, I don't mind that the police are being thorough. I'd rather that than them not looking at all. It's just a shame everyone got to know I'd been taken in.'

He paused and they both took a sip of tea.

'Oh, did I tell you me letter's been signed by the guvnor himself, George Oldfield.' Jim got an envelope out of his pocket and with a flourish opened the piece of paper inside for Dad to read, as though he'd got the autograph of a famous person.

'You must be relieved you've got this,' Dad said, handing it back after reading.

'Aye, man. No doubt I'll be picked up again before all this is done and I can just show them it. I just bloody well hope they catch him soon. First time in me life I've been glad of me massive feet.' Jim laughed. 'And it might be worth something one day,' he said, waving the letter in the air, like Charlie and his Golden Ticket.

As he left, he chucked me under the chin. 'See you later, lassie,' he said with a nod.

I found out later from Dad that in a macabre parody of *Cinderella*, Jim Jameson had eventually been cleared of all suspicion by his work boots, which were too large to match the footprints found at Josephine Whitaker's murder site.

It hadn't happened quickly enough for him to escape the beating of the lads at work, but it had secured Jim Jameson a letter from George Oldfield, confirming he was no longer a 'person of interest'. I sat on the settee wide-eyed while Dad explained all of this to me and Aunty Jean. Dad and I played dominoes together after Jim had left. I wished that life could always be like this.

But Mum came home the next day and the silence settled once more.

21

Miv

Number Six

It took longer than usual to get ready on the first day back at school. I had my new school clothes to wear and had decided to make more of an effort with my appearance, a decision entirely unconnected to the snippet of gossip that had filtered through to Aunty Jean via washing-line conversations – a route far more effective than the telephone – that Paul Ware would be joining our school.

'There's no more money for posh school fees,' Aunty Jean had said the night before, and I wasn't sure if she was telling me or Mum, who had taken up residence in her armchair once again and was sat silently, staring into space. The radio was playing quietly on the sideboard next to her and I could make out the strains of 'Don't Cry for Me Argentina' by Julie Covington, one of Mum's favourite songs. I wondered whether she could hear it, wherever she was, and whether she was singing along, like she used to. I could almost see her as she was before, floating around the house, gesticulating wildly along with the words, in full performance mode, her voice clear and pitch-perfect. Things never seemed any different after one of her breaks, and I often wondered what the point of them was.

'Not now they're getting divorced,' Aunty Jean had continued, jolting me back to the conversation. Although the news about Hazel and Mr Ware was expected, it was still shocking and all I could think about was Paul. Aunty Jean's words had been accompanied by a series of sniffs, 'divorce' and 'posh schools' both featuring on the list of things that she disapproved of.

Staring at myself in the mirror that morning, I put a slide with a plastic butterfly on the end of it into my newly washed hair, now grown out of its pudding-bowl style into something resembling a bob, and pinched my pale cheeks. My confidence was only dimmed slightly at the sight of Sharon waiting for me at the end of her road, her increasingly long blonde hair in a high ponytail, curls cascading down her back. She'd taken to flicking her fringe and spraying it with hairspray till it was so hard it moved as one, like one of Charlie's Angels. As I got closer, I noticed that her lips seemed to be sparkling. They looked like they had been covered in the glitter we used to glue onto our pictures what seemed like only a few months ago, and I stared at them. 'What have you got on your lips?' I asked. 'Is it one of them glosses?'

The latest craze was for flavoured rollerball lip glosses, which sat on Mr Bashir's counter, in raspberry, strawberry or cherry flavour. She nodded. 'Me mum let me have one,' she said. I felt a sliver of envy slowly unfurl inside me. Out of the pocket of her school bag, Sharon pulled the pink patterned see-through cylinder of lip gloss and held it out to me.

'I brought it so you could have some too.'

All feelings of envy disappeared as I took the top off and applied the sickly-sweet strawberry gloss with abandon. We looked at each other, pouting in unison, then dissolved into giggles. Everything and anything felt possible wearing my new bra and lip gloss.

On the way home, the day took a more sinister turn. We were meandering slowly, Sharon walking backwards while demonstrating the winning goal she had scored in netball, when I saw the headline on the newspaper stand outside Mr Bashir's and stopped still.

'What's the matter?' Sharon said, then followed my frozen gaze to the words emblazoned in bold black capitals:

RIPPER STRIKES AGAIN

Without saying anything we held hands like we had when we were smaller, cementing our togetherness, drawing strength from it. I became acutely aware of the street in front of me. Everything looked faded and bleak, as if someone had washed all the colour out. September had brought with it colder and windy weather, and I watched as a blue crisp packet blew across the street, swirling amid a cloud of grey dust which caught in the back of my throat.

We went solemnly into the shop to buy the newspaper. Mr Bashir seemed to sense the mood and just nodded at us, his customary smile gone.

There were already four women crowded around the newspaper shelves, and Valerie Lockwood, from the next street along, was poring over the *Yorkshire Chronicle*. '"Twenty-year-old Barbara Leach is confirmed as the notorious Yorkshire Ripper's eleventh victim,"' she read aloud to her audience. '"It has been 159 days since his last attack. She was a university student, murdered in Bradford. In what is becoming the Ripper's signature method of attack, she was hit on the back of the head with a hammer and stabbed. He dumped her body behind a wall where dustbins were normally left, covered with an old piece of carpet."'

At this one woman gasped, another put her hand over her mouth and a third shook her head vigorously.

'She wasn't even a prostitute,' said Valerie, her voice trembling with outrage.

One of her companions spotted the two of us and nudged her. She folded the paper and tucked it into the armpit of her brown coat. 'I'll take this home for our Brian – he likes to keep up to date,' she said, and nodded towards the door. We instinctively turned in that direction and saw the familiar sight of the man in the overalls standing on the opposite side of the road, watching the shop. I felt a shiver of unease. Valerie paid for the newspaper and left, followed by the others, and I picked a copy of the same. Mr Bashir shook his head, staring at the photograph of Barbara on the front as he rang the paper up on the till.

The photo showed a smiling short-haired woman in a tweed flat cap. She looked like the trendy students we sometimes saw spilling from the doors of the local arts college, where my mum had once gone too, to study music, though of course I couldn't imagine that now. Barbara looked like the sort of person I wanted to be when I grew up.

'It's just not fair,' said Sharon, as we stood outside the shop, devouring every word of the pages and pages of coverage. 'He threw her away like she was rubbish, and she wasn't. She was a person.'

'I know,' I replied. I couldn't think of anything else to say.

'Who's next on the list then?' she said, without hesitation. 'We've got to find him. I can't bear it.'

My heart leapt at the thought she might be interested in the list again – followed quickly by a flush of shame. How could I be excited right now? She looked directly at me, her eyes swimming and her face contorted with anguish. 'Don't the police care? What are they even doing?'

I had wondered the same thing myself. The only policemen I'd ever seen interviewed about the case were even older than my dad. The ones who weren't in uniform wore suits and spoke in posh voices – mainly to each other, it seemed. It was like they were a million miles away from us, and even further away from the young women the Ripper was murdering. I wondered if the distance mattered. If it made a difference to how much they cared, and whether they caught him.

'Let's find out,' I said. 'Let's look into the police investigation, see what they're missing.'

On the rest of the way home, the streets themselves felt unsettled, as though the news had seeped into the bricks and mortar of the town. Whispers of this latest murder seemed to be all around us: women were outside their houses in small groups, muttering his name, their eyes darting around as if he might appear at any moment.

Aunty Jean was waiting for me when I got in, sat at the yellow Formica table with a mug of tea in front of her. She hadn't even taken her coat off, which just added to the unsettled feeling in the air. Mum was nowhere to be seen, presumably upstairs in bed. Aunty Jean nodded at the newspaper I was carrying, then at the chair opposite her, and I sat down.

'You've seen the news then?' she said, looking almost relieved that she didn't have to explain to me that another woman had been murdered.

I nodded back.

Her grey curls were rigid. 'I think you're old enough to understand now,' she said, as though convincing herself, 'and I think it's time we talked about keeping your wits about you.'

'How do you mean?' I said, finding it hard to swallow.

'Well, when you're out and about, you should be

keeping an eye out for any strange men. Particularly anyone not from round here,' she said. She seemed to be struggling to keep eye contact with me and I wasn't sure why. 'And maybe as the nights draw in, you shouldn't be walking home from places in the dark,' she added. There was a silence in which I left the question about who would walk me home or pick me up unasked. 'And if there's ever anyone behind you, you cross the road. And if they cross the road as well, then you run.'

'OK,' I said, almost in a squeak, unsure of how to feel about this new state of affairs.

'Now, what do you want for your tea?'

The combination of Aunty Jean's unexpected fear, and this question, normally reserved for birthdays only, made me start to cry. Aunty Jean let me do so without comment as she took her coat off, hung it up and started clattering around the kitchen.

When Dad came home later, he placed another copy of the newspaper down on the table on top of mine. After tea he grunted at it and said, 'Has your Aunty Jean talked to you about minding yourself?'

I nodded, mutely.

We all watched the news together in silence.

Later the same week of Barbara Leach's murder, the sun returned briefly, as if it was teasing us, like a cruel reminder that the summer had passed and we were back at school. It also didn't feel right that the sun could be shining when another woman was dead – it felt as though the skies should be dark and sombre, to match the mood of the town.

Mrs Andrews was behind the desk at the library, fanning her face with a newspaper, and she waved at us as we passed her, and we waved back. We had decided to use the library reading room – which had back copies of all the main and local papers available for free – to conduct our review of the police's investigations so far, but regretted it as soon as we walked in. The smell of unwashed bodies and stale cigarette smoke was at its ripest in the small, stuffy room, and we did our best to breathe through our mouths as we gathered up copies of the *Yorkshire Chronicle*, past and present. There was a growing sense of frustration in every recent article about the lack of progress in finding the Ripper since the tape recording had been released. We too were frustrated as we hunted for holes in the police investigation.

Then I spotted a headline that read: *Who Are the Women in the Ripper's Life?*

I looked up from the paper and showed it to Sharon.

'Maybe he's married after all,' I whispered.

'Maybe, instead of looking for a man, we need to look for a woman who's hiding something. She might be hiding the Ripper,' she whispered back.

We left the library early. Ruby had started asking Sharon where she was going and what time she would be home. We presumed it was for the same reason I had been told to keep my wits about me, but Ruby hadn't said. When I left Sharon to walk the rest of the way home alone, I remembered Aunty Jean's words and looked in every direction carefully as I walked down the street and listened for footsteps when I turned into dark ginnels.

I considered all the women in our lives. Apart from Hazel Ware, they all seemed to be the same shape and size of drudgery, a kind of wallpaper to our lives with nothing that stood out as being of interest to our investigations. It was almost as if they were a different species from us. I couldn't imagine them having the kind of secret, inner life that I had, and that the wife of the Ripper must have. I was surprised to find that I felt strangely sad about this. Was that what we had to look forward to when we grew up?

I wondered if, from the outside, the women in my own family might look suspicious. No one else's mum was silent. And no one else's Aunty Jean lived with them. I shook my head to dislodge the thought before it got stuck, not willing to follow it to its logical conclusion. I had no interest in turning my gaze to my family. I was more interested in the strangeness of others.

The next day we went back to the library after school. It was much cooler, and Mrs Andrews was frosty with it. As we headed to the reading room, she barely acknowledged us, and her pale face and darkened eyes looked as though she had not slept since we'd seen her the day before. One eye looked almost purple. There was no waving. As we sat down in our usual spot, Sharon's eyes kept flitting back to the desk and Mrs Andrews' drawn expression. There was nothing new for the list that day, so we left shortly afterwards, but as we did so Sharon stopped at the desk.

'Hello, Mrs Andrews,' she said, as I turned back, surprised. I hadn't planned on speaking to her, sensing she wanted to be left alone. It was as if inside her head she was in a completely different time and place, and though I wanted to reach in and draw her out of wherever she was, I somehow knew it was better to stay quiet.

'Mrs Andrews?' Sharon repeated, having had no response.

Mrs Andrews stood with her back to us, gazing at an unfixed point on the wall. She seemed to rouse herself at the second greeting and turned to look at us.

'Hello, girls,' she said faintly.

'Are you all right?' Sharon asked. 'It's just we noticed you don't seem yourself.' She looked over at me as she said this and I nodded vigorously, going along with the pretence. At this, colour rose in Mrs Andrews' cheeks and she shook her head and said, 'No, no, I'm fine,' though the emotion now clearly visible on her face said the opposite.

'OK,' said Sharon, giving me a meaningful glance, and we left. As soon as we got outside, Sharon began making her case for Mrs Andrews to go on the list.

'Remember that the article said we had to look out for changes in behaviour?' she said. 'And what that policeman said about him being someone's family? I just think Mrs Andrews is suspicious. One day she's all happy and chatty, the next day it's like she doesn't know us, and she looks all sad and just, well, beaten down. And did you notice her eye? What if it's her husband? She's definitely hiding something.'

I couldn't deny the truth of this. I wrote Mrs Andrews down on the list.

6. The Librarian

- Mood changes
- Acts suspiciously
- Possible black eye/bruising
- Is she hiding something?

22

Omar

Omar propped the door open and stood on the door-step. He closed his eyes, letting the sun beat down on his face, and for a moment let himself believe he could be anywhere.

The latest murder had leached all the hope from the town. They had barely got over the last one, Josephine Whitaker, and all the worry and wondering that had happened after her death, all the chatter and speculation in the shop about them all being in danger now, before he had struck again. The horror was becoming com-monplace. Part of the landscape. After the initial shock of the news, Valerie and her friends had been back, talk-ing with each other about the number of stab wounds on Barbara's body as though they were discussing the state of Marjorie Pearson's unwashed net curtains.

He had just turned to go back in and restock the shelves when his neck stiffened in response to a differ-ent, more ominous set of voices. He knew, if he looked, he would see the short-haired boys at the other end of the street, where they sometimes liked to meet and smoke and stare. Never close enough to speak to, or do any damage in plain sight, but just close enough to make him aware of their presence, putting him on edge.

Except this time they *were* coming closer, the sound of their boots thudding rhythmically on the pavement, pounding out their aggression. He turned back to see where they were and inhaled sharply when he realised Brian was sandwiched between two of them, his yellow hat giving him away, still perched on his head despite the warm September day. They were heading down the street, on the opposite side to the shop. Omar immediately recognised one of them as the tall, rangy boy who had knocked the bucket of water a month or so ago. Ishtiaq had said he was called Richard and was in his class. The other was clearly older but had almost identical features to Richard – an older brother, perhaps?

Omar watched in silence. Every protective instinct was on high alert, almost as if Brian were Ishtiaq, not a 23-year-old. He stared at Brian closely, trying to work out if he was with them by choice or coercion. His eyes were on the ground as he walked, his face intent on the paving stones in front of him – which wasn't unusual for him – but something about the scene wasn't right. It was almost as though they were pulling him along with invisible chains, Brian shuffling slightly behind their exaggerated swagger. When the older of the two boys pushed Brian so hard that he stumbled, the word was out of Omar's mouth before he even had time to think it through.

'Oi!' he shouted.

They stopped in their tracks, clearly surprised. The tall one recovered first.

'Fuck off,' he said, laughing, and looked at Richard, who seemed to sense his cue and began laughing too. Brian kept his eyes on the ground.

'You leave him alone.'

Brian looked up at him, and for the first time ever their eyes met fleetingly. Then he looked down again, as doors on the street began to open, people peering out to see what the commotion was.

'See you later, Brian,' the taller boy said, and the two left him standing there while they sauntered off down the street, pausing only to spit in the road.

Omar felt himself begin to shake. 'Come on in here,' he said to Brian, trying to sound as calm and normal as possible, sensing that was what he needed. 'I've got your order ready.' Brian followed him into the shop, his hand in his pocket to count out the money when Omar turned back, putting his hand on the man's arm to stop him.

'Them two,' he said, 'what were they after you for?'

Brian's voice was quiet. Faltering. Omar had to strain to hear him.

'They want me to. To. Join them,' he said. 'To. Do. Things for them.'

'They're not good people, Brian.' Omar tried to keep his voice steady and not let his rage spill out. 'So you keep away from them if you can.'

Brian nodded, and Omar sensed the futility of trying

to warn this otherwise friendless man off some of the only people who had taken an interest in him. He handed Brian his paper and cigarettes, waving away his offer of payment, and watched him as he left the shop and wandered back down the street to home. Maybe he should talk to Valerie. Let her know about the boys if she didn't know about them already. Make sure she knew they were targeting Brian. But would she think he was interfering? While Yorkshire people could gossip as well as the best of them, they were tight-lipped about their own lives, full of pride and misplaced determination not to show any feelings. For a moment he smiled, imagining what the aunties would do with this. Maybe they were right. Maybe what he'd once seen as interference was actually a way to keep people safe. Maybe that's what being part of a community was. He would talk to Valerie.

23

Miv

I caught my next glimpse of Paul Ware during the following day at school, a day when, much to my dismay, I had forgotten to borrow any of Sharon's rollerball lip gloss. He was in the distance, at the other end of the corridor to me. I stood and watched as his long brown fringe flopped into his eyes and he gently blew it away. He was leaning on the wall outside a classroom, presumably waiting to go in, his lanky limbs betraying the anxiety I could somehow sense behind his attempts to look casual. He was alone, others bustling around him, paying him no attention as though he were an inanimate object. I couldn't stop looking at him. It felt like I was in one of the *Jackie* photostories that Sharon loved, except instead of 'swooning' at the sight of him, I felt something inside me pull at the thought of him having no friends yet. Even *I* had one – more if you included Ishtiaq, Mr Bashir and Arthur.

In fact, I'd been spending more and more time with Ishtiaq at school. On our first day back, Miss Stacey had announced that this year we were going to be streamed according to ability. She had told us to look at the sheets on the wall to find out which classes we were going to be in for English, Maths and Science. I had been horrified to see that I would no longer be sharing those classes with Sharon, as I was in the top sets.

'Of course you are,' she'd said, laughing at my downcast expression. 'You're much cleverer than me.'

'Am I?' I'd said, uncomfortable with the thought. She'd shaken her head at me, her puzzlement evident.

'Yes, you daft apeth. And I'll see you at break and in art class and that.'

I'd almost crept towards my new classroom that first day, peering around the door to see Ishtiaq ahead of me, walking confidently to a seat in the front row and sitting down, keeping his face to the front, not looking around to see what anyone else was doing. I followed, and sat down next to him, feeling a curious mix of pride and fear that I hadn't waited to see what anyone might think. We sat together and shared our books, and at the end of the lesson Ishtiaq said, 'Want to come over to mine to do our homework together?'

The two of us had sat at his kitchen table while Mr Bashir cooked our tea and sang 'Benny and the Jets' at full volume, until Ishtiaq told him we had to work, and the singing turned into humming, which was just as distracting.

Ishtiaq seemed to be entirely at ease in our new classes. He didn't seem to mind people knowing he was clever, and never showed off about it. I noticed he would often read at breaktimes but was just as comfortable playing cricket if the offer was there. He talked to boys and girls alike and it didn't bother him whether they included him or not, somehow making him more attractive to others, even the ones who had called him names.

I felt as if I was seeing him for the first time.

I decided to try and copy aspects of his behaviour; to believe that you didn't have to be the same as everyone else to make people like you. I was working hard at becoming less concerned with whether the small number of girls in the top set wanted to be my friend. This was helpful, as there wasn't exactly a queue forming and I always sat with Ishtiaq anyway.

'Lucky you,' Sharon said wistfully, when I mentioned it to her. 'I'm still putting up with Neil and Richard in my classes.' She paused. 'Richard keeps on pestering me an' all.'

'What do you mean, pesters you?'

'Oh, you know. One minute he's laughing at me, calling me names, and the next he's asking me if I want to hang out at breaktime. I always say no though.'

I nodded wisely, as though fending off boys was a daily occurrence for me. I noticed that Sharon's expression had grown graver.

'They frighten me a bit, those lads,' she said. 'They're just . . . hard . . . you know?'

I thought about the last time I'd seen Neil and Richard, their foreheads permanently set in an aggressive furrow. Their expressions were almost as much of a uniform as the ones we wore every day to school. I wondered what had happened to make them change from the funny, mischievous boys they used to be. What had turned Richard's shyness into brooding silence?

They frightened me a bit too.

The fear became intensified that Saturday. We had gone to Arthur's and were sat in the garden, telling him all about Jim Jameson and how we were planning to visit him later. I was surprised to see how much the story seemed to affect him. Tears began to form in his eyes, which I hastily rushed to prevent. 'It's OK, Arthur,' I said. 'He's been cleared and everything. He's got a letter.'

'Aye, love, I know. It's not that,' he said, not meeting my eyes.

'What is it? What's the matter?' said Sharon as the tears threatened to spill onto his cheeks.

'It's just . . . It's just him living in his lorry like that,' Arthur tried to explain while looking at our confused faces 'I don't expect you two to understand. I know I'm a soft old thing. But no one should have to be that lonely.'

Actually I did understand that.

'I might walk down there with you when you pop along and see him, if he's still parked up on t'lane,' Arthur said. 'Offer him a bath when he needs one.'

The three of us left not long afterwards and walked down the street more slowly than usual, due to Arthur's insistence on pointing out who lived where and identifying various flowers and birds. Sharon and I were pretending to admire a neighbour's garden when I felt a shift in Arthur, a sort of freezing, and a sharp intake of breath.

'What's the matter, Arthur?' Sharon had clearly felt it too, and we both looked at him, his face intent on a distant point. We turned to look where he was staring and immediately recognised Richard and Neil along with two other older boys we didn't know, both of whom looked so like Richard, they were clearly related.

'Don't worry about them, Arthur,' I said, more confidently than I felt. 'We know them. They're just some boys from school, like.'

'It's the same ones as came into t'scrapyard,' he said, his voice unsteady.

'Are you sure?' said Sharon, looking at me with alarm on her face. 'They're quite far away.'

'I, I think so. I mean, I can't be sure but . . .' I heard his breath quicken. 'I want to go home,' he said, so we turned and escorted him back. I noticed Sharon kept turning to stare at the gang of boys in the distance. Maybe we were right to be afraid of them if Arthur, a grown-up, was too.

The next day, we decided to head to Wilberforce Street after church to check on Arthur and make sure he was all right. To our surprise, he was on fine form and actually inside the house for once, clearing space in the kitchen.

'I've got Jim Jameson moving in next weekend,' he said to our evident amazement. 'I ended up going back to see him and we had a chat,' he added, by way of explanation. 'And I want him to feel at home an' that. You two can give me a hand if you don't mind?'

When I looked at Sharon, I saw her eyes were shining as brightly as mine.

I had never seen Arthur in such a good mood. I stayed downstairs, dusting around the numerous faded lace doilies that adorned every inch of furniture, while Sharon went upstairs to the spare room, packing things away into boxes to be stored in the shed. The room was dainty and pink, with everything matching, in direct contrast to the rest of the house, and Arthur himself.

'It was our Helen's room,' he said, misty-eyed. 'She was t'youngest and last to move out,' as if we hadn't heard this fact a hundred times already. Helen was clearly his favourite, and her husband his least favourite of all the additions to the family.

'He never wants to be wi' family,' Arthur would often say, 'and I wouldn't care if he'd let Helen come and go as she pleases, but he doesn't like it if she's wi' family either. When our Doreen passed, he didn't even let her come and say goodbye in the hospital.' At this, his eyes would glaze with a mixture of tears and fury.

I was just about to join Arthur in the kitchen to make tea, when I heard Sharon calling me from upstairs. I couldn't quite read her tone of voice, but she sounded excited about something. When I got to the top of the stairs, she was stood in the doorway to the bedroom, beckoning me over to look at the photo in an ornate brass frame she was holding out.

'Look,' she said, her voice filled with anticipation. 'Who does this remind you of?'

I looked at the black-and-white image of a school-girl in the frame. She had a familiar pixie-like face, with long plaits instead of the shorter cut she wore now. Her smile was wide, and she was beautiful in an ethereal way, even as a young girl. It was unmistakably Mrs Andrews. We both went downstairs, Sharon holding the picture.

'Arthur, does Helen work at the library?' she asked immediately.

'Aye, she does that,' he said, his face glowing with pride. 'Always had her head in a book, that one. Why? Have you met her?'

'We have!' I said. 'We see her all the time. I can't believe we didn't know she's your daughter.' I looked around at the photos downstairs, wondering how we'd missed it, then remembered the wedding photo where her face had been obscured. The rest were of the chil-dren at a much younger age.

Arthur saw me looking. 'I know you'll think I'm daft,' he said wistfully, 'but I like to remember them when they were little bairns, and me and our Doreen were young and first married.'

As we said goodbye that day, the space all ready for Jim Jameson, we agreed to return next Sunday to wel-come Jim to the house.

'I'll see if I can persuade our Helen to come, make a day of it, like,' Arthur promised, to our joy. We were just about to leave when Arthur called us back and stooped to our eye level as he said, 'Now, you be careful walking home, you hear me?'

We didn't need to ask why.

I couldn't work out whether the discovery that Arthur was her dad made Mrs Andrews more suspicious or less. On the one hand, Arthur, who seemed to like everyone, did not like her husband – therefore could he be the Ripper? Could she be protecting him? On the other, she had not long lost her mum, so could her strange behaviour simply be grief? We had seen at first hand the devastating effect that losing Doreen had had on Arthur. Was it that? Either way we hoped we would get the chance to see next weekend.

When we arrived at the house on that Sunday afternoon, there was a strong smell of burning. Arthur had attempted to bake a Victoria sandwich to welcome Jim but had failed spectacularly – never having baked anything before in his life. The windows and oven door were all wide open and Jim was sat in the lush back garden on a striped wooden deckchair, despite it barely being warm enough to sit outside. Arthur brought him a large mug of dark brown tea 'so strong you could stand a spoon up in it', as Aunty Jean would say, then sat on a matching deckchair next to him. In front of Jim there was a small crate, the kind we saw outside Mr

Bashir's with fruit or vegetables in, but this was stacked with random belongings: an alarm clock, a photo in a frame, a couple of books and some folded material, possibly clothes. It struck me that this might be all that Jim Jameson had.

Despite him having so little, it seemed already that he'd lived there forever, and his presence brought the house to life. The grief and neglect that had seemed to haunt the walls had diminished to a mere whisper. We were just about to join them when the sound of footsteps on the stairs stopped us and Mrs Andrews appeared.

'Hello, Mrs Andrews,' we chorused.

She smiled widely at us.

'Hello, you two,' she said. 'What a lovely surprise to find out that you are the ones who have been keeping Dad company. I think that's very kind of you.'

'Oh, we don't mind,' Sharon said, smiling back at her. 'He's our friend.'

'Is Mr Andrews with you?' I burst in. Mrs Andrews started a little.

'Er, no,' she said, looking puzzled at the question, 'but he will be coming to pick me up soon. Shall we go outside? And while we're at it, it's Helen. I don't feel old enough to be called Mrs Andrews,' and she laughed.

We all sat out in the September sun, Arthur and Jim trying to outdo each other with stories about the olden days that all started with 'When I were a lad . . .', despite Jim being at least twenty years Arthur's junior. Me, Sharon and Mrs Andrews – I couldn't bring myself to call her Helen yet – sat on a checked rug so rough it felt like sandpaper, nodding along indulgently and drinking cold dandelion and burdock. The afternoon was peaceful and I almost forgot that Mrs Andrews was on the list. But then, at the sound of a car pulling in and parking up outside, Mrs Andrews got to her feet and adjusted her hair.

'That'll be Gary,' she said in a fluttery voice. 'He won't let me walk home on my own these days. I'd better go.' Her eyes flitted between us and the gate. Before she could say her goodbyes to Arthur, a tall figure appeared.

'Hello, hello, hello,' the man said.

I couldn't stop myself staring at him as he peered over the side gate, and sensed Sharon beside me sitting up too. He had curly, shoulder-length hair, was wearing frayed bell-bottom jeans and had sparkling blue-green eyes. He was mesmerising. I was immediately smitten, even more so when he smiled at us both. He opened the gate and walked towards us.

'I'm Gary Andrews,' he said, with mock formality, holding his hand out. We shook it and he nodded and smiled at Arthur and Jim as well.

'This looks like a lovely little picnic,' he said, his voice full of charm. 'I should've joined you earlier.'

Arthur grunted and I noticed that Mrs Andrews was fidgeting and fussing with her handbag, seeming uncomfortable. I continued to watch until I caught a glance between her and her husband. It contained an intensity I couldn't name.

'We'll be off then, Dad.' She moved over to Arthur and kissed him on the cheek. 'Bye, Jim. Bye, girls.'

Arthur seemed quiet after they had left, and it took a while for Jim to jolly him out of it, but eventually he did, and we left later feeling that Arthur was in safe hands.

'I don't know if she is suspicious,' I said as we walked home. 'I just think Arthur doesn't like Mr Andrews, probably because he took her away from home.'

'Hmm, you might be right. And it makes sense she'd be sad. Her mum died.'

'And Mr Andrews didn't seem suspicious at all,' I said, smiling at the thought of him.

'No, he didn't.' I could sense Sharon was blushing in the way she sometimes did when Ishtiaq was mentioned.

'He's really handsome, isn't he?' I couldn't help adding, a giggle spilling out too.

'He really is,' she said, and we smiled broadly at each other.

We spent the rest of the walk home in silence. I have no idea what Sharon was thinking about, but I was definitely thinking about Mr Andrews.

The next day, Sharon said she had to get home straight after school because her mum needed her for something. I headed to the library alone in the hope that Mrs Andrews would be there and in the mood for conversation. She was stood behind the desk in pro-file, stamping books with the same faraway expression we had seen the other week. I wasn't sure she would want to talk, but I decided to go ahead anyway and approached the desk. As I did, she turned her whole face to me, and I took a step back at the sight of it. The right-hand side of her face was swollen and there was a large bruise underneath her eye.

'Oh no, are you hurt?' I asked, then blushed at my stating of the obvious.

'Don't worry,' she said with a smile that seemed full of effort. 'I took a tumble and didn't get my hands out fast enough to catch myself. I know it looks awful now, but it'll heal up in a few days.'

'Did you cry,' I said, 'when it happened?'

She looked around her, as if she was about to tell me a secret.

'Don't tell anyone, but yes, I did.' She tried to smile again, but it looked like it hurt.

'Anyway, how are you?' she asked, and I stared at her. No adult ever asked me that question and I wasn't quite sure how to answer it. Her face, despite its injuries, softened as she inspected mine. I could feel the prickle of tears in the back of my throat and couldn't under-stand why.

'You know, Miv, if you ever want to talk, about any-thing at all, I'm here,' she said, so softly it was almost a whisper.

She glanced at the clock on the wall behind me, her

hand flying to her face. 'Oh, I need to get sorted,' she said. 'Gary'll be waiting.'

As I left, I saw Mr Andrews in a car parked across from the library. He was smoking a cigarette through the open window, the smoke blowing out in a thin line then dispersing into clouds that obscured his face. I wondered if he had wiped her tears when she fell, imagining him wiping my tears when I cried at night-time, missing Mum.

24

Omar

Omar opened the counter to let Sharon through to the back, where Ishtiaq was waiting, having borrowed Omar's coconut oil to keep his neatly side-swept hair in place. The smell of it, mixed with the cheap deodorant Ishtiaq had sprayed liberally all over, now filled the shop with its sickly-sweetness, and Omar had propped the door open for fear of suffocating his customers.

He'd noticed that these solitary visits from Sharon were increasing, and Omar wondered how her friend felt about them. She and Sharon had formerly been joined at the hip, and Miv in particular had always struck him as having a layer of skin missing, her wide eyes taking everything in and her expressive face shifting with the emotions in the room. He felt an affinity with this serious-faced, skinny child.

He himself felt a mixture of heartache and joy at the blossoming relationship between Sharon and Ishtiaq. He loved watching his son smile whenever he said her name, which happened a lot as Ishtiaq crowbarred it into every possible conversation. But Omar was aware that the only thing it could lead to was a pain equal to the happiness Ishtiaq was feeling now. That was just the way of things when you were young, made even more likely given the colour of his skin. Omar combed his memory for the anguish and ecstasy that came with his own first crush, years before he was set up with Rizwana.

It was different for Ishtiaq and Sharon, of course. At least they got to spend time together, to become real people to each other. There was a time when he wouldn't have approved. A time when different things mattered to him, and the fact that Sharon was white would have made a difference to how he felt about his son falling in love for the first time. But Rizwana and he had talked about this. The inevitability of Ishtiaq wanting to try things, relationships included. They'd had plenty of time in the hospital for these discussions, him sat on a plastic chair next to her bed, keeping his head close to hers so she didn't have to speak too loudly while they talked about their son's future.

'Let him live a little, experience life. Let him *choose* tradition, not force it on him,' she'd said, and he'd agreed, mainly because at that point he would have agreed to anything she asked, though later he'd real- ised she was right. He could allow his son the joy of young love. It wasn't like they were getting married, right? His biggest worry was whether her parents knew. He couldn't imagine they did.

He turned the tape recorder up, but the mournful strains of 'Rocket Man' brought back the memory of his wife, swaying with him in the cold, damp kitchen of their tiny house in Bradford to this very song. Usually, music was his way of rewinding to these moments, but the line about missing his wife made him ache so much he picked up the *Post* and attempted to use the words he read to shock him back into the present, away from the painful wounds of the past.

It was page after page of the Ripper. Every time there was another death, every fact, photograph and quote from the previous murders was repeated on loop. But then his eyes were drawn to an article right at the bottom of page five. Just two paragraphs on a large demonstration in Leeds by the National Front. He shook his head, feeling anger ignite. A small photograph showed the streets crowded with Union Jacks and a placard proclaiming *Stop the Muggers*, meaning folks like him, not white, which he found ironic given that the entire country was in the thrall of a single white man in the form of the Ripper. At the centre of the photograph was a snarling bald man shaking his fist at the camera. All at once the thought of a relationship between Ishtiaq and Sharon became tinged with something more like fear.

The sound of footsteps shook him out of it with some relief and he was pleased to see that it was Helen, giving him an opportunity to ask after Arthur, when he noticed what she was wearing. Given the unseasonably warm September weather, the hat she had pulled down low over one eye seemed out of place and the long-sleeved, high-necked jumper would surely be suffocating. She looked around the shop as though she'd never been there before, an expression of confusion as she tried to work out where the things she needed were displayed.

'Can I help you with anything?' he said, the formality of the offer taking him by surprise. She looked up at him, clearly surprised too, then shook her head, giving him a brief glimpse of her injured face. He stopped the expression of horror just in time. He wondered what Rizwana would do if she was here.

Frozen by his indecision, he noticed her looking back at the door and spotted her husband on the other side of the road, watching the shop, his expression one of icy intensity. He'd heard talk about Gary Andrews. He heard talk about everyone in the shop, so often he wondered if people knew he could speak English, the things they would say to each other in his presence. Gary was often described as a 'right charmer', an expression usually accompanied with a wry smile and an indulgent roll of the eyes. Omar had never seen it himself. He'd always found him cold. Whenever Gary came into the shop, which was rare, he would silently place whatever he was buying on the counter and slowly count the correct change out, while staring at Omar intently.

Their eyes met now, and Omar thought he saw a flicker of something else pass across Gary's face. Helen quickly collected the rest of what she needed, came to the counter, paid and left.

25

Miv

That evening, Jim Jameson came round to see Dad. He wasn't expected, and I sensed the tension in the room when the doorbell went. On our street, everyone 'popped round' to everyone else's houses all the time, except ours. When Mum was at home, visitors were restricted to family, meaning no one except the people who already lived here. Mum silently got up from her chair and went upstairs to the bedroom as Dad let Jim Jameson in and Aunty Jean bustled to the kitchen to make a pot of tea, making more noise than was either usual or necessary. She seemed flustered, her skin turning so pink I could imagine it reaching as far as her grey curls, turning them that funny shade of lilac all her friends had rinsed into their hair once a month. For a fleeting moment I wondered whether she had a crush on Jim Jameson, then recoiled with horror at the thought of her harbouring such feelings.

'Do you need summat?' Dad asked, somewhat abrupt in his surprise at this unexpected visit.

'I were just passing,' Jim said genially. 'Wondered if you might fancy a quick pint?'

'I'm not much of a pub man meself,' Dad said.

I looked sharply at him, knowing that wasn't true. Dad's eyes looked upwards and he nodded, indicating upstairs.

Jim's face flushed and he stumbled over his words. 'Oh aye, sorry, Arthur did mention. I should've thought before I came over uninvited. Well, I'll leave you to it then?'

I could see Aunty Jean hovering at the kitchen door. I noticed she'd taken her apron off and her cardigan top button was undone. I found myself wanting to giggle: this was as shocking as if she'd walked into the room in her underwear.

'How do, Jean,' Jim said on his way out, blushing a shade of pink himself, presumably at his turning up unannounced. I followed him to the door and got the chance to ask, 'Has Arthur heard from Mrs Andrews at all?'

He frowned at me. 'Not since yesterday. Why, should he have? Is she all right?'

'Oh, it's just she fell,' I said, not really sure why I was telling him this. 'She's all right though, just bruised.'

He looked thoughtful for a moment. 'I'd better let him know. He worries about her a lot.'

Curiously, Dad still went out shortly after Jim had left, despite his protestation that he wasn't a pub man. He seemed to just slip out and disappear into the alleyway at the back of the house, with no explanation, while no one was looking.

*

I shared my thoughts about Mrs Andrews with Sharon the next day after school, keeping the rest of the night's events to myself. We were flicking through magazines in her bedroom.

'I don't know what it is, but there's definitely something the matter.'

'Do you think she might be poorly? What with the bruises and that? When my nan died, she got all these bruises to do with the cancer. No one told me that she was sick. They said they wanted to protect me. She might be trying to protect Arthur.'

I thought for a second. 'You might be right. Shall we go and see her? There's time before tea. See what you think about the bruises and that?'

As we walked into the library, I could see that Mrs Andrews was less than pleased to see us. She seemed to sigh as she turned back to whatever task she was engaged with, expecting us to go to the reading room. I nudged Sharon, attempting to point out the bruising while realising it seemed to have disappeared. Sharon marched up to the desk anyway.

'Mrs Andrews,' she said, her voice ringing out clearly and confidently, 'please can you direct us to the medical encyclopedias?'

Mrs Andrews looked up and directed us to where we might find what we needed, eventually moving closer to us. As she did so, I could see that the bruising was still there, just inexpertly covered over with make-up.

'Just before you go,' she said, her voice quiet but

steely, 'I know you told Jim about my accident.' She unconsciously touched the swollen part of her face. 'And he told me dad, who's now all worried about me.' She attempted to smile, but visibly winced in pain as she did so. 'And you know what it's like, I don't want me dad to be worried about me. I'm supposed to be a grown-up.' She attempted a weak smile, as though to demonstrate this was all light-hearted, which it clearly wasn't.

I wondered for a moment how old she actually was.

'Sorry,' I said, my voice matching hers for volume. 'It was me. I didn't think.' I cast my eyes downwards.

'Oh no, please don't be sorry,' she said, her words tumbling over each other as she saw my forlorn expression. 'Forget I said anything, I don't want you to feel bad, I just . . .' She stopped and took a deep breath. 'Just ignore me. I clearly took a blow to the head when I fell and have gone doolally.' She put her finger to the side of her head and moved it in a circle, and we all giggled then shushed each other as we remembered where we were.

When we left, Sharon was silent. She seemed cross about something, her lips set in a hard line. She looked as though she was about to say something when I saw the same car as I had seen the day before, parked outside. This time Mr Andrews was leaning against it, smoking. I nudged Sharon. As he spotted us, he casually flicked his cigarette on the floor, stubbed it out with his foot and walked over.

'Hello, hello, hello,' he said, the same greeting as he'd

given on Sunday when I'd met him. 'Have you just been to see my good lady wife? I've come to collect her,' he added. It felt like he was explaining his presence to us, which I thought was odd. Why did he need to explain himself to children? We nodded.

'You heard about her fall then?' he pressed on, looking at us intently. The eyes I had thought of as twinkling were as sharp as knives. 'Was it you two who got her dad all in a state?' He smiled, but something seemed different about him. 'It's probably best not to alarm our Arthur. He's getting on a bit now, and it's not good for him,' he added, and again we nodded at him in silence.

'So, we good then?' He seemed to think that we had come to some arrangement. I wasn't sure what that arrangement was, but we both said yes, nonetheless.

As we walked away, we both acknowledged with a single look that something was very wrong here. Mrs Andrews was staying on the list.

26

Miv

Number Seven

I was running late for church the next Sunday morning. The weather had begun to turn, and the relentless rain which seemed to cover the streets in silvery spraypaint had slowed me down as I hurried into the church, removing my cagoule while I scurried down the aisle. Steam from everyone's Sunday best rose into the air, and I squirmed in my seat at the stifling atmosphere. I was sat next to Stephen Crowther, who, along with me, had long found refuge in the church choir.

I looked around at the congregation. Every creaking pew was filled and had been since the latest murder. I looked at the faces of my neighbours, their eyes all intent on Mr Spencer, the vicar. Even the scrapyard-owning Howdens were there, taking up the front row, looking squeaky clean, as though they'd all had a hot bath in preparation.

I drifted off as the service began. I was only there for the choir. Singing didn't just remind me of Mum as she was before; all my awkwardness seemed to disappear too. There was also a new reason for my love of the choir: Paul Ware had joined.

I had managed to smile and say hello to him at the end of service last Sunday, when we were collecting a cup of fizzy pop and a Wagon Wheel from a table at the back of the church set up by Uncle Raymond and Aunty Sylvia. They helped out at church and were the sort of aunties and uncles who weren't really anyone's aunty or uncle but were just called that.

As soon as I had uttered the word 'Hi' to Paul, my plastic cup of cherryade trembling in my hand, I almost ran in the other direction, but when his eyes met mine and he nodded his head in acknowledgement I managed a smile instead. I couldn't sleep afterwards for two whole nights. That was the upside of being a choir member. The downside was the requirement to attend more church services. A thump from the pulpit jolted me back to the moment. Mr Spencer's face was tomato red. He looked like he was about to explode.

'*Beware the sins of the flesh,*' he said, spitting each word out. His wife, who was sat in the front row, had to duck to avoid being hit by his saliva. And I had to stop myself from laughing as I watched her mop her face with a pristine white handkerchief. She'd clearly not been quick enough. I tried to drift off again, but his sermon got increasingly loud, until it was almost a shout. As if wanting to remind everyone of the risks of bad things happening to bad people, he railed against temptation and what he called the 'dangerous streets' of the 'hotbed of vice', also known as Chapeltown in Leeds.

It was at this point that I sat up and began to pay proper attention. This was a place I had heard of many times in association with the Ripper. Wilma McCann, Emily Jackson, Irene Richardson and Jayne MacDonald all came from or were murdered there, and two other women had survived suspected Ripper attacks in Chapeltown. What if the way to catch the Ripper was to go to a place we knew he frequented?

That night I dug out an article I remembered seeing after the murder of Josephine Whitaker, one that warned 'girls' on the streets not to accept lifts from strangers, and I read it through again, devouring every word. I was so intent that when Dad came to say good-night, I was still sat cross-legged, the paper on my lap.

'What you reading?' he said.

'Cricket,' I answered, my voice coming out as a squeak.

'Don't be too late,' he said, kissing me on the forehead. 'Night night.'

'Do you think the police are right that he got it wrong? That he might've mistaken who Josephine and Barbara were and thought they were prostitutes?' was the first thing I said to Sharon the next morning on our way to school.

'What you on about?' she asked, her nose scrunched in confusion. I waited for it to dawn on her. 'Oh, the

Ripper you mean?' she said, her face darkening for a moment. 'Maybe.'

'I was reading about it last night,' I said. 'The police think he might've thought they were prostitutes because they were out late at night. And I think if he did make a mistake, then he'll make sure he doesn't make a mistake next time.'

'How?' said Sharon.

'By going back to where he knows he'll find prostitutes. I've worked out what's next on the list.'

'Hmm.' She looked down at her feet. 'We should hurry up, we'll be late to class,' she said, picking up her pace and leaving me stood in her wake. Not willing to ask her what was wrong, not wanting to know the answer, I hurried to catch her up.

I'd never been to Chapeltown, or indeed Leeds, but thought of it as a dark forest from the fairy tales I still secretly loved, despite being too old for them: a forbidding and violent place. News updates about the search for the Ripper were more often than not filmed in Chapeltown. Always shot at night, there would be blurry images of groups of women standing around smoking cigarettes behind whichever sombre-faced man with a microphone was doing the talking.

During one report on a particularly dark, rainy night, the reporter held his coat at the collar, as if defending himself against the women in the background. I didn't know what 'red-light district' meant, but it didn't sound good. I decided we should go and see Chapeltown for ourselves, and – while I worked out how to persuade Sharon to come with me – in the evenings after school I did whatever job was needed around the house, under the direction of Aunty Jean, to earn the money to pay for the trip to Leeds.

If Aunty Jean was surprised by my sudden enthusiasm for housework, she didn't say so, and managed to find tasks to keep me occupied. This meant that Mum spent even more time in her room, as my cleaning around her seemed to disturb her peace. But while I felt the thud of guilt, my aim was clear. We had to get to Chapeltown.

7. The Red-Light District

- It's where the prostitutes are
- The Ripper attacked five women there
- It looks scary/suspicious on the news
- The vicar called it a 'hotbed of vice'

27

Miv

'I'm not going to Chapeltown,' Sharon said, when I first suggested it. 'Mum would kill me.'

I had to admit there was probably some truth to this statement. It seemed the older we were getting, the smaller our lives were becoming; adults all over the place had started asking where we were going and what we were doing. And not just us – all girls. Even Aunty Jean no longer walked home from work alone. She caught the special minibus laid on for women in the town instead.

But I was too scared to go to Chapeltown alone. A few days later we were in Sharon's bedroom, getting ready to go into town so that she could buy the latest Boomtown Rats single, which I would then tape. While she was sat at her dressing table, I placed the latest police notice in front of her. It had been printed in the paper and contained pictures of all eleven victims. I hoped it would remind her why we had started the list in the first place.

SOME WERE COMPLETELY RESPECT-ABLE, it declared in capital letters. *NONE DESERVED TO DIE IN SUCH AGONY.*

Her response wasn't one I expected. 'How dare they?!' she said, her hands shaking in fury.

'Oh, I . . . what do you mean?' I said, confused. Who were 'they'?

'They're making out like some of them were better than the others,' she said, pointing at the words printed in capitals across the bottom. I looked from the words to her, then back again.

'It's like they're looking down their noses. As though they're not good enough. When they don't even know them.' She sighed, her breath blowing the piece of paper off the dressing table.

I held my breath to see whether this might mean she would give in to the trip to Leeds. She sat in silence, the rage still simmering, until she said, 'OK. Let's go to Chapeltown then.'

We knew every snicket and ginnel in our town, but Leeds was a very different prospect and we had to find out how to navigate our way around. In the end it was Sharon who resolved this for us. That Saturday morning she came to call for me.

'Bring the notebook,' she said. 'I've had an idea about how we can get to know Chapeltown, and we can check on Mrs Andrews at the same time.'

Thrilled that Sharon was taking the lead, I picked the notebook up and we headed to the library in silence. Sharon's expression was one of grim determination, matching the grim grey drizzle of the day, and I was unwilling to say anything that might upset her or make her change her mind. We went straight to Mrs Andrews at the desk. It was clearly a good day, judging by the wide smile she gave us.

'We're doing a project about local towns and cities at school,' said Sharon, without pausing for breath, 'and we're doing Leeds, so we need to know as much as we can about it, including maps and that.'

Familiar with our curious minds, Mrs Andrews directed Sharon to the reference library while I stood stunned at the story Sharon had made up and the flaw-lessness of her delivery. It is a source of some shame to me now to realise how often I underestimated her. We left the library armed with an *A–Z* of Leeds.

We agreed not to tell anyone that we were going to Leeds, let alone Chapeltown. There had been very little trouble at home for a few weeks and I was determined not to cause any. Admittedly the calm was mostly cre-ated by absence. Mum spent even more time in her room, Dad spent even more time at the pub, and Aunty Jean spent even more time at work.

Sharon told her parents that she would be at my house for the day, and I told Aunty Jean that I would be at Sharon's. We crossed our fingers that their new curiosity about our whereabouts would not cause them to check our stories.

On the Saturday morning we had chosen for the journey I woke up at 4 a.m., like I did in the days when we used to go on holiday. Dad always made us get up before daylight in order to miss the traffic, but I would be awake with excitement anyway and would join in with Mum when she came to wake me up singing, 'Oh, I Do Like to Be Beside the Seaside'.

That morning the excitement was tinged with fear. October was here, and autumn was just beginning to bite. It was a cold, damp morning, requiring coats and scarves for the first time that year. Our breath came from our mouths in plumes of mist, so as we walked to the bus station we pretended to smoke like the women did in the background of the Ripper news reports in Chapeltown, getting ready to blend in.

The bus station was a bustling hub of activity and we easily moved around unnoticed. Queues of people were waiting patiently under shelters, many carrying bags of shopping from the nearby covered market or trundling pull-along shopping trolleys behind them with tartan covers on them like Aunty Jean had. The only splash of brightness came from the red double-decker buses themselves, lined up on the kerbside.

I got my ticket first and went straight up to the top deck of the bus, our favourite place to sit, apart from the stench of tobacco that lingered on our clothes from the smokers who sat up there too. Sharon followed on a little behind me, and as she sat down, I noticed that the light in her eyes seemed dimmed.

'You OK?' I asked, a tremor in my voice, fearful of the answer.

Sharon looked out of the window as she answered. 'I'm just not sure that this is the right thing to do,' she said, her voice so low I had to move closer to hear it.

'What? Going to Chapeltown?'

'Yes. Well, not just that. I mean the list. All of it. Are we looking for the Ripper or . . . ?'

She had turned back to look at me straight in the eye as she said this. I wanted to stop her, to talk over her, about the list, school, lip gloss or anything really, to stop her words piercing me like hot needles. It felt like she was breaking one of the unwritten rules of our friendship by talking about things, questioning them, challenging them. That wasn't what we did, and I wasn't ready for it yet.

'I just worry about what we're doing here, and why,' she said. 'It feels, I don't know, like a game. And it's not a game, what's happened to these women. It's not.'

I was horrified into silence. Was it a game to me? It didn't feel like one. I started to protest, but Sharon put her hand up.

'Look, I'm here, and we're doing this, but I just want us to be sure it's right. The right thing, I mean.'

'OK,' I whispered.

Sharon turned back to look out of the window, and I sat there silently once more, trying to ignore the discomfort which bubbled up inside me. What if she didn't want to do the list any more? Who would we be together if we didn't have the list? I glanced at Sharon, taking her in. She had changed so much, was calmer, more measured somehow. Had I changed at all? If anything, the skin surrounding me had stretched thinner as I had grown taller and things seemed to affect me much more than they did her. If I gave up this thing that bound us together, what would hold her to me? And what would I do without it?

When our second bus finally got to Chapeltown it was early afternoon. As we waited for the queue of people climbing down the steps to get off, I could feel the anticipation increase with each thud of foot on metal. When we eventually made it off ourselves, that feeling was replaced by a sense of anticlimax, like flat lemonade, that almost made me laugh out loud.

I'm not sure what I had expected to see, but the streets around us looked the same as the ones at home. Row upon row of brown and grey terraced houses, with children playing football in the road and clothes lines strung across back alleys as far as the eye could see. Only the sounds were different. There was an ever-present hum of traffic and the faint clangs and clatters of the nearby city centre. There was nothing scary about it at all.

We decided to walk to a nearby park to eat our packed lunch and think about what to do next. I felt a desperate need to make the trip worthwhile, so I turned to the notebook for inspiration and as I flicked through the pages it came with a gasp.

'Did you notice the name of the park we're in? Is it Roundhay Park?'

I looked excitedly around for a sign or some evidence that this might be the case. Two of the Ripper's victims had been attacked in Roundhay Park. Just sitting in that very park would make the journey more than worthwhile. Sharon visibly shuddered and I felt her disgust, tempering my excitement with a shot of shame. Did it really matter this much to me, that I could be thrilled at being in a park where women were attacked by a monster? Was Sharon right?

We used our map to find out where we were, and I realised that Roundhay Park was some distance away and we were sat in Prince Philip Playing Fields, a much smaller patch of green. Sharon looked relieved. It wasn't until much later, after everything had happened, that I found out those playing fields were where the body of the Ripper's first victim, 28-year-old mother-of-four Wilma McCann, had been found. She had been hit with a hammer and stabbed fifteen times. Nothing about the small recreation ground in front of us gave away the horror that had taken place there.

The notebook and A–Z did spark an idea. There was a pub in Chapeltown called the Gaiety, outside which the Ripper had met a number of his victims. It was within walking distance, and I decided we would head there just to see it. I could tell that Sharon's enthusiasm for the trip was waning further and kept up a steady stream of inane chatter as we walked, all the while imagining what we would do if we saw the Ripper.

It had developed into an overcast afternoon, and as

we walked, Chapeltown finally took on the hue I had expected to find. The sky closed in further, and as the clouds turned ominously dark, the faces of the people we passed became harder, colder and more suspicious to our minds. Not even the pretty Victorian terraces could dispel the gloomy atmosphere.

We passed a bus stop, and I almost suggested returning home when I realised that the man I had thought was looking at the timetable was urinating against the concrete pole. We huddled into each other as the landscape seemed to move from sepia to black and white. The pub, when we got there, was a drab 1960s red-brick building with the word *GAIETY* in orangey-red capitals on the front, looking like the faded blood in Hammer House of Horror films. There was little about it that could be described as gay.

Emily Jackson and Irene Richardson had both been there on the night of their murders. They were named in the paper as 'prostitutes who had been soliciting in the area'. My understanding of the word *prostitutes* had developed, and I knew that they sold sex. I was less sure about whether I should be scared of them or not, and what to think about the men who bought it from them.

It was the middle of the afternoon, so the pub was closed, but two men were sat on a wall outside, drinking from green-and-brown cans, a collection of which sat in candy-striped carrier bags between them.

'Care to join us?' said one of the men with mock politeness. At a guess, he was in his twenties, scrawny and pale with acne-marked skin and one eye that looked in a different direction from the other.

'We're waiting for someone,' Sharon said, in her best school voice, a bit louder and higher than usual. Only I would be able to detect the nervousness behind it. We had been taught to be polite.

'Well, it's gonna chuck it down. We were just about to move,' he said. 'You probably should an' all.'

He looked up at the dark sky and I did the same, noting that he was right about the rain. The second man just stared at us, unblinking. He lit a cigarette and slowly blew a lungful of smoke in our direction. I caught the sharp tang at the back of my throat and coughed. I took a closer look at him. He was older than the first one, with receding sandy hair combed over at one side to cover the baldness. As he watched me observe him, a lazy smile spread across his face, and I could see he was missing a tooth at the front. I recoiled.

His colouring was all wrong for the Ripper, but it didn't matter. Every sense I had was on full alert that we were in danger, and I took Sharon's hand and gripped it tightly. She squeezed back. I looked around us. The streets seemed suddenly empty of people.

A crack of distant thunder made me jump and distracted us for a moment when the younger of the two men got up and began to move towards us, his face intent on Sharon. I had frozen to the spot when I became conscious of Sharon tugging on my arm. 'We've got to run,' she said, her voice quiet and urgent.

As I came to and turned to run, he started to do the same and within two strides had hold of my arm. Sharon was tugging me from the other side, shouting, 'Let go! Let go!' as we both pulled hard to release me from his grip. I looked at his face. No smiles now.

'Oi!'

A voice came from behind the Gaiety and a woman appeared in the space between the buildings.

'You leave them girls be, Ron Ainsworth.'

He let go of my arm immediately and shrugged, all smiles again, as if laughing off the seriousness of whatever he had been about to do.

'All right, Mags. Keep your 'air on. We were just keeping them warm and dry.'

'Course you were,' said the woman as she walked up to us and shooed him away. 'Come on, you two.' She grabbed our hands and set off back down Roundhay Road at such a pace we had to run to keep up. Once we were out of sight of the Gaiety she stopped and squatted down, looking right into our eyes. I could smell the cigarette smoke and chewing gum on her.

'What the bloody hell did you think you were doing?'

We both stared back at her.

'Are you dumb as well as fucking stupid?'

She stood back up and shook her head, reaching for a cigarette from her coat pocket. She was wearing a nylon minidress with green swirls on it and knee-high boots, the gap between the dress and boots showing chubby thighs made ruddy by the cold.

'Are you a prostitute?'

Sharon's blurted question shocked me so much I was struck mute again, but the woman threw her head back and laughed, a rich, throaty sound. I was mesmerised. I had an image in my mind of what a prostitute looked like – partially informed by the photos of the Ripper's victims, partially informed by an active imagination. I pictured them as either bottle-blonde, red-lipped sirens or downtrodden, unkempt, haggard-looking older women. She was neither.

'Where did a young lady like you learn that word? You look like butter wouldn't melt,' she said, still looking Sharon up and down. 'Well, not that it's any of your business, but yes, I am. And so will you be if you keep hanging round here. Now get yourselves off home.'

All this was delivered without a smile and ended with a dismissive nod down the road, indicating that we should leave. The sky chose that moment to break. Large drops of cold, heavy rain started to splatter onto the pavement, and I could see the woman's eyes roll as she muttered to herself, 'Fuck's sake,' then to us, 'Follow me.'

We hurried after her as she lifted her coat over her head and headed down the street, eventually stopping outside a small shop with a red-and-white awning. There was a phone box on the pavement, covered in cards with shapely silhouettes on them offering 'personal services'.

'Wait here,' she commanded, and stepped into the

phone box, pulling out a purse from her handbag as she did so and looking around before she opened it up. We did as we were told, too scared to do anything else, and stood shivering under the awning. After she had finished her call she ushered us into the shop, where the man behind the counter nodded at her and reached behind him for a packet of cigarettes. 'And I'll get these,' she added, picking up a packet of Opal Fruits, which she handed to us. 'That's to keep you quiet for t'next ten minutes.'

'Thank you,' we both muttered, scared of saying anything that might make her swear at us again. We left the shop and the three of us stood under the awning again, watching the rain pour down. Cars passed us, sending splashes of water our way and sometimes honking at us. One man shouted, 'Is it three-for-two week, Mags?' and laughed as she stuck two fingers up at him.

As I stared down the street, hoping to see the Ripper, I caught sight of a face I recognised. I couldn't place who it was at first. I was fooled by the clothes he was wearing – the combination of a sheepskin jacket and jeans. He looked younger, fashionable. I was about to grab Sharon's arm to point him out when he headed into a boarded-up shopfront with the words *Private Shop* printed above it. Maybe it was seeing him out of the safety and sanctity of the church, but it was unmistakably our vicar, Mr Spencer. Maybe he wasn't so righteous after all.

Before I got chance to tell Sharon, a police car drew

up next to us and fear gripped my chest hard, like a fist. The driver wound the passenger window down and Mags leaned in to talk to him.

'All right, Maggie?' he said. 'Are they all right? You found out their names or owt? Where they're from?'

'I'm not the bloody copper,' she said. 'That's your job. I've got to go to work.'

The policeman sighed and shook his head. 'You're mad. I've told you before it's not safe out there till we catch him.'

'Do you want to pay me bills?' She paused as the policeman looked down. 'Thought not.'

She stood up and indicated to us to get into the back of the car. 'He'll make sure you get home. Don't let me see you round here again,' she said as we climbed in. She walked off down the rain-drenched road without another word or a backward glance.

As the car drew off, the enormity of the situation we found ourselves in seemed to hit us both and I burst into tears first, closely followed by Sharon.

'Now, now,' said the policeman. 'There's no need for that. Big brave girls like you shouldn't be crying. I'm Constable Blakes. Why don't you tell me your names and where you're from and we'll start from there.'

By the time we got to the police station, Sharon had spun Constable Blakes our now well-used story about visiting Leeds for our 'school project' and getting lost and wandering into Chapeltown. She reassured him that no one would be worried about us as we weren't expected home before dark. I sat there in silent fear that he wouldn't believe her, but her confident expression seemed to win him over in a way of which I was in awe.

We sat in the uncomfortable plastic chairs he pointed to on our arrival at the police station, distracting ourselves from our fate by eagerly watching all the passers-by, wondering why each of them was there. Despite the drama of the day, and the underlying fear that we were in trouble, it felt like we were together again.

Eventually Constable Blakes reappeared, joined by a tall, striking man with dark hair wearing a black leather jacket. I felt the faintest flicker of recognition as Constable Blakes said, 'This is Detective Sergeant Lister. He lives over your way, so you're going to get a special police escort home.'

On the journey back, Sharon retold the story of the school project and how we had got lost in Chapeltown. It was not so unquestioningly received. DS Lister asked more questions and eventually I had to kick Sharon to prevent her from tying us in knots we might never be able to undo. I sat mutely until he said, 'You realise I'm going to have to talk to your parents.' I felt sick.

The last time I had been in trouble, I had barely been able to look at Mum and Dad for weeks. Not because there had been any real punishment, but because of the guilt that had been thrown in my direction by Aunty Jean. 'They've enough on their plates without the likes of you,' she had told me. But that had been for being late for school during the Russian-spy hunt, a far lesser crime than this. I had learned to deal with Aunty Jean's wrath, but trouble of this magnitude would probably mean the end of my freedom. At the back of my mind there also lay the worry that it might lead to the separation of Sharon and me. And after today I wasn't sure she would mind.

'Please, Detective Lister, please. Me mum's not well and if she hears about this it'll make her worse, I know it will. Please. We're good girls, I promise. We won't do it again, I mean it. Swear on our lives.' The words ran into each other in my eagerness to get them out. Sharon tearfully nodded her head vigorously, and we both looked at him pleadingly through the car mirror.

'I'll think about it,' he said, and turned the radio on. As the smooth-as-honey voice of Karen Carpenter singing 'Rainy Days and Mondays' filtered through the speakers, my head began to nod and I fell asleep against Sharon's shoulder.

'Come on now, wake up.'

As I blearily came to, I realised that Sharon was no longer sat next to me. I sat up, ramrod-straight, to see DS Lister stood there with the car door open.

'I've already dropped her off,' he said, 'with a promise that she will never ever do anything that daft again. Can I get the same promise from you?'

I nodded my head. 'Yes,' I said.

'Against my better judgement, I'm not going to tell your mum and dad. This time.'

He smiled at me for the first time, and the glimmer of recognition grew stronger. 'Go on then. Off you go.' I jumped out of the car and he drove off, leaving me stood on the pavement with a relief so overwhelming I felt faint. I pulled out the key tied to a ribbon round my neck and opened the front door.

For once, the silence in the house was welcome. It gave me a chance to calm the shakes that had overtaken my body. As I stood there, I wondered whether what we were doing was still the right thing. Was what happened in Chapeltown a step too far? Had *I* made us go too far? I switched on the television, only to see Barbara Leach's mum being interviewed on the news. Her anguished, grief-stricken face was hard to look at. What would have happened if the men in Chapeltown hadn't been interrupted? Would it have been my mum on the television, haunted by the loss of me? Was that really what I wanted?

As if powered by that thought, and some internal clockwork, I went to the kitchen and made a strong cup of tea, one sugar. I carried it carefully upstairs and set it down outside Mum and Dad's bedroom door.

'Mum,' I said, the word unfamiliar on my tongue. I usually just placed the tea outside, knocking as I left. 'There's a cup of tea here for you.'

Then I went into my bedroom and closed the door.

28

Helen

She kept her eyes out for the girls coming to return the *A–Z* she'd lent them, intending to disappear behind the desk or run into the back room at the first sight of them, but to her relief they didn't come.

While being at work with bruises and black eyes was uncomfortable, and embarrassing, it was easier to get away with it among adults. Her colleagues' glances would slide over the injuries she had attempted to cover up and focus on something else while they spoke to her quickly, desperate to get away. They seemed to buy whatever story she came up with – nodding in sympathy in order to avoid having to ask any questions that might mean getting involved. For all the talk about community and 'looking after our own', when it came down to it 'our own' had a very narrow definition, Helen thought.

It didn't help that Gary charmed almost everyone he spoke to. She understood. She'd been exactly the same. She had completely fallen in love with this handsome, charming man, who treated her 'like a princess', as he used to say when they were just going out with each other. She'd felt seen by someone outside her family for the first time and had blossomed under his gaze. She hadn't got to see who he really was until they were married, and by then it was too late. Women like her didn't leave men like him. It just wasn't done. You had to put up and shut up.

It was different with children. They would stare. And ask questions. And look at her quizzically when she replied, as though they could see right through her excuses. She'd seen the concerned expressions on the two girls' faces the last time. They were just on the cusp of learning the conventions of the world of women: when to say something and when to stay quiet. In another year or so they would have learned the rules and wouldn't enquire, but she knew if they had seen her face and neck that day, they would have noticed she had more bruises and asked what had happened and wouldn't have taken 'It was a silly accident' for an answer. It was better to hide.

Among the adults, only Omar didn't follow the rules as strictly as the others. He had done so that day in the shop, in that he hadn't asked her directly what had happened, but he had looked at her with such com-passion that it made her want to tell him everything. She had been avoiding going in there for days, even though they'd run out of milk, and as she neared the shop now, she wasn't sure what was worse: seeing that expression again, or going home without and facing the consequences.

Her step slowed as she approached the corner, and she felt her heart rate quicken. Maybe there would be enough people in there that he wouldn't notice her, or at least not look too closely. She stopped on the opposite side of the street and leaned forward to try and see through the shop window and assess how busy it was. So intent was she that when the man coughed, she swung round and nearly shrieked in fear.

But it was just Brian.

'Oh my goodness, you almost scared the life out of me,' she exclaimed, holding her hand to her chest to steady her breathing.

'Sorry,' he said, looking at his feet.

She couldn't work out where he had come from. She hadn't heard any footsteps, and now he was stock-still, as though he'd always been stood there and she was the one who'd just appeared. She was about to ask him, when she heard the sound of the shop bell and turned to look as Valerie exited the shop, waving the two carrier bags she had up in the air in Brian's direction. He mumbled something Helen couldn't make out and scurried over the road to help his mum. Free of the carrier bags, Valerie waved at her.

'Hello, Helen love,' she said. 'Can't stop.'

Helen almost cried with relief as she waited for her breathing to return to a regular rhythm, then turned round and headed back into town. She couldn't go in. Even the thought of his kind looks made her throat tighten, causing the marks on her neck – the fingerprints she had hidden under a polo-neck jumper from where Gary had tried to throttle her last night – to throb.

29

Miv

Number Eight

'This is the last year we're doing this,' Sharon said, her voice low. 'Remember. We agreed. We're getting too old for this now.'

We were sat next to each other on little wooden chairs made for smaller children than us in the dusty, high-ceilinged room at the back of the centuries-old church.

'I remember,' I said, while hoping that it might not be the last year. Since Chapeltown, I had felt like I wanted to cling hard to the rituals of our childhood. I wasn't sure if I was ready to be in the world as a grown-up, and the October half-term Church Holiday Club was one of those rituals. It involved games and singing, and a lot less God than Sunday school, and that year it was the intention to put on a show at the end to mark All Saints' Day.

Things had been uncomfortable between us since Chapeltown. It felt as though we were learning a new dance and neither of us knew the steps. Sharon had been quiet, and I had got louder to compensate. I stared hard at her, while her eyes fluttered downwards and her cheeks, pale in the dark October gloom, began to glow pink, as if someone had turned the heat up. She looked awkward, out of place. I, on the other hand, took comfort in the familiar surroundings and the fact that I didn't have to pretend to be grown up.

'What about Mr Spencer?' I asked, hoping that this might pique her interest in the week ahead.

'What about him?' She looked over at me, frowning.

'Oh. I forgot to tell you that I saw him. When we went to Chapeltown. He was going into a boarded-up shop.' I paused, letting that sink in for a moment. 'I think it's weird he was in Chapeltown, given that he spends so much time warning everyone else off the place. Don't you think it's weird?'

Her eyes narrowed. I could see I had her attention.

'Anyway, it's just that this week will be a brilliant time to watch him,' I said airily, in an attempt at not caring.

'I know we haven't talked about what happened . . . in Chapeltown, I mean,' said Sharon, her voice serious. 'But I think we should. Don't you?'

'Course,' I said. Meaning: *No, I really don't want to.* 'And we will. But let's have this week first. It won't hurt to keep an eye on Mr Spencer, will it? And it's not like we can get into trouble. We're in church.'

Sharon shook her head at me and was about to say something else when the door at the back of the room creaked open and Mr Spencer walked to the front, his stride bouncy and his smile wide.

'Good morning, children.'

'Good morning, Mr Spencer,' I chanted back with the others while Sharon sat silently next to me, arms folded. The vicar started to write on a big blackboard behind him while I looked around to see who else was there, nodding at Stephen Crowther, when a thought occurred to me.

'Why don't Mr Bashir and Ishtiaq come to church?' I whispered to Sharon. It seemed a shame to miss a week of laiking out with him.

'Don't be daft,' she said. 'They're Muslims.'

I nodded as though I knew what she was talking about while looking around at the rest of the group. I made a note to research what being 'Muslim' meant, ashamed that Sharon knew something that I didn't and wondering why that was the case.

The first order of the day was to decide which Bible story our end-of-week show would be based around. Half of the room wanted 'David and Goliath', presumably as it offered the opportunity to playfight with abandon, and the other, kinder half, 'The Good Samaritan'. I whispered to Sharon that she should put her hand up and ask if we could do the prostitute who washed Jesus' feet, just to see what his reaction to the word was. Her eyes came alive for the first time that morning. We grinned at each other, and she did.

I watched in triumph as Mr Spencer visibly squirmed.

'See,' I said to Sharon, smiling.

Someone else piped up. 'What's a prostitute?'

It seemed to me that that question had endless power to make grown-ups uncomfortable, Mr Spencer particularly so. Sharon and I swallowed down giggles.

Mr Spencer's usually confident face flushed bright red and beads of perspiration appeared on his brow, despite the October chill which the building did nothing to keep out. As he stuttered and tried to change the subject, I took a closer look at him. He was tall, with strikingly dark eyes, large features and bushy, black caterpillar-like eyebrows that seemed to have a life of their own. He had also recently shaved off a particularly striking moustache.

He was definitely going on the list.

8. The Vicar

- He was in Chapeltown
- He has dark hair
- He used to have a moustache
- Is he too good to be true?

30

Miv

We eventually settled on 'The Good Samaritan' as our end-of-week play. When he let us stop for a break, Mr Spencer left the room and I was about to point out his recently shaved-off moustache to Sharon when we found ourselves swept into a rowdy game of tig, and even Sharon threw off her cloak of maturity and thundered across the worn floorboards, running and jumping to dodge the person who was 'it'.

The door burst open and Mrs Spencer peered in, eyes ablaze.

'This . . . is . . . a . . . house . . . of . . . worship!' she shouted, as we all froze. Mrs Spencer was all stiffness and spikes in contrast to her husband's easy-going nature. I often wondered how they could be married to each other, they were so different, then I remembered how different Sharon and me were. Maybe it worked for them too.

She looked around, presumably searching for Mr Spencer.

'Right, back in your seats, while I . . .'

She turned round to see that Mr Spencer had appeared

behind her, and she closed the door until just a sliver of light showed. Pulling our chairs back into a semi-circle, we could hear furious whispers between the pair.

As Mr Spencer walked back into the room, we steeled ourselves, ready for a further rebuke, but he seemed more jovial than ever and we relaxed as he retold 'The Good Samaritan' parable, wildly gesticulating as he did so, at one point knocking over a stack of Bibles that had been precariously balanced on a table next to him. 'Oops,' he giggled as a girl ran to pick them up.

We ate our dinner in a small building next door, a Portakabin-like community centre used for church functions, jumble sales, and the birthdays, weddings, anniversaries and retirement parties of everyone on the neighbouring streets.

Inside, there were several long tables with benches, reminiscent of the school dining hall. A large table had been set up at the side of the room, with polystyrene cups of warm orange squash on it. Sharon and I had brought warm potted-meat sandwiches wrapped in foil by Ruby that morning and a packet of crisps to share that we'd purchased from Mr Bashir's on the way. While I was paying in the shop, Sharon had run behind the counter to say hello to Ishtiaq and reported he was in the darkened back room doing homework.

I walked over to a bench away from everyone else so we could discuss Mr Spencer's addition to the list, when I spotted a familiar face. He was sitting with a group of older children, part of the youth club that we would join when we were teenagers.

I nudged Sharon. 'Look, it's Paul Ware,' I said, whispering the words with reverence.

'What you blushing for?' Sharon said with a knowing smile.

We'd never spoken about it, but she knew exactly why I was blushing. He was sat on his own too, book in hand, his fringe flopping in his eyes. I got the sense he wasn't really reading. He had the imposing height of his dad, combined with the exquisite, fragile features of his mum, a striking mix.

'Where do you think they live now?' I wondered out loud. 'They can't live with her new boyfriend, can they? It wouldn't be allowed.' I frequently confused the morality prescribed by the church with the law, and took Bible stories and the rules of Christianity quite literally.

'Right, my group, back to the church,' Mrs Spencer called before Sharon was able to answer. I watched as Paul slowly got up and trailed behind the others in his group, keeping his eyes on the floor as he did so.

Mr Spencer seemed less energetic in the afternoon and divided us into groups to act out scenes from 'The Good Samaritan' story while he sat to one side, a mug in his hand. More than once I noticed his head nod and at one point the mug almost fell to the floor as he jerked awake and looked around to see if anyone had spotted him.

At the end of the afternoon, he announced that auditions for the show were to be held the next day and that we should come prepared to 'act and sing your little hearts out', an instruction he gave with a dramatic flourish of his hand that almost saw the Bibles toppling once more. All thoughts of the list were forgotten as I screwed up my eyes during the closing prayer and begged for God to give me a lead role.

'What part do you want?' I asked Sharon on the way home. 'I bet you'll get the Good Samaritan.'

She visibly shuddered. 'I don't really want a part. I don't like it like you do.'

'Like what?'

'Acting and performing and that,' she said.

I was struck by the irony that she didn't like the spotlight when nature had determined she would be in it, while I was desperate for someone to notice me. But I was secretly pleased that she wouldn't be auditioning. It meant less competition for me.

I spent the evening in my room, practising a song, until eventually Dad knocked on my bedroom door and said, 'Enough now, love. Your mum's in bed, and Aunty Jean and me . . . well . . . we've had enough of the same song over and over.' He laughed and ruffled my hair to show he wasn't cross with me. 'I'm off out,' he said then. 'Don't stay up too late.'

He turned back just before he closed my bedroom door, his head cocked slightly to one side. 'You've got your mum's voice,' he said, his voice so low I almost didn't hear him.

When I eventually got into bed, unable to sleep with excitement and nerves about the following day, a memory of Mum suddenly came to me. She was stroking my hair while I lay sleepless for one reason or another and was singing the song we'd heard being whistled in the mill, 'You Are My Sunshine'. I wrapped my dad's words around me like a blanket and hummed the song quietly to myself until I fell asleep.

I thought I'd made a mistake when Ruby opened their front door the next morning and said that Sharon had left already – I'd hoped to practise on her too and couldn't remember her saying she wouldn't be at home as usual. She wasn't at the church when I arrived either, but any worry I might have felt about that was soon overtaken by auditions. As always, I was awarded the role of narrator, where at least I would be heard, if not seen.

The morning was spent happily learning my lines and the songs that we would all sing, so much so that I didn't even miss Sharon and barely even noticed Mr Spencer. But when she hadn't arrived by midday, when we broke for dinner, I decided to go and look for her. I headed to Mr Bashir's first, to see if she'd decided to avoid the auditions by going to call for Ishtiaq. I took the back way, weaving my way through the dark snickets and ginnels, mouthing my lines as I walked, cold mist streaming from my mouth as I did so. When I neared the shop, I heard the tinkle of a giggle that sounded like a waterfall. I knew instantly it was Sharon.

I peered around the end of the hedge-enclosed snicket, just to make sure, and saw Sharon and Ishtiaq leaving the shop and walking down the street together. After looking around, presumably to make sure that no one else was on the quiet street, Ishtiaq took her hand. My own hands started to tingle, not just from the cold, and I shook them, trying to get the feeling back, keeping my eyes trained on Sharon and Ishtiaq.

They were totally absorbed in each other, Ishtiaq talking more than I had ever seen him, his eyes flashing with expression, while Sharon nodded and smiled, her eyes intent on his face. She looked beautiful, radiant. As she threw her head back and laughed again, I stepped back, making sure they couldn't see me, only peering out when I was sure they were far enough away.

Watching Sharon's ponytail swing with each step as she walked into the distance, I was more aware than ever of how much I wanted to be like her. But I knew that would mean being a different person altogether. An entirely different girl, born to a different family, with a different life. I had always settled for being close to her, but now my two best friends had formed a unit without me. They fitted together perfectly, like one of those interlocking puzzles that she and I used to spend hours trying to solve. What if I became a leftover piece, surplus to requirements? What if there was no place for me any more? It would be just like home. The thought formed a hollow inside me which expanded with each breath.

Sobbing, I turned and went to run back down the snicket to the church, when out of the corner of my eye I noticed a flash of yellow to my right, on the opposite side of the street, and saw the man in the overalls watching me.

Maybe it was seeing Sharon and Ishtiaq together that made me decide to follow Paul Ware home at the end of the day's activities. I told myself it was because I wanted to see where he lived and to get a glimpse of Hazel if I could. As though this were a normal thing to do. As soon as we were let go for the day, with a prayer which I sulked through, not feeling like God was on my side at all, I ran out of the church. I headed down the cobbled path through the crumbling cemetery to the gate, waiting for Paul Ware to leave too and hopping from one foot to the other in the cold.

Eventually he came out of the church, his eyes on his book, which he read, or pretended to read, as he walked. I hid behind a bush as he came down the path, then followed on at what I thought was a safe distance, observing him and making mental notes to repeat to Sharon, though the thought of her caused my chest to tighten.

I couldn't help noticing every detail about him. His

trousers were the newly fashionable drainpipe jeans, which he wore with black-and-white trainers and a black T-shirt with a picture of Debbie Harry on it and *BLONDIE* written in white across the bottom. He carried his coat in one arm, despite the cold. His brown hair curled around his face and collar, in a style that managed to look fashionably unkempt. He was just cool.

I was surprised to see that we were heading into familiar territory, and the streets where I lived. I couldn't imagine Hazel Ware living there though. Row upon row of uniform houses. Row upon row of uniform people. It felt too plain and poor to contain her, and I was right. The grey, cracked, uneven flagstones with weeds growing up in between them eventually made way for wider roads with neatly manicured bushes at either side.

He remained in sight. I kept one eye on him, the other taking in the streets in front of me so I could safely make my way back again. I was so absorbed that I don't know how long it was before I became aware of the heavy-booted footsteps gaining ground behind me.

I was caught, not wanting to risk losing Paul by turning away to see whoever was on my tail, but unable to dislodge the thought of the Ripper coming up behind his victims and hitting them on the back of the head with a hammer. I stopped momentarily, my instincts spiking, and as the footsteps stopped too, I began to run, my heart pulsing in my temples with every sharp breath I took. The footsteps pounded, increasing in speed, and I felt a pull on my jumper as whoever it was got hold of it.

I called out a weak 'Help' as I tried to get away and tumbled to the ground, grazing my knee underneath my jeans and slapping my hands hard against the pavement.

I looked up.

Leering down at me was Richard Collier. He was wearing his same uniform of rolled-up jeans and monkey boots, but they seemed worn in now, like they were part of him. He was carrying a heavy-looking sports bag, the strap across his body, with pieces of paper spilling out of it from running. His expression was strangely blank, as though someone had switched him off at the mains. In the distance, I could see Neil watching us, laughing. I went to speak but found the words wouldn't form themselves in my mouth. He pulled at my jumper neck again, dragging me up by it.

'You're Sharon's friend, right?' he said, as if we had stopped on the street for a natter.

I nodded.

'Does she have a boyfriend?' he said, his gaze intent on me.

The word 'no' escaped me, the strangled sound a surprise. I hadn't had time to get used to the fact that she clearly did.

'What's going on?' I heard Paul's voice ring out. He was nearing us, staring straight at Richard. He must have turned back at the noise.

'Nowt,' said Richard, his voice breezy. 'She just tripped and fell.'

I watched his face change as he smiled at Paul. It was

just like it had at the pool when moments before he had been drowning Stephen Crowther, then let him go.

'You all right?' Paul said to me.

I nodded.

'See you at school,' Richard said, as he sauntered off back to Neil, who was still smirking at us.

'What just happened?' Paul asked, bending to pick up the pieces of paper that Richard had left littered on the street, while I dusted my knees, realising in horror that the fall had made a hole in my trousers that I would have to explain to Aunty Jean. I kept my face down so he couldn't see the tears in my eyes. I was experiencing a painful cocktail of fear and embarrassment, mixed with a tiny droplet of joy that he had come back to help me.

'I don't know,' I said. And I really didn't. Was Richard really chasing me? Had I overreacted? Was it my fault?

Paul and I continued to walk down the street together in silence until he came to a stop outside a small Georgian semi-detached house with a large garden at the front. Unlike Sharon's house, it wasn't pristine – muddy wellies sat on the doorstep and stripes of different coloured paints were daubed on the front door – but it looked like a home.

'Why were you following me?' he asked, looking at me square in the eyes for the first time.

I felt the hot flush of shame infuse my body. I pulled at the hem of my faded jumble-sale jumper, wanting to make myself into the sort of girl that boys took notice of in a different way to the way he was looking at me now.

'I . . . I wasn't.'

'Yes, you were. You'd been following me since church. I'm not daft,' he said, the edges of his mouth moving up into a half-smile.

'Oh. I, er, is Mr Ware your dad?' My mind started to concoct a possible reason I might be trailing him, and the words were out of my mouth before I had thought them through.

'Yes,' he said, his eyes narrowed.

'Well, he used to be my teacher and I thought you might still live with him and so I followed you and . . .' I trailed off, aware that my story wasn't helping to change his view of me as a weirdo. My shoulders slumped. 'I just wanted to see where you live,' I mumbled.

He looked at me as though I were a puzzle he couldn't work out.

The door of the house opened, and I saw Hazel step outside. I was immediately struck mute. A paisley silk headscarf kept her long hair out of her eyes, and she was wearing paint-spattered dungarees.

'Paul?' she said. 'I thought I heard you.'

She looked at me, her eyes smiling.

'Hello. We've met before, haven't we, Miv? At the coffee morning.'

I nodded, thrilled that she had recognised me.

'Do you want to come in for some pop?'

I wanted nothing more than to say yes. In fact, just

in that moment I wanted to run into her arms and sob and tell her everything, about Richard, about the Ripper, about Mum, but I could see Paul widen his eyes in horror.

'No thanks, Mrs Ware,' I said, the words escaping in gasps.

'OK,' she said. 'Well, any time. You know you're welcome. We haven't lived here for very long and Paul doesn't know many people round here yet.'

Paul looked at her with undisguised fury, his neck turning scarlet. He walked past Hazel and into the house. 'Say goodbye, Paul,' she called over her shoulder to him, her eyes on me, sparkling with amusement.

'Bye!' I heard him shout from inside the house. It sounded more like a bark than a human voice.

'Bye, Mrs Ware,' I said, and turned and ran.

My shaking legs automatically took me in the direction of Sharon's. So much had happened and I was desperate to tell her. Then I remembered the thing that she hadn't told me. My body slowed with the realisation and instead I went home, thinking about the blankness on Richard's face and how unsettling I had found the switch to his smiling, friendly response to Paul.

I wondered about the Ripper. Did he have two faces too? Was that why no one had caught him? Did he look like a normal, good person on the outside? Like Mr Spencer? I swallowed my words and feelings as I opened the front door to the silence of Mum in her armchair and the rest of the empty house.

31

Mr Ware

As he pulled up to the house, Mike saw two familiar figures, one carrying a large sports bag, both doing what he could only describe as 'loitering'. He sat in the car, the engine idling while he waited for Paul, watching them closely. He had told Hazel he wouldn't be coming up to the house to collect his son, nonchalantly implying it was for practical reasons when it was really because he couldn't bear to even catch a glimpse of her.

His instinct was to question them. What were they doing here? What was in the bag? But of course, he was no longer their teacher; they were nothing to do with him. He couldn't stop watching them though, and as he stared, seeing them go from house to house, he realised that they were posting pieces of paper taken from the bags, and it made him smile. Maybe they had turned over a new leaf? Maybe they were gainfully employed now? He was surprised by how much they had changed in the months since he'd left Bishopsfield. They had broadened and hardened.

The tap on the car window made him jump.

'Hi, Dad.' Paul opened the car door and folded into the seat next to him, all limbs and awkwardness.

'Hi, son,' he replied, suddenly self-conscious, as if this were a stranger.

They set off in silence, and as they passed the two boys, Mike became aware that Paul had turned to stare at them, only settling again when Neil and Richard were in the distance. Mike turned the radio on to cover up the silence between them and sat thinking about what he might say. Before the separation, he and Paul had never spent time alone together unless it was to complete homework. Conversation between them was as difficult to navigate as learning a new language.

'Have you come across those two at school?' he said, unable to let the two boys go.

'Yup,' he said, his voice low.

'I can't imagine them being reliable paper boys,' Mike said, aware that his attempt at a joke was weak.

'Hmm,' Paul replied, turning to look out of the car window. Mike took that as a sign that the conversation was already over and turned up the volume on the radio to hide his embarrassment.

When they arrived at the flat, Mike found himself desperately wanting to make excuses and prepare Paul for what he was about to see.

'It's the best I could get, and it's only temporary,' he said as they walked up the empty, echoing stairs.

His sense of embarrassment and shame only increased when his neighbour, Gary, appeared from his flat and leaned on the grubby magnolia wall, observing them.

'Hello, hello, hello,' he called out, in that matey way he had, which made Mike cringe from the bottom of his feet upwards. He hated his snobbishness, but this artfully dishevelled young man with his overconfidence brought out the worst of his father's judgemental beliefs, reincarnated in him.

'Gary.' He nodded his head briefly at him, hoping to discourage any further conversation.

'And this handsome lad must be yours. I can see the resemblance,' Gary said, looking at Paul.

'Yes, this is my son, Paul.'

'Gary Andrews,' Gary said. 'Pleased to meet—'

'We'd better get on,' Mike cut in, and turned to open his door. He tried to avoid Gary as much as possible, suspecting that, given the yells and bangs that came from the flat he shared with his wife, Gary's mask of charm hid something more sinister.

'Of course!' Gary said, his sneer only half hidden by his smile. 'We all know you're always busy, busy, busy, Mike.'

Mike knew this was intended as a slight, from the expression that accompanied it, but chose to let it go, especially in front of Paul. His son had seen too much of his anger already.

'Hah,' he said, and ushered Paul inside.

*

The emptiness of the flat felt more pronounced now that Paul was with him, despite more of the space being filled by the two of them. He looked around at the tiny room in which he now existed. There was a kitchenette, with a barely used hob and an old, rusted fridge to the left; a single bed, which doubled up as his sofa, to the right; and a small square table and two chairs. While he could have asked his father for help, he felt unable to, pride getting in the way of confessing to the mess he'd made of his marriage.

'I thought we'd get fish and chips from Barry's for tea, as a treat,' Mike said, his voice overly bright.

'Sounds good,' Paul replied, putting his bag down on the chair that Mike pulled out for him.

'Like I said, it's only temporary,' he repeated. 'There's no TV yet, but I'll get one . . .'

'It's OK, Dad. Really,' Paul replied, with a sincerity that made Mike tearful for a moment, the sudden emotion surprising him. 'I don't mind, I brought my book and my homework with me.'

He opened his bag and pulled out the battered copy of *Fahrenheit 451* Mike had given him, and Mike experienced a wave of pride.

'Good lad,' he said. 'I can maybe help you with that.' He reached for the sheet of paper that had come out of Paul's bag.

'That's not my . . .' Paul started.

Mike read the words in front of him, written in red, accompanied by a garish Union Jack.

PUT BRITONS FIRST

STOP immigration
REJECT common market
RESTORE capital punishment
MAKE Britain great again

Mike looked up at Paul's pale face, two burning-red patches on his cheeks giving him a doll-like appearance. 'What the hell is this?' He couldn't contain his fury.

'It's not mine,' Paul said firmly, his voice echoing off the bare walls.

Mike had heard similar from pupils over and over down the years, and looked at his son hard, hoping that the truth he saw in his face was genuine.

'If it's not yours, whose is it?'

'It's a long story, Dad.'

'Well, I've got all night.'

He hated the scolding tone that overcame him, the well-worn teacher's phrase.

'It belongs to Richard, or at least I got it from him. I was talking to him earlier. It fell out of his bag and I picked it up,' Paul said, now looking down at the floor.

What Richard and Neil had been doing clicked into place, like a puzzle he hadn't realised he was trying to figure out. Mike sank onto the chair, indicating for Paul to sit down too.

'Those boys, they're not your friends, are they? What they're involved in, it's . . .' He thought about his father and what he would say about them, probably something along the lines of 'I didn't fight against Hitler to see my own countrymen turn into him.' Mike could even picture his father's face, puce with rage, as he said it.

Paul perched on the edge of his seat as if ready to run.

'It's dangerous, not to mention ignorant.' Mike tried to modulate his voice to take out the echoes of his father.

'I know. I really do. I wouldn't have anything to do with them and I won't. I was helping someone else. A girl,' Paul replied, the high pink on his cheeks spreading over his face and neck.

'A girl, eh?' The realisation that he had underestimated his son made him begin to smile.

'Daaadddd,' Paul said, the blush deepening.

The relief was enough to make Mike laugh out loud. He looked at Paul's cross, embarrassed face and watched while it changed, infected by his laughter, and they smiled at each other for the first time since Mike could remember.

32

Miv

'I saw you yesterday,' I said to Sharon as we walked to church the next day. 'You were with Ishtiaq.' I kept my eyes on the pavement in front of me.

There was a pause before Sharon replied, 'Oh, right. Why didn't you say anything?'

'I felt weird about it,' I said, and shrugged. Then, because I couldn't resist, even though I'd promised myself I wouldn't, I asked, 'So is he your boyfriend?'

'Yes. Yes, he is.'

Her nervous voice was accompanied by a shy smile.

'Why didn't you tell me?'

'I didn't want you to be upset. I thought you might feel left out or something.'

'I'm upset cos you didn't tell me,' I said, though I knew this wasn't strictly true. I was upset because if Sharon loved someone else, she might not have enough room to love me.

'I'm sorry. It's just . . . well . . . me dad. He wouldn't want me to be with someone like, like Ish. And I know you wouldn't tell him, or anyone, but I also know how things can be for you. At home, I mean. God, this is hard.' She fell silent for a while, her face serious and sad. 'The thing is, I was worried. About how you might feel. I didn't want to make you any sadder.'

We carried on walking in silence. We never spoke about things at home. I didn't even know how much she knew. Was she only going along with things like the list because she felt sorry for me? The thought made my throat close.

'Is it serious? I mean, do you think you'll stay together?' My voice wobbled with wanting to know and not wanting to know.

Sharon gave a small laugh. 'I don't know,' she said, her voice quiet, hesitant. 'All I know is that I really, really like him.'

We were nearing the church as she put her arm on mine to turn me towards her. 'But we'll always stay together. Me and you, I mean. We'll always be friends.'

I nodded, unable to speak.

Much of the day was spent separately, as I was rehearsing 'The Good Samaritan' story at Mr Spencer's direction, and Sharon disappeared happily into the back row of the chorus, led by Mrs Spencer. I got totally lost in the story, and Mr Spencer remained on the outskirts of my awareness.

At dinnertime we went to sit in our usual spot, and as we passed Paul Ware he nodded at me. I nodded back, trying to look nonchalant but failing, the heat rising in my cheeks. I decided not to tell Sharon about following

him home. I could have my own secrets. Over jam sandwiches and warm orange squash I described to Sharon
the limited observations I had made of Mr Spencer's
behaviour and we both decided that we needed to
keep a closer eye on him. Even though I suspected
that Sharon was only doing so to please me after the
awkwardness of the morning, I didn't mind if it meant
that we were united.

Thanks to some unexpectedly sunny weather,
brightening the day if not warming it, the afternoon
session was a game of British Bulldog, held outside.
As we ran from one end of the church garden to the
other, kicking leaves as we went, avoiding being caught,
Sharon and I didn't let Mr Spencer out of our sight. He
seemed to spend much of the game slumped against
the church wall, a flask of tea beside him, his only con-
tribution an occasional call of 'Be careful!' or 'Now,
now!' if the game got rowdy. As the day drew to a close,
he slowly got up from the floor, staggering slightly and
holding on to the wall for balance. He picked up his
flask and steadied himself again. 'Right, everyone' – he
clapped his hands – 'home time!' It wasn't until that
evening that I realised he hadn't closed the day with a
prayer.

The next morning, we were back to rehearsals. I had
spent the previous evening learning my lines to make
sure I was of the same standard as Stephen, whose
acting had become more impressive each time we

ran through the story. Mr Spencer was full of energy, praising our efforts in a voice so loud it jarred, and clapping furiously whenever a scene was particularly well done. I found myself feeling tense and unable to explain why.

At one point I noticed that the unsteadiness we had observed the day before was back again, and after one exuberant round of applause he seemed to trip over his feet and was only saved from falling head-first by gripping on to a pew at the last minute. I wondered if he was unwell.

I discussed this possibility with Sharon at dinnertime. She was still indulging me, if a little less enthusiastically as the day passed.

'There's definitely something wrong,' I said. 'He's all wobbly and slurry.'

'I know,' she nodded, and I was relieved.

'And it's not just that. It's like one minute he's all happy and that and the next he's asleep and the next he's cross,' I said. 'Do you see what I mean?'

Paul Ware leaned in. He was stood next to our table, and I hadn't even noticed.

'I know exactly what you mean,' he said, and we both jumped, startled.

'Sorry, it's just I heard you talking as I was going to get a drink. I think it's weird too. It's not just this week, it's when we have youth club as well.'

Before I had thought it through, I found myself saying, 'Do you think he's suspicious?' to Sharon's obvious surprise at my asking the question in front of someone else.

'Actually, I think he's drunk,' said Paul, and I felt my eyes widen. The thought was shocking to me. Then I remembered that what had sparked all this was seeing him in Chapeltown. There was more to Mr Spencer than met the eye.

Before I could respond, Mrs Spencer called Paul's group back in, and I just got chance to say 'Thanks' before he disappeared. Sharon and I looked at each other, and I jumped up and down inside, not only at the thought that we were on to something, but also because I'd managed to have a relatively normal conversation with Paul Ware.

The following day was the church concert. That afternoon, we would perform for the parents the play, songs and skits the groups had been working on all week. All thoughts of Mr Spencer, the Ripper and even Paul Ware were put to one side as I repeated my lines over and over until I was word-perfect and required no script, even though as the narrator I was allowed one. I wanted to be as good as Stephen. I had no expectations of anyone coming to watch me but decided to mention it anyway – just in case – saying to Mum, Dad and Aunty Jean the evening before, 'We're doing our show tomorrow and I'm narrating. I just thought I'd say cos all the mums and dads are coming to watch . . .'

I left the rest unsaid.

Mum didn't react. Aunty Jean nodded tightly.

'Is Ruby going to watch Sharon?' Dad asked.

I nodded.

'Well, I'll leave work early and come and pick you all up afterwards, how's that?' he said. 'We could go to Caddy's for an ice-cream float?'

Caddy's Café was a magical grotto of good things to eat and was known for its cherryade ice-cream floats. I was momentarily stunned at this unexpected offer. All my concerns that no one was coming to watch me vanished. There was also the hope that Hazel Ware would come to see Paul and the promise of a glimpse of her elegance.

As parents started arriving the next afternoon, Sharon ran to join the chorus and I stepped behind the hastily put-up curtains that divided the makeshift backstage area from the stage. Peering around one of the curtains, I sneaked a glimpse at the audience, their heads bobbing and bodies bustling. Stephen was back there too, standing tall and smiling. I smiled back, noticing how different he was from the cowering little boy he'd been at school. I felt oddly proud of him. After a while all the parents and choir were seated. Uncle Raymond, who was the photographer for the concert, was ready with his camera and the full cast was assembled behind the curtains.

We waited for Mr Spencer to open the show.

And we waited.

I looked around, realising that I couldn't remember having seen Mr Spencer for a while, and started shuffling uneasily. Eventually Mrs Spencer's head appeared around one of the curtains. Uncle Raymond peered over her shoulder, so close behind she had to move forward, making him stumble.

'Where's Peter?' she hissed, glaring at us as though we had hidden him somewhere. We all looked at each other and shrugged. I could see a giggle rising in Stephen's body and had to look away to avoid becoming infected with it. After some discussion it was determined that Uncle Raymond would have to open the concert as Mrs Spencer had to conduct the opening song.

'I can't be in two places at once!' she said, talking to him like she talked to us.

I felt sorry for him as he stood there, perspiration forming on his forehead and under his armpits. He finally stuttered some words of welcome, then Mrs Spencer instructed the choir to begin, her face frozen in a furious rictus. As the audience's attention turned to a loud rendition of 'Cross Over the Road', Uncle Raymond scuttled to the back of the church and put his camera up to his eyes, hiding behind it, training its gaze firmly on us.

Peering out from the side of the curtain again, I spotted Ruby in the crowd and waved wildly at her. She waved back. Then, two rows behind her, I spotted Hazel, wearing the same headscarf she had worn the day I went to their house, and when she caught my eye, she smiled and waved too and I blushed, feeling the warmth of her attention like the summer sun. The glow of being watched, even if it wasn't by anyone related to me, made my heart soar and when it was time I gave my performance my all, even garnering an unexpected round of applause after my introduction.

After the play the older group sang some songs and performed sketches, so Stephen and I headed to the back room to get changed out of the towelling robes which constituted biblical costumes. Thanks to my newly found shyness about getting changed, I headed to a small storeroom at the side, which contained spare Bibles and hymn books. As I opened the door, an acidic, foul smell hit my nose and I recoiled.

'Eurgh. Yuck!' I said, stepping back.

'What is it?' said Stephen, walking over to me. 'Oh, that's disgusting,' he said as soon as the smell caught his nostrils. We both held our noses and looked into the darkness. In the corner I could just make out a mound of clothes, which was where the smell seemed to be coming from. I pointed it out to Stephen, and as I did so the mound moved and we both took a step back.

At the sound of a muffled groan, my thoughts went straight to the Ripper and I gave a little gasp at the idea that we might have come across someone who had been attacked. But as the mound unfurled, I recognised the eyes now trying to focus on us, and the mouth with trails of vomit dripping from it.

'Oh, Mr Spencer,' I said. 'Er, are you poorly?'

Paul's words from yesterday were ringing in my ears. I couldn't quite bring myself to ask if he was drunk.

'I'll go and get Mrs Spencer,' Stephen said, backing away from the miserable sight in front of us. Mr Spencer looked like a man on the streets, not a man of the cloth. I probably should have tried to help him, but something kept me rooted to the floor as I watched him try to get up. Alongside the acrid smell of sick, there was a strong sweet smell that I recognised from Christmas and special occasions.

Mrs Spencer strode up to us, Uncle Raymond and Stephen not far behind her. She was so furious she looked almost purple in the half-light of the gloomy room.

'Good grief, Peter. What have you done? What will people say?' she hissed, looking down at her husband. She shooed Stephen and me to one side, and she and Uncle Raymond hauled Mr Spencer up. As Uncle Raymond put his arms around the vicar and they slowly made their way out of the back door, it looked as though this was something that had happened many times before, like a well-rehearsed dance. Uncle Raymond turned back just as they left the room and, seeing me watching, winked in a way that made me wince, though I had no idea why. Mrs Spencer turned to us. She took a deep breath and seemed to compose herself.

'My husband is unwell,' she said calmly. She looked almost regal, poised. Like the Queen.

'I would appreciate it very much if the two of you were not to mention this to anyone. I wouldn't want anyone else to worry.' Each word was delivered in staccato, like a soldier issuing a command. 'If anyone asks, you can say he was called to attend to a needy parishioner.'

'Yes, Mrs Spencer,' we both said, and I very nearly curtsied while swallowing the urge to point out that lying was supposed to be a sin. She smoothed her clothes and hair and shook her head, seemingly to shake off what had just occurred, and we followed her back into the main hall.

At the end of the concert, after we had taken our final bows, there was a swarm of parents as they went to collect and congratulate their children. I stood quietly to one side, hoping that Ruby would come and get me after she had finished hugging Sharon, when Hazel made her way over to me, the milling group seeming to part to let her through as though she were a Hollywood film star on the red carpet.

'Well done, you,' she said. 'You were a bit of a revelation.' I had no idea what she meant but my body hummed with pleasure and pride anyway.

'Thank you,' I said shyly.

Paul appeared at her shoulder.

'Yeah,' he said, 'you were dead good.' His words were quiet but clear, and my pride turned to astonishment at the compliment.

JENNIE GODFREY

'Would you like to come to ours for dinner one evening?' Hazel said.

I was confused by the question.

'She means tea,' said Paul, smiling.

'Oh. I . . . yes please, I can come whenever. I mean,
I can come any time,' I said, tripping over my words,
and I felt the heat of embarrassment rising through
my body.

'I'll talk to your dad, and we'll sort out a date then.'

I was too shocked to point out that there was no
need to talk to my dad, that I didn't need permission
to go anywhere, then I remembered that, thanks to the
Ripper, these days I did.

I hardly noticed the laughter and chatter of Dad,
Ruby and Sharon at Caddy's after he picked us up, but
there was no need for me to join in. Dad was on fine
form, making Sharon laugh while Ruby watched on,
smiling. My head was filled with the knowledge that
I was going round to Paul and Hazel's for tea, and I
replayed Paul's compliment about my performance over
and over again.

By the time we dropped Sharon and Ruby back at
home, the sky was darkening, and my head nodded on
my chest, worn out from the excitement of the day.
Dreams were beginning to descend when the sound
of sirens jerked me awake. Dad silently slowed the car
down as we passed the street that Mr Bashir's shop was
on, which seemed to be where the noise was coming
from. Flashing lights lit up the sky like fireworks, and

people were stood in the road, faces all turned in the same direction. Dad wound the window down, leaning out to ask someone what was going on, but the throat-catching smell of smoke made it clear, and he wound it back up again.

'Let's get you home,' he said.

33

Omar

Every Friday afternoon Omar shut the shop early and went to the cash and carry to stock up for the week ahead, Saturday being his busiest day. Ishtiaq usually joined him – ticking everything off the list of what was running low which Omar kept pinned behind the shop counter, next to the little exercise book in which he kept a running tally of who owed what – but today he'd insisted on staying at home. He claimed to have homework to do before school started again, but Omar knew he was hoping that Sharon might come round and call for him after the church concert.

Omar was aware that the point when he needed to talk to Ishtiaq about his budding relationship was getting closer. He worried that they were far too young, he worried that Sharon was far too white, he worried that Sharon's parents most likely didn't know, he worried that if anyone said anything disapproving to him about it, he might say something he would regret.

Yet the expression on his son's face melted his heart. When Rizwana had died, Ishtiaq had been of an age to really feel the empty space where his mother should be. Omar had watched his son's sadness with an aching heart, but he himself was unschooled and unfamiliar then with the expressions of love and affection that might give his son comfort, and so he'd just looked on, feeling powerless to help. Sharon had brought him out of the fog of grief, and whenever Omar heard them laughing together in the back room, his heart sang at the sound of life in his son's voice. Omar sighed and refocused on the task in front of him. Having been round and round this issue many times already in his head, he knew there was little point dwelling on it.

He nodded at the familiar faces as he pushed the large trolley around, picking up boxes of sweets and packs of washing powder, ticking off his customers' wants and needs on his list. He picked up the midget gems he knew Helen would buy for Arthur next time she was in, and the lime cordial that Valerie and her son Brian preferred. He could win whole quizzes about the likes and dislikes of everyone who came into his shop, even though many of them didn't even know his first name.

He was loading everything into the boot of the car when he heard the shout from the door of the cash and carry.

'Oi!'

He turned back to see what was going on and was surprised to see one of the store staff running towards him in the navy-blue uniform they all wore. He felt a flicker of anger ignite; he was a familiar enough face now not to be accused of shoplifting, surely? The young man stopped in front of him, bending slightly, his hands on his knees, panting.

'You. Need. To hurry,' he said. 'Someone rang here. Trying to find you. Police.'

Omar stared at him, trying to put the words into an order that made sense.

'Fire. There's a fire. The shop.'

Without saying a word, Omar slammed the boot, got in the car and drove off, leaving his half-full trolley abandoned in the car park. If he had been in any way aware, he would have been surprised at the deals he tried to make with Allah as he drove home, gripping the steering wheel so hard his hands and arms ached for days afterwards. The muscle memory of faith had kicked in.

He heard the fire before he saw it. Sirens echoed through the sky from streets away. He turned into their road and, faced with the crowds and emergency vehicles all watching as though it was Guy Fawkes Night, he abandoned the car in the street and ran forward. A tall man in a uniform stepped out from the throng, steered by a neighbour who was pointing at him. There was a formality to his bearing as he stood in front of Omar, whose face creased in anguish as he opened his mouth to ask the question that wouldn't come.

'Mr Bashir?' he said, to which Omar nodded, his eyes wildly searching the mass of people before him.

'Your boy is safe.'

With that, Omar's knees gave way, and he fell.

34

Miv

Number Nine

'I heard it was a bomb.'

'I heard their fridge blew up.'

'I heard it was a rag soaked in petrol shoved through the letterbox.'

The news of the fire swept the playground as fast as the flames had devoured Mr Bashir's shop. The petrol-soaked rag turned out to be true. Ishtiaq had escaped but had been taken to hospital suffering from smoke inhalation, then on to stay with family in Bradford once he'd been discharged.

Our whole class was unusually silent and sad, even Neil Callaghan, though Richard Collier had sniggered at the news and was sent to the headmaster. Later that morning I watched out of the clouded classroom window as Mr Collier came and took Richard home. I vaguely recognised him from parents' evenings and school plays as one of the dads who would sit there, arms folded, faces set like stone, showing how little they wanted to be there. He was a bulldog of a man.

For a moment I felt sorry for Richard, imagining the trouble he would be in, but then Richard's dad patted him on the back, so hard it made Richard stumble, and then he smiled at his son. I shuddered at the strangeness of the sight.

At home, Aunty Jean was in full bustle, furiously wiping down the fridge and kitchen at the same speed as her words tumbled out. Apparently, the whole town was ablaze with the news. 'It were deliberate,' she told us with a shaking head as though unable to comprehend it. 'The police have said it were arson.'

For days, two policemen made their way from house to house, questioning residents about the blackened shell where the shop had once stood. Sharon was a shell too. She was like a ghost of herself, her skin almost translucent and her eyes welling with tears at the smallest of things. I didn't comfort her. I didn't know what to say.

One breaktime I walked up to her while she was talking with two of the pretty girls and Neil Callaghan. They seemed intent on something, their heads close together as if sharing secrets, but suddenly Sharon took a step back. The closer I got to them, the more confused I felt. Since the fire Sharon had been consumed by sadness, but I could feel the simmering fury almost visibly flowing from her now in waves.

'Don't. You. Dare talk about him like that.'

She almost spat as she pronounced each word fully, with barely controlled rage. Neil took a step back too, laughingly putting his hands in front of him while one of the girls said, 'What's the matter, Sharon? Are you in love with a P—?'

I saw her body go rigid, and as she stepped forward, I pulled her away.

'What's going on?' I asked her.

I could see her swallowing, and as she tried to form the words, I noticed her hands were shaking violently.

'I should've told people,' she said. 'I should've been proud that he was my boyfriend.'

We walked to school a different way now, to avoid looking at the charred remains of the shop, until one day Aunty Jean sent me out on an errand, asking me to collect some Tupperware she'd lent to Mrs Weatherby from two streets over. Tupperware went up and down the streets of our town faster than the traffic. I was surprised anyone knew who the original owners were, but I agreed anyway.

My legs moved automatically, and without Sharon there to steer me away, I found myself at the bottom of Mr Bashir's street, staring at the cordoned-off shell of the shop and wondering who could have done this. My heart began hammering in my chest as I sensed another presence nearby. The man in the overalls was on the opposite corner, also staring, unmoving, at the site of the fire. I took a sharp breath in and held it as I watched him. His yellow hat was in his hand for once, revealing a shock of curly black hair I couldn't remember having seen before. He was unshaven, a dark moustache forming on his top lip, and his eyes looked dark and unblinking.

Images of him flashed up in my mind and clicked into place, like on the clunky carousel projector we had watched the French holiday slides on at Irene Blackburn's. Here he was, walking down the road, head down, never acknowledging us. Here he was, outside the shop, watching, only going in if no one else was around. Here he was, with Richard and Neil, when we were walking along the road with Arthur. I hadn't put him on the list yet for reasons that were not clear to me, but surely he was the most suspicious of all? He seemed to avoid human contact, and yet I now remembered all the times I had seen him hanging around the shop. What if there was a reason for that?

On the way home, I thought about all the things I knew about him. I knew that he lived with his mum, Valerie Lockwood, on a narrow-terraced street called Thorncliffe Road and that his name was Brian – though I still called him 'the man in the overalls' in my head. I'd once heard Aunty Jean say to Dad that she felt sorry for the two of them, but I wasn't sure why.

There was something unsettling about his lack of eye contact and shuffling walk, and I wondered if this might mean he had a criminal past. Did he have something to hide? I realised then that he needed to be the next subject of investigation, especially now that the fire had happened.

It was less easy to convince Sharon of this.

'Are we still doing that?' she asked. 'Given everything that's happened? I thought we were done.'

It was a cold grey Saturday, and we were on our way into town. Since half-term we had started to hang around the High Street, like the older girls did, and Sharon wanted to go to Boots to look at lipsticks. I pulled the hood of my anorak up and zipped it to the top as the wind whipped up the few spots of rain into hard pellets that stung the skin as they landed.

'The Ripper's not been caught yet. He's still out there,' I said, but as I finished, I could sense her exasperation.

'That's as maybe, but we're no closer to finding him than we were when we started,' she said. 'And, well, I'm not sure it's good for you. I mean us. It's not good for either of us.'

The words stung like the rain, and we walked along in silence for a few steps while I swallowed down the tears that threatened to show themselves. I didn't know how to bring up what I suspected about the man in the overalls. The topic of the fire was so upsetting, we tried not to speak about it. I took a deep breath.

'And then there's the fire,' I said.

Sharon stopped and turned towards me. With her hood up, hiding her carefully styled hair, and her face free of make-up, she looked more like the girl I used to know.

'What about the fire?' she said. 'Do you think he had something to do with it?'

I nodded slowly, carefully weighing up my words,

knowing how much it would upset her but at the same time wanting her to know what I suspected.

'Think about it,' I said. 'Whenever we see him, it's always around the shop. And remember we saw him with Richard that day, when he was saying mean things about you and Ish.' I paused, to let these facts sink in. 'And I've seen him too. Twice. Once when I saw you and Ish together, and he was watching me, and once the other day when I went past the shop, after the fire I mean, and he were just staring at it.'

I stopped then, panting slightly. The words had rushed out of me in a torrent.

'OK.'

She said it so quietly, I almost didn't hear it.

9. The Man in the Overalls

- He never makes eye contact
- He's weird
- He looks dirty and smelly
- He has no friends (apart from Neil and Richard, who are not very nice)
- He's always watching the shop

35

Miv

After church the next day we took a bucket from the garage at Sharon's and made our way to Thorncliffe Road. I'd thought up a story about raising money for the church and decided to offer up our services to complete odd jobs for people, giving us the perfect excuse to knock on the Lockwoods' door.

Sharon trailed behind me, sighing. I knew she was having second thoughts about the whole enterprise. Eventually I stopped us both. 'Look. Leave the talking to me. I've planned everything I'm going to say and it's going to be fine. You just need to smile and look innocent.' I had decided that I was going to show Sharon that I could use my voice too. We knocked on the door of number 75 and stood there, our hearts thumping.

'What do you two rapscallions want?'

Valerie, wearing a densely patterned housecoat, opened the door, looked down at us and smiled. I felt Sharon shrink back as I explained that we were doing a special bob-a-job for the church.

'We don't mind what we do,' I said, trying to look

around her to see if I could spot Brian. I couldn't. 'We'll do anything you want, cooking, cleaning, tidying—'

'Aye, well, I'm on nights this week,' she interrupted, indicating her housecoat. 'And I need me sleep, so can you come back on Friday? You can do some dusting for me.'

I jumped at the offer. Dusting meant we'd be in the house and could conduct a search if need be. All my enthusiasm for the list had returned, even if Sharon's hadn't.

On the way home, I decided to ask Aunty Jean why she felt sorry for Valerie and Brian, curious to know what it was about the two that aroused her sympathy, an emotion not usually evident in her. As soon as I opened the door, however, I could sense the discord in the house. Even the air seemed to be on edge. I crept slowly in.

The television was on low, and I peered into the living room to see Mum staring at it, her eyes blank and unseeing. Then I realised that the back door was open, and Dad and Aunty Jean were in the garden, arguing in hissed, quiet voices. I froze. Conflict in our house was normally of the unspoken kind. I tried to tune into the voices, listening for my name. Aunty Jean was on the attack, her whispers packed with anger. Dad's voice was quieter, more defensive, and when I stepped closer to the kitchen and the open back door I heard him say, 'You don't understand how hard it's been.'

'I don't understand how hard it's been?' Aunty Jean's

tone was incredulous, and I moved back as her voice grew more distinct and she walked into the house. 'It's been hard for us all, brother, but what you are doing is wrong. It has to stop.' She began emptying the draining board of washed pans and cutlery, slamming them into their places with a clang. 'Maybe it's time I left you to it.'

I had forgotten that Aunty Jean had ever lived anywhere but our house; that she had rented a small, one-roomed council flat, in one of the grey concrete-box structures on the outskirts of town. In fact, I was surprised to realise that I knew very little about Aunty Jean's life outside of the role she played in our family. Had she ever been in love? Wanted a family of her own? More of a shock to me was the revelation that I didn't want her to go anywhere. Somewhere along the line, Aunty Jean had become the glue that held us together. I crept slowly upstairs, shutting my bedroom door on the feelings, and turning instead to my notebook and the list. It was easier to focus on that. Hunting a killer was simpler to deal with.

After school on Friday, Sharon and I headed off to the Lockwoods' house.

'This is the last time,' said Sharon. 'I mean it.'

And I knew she did. This was my last chance to prove I was right.

This time the door was answered by a different woman, just as large, with tight dark curls set in place, hard as concrete.

'Valerie, you've got visitors,' she shouted, looking back inside the house. 'Come on in, young ladies,' she said, and we wiped our feet on the mat and stepped into the hallway.

The house was an almost exact replica of ours, with a living room, front room and kitchen downstairs and two bedrooms and a bathroom upstairs, the only difference being that, like some of the houses on our street, there was an outside toilet.

The inside of the house was a combination of faded swirls and patterns on wallpaper and carpets, and kitchen appliances and furniture which had seen better days – though they were scrupulously clean, which surprised me, given Brian's generally dishevelled appearance.

In the front room, a large carriage clock was centre stage on the sideboard, ticking loudly. The rest of the room was covered with a proliferation of crochet: there were doilies on shelves and tables, and blankets of sewn-together crochet squares over threadbare chairs. Clearly Valerie loved doilies as much as Doreen, Arthur's wife, had. I couldn't see the attraction. They seemed to me to serve no useful purpose, and Aunty Jean said they were for people with ideas about themselves. She wasn't keen on anything that was purely decorative. The room looked unused, as though all activity took place in the kitchen and living room. Just like at our house, before Aunty Jean had moved in.

This was where Valerie wanted us to dust, while she

and three of her friends drank tea in the next room. I was beside myself. While there was no sign of the man in the overalls, we were perfectly placed to eavesdrop and I looked at Sharon and smiled. She grimaced back – still not comfortable with the situation, but she was there, and I was grateful for that.

We began our work. Picking up ornaments and cleaning them with yellow dusters and Mr Sheen. I tried to tune into the conversation next door, punctuated as it was by drags on cigarettes and howls of laughter. There was talk of work – all of them worked at the local biscuit factory, the main industry in the area – followed by the comparison of various ailments and remedies, the mysteries of women's bodies making me squirm and blush.

We struck gold when the conversation moved on to families and Valerie said, 'I'm worried about our Brian. He's not himself and I just can't get through to him.'

We both froze, listening carefully.

'He's never been a talker, but it's like living with a bloody ghost. He never says a word. He just floats in and out, then has his tea, then bed. I don't even know where he goes when he goes out any more. I mean, he can't get any work, and the only other place he used to go on his own was the corner shop.'

'Do you think it's that that's upset him? What happened to the shop, I mean. You know he likes his routine,' said a voice I didn't recognise.

'Aye, you might be right,' said Valerie.

I let out the breath I'd been holding while she talked, and nodded at Sharon, who shook her head at me.

'Are you still going to get the bus home after nights?' I heard the lady who answered the door ask.

'I'm going to carry on as normal,' said another of the group. 'I'm not letting them win.'

'Them?' said Valerie.

'Aye,' the voice carried on. 'Men. It should be bloody men who shouldn't be out after dark, not women. We're not the bloody murderers.'

'You'll be burning your bra before we know it,' said the first woman, to gales of laughter.

'Our Brian is going to meet me at the bus stop until they catch the bastard,' Valerie said. It was followed by lots of shushing and I visualised them pointing to us in the next room.

'Our Jeff isn't letting me go out on me own any more – it's quite sweet,' said the first woman. 'Mind you – he's probably just worried. If t'Ripper catches me, he'll have no one to cook his tea.'

Loud cackles accompanied this declaration and the subject changed to the familiar grumbles of long-married women. But I had noticed that the laughter had had an edge to it. It sounded forced and tinged with an anxiety I didn't expect from such formidable women. I thought about Aunty Jean in her little flat again. How would she feel if she moved back there? Would she be scared too?

We drew out the dusting and tidying as long as we could, but eventually we ran out of things to clean and went through to Valerie to be paid.

'Is there owt else we can do, Mrs Lockwood?'

'I tell you what,' she said. 'Our Brian might want his shed cleaning. Why don't I ask him when he gets home, and if you pop back tomorrow, I can let you know.'

I was almost shaking with excitement.

'That would be dead good, Mrs Lockwood. Shall we go out back now and have a look at it? See how long it might take?'

She led us out the back into the postage-stamp-sized garden, which was almost entirely taken up with the outside toilet and a similar-sized rickety shed. I looked around. What grass there was, was weedless and neat and unexpectedly cared for. The door of the shed creaked loudly as Valerie opened it, and I gripped hold of Sharon's hand and held it tightly. We peered into the darkness, inhaling the musty smell that I realised imme-diately had a chemical tang to it. 'Is that petrol?' I asked, widening my eyes at Sharon for emphasis.

'Oh aye, our Brian keeps a can just in case,' Valerie said, and pointed to a small green container in the corner. I stepped into the shed, looking around as though sizing up the job ahead of us, though all the tools seemed clean and tidy. As soon as Valerie turned to go back into the house, I picked up an item I had

THE LIST OF SUSPICIOUS THINGS

spotted lying next to the petrol container and followed
her and Sharon.

'So Brian's "not himself" lately,' I said, as we headed
home. 'I wonder why.'

'It could be because he's not in work,' Sharon said.
'Think about your dad and what happened to him.'

I thought about it. Before working at the delivery
depot, Dad had been a steelworker and had lost his job.
It took almost a year for him to find another, and
although I was only little then, I could still remember
the grey mashed potato and whatever cheap cuts of
meat Mum could scavenge off the butcher that we had
daily for our tea. Dad had snapped at every question
or request and would sometimes slam the door as he
left for frequent long walks. I walked on the same egg-
shells I walked on now, just around a different parent.

'Don't you think he's suspicious any more?' I asked.

We were at the point where we usually parted, Sharon
going off to her house, me to mine. She stopped and
looked down silently for a few moments.

'I'm not sure I ever did,' she said. 'I don't know
if any of the people we know are suspicious or
whether they're just trying to live their lives. Maybe we
should let the police find out who set the fire. See you
tomorrow.'

I felt as though she had slapped me, and watched her
walk off, stunned. As she turned out of sight I reached

into my pocket and pulled out the item I'd taken from the shed. I sniffed it and recoiled. It was an old, discarded T-shirt, covered in oil and dirt and clearly used as a rag. The smell of petrol on it was overwhelming. I toyed with the idea of calling Sharon back, but decided I would show her I'd listened instead. Rather than going home, I walked into town and went to the police station.

I stood outside for a few minutes, looking at the urban block of a building. I had seen it on television in the background of some of the local Ripper reports, where it seemed formal and imposing. In real life it was dirty and bleak. It took a while, but eventually I summoned up the courage to go in and approach the desk.

Inside, the building reminded me of school. The walls and furniture were bland and functional; no one cared what it looked like. It was busy, with men in uniform going in and out, and people sat waiting on plastic chairs. No one looked at me.

'I want to speak to DS Lister, please.'

The desk sergeant looked down at me and smirked.

'And what might you want to speak to DS Lister for?' he asked.

'It's important,' I insisted. 'I know him already.'

'What could a young lady like you have to say that's so important?'

Still smirking, he disappeared into a back room and I felt my cheeks burn. I wondered if this was how the police usually treated important information, or if it depended on who was bringing it. I sat on one of the plastic chairs and waited, until a few minutes later DS Lister appeared.

'Come through,' he said, beckoning me over. His expression was grim, and he appeared tired, dark circles under his eyes and his face unshaven. Before I even sat down in the small stuffy room he led me to, I started to tell him about Brian – from how strange he was, to how I had seen him staring at the shop after the fire, to the petrol can in the shed. The story fell out of me in a jumble of words, and I finished by handing over the rag.

'This is evidence,' I said, my voice suddenly strong and clear, if slightly breathless from racing through the story. To his credit, DS Lister didn't laugh at me like the desk sergeant had. Instead, he stared at the rag, then at me, then explained that he wasn't working on the case but that he would pass the information on.

'You did the right thing,' he said, 'coming to tell me.' He smiled at me briefly, and any fear and hesitancy I had felt about coming there fell away, replaced by relief and adrenaline.

As I left to go home, I spotted a familiar lanky figure leaning against the wall outside, scuffing his trainers on the pavement. It was Paul. He looked up, his face as closed as it had been the first time I met him. A hint of pink flushed across his cheeks at the sight of me, and I fleetingly wondered why.

'Hiya,' he said. 'What you doing here?'

Suddenly shy, I shrugged.

'A school thing,' I muttered. 'And anyway, what you doing here?'

'Oh,' he said, the shutters coming down once more. 'I'm waiting for me mum's boyfriend to give me a lift home,' and he went back to kicking the kerb. All at once I knew exactly where I had seen DS Lister before. He was the man who had been holding hands with Hazel Ware the day we saw her in the market from Arthur's cart.

The next afternoon I headed back to Thorncliffe Road alone. I knew Sharon hadn't wanted to return and I was also concerned that if we tidied the shed, we might be destroying evidence, but in the end it didn't matter.

'Hello, love.'

Valerie answered the door, but her undone hair and flattened tone told me immediately that something was wrong. She looked down at me, then around at the street.

'Are you all right, Mrs Lockwood?' I asked, concerned.

'Our Brian didn't come home yesterday and I'm just right worried,' she said, her voice almost a murmur as she continued scanning the road.

'Is there anything I can do? Can I help you look for him?' I said, my voice taut. Valerie looked at me properly then.

'Bless you. There're people searching, so don't you fret. It's not the first time he's gone walkabout,' she said. 'You can come back when he's home and do the shed then.'

I said goodbye and walked back down the street, humming loudly to myself to stop the thoughts that this might have something to do with my visit to the police. Maybe he had run away because he was the Ripper. Maybe it was because he was unhappy, like Valerie's friend had said. Maybe he hadn't disappeared at all, but had just gone 'walkabout', as Valerie mentioned.

I didn't know it then, but Brian would never go back to 75 Thorncliffe Road.

36

Helen

It wasn't just the inconvenience of having to trudge into town to buy the smallest of things, Helen realised, as she pulled her headscarf tighter and held her mac at the collar to keep the wind out; it was that she missed the comfort of Omar's quiet concern and care. After the bruises had faded the last time, and she'd gone back to the shop, he'd given her some food stored in Tupperware for her dad, who'd developed a taste for the rich spicy meals Omar made.

'And for you,' he'd added.

She'd nodded but known she couldn't try any in case Gary noticed the taste on her lips when he kissed her. With a sickening swallow, she realised that Omar was more than just a comforting presence in her life. He was one of the few people she could be herself with. He had a way of asking questions about *her*, her likes and dislikes, hopes and dreams, and left space for her to talk. She was also sure that somehow he knew her secret. She wondered how she might find out how to get in contact with him, to maybe send a card or something. Maybe the two girls might know: they were friends with his son. She would ask the next time they came in.

The one positive to the situation was it meant that she could be out for longer. The walk to and from town to go to the supermarket took a while. If she went before Gary got home from work, like today, she could avoid his offer of a lift, which he would make in a tone of voice that suggested it would be at great cost and sacrifice to himself. Although it was a Friday evening anyway, meaning he would be both late and too drunk to drive by the time he got home.

She felt the familiar catch in her throat and turned her attention to her surroundings, wanting to chase all thoughts of him from her mind and fill it instead with the sights around her. She found great solace in doing so. There weren't many bright colours in the street where they lived, in a flat they rented from a landlord they had never met, but as she walked, she noticed the textures of the houses: the dark brown, worn stone that spoke of lives lived. She could work out, from the state of the windows and doors of each one, which houses were loved and which were uncared for.

She was deep in thought when she noticed the buzz in the air. The sound of women talking, exclaiming over something in hushed tones that meant whatever had happened was serious. Another Ripper attack? she wondered.

She thought sharply of Omar and his son. Maybe it was to do with them? Had something else happened?

She usually avoided gossip, knowing that she could so easily become the focus of these women's attention if she wasn't careful. But today she had to know. She steeled herself, patting her headscarf, and walked up to the small group gathered on the front step of the house nearby, reckoning that she would know at least one of them – that was how it worked in towns as small as this one.

'Helen,' said Marjorie Pearson, nodding her head in Helen's direction. The rest of the women parted slightly and turned to look at her.

'How do?' she said.

'It's a terrible business,' Marjorie clucked, as though Helen had been there for the whole conversation.

'Aye, it is,' she replied, while the rest of the group murmured their agreement and nodded in a seemingly synchronised wave. Helen found herself looking around at the women, catching each of their eyes, and nodding too.

'Do they know why he did it?' said one of the women, someone who Helen didn't recognise but who wore the same brown, buttoned-up uniform of the rest of the biscuit-factory workers.

'Well, he was never right in the head, was he?' Marjorie said, an authority to her voice which made it clear she was the leader they all deferred to. More nods.

'It's Valerie I feel sorry for,' she carried on. 'It's not right, a child going before the parent. And you know what they say . . .' She lowered her voice to a whisper. 'Suicide. It's the coward's way out.'

'I'm sorry,' Helen said, 'can you say that again?'

'You heard me right,' Marjorie said. 'Brian's done away with himself. He were found t'day before yesterday apparently. Hung himself in the woods.'

37

Miv

I found out about Brian's suicide from Dad. Before the following Saturday was out, everyone knew. The warning signs that something was wrong were there when Aunty Jean sent me to my bedroom, saying that Mum was feeling poorly, and she even distractedly ruffled my hair, so I realised it was something serious.

I knew what suicide was. It was the word that I had overheard muttered many times to describe what Mum had tried to do the day I found her on the floor.

When Dad came upstairs to tell me, he looked worn out and beaten. He kept glancing up at the ceiling, as if to find guidance from somewhere else, as he explained what had happened to Brian. It felt as though everything I had to say had curled itself into a ball, now lodged in my throat.

'Why would he do that?' I eventually whispered, sickened, and unable to stop thinking about my visit to the police the previous weekend.

'Sometimes grown-ups feel a lot of pain, and they think the way to cure it is to hurt themselves,' he said. He paused, seeming to weigh up the wisdom of saying the words that came next. 'Your mum once thought that too – you remember – the day you found her? It's why she is so upset. She knows about Brian.'

Panic rising, I swallowed it down before it consumed me. That was a moment I tried hard not to think about. A day I didn't want to remember. But I didn't want to think about Brian either. I tried desperately to convince myself that maybe his death had nothing to do with me.

Maybe he was even the Ripper.

After Dad had left, with a peck on my forehead, something he hadn't done for a while, I tried to think about something, anything else, but each time I managed to distract myself something yellow would catch my eye and the vision of Brian, hanging, his old woolly hat on his head, would appear in my mind. The image made me catch my breath and I'd blink hard, trying to clear it away.

Later, Aunty Jean packed a bag and wrapped Mum in a blanket, and I watched from my bedroom window as Dad carried her out to the car. She looked like a small child in his arms. This time there was no talk of it being a 'break'. We all knew she was going to hospital. After they'd gone, Aunty Jean called me downstairs. She made chip butties for tea and we sat in front of the telly to eat them, which was unheard of in our house. I resisted pointing out that according to her this was *letting our standards slip*.

When she came and kissed me goodnight in my

bedroom, I couldn't stop the tears. It should have been a cherished moment, but I didn't feel I deserved it.

I knew I had to tell Sharon what I'd done and walked slowly to hers the next morning before church, going over and over the conversation with DS Lister and wondering whether it had had anything to do with Brian's actions. She opened the door on my arrival, her eyes red and swollen, and walked straight upstairs to her room before I'd even had chance to say hello.

I followed her up to her room and sat down on the bed, playing with the corner of the red chequered bed-spread while she sat at her dressing table and looked at me. Her expression was hard to read. I took a deep breath.

'I need to talk to you,' I said. 'It's about Brian.'

'I know about him,' she said, her voice flatter than I'd ever heard it.

My hands began to shake.

'It's not just that,' I said. I knew my voice was too loud, that my words were coming out too quickly, but I also knew I couldn't keep this from her. If I did and she found out, our friendship would be over if it wasn't anyway. I felt physically sick, like the ground was moving underneath me. *What had I done?*

'I went to the police. About Brian and the fire.'

I waited for the realisation to take place and I watched as her face crumpled like a piece of paper in my hands.

'Do you mean they might have gone to see him? And then he . . . ?'

I nodded, closing my eyes as if doing so might shut out the consequences.

When I opened them, she was pale and her expression was blank again. For a moment she reminded me of Mum.

'But . . . he might've been the one to set the fire,' I said, not sure who I was trying to persuade. I had been *so* convinced of this when I went to see DS Lister last Saturday, but I could no longer hold on to that feeling. Sharon shook her head slowly, with a look of sorrow – whether at Brian and his fate or my pitiful attempts at trying to justify myself, I didn't know.

'I think you need to go,' she said, her voice sounding like that of a stranger.

So I left.

That night when Dad appeared at my door, he took one look at my face and before I knew it his arms were around me.

'Shhh,' he said, while I cried. 'It's all going to be all right.'

But he didn't know what I'd done. And that things would never be OK again.

I rose earlier than usual on Monday morning, groggy and nauseous from lack of sleep. I went to call for Sharon before school. Normally, I never had to ring the bell as she would be downstairs with the door open before I made it up the path.

Not that day.

Ruby answered the door.

'Sharon's not going to school today,' she said. 'She's not well.'

I called for her every day that week. Sometimes I saw the curtain upstairs move when I rang the doorbell, sometimes Ruby answered and said she still wasn't well, sometimes there was no answer at all.

All I knew was that I had lost Sharon and I didn't know how to find her.

38

Miv

Number Ten

The day that Sharon returned to school I had gone to
call for her as usual. The weather was bitterly cold, and
it was still so dark it felt like it was the middle of the
night. I was more unsure of my way to hers, as though
the landscape had changed, and I wished I had brought
my torch, as much for comfort as for light. Aunty Jean
had made me porridge that morning and had told me
to put a bobble hat on before I left.

'To keep the heat in,' she said.

But all I could think about was Brian in his bright
yellow bobble hat, and hot tears streaked my face
as I walked round to Sharon's, determined to talk to
her whether she was ill or not. She was waiting for
me when I arrived, and when she handed me a tissue
so I could wipe my eyes, I blew my nose on it loudly.
She looked like she hadn't eaten during the week she'd
been off, her usual soft lines hardened into angles
more like mine. She wasn't wearing make-up and the
collar of her school blouse looked too big for her neck,

but I didn't know how to ask her about it. It felt as if our friendship was teetering on the edge of something, like a rollercoaster that had slowly climbed to the top, and I didn't want to be the one to send it hurtling down the other side. Sharon was the one to begin.

'I want to talk to you about the list,' she said, her voice unexpectedly firm, her eyes staring straight ahead as we made our way to school.

I stayed silent.

'I know how much it matters to you, and I know you want to catch him, but . . .'

'It's all right,' I said, not wanting to hear the next bit.

'I'm not going to do it any more,' she said anyway.

I nodded.

'It's not right,' she continued, 'what we've been doing. Messing with people's lives.'

She stopped for a moment and turned to face me.

'A man died,' she said, 'and we'll never know the part we played in that.'

I closed my eyes, feeling the words jab hard at every part of my body.

She started to walk again, and I ran to catch up.

'And Ishtiaq's moved back. I want to spend time with him, with people who are real, not the Ripper. I mean, I know he is real, but he's not . . . oh, I don't know what I mean.'

I started at the news that Ishtiaq was back, momentarily warmed by the thought of him, and Mr Bashir.

'It doesn't mean things will have to change.' Sharon's voice had speeded up. 'We'll still hang out all the time and . . .'

'But it does.' I forced the words out. 'It does change things. What if you don't want to be my friend any more? I feel . . . I feel . . .'

I wanted to tell her how awful I felt about Brian. About how I couldn't sleep. About how I felt like a terrible person and only her friendship would convince me that I wasn't. But I couldn't stop the tears, so I let them come. Sharon reached for my hand and squeezed it tightly.

'You are the cleverest, funniest and most loyal person I know. We will always be friends,' she said. 'Always. But you've got to stop this, this . . . *obsession.*'

I nodded and thought about the list for the rest of the way to school in silence. Was Sharon right? Images of Brian kept coming to me, no matter how hard I batted them away. It was like swatting flies. Each time I thought of him – stood outside the shop, hanging around with Neil and Richard, stroking Mungo's nose – I would remind myself that he might've been responsible for the fire, or even be the Ripper, and that his death might have nothing to do with me at all.

But the thoughts kept coming anyway.

Ishtiaq was waiting for us in the playground, and Sharon held his hand as they walked down the corridor to class. Our classmates parted, clearing space for them to walk through, like some biblical scene. I trailed behind them and ignored the sideways glances and comments aimed in their direction.

Richard and Neil, both leaning against the classroom door as we entered, quietly muttered what I assumed to be threats against Ishtiaq and insults at Sharon, judging by their expressions, which were full of hate. They were less easy to ignore. It had felt for some time as though something further had shifted in them, that somewhere along the line they had curdled, like gone-off milk. I remembered an article I had read that said the Ripper's behaviour was 'escalating'. It felt like these boys were escalating too. Into what, however, I just didn't know.

Later that week I was leaving choir practice when I saw one of the younger members, Alison, a quiet slip of a girl with blue sparkly eyes and freckles, standing alone in the church car park, crying. I liked Alison. Her shyness and intense expression reminded me of my own.

'What's up?' I asked.

'I don't like him tickling me,' she sniffled. I looked around. There was no one else there.

'Who you on about?'

'That man,' she said. 'Uncle Raymond. When he gives out the orange cordial. I don't like it. He's always doing it and I always tell him I don't like it, but he does it anyway.'

'Why don't you like it? He's only playing,' I attempted to reassure her.

'I don't want him to touch me,' she said, and I took a

step back, momentarily wrong-footed by her fury. She began to wave at a car which had turned into the car park, and I watched her run and get in, her mum kissing her on the cheek as she climbed into the back seat.

At our next practice we started to rehearse our Christmas concert, which was only a few weeks away. We were practising a medley of carols, and I was hoping that I might persuade Dad to come and maybe even Aunty Jean, as I was to sing a solo rendition of 'Silent Night'. Uncle Raymond was there with his camera, taking photographs for the church newsletter, and I was at the front and in the middle of the shot due to my starring role. Once the photographs had been taken, Uncle Raymond said, 'Well done, everyone. Take a bow.'

Instead of bowing, I did an awkward curtsy, accidentally putting too much weight on my left foot so that my hip cocked. Embarrassed, I looked around to make sure no one had noticed, but the rest of the choir were laughing and bowing, completely oblivious. Uncle Raymond, however, licked his lips and gave me a strange smile that made me stop and stand up straight again immediately, heat rising to my face.

He was looking at me in a way that no one else did.

This took place in a matter of seconds before he was back to being jolly Uncle Raymond, and only then did I really register the turmoil in my stomach. I knew at once that this was why Alison didn't want him to touch her.

I thought of all the things Sharon had said about the list.

I thought about Chapeltown.

I thought about the Bashirs and the fire.

I thought about Brian.

I thought about Mum.

I knew I couldn't fix what had happened to any of them.

But I might be able to fix this.

So I went ahead and put Uncle Raymond on the list.

10. Uncle Raymond from Church

- The tickling
- He isn't anyone's uncle
- The papers said the Ripper might be hiding in plain sight
- Something about him doesn't feel right

39

Miv

As I started to watch Uncle Raymond, I was surprised at how much can happen under people's noses without them noticing. According to the *Yorkshire Chronicle*, the failure of the police to identify any credible suspects had to mean the Ripper was 'hiding in plain sight'. I hadn't understood what that meant. Now I did.

Uncle Raymond had three or four favourites in the choir. Alison was one, and at nine years old she was the youngest. He would add more sugary cordial to their drinks and hand them out first when we queued at the table at the close of practice. He would ruffle their hair, chuck their chins and play tickling 'games' with them. When we were singing, he would catch their eyes and wink. They in turn squirmed in his presence, fleeing when it became too much.

Watching him made me physically uncomfortable too, but the meaning of his actions remained just outside my reach.

One night after practice I sat on the wall outside the church and wrote down what I had seen in the notebook, avoiding looking at pages past and any reminders of where the list had taken us – particularly of Brian. When I looked up, Paul Ware was stood in front of me, his expression curious. 'What you up to?' he asked, as I closed my notebook and we set off to walk home.

We occasionally walked a little way together, engaging in a tentative friendship that was so fragile I hardly dared look at it in case it fell apart. He had started to wear glasses, the thick black frames making him look studious and even cooler. The mix was intoxicating.

'What do you think about Uncle Raymond?' I asked.

He was quiet for a moment.

'It depends on what you mean,' he said finally. 'If you mean, is there something off with him, then yes. Definitely.'

I nodded, pleased he could sense it too.

'Be careful around him, won't you?' He kept his eyes straight ahead as he said this, and I was glad of it. It meant he couldn't see my deep-pink blush.

'Why do you say that?'

'I just . . . I don't know.'

I had to stop myself from smiling as it popped into my mind that Paul was like Julian from the Famous Five – sensible and mature. 'Don't worry,' I said, revelling in the momentary thought that someone cared about me. But then I thought again about Uncle Raymond. The trouble was that all these suspicions were just feelings. We both knew there was something not right about Uncle Raymond and his interest in the girls in the choir, but we had no way of voicing that, even to ourselves.

Later that night after tea, I asked Dad and Aunty Jean about him. It was a way of getting more information, but also of breaking the atmosphere between them, which had felt as frosty as the winter streets since the argument I had overheard a few weeks back. For once, Mum's absence seemed to make the tension worse, rather than dispelling it.

'You know Uncle Raymond at church?' I started.

'You mean Raymond with the glasses? Married to Sylvia?' said Aunty Jean, followed by a sniff that communicated her disapproval. I found it interesting that such an upright, God-fearing man should deserve one of Aunty Jean's sniffs and felt brave enough to continue.

'Aye. Do you think he's funny?'

'Funny ha-ha or funny strange?' she asked, placing her mug of tea on the table and looking at me with narrowed eyes.

'Funny strange,' I said.

'In what way?' said Dad. 'We're going to need a bit more to go on than that.'

They were both staring at me now.

'Well. He tickles the girls at choir, and he makes me feel weird.'

'Tickling? That's it?' said Aunty Jean, breaking the

spell by getting up from the table and beginning to clear it. 'There're worse sins than that.'

Dad looked at me, smiling. 'You're a funny bairn,' he said, and Aunty Jean shook her head and rolled her eyes.

When I left the table shortly afterwards, I heard Aunty Jean say, 'I mean, she's not wrong that he's a funny one. I'd always thought he was destined to be a confirmed bachelor before he married poor Sylvia.'

I could imagine her eyebrows waggling with the words *confirmed bachelor*.

Dad snorted with laughter.

I smiled briefly as I headed upstairs. It seemed my question had at least led to a truce between the two of them.

The following weekend, Sharon and Ishtiaq invited me to spend the day with them, but I said no and instead decided to trail Uncle Raymond. I sensed their relief and it hurt more than if they'd not asked.

I knew there was a park opposite where Uncle Raymond lived, and while girls who were nearly thirteen mainly hung around bus shelters and shops, I hoped I wouldn't be too out of place on the swings and roundabouts that would allow me to keep an eye on his movements. The house Uncle Raymond and Aunty Sylvia lived in was a grey, boxy, 1950s bungalow that had all the neatness of Valerie Lockwood's and none of the heart. I made sure it was in sight as I climbed onto a swing, wishing I had worn gloves as my hands practically froze to the grey metal chains either side of the battered blue plastic seat.

I kept my eyes so closely on Uncle Raymond's door that I almost missed two familiar figures making their way down the street. Mr Andrews was ahead, walking purposefully, his mouth set in a hard line. Mrs Andrews trailed behind, loaded with carrier bags full of shopping, her eyes on the pavement.

I watched as Mr Andrews opened the door of a large, dilapidated-looking house and stepped inside, the door shutting in Mrs Andrews' face. She placed the carrier bags on the ground, presumably to free her hands to look for a key, and as she did so she looked around her, as though assessing whether anyone had seen what had happened. She didn't see me, and I wanted to shout, 'I'm here! I see you!' But something told me she didn't want to be seen, so I didn't.

On an equally battered metal roundabout on the other side of the park, two younger girls appeared. I knew them vaguely. After a little while they nodded at me, their chapped faces glowing in the cold. I nodded back.

'What you doing here? You don't live round here,' one said.

I thought for a moment and decided to let a little of the truth out.

'I'm watching for him over there,' I said, indicating Uncle Raymond's house.

'Why? He's a perv!'

'What d'ya mean?'

One of the girls stuck out her tongue and wrapped her arms around herself.

'He wants to snog little giiirrrrls.'

'How do you know?'

The other girl looked at me straight in the eyes. 'Everyone knows! And he tried it on me, and I kicked 'im in t'goolies.'

I held my breath. I was right. And I had a real live witness.

'Did you tell anyone?' I asked.

'Why? He didn't get to do it, and he'll never come near us again,' said the same girl and they both exploded into laughter, bending over in pretend agony, presumably an impression of Raymond post-kick.

Eventually the girls wandered off and I was just debating whether I could bear to stay any longer, my hands turning blue, when the glossy white door to the house opened and Uncle Raymond stepped out, wearing a uniform and heading in the direction of the bus station. I jumped into action and followed him, just far enough away that I could still see him, wishing Sharon was with me.

The crowded bus station made it more challenging to keep an eye on Uncle Raymond, but his hat, uniform and distinctive glasses helped, and when he finally got on a bus, I joined the queue. He chatted away to everyone who got on, sometimes getting out of his seat to help old ladies with their bags and chucking the chins of children with their mums watching on indulgently.

Finally I got on.

'I don't know if I've got enough for me ticket,' I said, and saw the same lazy smile start to spread across Uncle Raymond's face as when he'd taken my picture.

'Well, who's a silly little girl then,' he said. 'How much have you got?' His eyes didn't leave mine. I emptied out my purse and smiled back at him, my insides turning violently under his lingering gaze. I had to steady my palm to stop it shaking with fear.

'Ooooh, you've just enough,' Uncle Raymond said, taking the money and slowly stroking my hand as he withdrew it. 'Or else I would've had to ask you to come back with the rest another day.'

He winked at me, and I almost turned and ran, but instead found a seat near the front, all the while watching Uncle Raymond leering at me through the mirror. I got off again at the next stop and ran for sure this time, stopping only to be sick in the bushes.

40

Omar

He hadn't intended to move back. He'd decided they would stay in Bradford and give up on this failed experiment at a new start. He could have easily worked for Rizwana's brother at his place. But Ishtiaq's sadness had become unbearable. In the end, Ishtiaq had sat him down and told him that they needed to move back, his face solemn as he explained his reasons in logical order, all relating to school and his education. Of course Omar knew the real reason he wanted to return and would have laughed if he hadn't seen the pain behind his boy's eyes as he tried to persuade him.

Finding somewhere for them to live, if only temporarily, had been the usual challenge: offers of viewings were cancelled as soon as he gave his name, something he'd forgotten about when they'd been settled in the shop for a while. However, he'd been lucky to find that a family connection a few times removed owned a flat in the town that he was able to rent until they found somewhere more permanent. He also needed time to think about whether he had the heart to try another shop. There was more than a small part of him that wanted to do so in defiance, showing everyone that they weren't going anywhere.

As soon as they were back, he went to pay his respects to Valerie Lockwood. He'd been deeply affected when he heard about Brian's suicide, the news going straight to the place where he held the loss of Rizwana. He'd felt it as hard as a punch to his guts.

He'd expected Valerie to have changed, knowing how grief had aged him, but was shocked at her appearance, nonetheless. All her previous solidity and vigour had left her, and she looked somehow insubstantial, as though if you touched her, she might just melt away into the lumpy settee she was sat on. The flowers that were crammed into jugs and vases around the room were now wilted and dying, and the cloying smell only added to the sadness she exuded.

'How are you doing?' he asked her.

'You're the first person to ask me that,' she said. 'Isn't that funny?'

Omar shook his head.

'I remember the same,' he said. 'No one wants to face the answer.'

She nodded at him, her eyes filling with huge tears that spilled onto her cheeks unchecked. There was no vanity in grief.

'He had nowt to do with the fire, you know,' she said to him.

Some mutterings had already reached his ears about this. The local rumour mill seemed to have Brian pegged as the number-one suspect. Omar suspected it was just because Brian was 'different'. He had no expectation that the police would catch whoever had done it, or even try. He waved his hand at Valerie, as she continued.

'No, I need to tell you. I need you to know. He was with me when the fire was set. Funnily enough we'd gone to Morrisons. For a change, like. Sorry about that,' she said, as though embarrassed at their treachery in going to a supermarket.

He shook his head again. 'It doesn't matter.'

'It matters to me. It matters that you know he would never have done anything to harm you – or your boy. You were one of the only people who just accepted him as he was.'

'I knew that already, Valerie,' he said, instinctively reaching over and patting her hand. 'He was a good lad.'

'He was,' Valerie said, taking hold of his hand for a moment before patting and releasing it. 'I always knew that this might happen. That he might finally hurt himself properly. It started when he was a boy. The sadness, I mean. I just never knew how to help him.'

There was a long moment of silence.

'How do you do it?' Valerie said eventually. 'Keep going, I mean?'

Omar thought about this, letting the silence settle once more, like a light coating of snow over the room. He wanted to give her an answer that might ease her suffering but wasn't sure he had one.

'I suppose what I do is try not to think too far ahead,'

he said at last. 'If I'd considered for a second that I had to live months, or even years, without her . . .' Omar stopped for a moment and cleared his throat.

'I'm not sure I could've . . . kept going. But if I only think about the day in front of me, sometimes the hour, or even the minute, then I can do it. I can keep living.'

'I'm glad you came back,' she said, when he left.

As he walked back to the flat, he was wondering if he agreed when he spotted Ishtiaq up ahead. He was with Sharon, the two of them hand in hand, swinging their arms exaggeratedly. Sharon turned to say something to Ishtiaq, her expression serious, and Ishtiaq listened intently, using his free arm to gently move a flyaway hair from her face. The two of them seemed to glow, in contrast with the grey drabness of the street, and Omar had an overwhelming need to protect the two of them. He thought that, in that moment, no matter what happened, he was glad they had come back too, and decided that he would do whatever it took to make this place, this town, their world, safe for his son.

41

Miv

I realised I would have to get Uncle Raymond alone and somehow catch him in the act. An ideal opportunity would be when he collected all the cups and cleared up after choir – as Aunty Sylvia didn't usually come to rehearsals – but I would need help in Sharon's absence, and I wanted witnesses too. My first thought was to ask Paul, but I quickly dismissed the idea, not only because he was too sensible and mature, but because I needed girls.

At the next choir practice, I sought out two of Uncle Raymond's favourites, Linda and Gail. Both were smaller, younger-looking girls than me. Linda had long brown hair in a thick plait down to her waist, and Gail had a ballet dancer's bun and a kind of fragility to her, a smattering of freckles covering her nose. I asked them what they thought about Uncle Raymond, wondering what response I would get, given I had seen them both giggling with him at one point or another, but they went silent. They looked at each other and an unspoken agreement seemed to take place.

'I talked to my big sister about him cos he wouldn't

leave me alone,' Linda eventually said. 'She said that I mustn't let him get me on me own, and to make sure that I always had someone with me, and so I told Gail and we stick together now.'

'Why didn't you tell your mum?'

'Tell her what?' Gail jumped in. 'That we don't like a man tickling us? They'd say to stop being soft.'

I thought about my own attempt to talk to Dad and Aunty Jean about Uncle Raymond. It was hard to explain the discomfort he made us feel. What could we expect them to do about it?

'How would you feel about staying behind with him after choir if I hid?' I said. 'So that we catch him doing whatever it is he wants to do, so that we can tell somebody.'

'No way.' Linda shook her head.

'I will,' Gail said. 'I want him to stop. I can't stand him.'

With that, we agreed that after next rehearsal, Gail, as the smallest and youngest of us, would offer to help Uncle Raymond to clear up. Linda and I would leave together but would find somewhere to hide so that we could hear and hopefully see what was going on. Once he made his move we would reappear, pretending to have left something behind. We would rescue Gail and go straight to the police to tell them what had happened. From the little I knew about him, I was almost sure that Uncle Raymond would try to do something.

*

As the next choir session came to a close, we waited for everyone else to go before Linda and I locked eyes with Gail, loudly declaring that we were leaving. Once out of the main hall we stood in the corridor, listening out for what we hoped and dreaded would take place. My heart was thumping so loudly I could feel it pulsing in my ears.

'Shall I help you clear up?' we heard Gail ask, and we strained to hear Raymond reply.

'What are you two doing, loitering out here?' We jumped, automatically standing to attention as Mrs Spencer came out of the toilets and marched down the corridor towards us.

'We're, er, just waiting for our friend,' Linda said. 'She's helping to tidy up.'

'Well, why aren't you helping her? The devil makes work for idle hands. Go on. In,' she said, gesturing towards the main hall.

Both of us did as we were told. Gail was nowhere to be seen, but Raymond was sweeping the hall.

'I've recruited some young ladies to tidy up, Raymond,' said Mrs Spencer. 'Why don't you take the opportunity to leave early, get home to Sylvia, and I'll put them to work.'

Uncle Raymond eagerly did as she suggested, and Gail reappeared from the kitchen, where she had been washing up. The three of us set to work under the watchful eye of Mrs Spencer. I tried to exchange meaningful glances with the others, frustrated that my plan had come to nothing. When we eventually left, it turned out that the arrival of Mrs Spencer had not foiled our masterplan, because nothing had happened to Gail – in fact, Uncle Raymond had seemed eager to get on with the task in hand. We were confused and not sure what we were missing. We found out not long after.

A few days later, all anyone could talk about was the fact that Uncle Raymond had been arrested the day before, though no one was talking about why. It was discussed in hushed tones. The news was apparently so shocking and the gossip so rife that Mr Spencer addressed the matter in the Sunday service, at which Aunty Sylvia's flowers were noticeably absent. He now seemed as spick and span as his wife and as full of right-eousness after a short time away – 'being treated for an unknown illness' Aunty Jean had told us, with a knowing look at Dad. 'I wonder how long that will last around the communion wine,' she'd continued, with a sniff.

That week there were more people in attendance than usual and tension was in the air as they took their seats. Parents held their children's hands. Dad even came too, instead of just dropping me off as he normally did. Mr Spencer stood at the pulpit, arranging then rearranging his notes and Bible and adjusting his glasses.

'Many of you have been asking about Raymond and his recent arrest,' he said finally. 'While it would not be right to discuss the crime he has been accused of, nor speculate as to whether he is guilty of that crime or not, I will say this.' He paused for a moment, then said, his voice louder and more resolute, 'None of us had any knowledge of or suspicion about him, and the alleged crimes did not take place under this roof.'

Whispers and murmurs broke out, and as I caught Paul's eye, who was sat with Hazel across the aisle from us, I shrugged, trying to show him I knew nothing about it. But inside I felt a mixture of horrified curiosity about what had occurred, glee that I was right about Uncle Raymond and some annoyance that we were not the ones to catch him. I felt redeemed by the fact that he was definitely a bad man, and I wondered if he would be revealed as the Yorkshire Ripper. I even thought about telling Sharon – that it might make up for what had happened with Brian.

I didn't have long to wait for more information. I was getting into bed that night when Aunty Jean knocked lightly on my bedroom door. I thought it was Dad coming to say night night, and her appearance in my bedroom was so unexpected that I was momentarily speechless. She sat down on the end of my bed and picked up the Famous Five book lying beside it, flicking through it as she talked.

'Remember you asked about Raymond and whether we thought he was odd?' she said. 'Well, me and your dad were wondering . . . did he ever do owt to you?'

She continued to look at the book rather than at me.

'No,' I said, then thought about how to express what had happened. 'But he made me feel funny. Has he hurt someone?'

She finally looked at me, then back at the book, placing it carefully on my blanket.

'You know Alison Bullen from choir?'

I nodded, curling in on myself in an effort to guard against what I knew was coming.

'Well. He took her into his car and he, well, he hurt her. She's going to be OK,' she added, seeing my distress, 'but you might not see her for a bit.' She paused, then sighed. 'Promise me that if anyone ever tries to touch you, you know, in a way that's not right, you will tell us,' she said, holding my chin up and looking me straight in the eyes.

I'm sure she must have talked to me with such stern care before that moment, but that's the only time I could remember it happening. I felt like I mattered. I found myself telling her what had happened that evening and about the trap we had set for Uncle Raymond, omitting the bigger picture and the search for the Ripper. She stared at me, as if seeing me clearly for the first time.

'You worked all that out?'

'Yeah.'

'And you tried to catch him?'

'Yeah.'

She shook her head. 'I feel like I should be telling you off, but actually, good for you.'

She then settled me down to sleep with a hug followed by a peck on my forehead.

My nightmares were layered that night. I would wake up from being pursued with relief that I had been dreaming, only to realise that I was still dreaming and being pursued from a different direction. I slept unusually late that morning and was eventually woken by a light tapping on my bedroom door. Dad's face peered around it.

'Wake up, love. I need you to come downstairs, you can leave your pyjamas on,' he said.

A man and woman in police uniform were in the front room. I recognised the man, who was pacing with his hands behind his back. The woman, who was sat on the settee, patted the seat next to her and I looked at Dad, who nodded for me to sit.

'Hello,' she said. 'My name's Beverley. Constable Beverley Halliwell – I'm a policewoman.'

I nodded.

'And this is Detective Sergeant Lister.'

He looked at me and smiled briefly. To my relief, he didn't acknowledge that he knew me already.

'We're here to talk to you about Raymond.'

DS Lister sat on the armchair next to the settee and Constable Halliwell bent forward kindly so that her head was level to mine.

'We think you might be able to help us by telling us what happened that afternoon after choir.'

I sat up and slowly and carefully told them the events of that day.

'I'd been watching him. Uncle Raymond, I mean,' I said.

Constable Halliwell looked at me, clearly confused.

DS Lister's expression didn't change, his eyes intent on me.

'Why? Why were you watching him?' she asked.

I knew I couldn't tell them about the list. Not after Brian. And certainly not with Dad stood there.

'Because he made Alison cry. He tickled her when she didn't want him to,' I said, and cringed, not knowing if they would understand, but the two exchanged meaningful glances and Dad nodded encouragingly.

'And what happened then?' asked Constable Halliwell.

'Well, me and two other girls decided we might try and catch him doing . . . something . . .'

There was a silence, and I heard my dad draw a deep breath.

'So, we tried to get to be alone with him, but he left anyway . . . Did I do something wrong?' I said, my voice wobbling. If what I had done had in any way caused what had happened to Alison, I knew I wouldn't be able to live with myself. Not after Brian.

'No, love,' Dad jumped in. 'It's just that it was that night that Alison was taken. It must've been after he left early – she was in the car park, waiting for her lift.'

I shuddered. My imaginings of what might have happened to Alison were blurry and dark, like an under-developed photograph. I didn't want them to be any clearer.

I decided not to tell Sharon about what I had done, or about the police coming to the house. It felt too close to what had happened with Brian after all, even though I had been right this time. Luckily, she was so wrapped up in Ishtiaq's return that the gossip about Uncle Raymond got only cursory attention from her, and the only people that knew about my connection to it other than Dad, Aunty Jean and the police were Linda and Gail.

It wasn't until the next choir practice that I got chance to talk to them about it. I was eager to tell them about the police coming round and wanted to know if the same thing had happened to them, but before I managed to say a word Linda spoke instead.

'I told me mum what we did,' she said. 'She was really cross and said that I shouldn't have got involved.' Gail nodded beside her, their faces a mixture of seriousness and something else I couldn't quite identify. Linda took a deep breath.

'Me mum said that you're a bad influence, and that it's no surprise given what goes on at home.'

Her words came out in a rush, tripping over each other, and I realised that the expression on their faces was one of disdain. They held each other's hands tightly, their solidarity clear. I was momentarily stunned. Surely the person who was to blame was Uncle Raymond?

In the following days I waited for an announcement about Uncle Raymond's connection to the Ripper. But there was no announcement and the search for the Ripper continued.

Gail and Linda never spoke to me again.

42

Miv

My thirteenth birthday began exactly as every other day did. It was the run-up to Christmas, and I had always felt cheated to have a birthday then, my presents and celebration wrapped up into the festive season.

Mum had come home a few days before, but she felt less present than ever, and was rarely out of her room. Aunty Jean was teaching me to cook and do more around the house, which I took as a sign she might still be planning to leave us or that we might yet be moving away, though I didn't dare ask, so I made my own porridge on the stove, leaving enough for everyone else in the big copper pan, and headed off to school early.

I slowly walked to Sharon's, my thoughts ricocheting between excitement at being a teenager at last, anxiety that Aunty Jean might leave or we might move, and complicated feelings about Sharon, Ishtiaq, Paul, Brian, the Ripper and the list. I seemed to move from one emotion to another at frightening speed. Sharon was waiting for me at the end of the road, a small parcel and card in hand. I ran the final stretch to meet her.

'Happy birthday!' she called. 'I got you something I thought you'd love.'

I hurriedly opened the parcel, my smile so broad it almost hurt as I ripped the wrapping paper off to reveal a cherry-flavoured rollerball lip gloss and a bubblegum-pink blusher. I wanted to say thank you but the sob forming in my throat meant I could only nod.

Sharon nodded too. Eyes shining.

We walked and talked about trivial things, staying away from murder, fire and investigations. A fragile harmony had been restored. As we neared the school gates, Ishtiaq was waiting for Sharon as usual, but I was surprised to see Paul Ware stood there too, his eyes firmly on the book he had open. At the sight of Paul, I became hyper-alert, the volume of my voice rising as I chattered away to Sharon, and she smiled knowingly. When we reached them, both boys handed me enve-lopes at the same time.

'Jinx,' Sharon and I said, and I found myself unable to speak or move. There was an awkward silence until Sharon introduced the boys to each other. I hadn't real-ised that they'd never met.

'All right,' said Paul, peering through his ever long fringe.

'All right,' said Ishtiaq. 'Ace book,' he added, nod-ding at the cover.

'Yeah, it's brilliant.'

While they began to chat in that halting way that boys had, I looked at the title of Paul's book – *A Kestrel for a Knave* – making a note to myself to get it from the library. I turned my gaze back to them and glowed at the two of them talking.

'Aren't you going to open your cards before we go in?' Sharon said.

Ishtiaq's card was from him and Mr Bashir, each signing just their names in biro.

'Thanks, Ish,' I said, wanting to cry and not understanding why.

Opening Paul's was more challenging, given that my hands had started shaking, but I carefully prised the envelope open, making sure I kept it intact, determined to keep every part of it. He'd written just two things. *Paul* and an *x*. That *x* was worth more than any gift anyone could give me, and I stared at it as if it were an actual physical kiss.

There was a little note from Hazel in there.

Come for lunch next Sunday, it read, and when I looked up at Paul his expression was expectant.

'I'd love to,' I said, and looked down at my feet to hide the smile which threatened to take over my face.

That evening, I opened the door to the sweet smell of polish, underpinned by fresh baking, and the house, which was of course always clean and tidy, was unusually so. I walked into the kitchen, and Aunty Jean removed her apron with a flourish, revealing her best matching cardigan and skirt. 'Surprise!' she said and indicated a Victoria sponge sat on the side. It was a little wonky but had an inch-thick layer of buttercream oozing out from the middle.

'I put extra in. I know how much you like it,' she said, and without thinking I kissed her on her dry, ruddy cheek, making both her and me jump a little.

She and Dad sang a rousing 'Happy Birthday' while I blew out the candles that Dad had bought from the Co-op.

'Make a wish,' said Dad.

I remembered the wish I had made many months before at Mother Shipton's Well and wondered whether catching the Ripper was still my heart's desire or whether I wanted to wish for something closer to home. In the end I didn't wish for anything. Wishes only seemed to bring trouble.

After tea, Dad and I sat alone in the kitchen, and he gave me my present – a much coveted pair of drainpipe jeans to replace my flared ones. I jumped up, unable to contain my excitement, and was about to rush to my room to try them on when Dad announced he had something he needed to talk to me about. He seemed agitated, shifting in his chair and avoiding my eyes. I felt a wave of fear rise from the pit of my stomach, mixing with the sugar from the cake and making me feel nauseous.

'What is it?' I said, before he could say anything.

'Well, I've been offered a new job,' he said. 'A manager's job. Less hours, more money, and I'd be a proper boss, like.'

I was confused about why he would be telling me this, as though asking for permission. I shrugged, itching to get out of my chair and run upstairs to try my jeans on.

'OK?' I said, my eyes scrunching up in confusion.

'The thing is . . .' He paused, this time his eyes directly seeking mine. 'We'd have to move.'

Now I was baffled.

'Why?'

'Well, because it's not in Yorkshire.'

The words didn't seem to make sense to me. I felt unsteady and faint and wondered if I had simply misheard. After all my work on the list and the threat that had started it all, was it happening anyway?

'What?'

'The job isn't in Yorkshire. We'd need to move away to a different place. To a bigger house – a nicer one where you'd have a bigger bedroom, mind. And you'd go to a new school and make new friends,' he said, as if making new friends was a good thing.

'Why are you saying this?' I said, wanting him to unsay it.

He misunderstood and laughed.

'Well, you're officially a teenager now, and I thought I should talk to you about it, given you're almost grown up.'

'Does Mum know?' I asked, nodding in the direction of the television, in front of which she was sat silently, her only acknowledgement of my birthday being that she was dressed and downstairs.

'Aye, she does, and I think she thinks it's a good idea for all of us.'

'And Aunty Jean?'

'Hmm.' That must be what they had been arguing over.

'Just think about it,' he said.

Upstairs I sat on my bed, my body rigid with mute shock and burgeoning fury, wondering how he could have delivered such devastating news so casually. Aunty Jean had bought me *The Girls' Handbook* as my present. In the card she had written, *Now that you are becoming a young lady.* The book contained instructions on how to sew, make a bed neatly, cook various meals and look after your skin and hair. As I thumbed through it, I found it did not contain any helpful advice about what to do if your life was turned upside down.

A little while later I was curled up in bed, reading, when I heard the heavy tread of my dad on the stairs. I closed my eyes and pretended to be asleep as my bedroom door opened a crack. He stood there for a moment, and then he left, but not before he whispered, 'Happy birthday. Night night.'

43

Helen

Earlier that week, Helen had been to see Valerie Lock-wood and taken her some books to read. She'd been surprised by her eagerness to talk about Brian, his sadness and her grief, having expected the usual stoical Yorkshire response of 'I'm just getting on with things.' It had done her heart good to hear the older woman talk with such insight and affection about her son.

'He were too sensitive for this world,' she'd said. 'I always knew it. That life would be too much for him, you know?'

Helen had nodded. She did know.

While she was there, Valerie had mentioned that Omar had been to see her, and that he and Ishtiaq had moved back, and were living in a flat which was only round the corner from where she and Gary lived. A little spark of happiness was lit which warmed her as she'd walked home, making her realise just how much she'd missed him. She waited until Friday, when she knew that Gary would go to the pub after work, and decided to go and see them both.

It was freezing, the kind of cold that burrowed its

way into the body and settled into the bones, so she dressed warmly, wrapping herself up in a vest, blouse, jumper and duffel coat. Winter was her favourite season for more than one reason. She could cover the bruises and no one would look at her strangely; there would be no unspoken questions hanging in the air.

As she stepped out of the front door of the building they lived in, she shielded her face: despite the cold, the sun was blindingly bright. She struggled to focus on the car that pulled up beside her. It took the window winding down and the smoke escaping out for her to register who it was. He must have decided to come home after all.

'And where are you off to?' Gary asked.

'The shops. We . . . we need some teabags.'

'Do we? I hadn't noticed. I wouldn't want you to tire yourself out by making an unnecessary trip. Why don't you get in the car and I'll drive you?'

She had no excuse. No reason at all why she shouldn't accept the lift. He leaned across and opened the passenger door for her.

'I don't mind walking,' she said weakly. 'You know, fresh air and that?'

He didn't say a word, just carried on looking at her. She climbed into the car, almost choking on the smoke, and he drove off; the silence was like a physical entity, filling the car.

'I'm worried about you,' he said. 'Are you OK? Feeling all right?'

She nodded.

'It's just you weren't going in the right direction for the shops.'

She stiffened.

'Do you need to see the doctor? I will take you and we can talk to him together again.'

It was then she knew she was in trouble.

When they got back from the shops, he opened the flat door for her and she went into the tiny kitchen, holding on to the box of teabags, her hands shaking. She was poised. Waiting.

'If you'd carried on walking the way you were going, you might've bumped into the bloke who ran the corner shop you were so friendly with. What was his name? The P— fella?'

She took a deep breath, cringing.

'Apparently, he's living on Featherstone Place now, in one of the flats there. I mean, at least then you wouldn't have had a wasted journey.'

'Oh. Right.' Her voice was high, wavering. There was nothing she could do to stop it, even though it was giving her away with every word.

'Such a *shame* about the shop. That someone could do such a vicious thing to such a nice, nice man.'

Helen froze.

'I mean, he's one of them people who *listens*, he's so *caring.*'

He pronounced each word fully and the clarity was like a knife.

'Was it you?' she said. The words were out before she realised it, and she immediately wished she could reel them back in.

'Me? Why on earth would I do such a terrible, terrible thing? I mean, it would have to be a really good reason to do something like that. He'd have had to do something as awful as, oh, I don't know, trying it on with someone's wife.'

She swung round.

'He never did *anything* to me, except be nice, listen to me, be kind. All the things you never—'

She didn't get to finish the sentence before the first blow landed.

44

Miv

Number Eleven

I told Sharon about the move the next day. We were in her bedroom, the space as familiar to me as my own. She bombarded me with questions, and I noticed her face had turned pale and wondered if mine had when Dad had told me too.

'But where will you be moving to?' she asked. 'When? How far away is it?'

All things I had failed to ask my dad in my shock. I shrugged and mumbled that I would find out, while at the same time knowing I wouldn't ask. I didn't want to know the details. I wanted to believe it wasn't happening. Instead, I suggested that we go and visit Arthur and Jim, who we hadn't been to see for ages. They were like a hot-water bottle for the soul. The decision to visit them was a wise one. Jim opened the door with mock ceremony and announced, 'A little bird told me that a young lady we know became a teenager yesterday.'

He and Arthur launched into a tuneless rendition of 'Happy Birthday', replacing the middle with '*squashed tomatoes and stew, bread and butter in the gutter'*. They both hugged me, and Sharon squeezed in too. I was unable to stop my tears, which fell silently in the centre of their arms. I thought about all the times I had cried over the past few months and wondered when, now I was a teenager, the tears might stop.

Later that night, I was drifting off to sleep when the phone rang. Dad answered. It wasn't the first time he'd had a late-night phone call. I was instantly awake and tiptoed halfway down the stairs to listen. His voice sounded tense and strained.

'How could I tell you first? Before my own daughter?' he was saying. There was a long gap then, before he said, 'Of course I was going to talk to you about it. We knew this was going to happen one day. It were never going to last forever.'

I wanted desperately to know who was on the other side of this conversation. I strained further.

'There's summat else we need to talk about.' Even from the stairs I could hear the deep sigh as Dad said, 'They came into the depot again. The police. They wanted to talk to each one of us, ask us about our whereabouts and that.'

With a start I realised he was talking about the Ripper investigation.

'They said that they preferred to come to work as they didn't want to ask questions that might be difficult in people's homes.' He gave a short laugh. 'They said that when they have to go to people's houses, they ask for a cuppa so that the wife will go and get one. Then they can ask the questions that matter while she's not in the room.' He paused. 'The thing is, they gave me a list of dates, and they want to know what I was doing on each one. I don't know what I'm going to say.'

I couldn't contain the 'Oh' sound that escaped from me, and I held my breath immediately to check that Dad hadn't heard.

'Hold on just a minute . . . I just . . . shhh, I just need to check something.'

I half ran and half tiptoed back to bed as footsteps came down the hall.

As I lay in bed, my heart throbbed in my ears. Why would my dad be worried about what he might say to the police? Why would anyone need to be worried about that unless . . . unless?

It was unthinkable, and yet all the ways in which my dad had been acting suspiciously were now clamouring for my attention. Had I chosen to ignore them? The late-night phone calls, the creeping around at night-time and now being questioned by the police?

Should my dad be on the list?

I got the notebook out from under my bed. Sitting on the edge of it, I looked up the date and time of each of the murders and thought about all the times when Dad had gone 'for a pint' or crept out in the night. Frustratingly, while I could remember where I was when I heard the news of each murder, I had no way of knowing whether he had been in or out of the house when the actual attacks took place.

The words of George Oldfield tolled like a funeral bell in my mind: *The Ripper is someone's neighbour. He is someone's husband or son. Someone has to know him.*

What if he was someone's father? And what if that someone was me?

I went to stand up, propelled by shock, but it felt as though my legs had been taken from under me. They couldn't hold me up and I slowly slid onto the floor, curling into a ball like a hedgehog, as if doing so might keep me safe.

I slept the night there.

11. My Dad

- He's keeping secrets
- He keeps disappearing
- He's been questioned by the police
- Is he 'hiding in plain sight'?

45

Miv

The cold, fresh air of the morning seemed to bring with it a clearer state of mind. The Ripper *couldn't* be my dad. Surely, I would have known. But when I arrived home from school that day it was as though I was seeing the house for the first time.

The familiar sight of Dad's work boots, scuffed and muddy, left on the floor underneath the coats hung in the hallway, now took on a new significance. I hung my own coat up, and for the first time I noticed that there was a navy donkey jacket hung among them. I got the notebook out to write this down, and as I did so I became aware of Mum, stood in the doorway of the front room, the cup of tea in her hands shaking slightly as she trembled. It looked as if she was watching me, without seeing.

As she turned to go back into the living room, it occurred to me that maybe her silence was to do with Dad. Was that why we were leaving? Were we running away? I stood in the hallway as if rooted to the spot, my fingers and toes fizzing with fear, wondering what to do next. I desperately wanted to talk to Sharon about all of this, but it simply wasn't possible. She didn't want to know about the list any more, and what if I was wrong? It all felt too big for me.

In that moment, I yearned for my mum as she used to be in every cell of my body. How can you feel a physical ache for someone who is right there? Even though this was the last thing I could have talked to her about, I just wanted to feel her arms around me and to lose myself in the sound of her voice.

While I stood there, Mrs Andrews' face drifted into my mind, together with the offer she had made all those weeks ago. I decided that as someone with secrets of her own, she might actually listen and understand, and I could take the risk to talk to her about everything. Before I knew it, I had headed back out of the door. I hadn't thought to put my coat on, so I ran through the darkening streets to beat the biting wind, feeling my cheeks redden and my heartbeat pound in my ears.

As I neared the building I'd seen Mr and Mrs Andrews go into the day I'd been watching Uncle Raymond, my footsteps seemed to slow. Would it be all right to call in uninvited? I wondered. It was the Yorkshire way to pop in unannounced, but something told me that Mrs Andrews' home might be like my own – one with situations that she might not want any eagle-eyed visitors to see.

The door opened, making me jump back. It wasn't Mr or Mrs Andrews though, and as a man walked out, puffing on a cigarette, leaving the door wide open behind him, I realised that this was the communal entrance to a number of flats. I slipped in before the door closed, and found myself in the entrance hall of what had once been a large house. As I looked around the hallway, with its flaky paint and threadbare carpet, I counted four doors on the ground floor, and noted the flight of stairs at the far end. There were probably more flats upstairs. Set to one side of the front door there was a grey payphone with a dog-eared telephone directory on a chain hanging from the bottom of it.

Just as I was wishing I had asked the man who was leaving which flat Mrs Andrews lived in, I noticed that the nearest door had a name above a little door-bell to the right-hand side. I had only taken one step towards the door to read the name when I heard a thud, followed by a cry. It had come from upstairs, and my legs carried me up the uneven, steep stairs almost instinctively. When I reached the first flat on the left, I stared at the name *Andrews* written above the doorbell, my heart thumping as though I had run back through the streets and home again.

I wasn't sure whether to ring the bell or not. Had the thud and cry come from this flat? I crept slowly to the door and put my ear against it. Mrs Andrews was crying. The kind of hiccupy sobs that meant some-thing was very wrong. I wanted to comfort her and was about to knock on the door when I heard Mr Andrews' voice.

'Shut the fuck up.'

It wasn't loud. He didn't even sound angry. But my heart began to race even faster and I took a step back from the door, and away from him. The black eye Mrs Andrews had sported at the library floated in front of me, and I forced myself to listen again. There was another thud, this time the cry so clearly one of pain that I winced. It was followed by another, then another cry, then a sickening crack that set my teeth on edge. Every nerve in my body came alive. I knew that he was hurting her, over and over.

I ran back down the stairs and dialled 999 on the phone, my hands shaking so violently I struggled to keep my finger in the dial as I pushed it around. I held the receiver to my ear.

'You've got to help her,' I whispered into the phone at the operator who was asking me what service I wanted. 'She needs an ambulance.'

After they had taken all the details I had, I crept back up the stairs to the closed door. There was silence. I debated knocking, and innocently pretending not to have heard what I had heard. I wondered for a moment if I could have been wrong. But I knew I wasn't. In the end I left the building, stood on the other side of the road and watched as the ambulance arrived minutes later. I cried as a stretcher was brought out with Mrs Andrews on it, looking like a small child, so tiny was her body. Mr Andrews was holding her hand and stroking it, walking alongside her. As they moved her into the ambulance and he had to let go, he didn't let his eyes leave her face. For the first time in a while, I knew I had done exactly the right thing.

I got home and went immediately to call Sharon. I no longer cared whether Dad would tell me off for using the phone. 'You only left her five minutes ago and you'll see her in the morning,' he always said.

Ruby picked up the phone and said their number, sounding flustered.

'Can I talk to Sharon?' I asked.

'She's busy,' she replied.

'Oh, er, can you tell her that I called?' I said, momentarily stunned. It was so unlike Ruby to be short with me.

'Yes, I'll let her know.'

'OK then. Bye,' I said, my voice faltering.

But Ruby had already put the phone down. I stood there, dizzy, listening to the dial tone with the phone held to my ear. No one was behaving how they should be. First Dad, then Mr Andrews and now Ruby. The world felt like it was spinning away from me. Thankfully, Aunty Jean behaved exactly as I expected when she bustled in later full of the news.

'Helen Andrews is in hospital . . . she fell down the stairs and broke her arm, apparently. She'll be going to stay with Arthur and Jim for a bit when she gets out, so they can look after her while Gary's working.'

I looked at my watch. It had only been a few hours since I had called the ambulance. I was always amazed by how much gossip Aunty Jean could gather, but this was in record time. Sometimes I regretted not telling her about the list. She would never have approved of such dangerous antics, but she'd have found the Ripper in no time at all.

'I don't understand,' said Sharon, turning to face me. 'Are you sure?'

It was Saturday afternoon, and we were on our way to Arthur's to see Mrs Andrews. I had just told Sharon what had happened, and she stopped in her tracks as she tried to take it all in.

'I'm sure,' I said. 'And remember that day when we saw her black eye?'

Sharon nodded slowly, understanding dawning. 'But what were you doing there?' she asked, starting to walk again. I paused, knowing I still wasn't ready to tell her my suspicions about Dad. I still wasn't sure about them myself. It seemed impossible, and yet George Oldfield's words kept echoing in my mind: *Someone has to know him.*

'Oh, was it to do with the list?' she said, and I nodded, relieved I didn't have to answer. Neither of us said another word until we arrived at Arthur's.

Mrs Andrews was staying on a camp bed in Arthur's front room. Jim was away, visiting his children, and Arthur was bustling around the house, clearly thrilled to have his youngest daughter there, despite the circumstances. As we sat down beside the camp bed, he plumped her pillows and made sure her arm was comfortable, then went to make us drinks.

I looked at Mrs Andrews properly for the first time since we'd arrived. She was wearing a short-sleeved nightdress, covered in flowers. I suspected it had belonged to Doreen, as Mrs Andrews looked like a little girl who had raided her mum's dressing-up box, her tiny arms sticking out, twig-like. Along with her plastered arm, encased in a sling, she had bruising on the other arm, a swollen cheek and an almost purple, half-shut eye.

The conversation was stilted. I was finding it hard to think of things to say, and Sharon's usual conversational charm and confidence seemed to be eluding her.

'She's always been the same,' said Arthur, appearing in the doorway. 'Clumsy, like me. Always falling over. I managed never to break me arm though.'

He put the drinks down on a little side table.

'I'll just go and get the biscuits,' he said, disappearing into the kitchen.

'Mrs Andrews,' Sharon said, 'how did you get them bruises?'

I gasped, putting my hand over my mouth. Mrs Andrews' face paled.

'Sharon,' I said, 'you can't ask that.' I had learned from my own circumstances not to talk about things that were painful, not to bring them out into the open. It was better to pretend they weren't there.

'I can and I will,' she said. 'Mrs Andrews, how did you get them bruises?'

The silence seemed to stretch for minutes before Mrs Andrews replied.

'You know how I got them,' she said quietly. 'I fell.'

'You don't get bruises like that from falling,' Sharon said, pointing at the fingermarks, as clear as a child's nursery-school painting. 'That's someone holding on to you.'

'Yes. Yes, that's right. It's where Gary tried to save me from falling.'

The air was heavy with the weight of unsaid things.

'Mrs Andrews,' Sharon said, almost whispering, 'we know that Gary did this to you.'

She nudged me hard, in the side. I nodded.

'It was me that called for an ambulance,' I said. 'I heard what he said to you.'

A strangled sob escaped from Mrs Andrews' mouth as she could no longer hold the emotion in.

'Helen?' None of us had noticed Arthur appear at the door. The expression on his face was the same as when we had met him at the scrapyard: grey and stricken with grief. Mrs Andrews just stared at him, her face blanching with shock.

'Dad? Dad, please don't cry. He's sorry, I promise you he's sorry. He didn't mean to do it, he didn't. He'll never do it again,' she sobbed.

He moved towards her, gently wrapping her in his arms.

'Girls, do you mind leaving us?' he said, his eyes not leaving hers.

We left father and daughter in a tight embrace.

The next day was Sunday, and dinner at the Wares' house. After getting home from church that morning and getting changed, I stood in front of the mirror, appraising my reflection.

I was wearing my new drainpipe jeans, with a frilly, high-necked blouse. The blouse was the prettiest item of clothing I owned and was usually reserved for choir concerts and special occasions, but in case of any embarrassing questions from Aunty Jean or Dad, I had an excuse lined up: the choir was dress-rehearsing the Christmas concert, I would say. I hurriedly put on my duffel coat and was relieved when I managed to sneak out of the house unnoticed.

As I walked to the Wares' house, my legs felt as wobbly as a new-born deer and I realised how nervous I was with every self-conscious step. I'd not been round to Paul's since I'd followed him home months ago, and still hadn't quite got my head around his parents' living situation, so when I knocked on the door, I was momentarily surprised when DS Lister opened it. He looked different from how I'd seen him before, his jumper and jeans making him seem softer and less imposing.

'You can call me Guy,' he said. He was still very handsome, and I felt my cheeks flush. I no longer needed blusher, that was for sure. But then I noticed that Paul blushed too as he came out of his room to say hello to me, his voice stumbling over the word.

Over dinner I watched carefully how everyone behaved, wanting to fit in with these people I admired so much. They did things differently from how we did them at home. The food was served from dishes on the table and there was no bread and butter to mop up the gravy. DS Lister and Hazel drank wine instead of the mugs of tea that Mum, Dad and Aunty Jean had. I noticed with pleasure that DS Lister talked to Paul about music, his favourite subject, and let him carve the beef, treating him as though he were an adult too. He still let Hazel do all the serving and clearing away though. Maybe things weren't that different from home after all.

Paul was quiet, but Hazel kept the conversation flowing, asking everyone questions, including me, which I stuttered my way through, though no one seemed to mind or laugh at me. I was just beginning to find my feet and relax a little when, unwanted, the thought of moving away hit me like a punch in the stomach and I realised that this might be the only time I would have dinner here. I put my knife and fork down for a moment while I steadied myself, holding on to the table.

'Now, we know Paul is going to be a pop star when he's older, but I was wondering about you?' Hazel was saying when I tuned back into the conversation.

Before I could respond, DS Lister jumped in,

chuckling, as he said, 'You want to be a detective, surely? You're already doing a good job as an amateur one,' and winked at me.

'I do want to be a detective,' I said, surprised at the clarity of the words coming out of my mouth. I wasn't used to people showing an interest in me like this and had never really thought about what I wanted to do before. Paul looked at me, astonished – whether at the fact I had spoken so confidently or at my wanting to be a detective, I don't know.

'Well, here's your chance to ask Guy any questions you have,' said Hazel, nudging him. 'I'm sure he'd be happy to answer them.'

I thought about the list and how our suspicions so far had not led to catching the Ripper.

'How do you do it?' I said. 'Investigate crimes, I mean. How do you go about it?'

'Ahh, it's nowhere near as exciting as folks think from watching Z-Cars and that,' he said. 'It's more methodical, like. You have to look at every single bit of information you get in detail, without getting waylaid by emotion or what you think the answer's going to be. You can't ignore anything.'

I thought about Dad and how maybe I'd been ignoring a suspect right under my nose because I didn't want him to be the answer. I could feel the blood drain from my face, and my voice felt like it was coming from far away as I said, 'Why do you think they've not caught the Ripper yet then?'

Hazel's eyes widened, and I wondered if I had crossed the line of polite Sunday-dinner conversation.

'That's a good question,' DS Lister said, seemingly unperturbed. He took a sip of wine and leaned back in his chair for a few moments.

'Sometimes, there's so much information it's hard to make sense of it all,' he said, after a while. 'And what I said about emotion comes into it. The amount of pressure from all sides, the papers, the public, even Thatcher, means mistakes get made. People get distracted by the noise.'

On the way home I thought about what DS Lister had said. I didn't want to get waylaid by my feelings any more. No matter how difficult it might be to accept, I needed to treat my dad as we had every other suspicious thing on the list and investigate him. This meant finding out more about what he was up to and where he was going at night when he wasn't at home.

I knew that something was wrong as soon as I opened the door. Sunday evenings had a particular rhythm to them: Dad would be sat on the settee, reading the papers and listening to the radio; Aunty Jean would be humming along, with the ironing board set up, piles of fresh-smelling laundry fighting with the leftover smell of the roast dinner she'd made earlier; and Mum would be in her armchair, or upstairs in her room.

Instead of this usual scene there was silence and a

feeling of stillness, as though the house had been abandoned, like Healy Mill.

'Hello?' I called out.

The door to Aunty Jean's room was open, which was unusual. She insisted on keeping every door in the house closed, telling me and Dad off regularly by saying, 'Were you born in a barn?' then theatrically closing any door we had left ajar. I peered around it, taking in the sight in front of me, my body going cold. Her room was always immaculate, with most things hidden away from view, just like her. It had never looked lived in; it was as if she still considered herself a guest, even though she'd lived with us for a couple of years. That day, though, it was entirely emptied of any sign of her – her hairbrush and reading glasses, even the picture of Grandad, which she kept in a brass frame by her bed. I had never known him – Dad said he 'went before his time', whatever that meant, but I had looked at the photograph many times. He was stiffly upright, like Aunty Jean, and handsome, like my dad. The absence of the photograph told me she was definitely gone.

I made my way through the rest of the house, tiptoeing as if to honour the silence. There were no cooking smells in the air, and no one was downstairs, so I crept quietly up to my room, noting that the door to Mum and Dad's room was shut, meaning it was likely that Mum was in there at least.

When Dad eventually arrived back home a few hours

later, he shut the door quietly, and I watched over the banister as he closed his eyes and shook his head before calling hello. I went to the top of the stairs.

'Where's Aunty Jean gone?' I said, before he had chance to speak. I couldn't keep the note of accusation from my voice. He slumped, visibly.

'She's gone back to stay at her flat for the time being,' he said. 'What with us planning to move and that.'

I wanted to say that *I* wasn't planning to move, *he* was, but something about his beaten expression stopped me. Despite my resolution not to let my emotions get the better of me, I felt the tears prickling at my throat.

'OK,' I said, and went back to my room, listening out as he put a record on and the sounds of his favourite song, 'Leaving on a Jet Plane', filled the house.

'*Don't know when I'll be back again,*' Dad sang along with John Denver.

Sat in my room, I made a plan. I decided to follow Dad after school the next day, but as it turned out, I didn't have to wait that long. I was so consumed with my thoughts about everything that I very nearly missed the sound of him dialling the phone, long after I'd gone to bed. As I tiptoed down the stairs, I heard his voice and stopped to listen.

'I'll be there in ten minutes,' he said. While he was putting on his coat and boots, I went back to my room and pulled a coat over my pyjamas, put my pumps on and hung the ribbon with my door key on it around my neck. The front door creaked open and closed, and I quietly went down the stairs after him. By the time I gingerly opened the door and stepped outside, he was halfway down the street. I closed it, looking both ways to make sure there was no one else around.

The pale street lighting was just enough to make him visible, but I made sure to keep in the shadows as I trailed after him. My heart felt as though it had taken over my body; I could feel it beating everywhere from the tips of my toes to the top of my head. I didn't dare think about where he might be going.

The familiar streets looked eerie and menacing in the darkness. My dad's footsteps, thudding with purpose, were the only sound. I felt almost consumed with the desire to call out to him and pushed my hand into my mouth to stop myself. At the end of our road, he turned left and I ran the rest of the way up the street – grateful for the soft soles of my pumps – to make sure I didn't lose sight of him.

He was getting further in the distance as I rounded the corner, but I watched as he turned right this time, into a small snicket I was familiar with as it was the way to Sharon's. I sprinted to it, just in time to see him turning left at the end. As I made my way to the bottom of the snicket and peered out, a realisation started to dawn on me: was he was going to Sharon's house?

Confused, my feet trod a path I could have walked

blindfold. I took a sharp breath in every time he came to a junction, half hoping he would choose a different direction, but every step took us closer to my best friend's house. When we got to the corner of her street, I hung back slightly, concealed by the bushes, and watched as my dad knocked on Sharon's front door and Ruby came to answer it. They looked around as she ushered him into the house, and as he passed her his lips met hers.

The meaning of the kiss was unmistakable.

I stood there for what felt like hours, my heart thumping in my ears as I tried to make sense of what I'd seen. Eventually I turned round and trudged slowly home, my mind swirling. Events, conversations and phone calls started to become clearer in my brain like a scene in a snow globe when the snowflakes settle.

I wondered if Sharon knew. Their house was bigger than ours, and Sharon's bedroom was part of an extension built over the garage. Could she really have not heard my dad creeping in and out of their house while Malcolm was away?

What should I do now?

The tears began as I opened our front door. My relief that Dad wasn't the Ripper dissolved into a white-hot rage that bubbled up inside me as I thought about what he'd done. How could he?

I reached for a scarf of his which was hung on the coat hooks and took it to my bedroom with me. Taking off my coat and pumps, I climbed back into bed with the scarf, held it to my face and took a deep breath in. It smelled just like him. Musky sweat, Swarfega and a warm woodiness peculiar to him.

Or at least the person I thought he was.

I realised I no longer knew him at all.

46

Miv

Number Twelve

I lay awake into the early hours of the following morning, my mind churning as I went over the events of the last few months. I'd wanted to do good, but it seemed I had only succeeded in breaking things. Now I was holding on to a huge secret about Dad and Ruby. I thought about Sharon, and knew I didn't want to break her heart the way mine was slowly cracking.

I made a decision. A plan unfurled. I was going to finish looking into whatever was left on the list, then stop, whether I found the Ripper or not. It was time to focus on real life. I got my notebook out and read through everything, shuddering as I was reminded of what had happened, my eyes filling with tears as I read about Brian. Everything seemed to have been completed, apart from one thing.

When morning came – though it was impossible to tell from the darkness outside – I felt strangely detached, as though I was floating. It was like watching the world on our black-and-white television with the volume and contrast turned down. Over breakfast I watched Mum, who had got up early for a change, making herself a cup of tea, while in a different place entirely in her mind. Now I knew exactly what that felt like. Dad rushed through the kitchen, late for work, and grabbed a piece of toast.

'Bye,' he said through a buttery mouthful as I tried to look at him objectively. I'd always known that he was considered handsome. I'd overheard Valerie Lockwood once saying that he reminded her of the dark-haired one in *The Dukes of Hazzard*, and I found it funny the way that women sometimes changed their behaviour around him. I'd just never imagined him acting on that. I could hardly bring myself to speak to him, and I just about managed to say 'bye' back.

A frost clung to the ground, glistening cold and white on the grey streets and buildings as I walked round to Sharon's, hoping I wouldn't see Ruby when I got there. I knocked on the door and was both surprised and relieved that there was no answer. I had forgotten that Sharon was going to the dentist that morning and would be late for school. The relief almost made me cry.

As I carried on to school, the cold entered my veins and sent a surge of energy and determination through my body. I outlined my loose plan to myself. After school I would head to Healy Mill – we'd been interrupted the last time we were there – and investigate it thoroughly, ghost or no ghost. Everything else on the list had been crossed off. This was the one thing left.

12. The Mill

- It's the last thing left on the list

47

Miv

The day passed in a haze, and more than once I had to be nudged into consciousness by Ishtiaq when a teacher called my name, though they all sounded like the teacher on *Charlie Brown* that day. I opened my schoolbooks and pretended to work, but the words danced in front of my eyes.

At lunchtime I went to the school canteen and took my tray over to a quiet corner where I could sit alone, Sharon not being back yet. I could barely swallow my food and was lost in my thoughts when Paul came and joined me. 'You all right?' he said, staring at me so closely I had to look down. I nodded, and he ate his food in silence while I pushed mine around my plate.

'What you doing after school? Shall we go to choir together? Hang out before?' he said, as I got up to leave.

'Er, I'm busy with Sharon,' I said. In my determination to finish what I'd started, I had forgotten about choir; I wasn't going to change direction now. I would have to go afterwards, maybe be late. Paul looked so disappointed I almost laughed. I had spent years wanting to be noticed and cared about, but today of all days it was the last thing I needed.

At home time I told Sharon that I had arranged to meet Paul before choir, so I was going straight to the church, and set off to the mill. I passed the now-derelict corner shop, still a shell of a building with *Danger – Do Not Enter* signs all over it. Images of Mr Bashir's smiling face and Ishtiaq's refined features came to mind, and a lump formed in my throat as I realised how much I had missed them while they were in Bradford.

This thought opened the floodgates, and with each step I was assaulted with images of the people we had met while investigating the list, clicking through my mind as if they were on a View-Master. Hazel Ware, DS Lister, Arthur, Jim, Mrs Andrews. There was a part of me that felt sad it would be over, despite knowing what it had caused. What I had caused. I stopped for a moment and a familiar car drew up beside me. The passenger window was slowly being wound down by someone leaning over from the driver's seat, and the opened window released a cloud of pungent cigarette smoke.

'Hello, hello, hello,' said a voice I recognised as Mr Andrews. I started to walk again, fixing my eyes on the pavement ahead of me as the car kept pace, crawling along the street.

'What's the matter?' His voice, trying for lightness, sounded like one of the mean boys at school. 'I hear you and your mate have been interfering again. I thought we had an understanding. I must've been mistaken.'

I almost started to defend our actions. Then I thought about what he had done to Mrs Andrews, and I stopped. The car stopped too, and I looked inside. Mr Andrews had lost the slightly rogue-like handsomeness he'd once had, and just looked dishevelled. Like he'd not washed or slept for days.

'You hurt her,' I said, my voice quiet but resolute.

'What?' he said.

'You hurt her!' I repeated. Louder.

'Get in,' he said, opening the car door. 'Let's have a chat. We could go and see my lovely lady wife. She'll tell you it wasn't me. I was just heading round there now. It's time she came home. We don't want her getting spoiled by Arthur and Jim now, do we?'

I looked into the bright blue-green eyes that I had once thought of as twinkling and saw the cold glint of steel in them. Some sort of survival instinct kicked in and I started to run towards a nearby snicket. As soon as I realised he wasn't following me I slowed and took stock. The same survival instinct warned me that Mrs Andrews was in danger.

For a moment I considered going round to warn Arthur and Mrs Andrews, but realised that if I did that, there would be no going to the mill. Instead, I ran to the nearest call box. Pulling out a 2p piece from my purse and putting it into the slot, I dialled Arthur's number.

'Arthur?' I said as he picked up the phone, before he could even say anything.

'Aye, love. Are you all right?' He must have recognised my voice, and the urgent, frightened tone in it, straight away.

'Yes, no, it's just I saw Mr Andrews.'

'Where was he?'

'He's on his way round. He said he's coming to get Helen.'

'Thanks, love. I'm hanging up now and calling t'police. You did right ringing.'

He put the phone down and I slowly breathed out, like a sigh. I felt a renewed resolution. Maybe I had just saved Mrs Andrews. Maybe I still had it in me to do something good. I carried on to Healy Mill.

48

Omar

As always, he thought about what Rizwana would have done had she heard about Helen's injuries. She would have made food, taken it round there and talked to her, woman to woman. So he made biryani and gulab jamun, and put the curry and little balls into separate Tupperware containers, and the syrup in a cup with clingfilm over it, ready to take round to Arthur's. At the last moment he wrapped some chapattis up in foil to take too.

He'd heard about her fall down the stairs from more than one person, the story told with knowing nods and eyes occasionally raised to the ceiling, the gestures a replacement for unsaid things. On his way round to the house, he decided he was going to talk to Helen about it, no matter how awkward it was. He also wanted to discuss the now fully shaven-headed boys with Arthur, determined to find out if they were the arsonists. According to Ishtiaq and the girls, they had been responsible for the attack on Arthur. No more of this Yorkshire way of talking around the things that mattered, of carrying on regardless.

Jim opened the door and let him in. He'd only met Jim once or twice when he'd come into the shop, and he'd been perfectly pleasant and chatty then, but today he looked downcast, as were his eyes, which would not meet Omar's.

'Come through,' he said, and nothing else.

Helen looked up when he walked into the room, and he tried not to show his shock at her appearance. She too seemed different with him, her voice wavering as she said hello, her eyes flitting from him to Jim, then at the floor. It was understandable though, he thought, given what she had been through. Helen indicated the armchair next to her with a nod of her head and he sat down, perched on the edge, no longer sure about the wisdom of coming here, as well as overcome with a shyness he couldn't fully explain. He held out the carrier bag, as if that might provide something to talk about.

'I brought you this,' he said. 'I made it.' He felt embarrassed, realising that he sounded like a child.

Jim stepped forward to take the bag. It looked like he was grateful for something to do, to get him out of the room with its awkward atmosphere, and he took the bag into the kitchen.

'Is Arthur here?' asked Omar.

'He's out back with the pigeons,' Helen said. She smiled and rolled her eyes, and he felt himself relax a little, her smile so familiar.

'So, how are you?' he asked.

She nodded, her lips tightly together, and he could see she was trying not to cry. He wanted to hold her, to tell her it was all going to be OK, that he wouldn't let this happen again. 'Look, it's none of my business,' he said instead, 'but—'

Before he could finish, a sob broke out from her with such force he jumped.

'I know you know. You've always known.'

He nodded slowly.

'Dad knows now too. And we're, well, I'm going to go to the police.'

He nodded again, not sure what to say.

'The thing is,' she said, 'there's something more.'

'More?' he said, surprised.

She sighed and looked up to the ceiling, and he let her draw strength from wherever she was seeking it. 'I think' – her voice was overtaken by another sob – 'I think he had something to do with the fire.'

The words didn't register for a moment. Instead, he just stared at her.

'What did you say?' he said, shaking his head as though to clear his ears out.

'I think he had something to do with the fire. He said some things to me, while he was doing this.' She looked down at her broken arm. 'And I think he might've been the one who did it. I was going to tell you. I mean, I'm going to tell the police too. I just needed to get my head right first. And talk to me dad.'

Omar was standing before he'd even registered that

he'd moved at all. The rage was a fierce burning in his hands and legs.

'Omar?'

Arthur appeared at the door, having come in from the garden. He looked at Helen.

'You've told him then?' he said, his expression resigned.

At that moment the phone rang, and Arthur walked to the hallway to answer it.

'Aye, love. Are you all right?' he said, followed by 'Where was he?'

'Thanks, love,' he said a moment later. 'I'm hanging up now and calling t'police. You did right ringing.'

He put the phone down and immediately picked it up again, closing the door between the hallway and the front room. There was only one reason Omar could think of for ringing the police, and he clenched his fists in anticipation. After a while, Arthur came back in and sat down, Jim following him.

'Gary's on his way here,' he said. 'But I've rung the police. I've told them about you' – he nodded at Helen – 'and about the shop, and that you're here.' His gaze moved to Omar.

The four of them sat in the front room, waiting, the only sound the loud tick of a grandfather clock in the hallway. Helen eventually broke the silence saying, 'I'm so sorry, Omar.'

He looked at her, incredulous. How could she even think he would blame her?

'What are you on about? You've nothing to be sorry for.'

'Well, that I didn't tell you straight away. That I didn't call the police straight away.'

He shook his head at her. He'd long mistrusted the police. For different reasons maybe, or perhaps they were the same. He knew how it felt not to matter to them. He also knew what it was like, to be paralysed by feelings so strong that you didn't know what to do with them. All this he wanted to say, but for once words had left him. Instead, he reached out and touched her hand, removing it immediately, not sure whether that was the right thing to do.

Jim made them what seemed like endless cups of tea while they waited. When the doorbell rang and the sound of a fist thudded on the door, more than an hour had passed. Omar was up before anyone could stop him, flinging the door wide to the sight of a uniformed police officer.

'Did you get him?' he asked.

The policeman looked confused.

'Can we come in and talk for a moment?' he said.

And Omar knew this wasn't about Gary.

49
Miv

Snow began to fall heavily, and as I walked up to Healy Mill, I stopped for a moment to stare at the scene. It looked like a Victorian Christmas card. Of course, underneath the clean white layer lay grime and dereliction, but in that moment the mill looked almost picturesque. Entering was trickier than last time. The door that had been propped open before was now locked, so I made my way around the building, looking for routes in, when I spotted that a board covering a large, low window on the ground floor was only partially secured, making it possible to slide through.

I recalled instantly how scary it had been on our first visit, though that felt like a mere echo now. The dank atmosphere seemed even denser in the winter cold. The air inside felt solid, like something you could take a bite of and taste. I switched my torch on and looked around nervously, keeping my eyes out for anything suspicious.

Spotting what I thought was a small side room at the end of the ground floor, I made my way over there, carefully treading across the dusty wooden floorboards, avoiding the large pillars and abandoned machinery. At one point I stopped sharp. There was a large sports bag in the corner of the room.

I tiptoed over, as though somehow the bag might hear me, and slowly unzipped it. Inside were leaflets, piles of them, along with various lengths and widths of metal piping. As I stared at them all, a memory came to me. Arthur had said that piping had been taken from Howden's Scrapyard the night he was attacked.

I stood and contemplated what this might mean. The leaflets and piping could have been left here a long time ago, but if they weren't, then there was a chance that I could find myself in unwanted company. I shuddered, tears threatening to override the adrenaline for the first time since I'd left school that day. I decided to search the top floor first, hoping that if anyone came for the bag, they wouldn't get that far. I automatically reached for Sharon's hand, grasping only empty, cold air.

We'd not made it as far as the top floor when we had come before, so hadn't known that it consisted of a series of rooms, one with a substantial amount of old furniture in it – shelves, tables, chairs – and I made a note of it. There were now at least places to hide if need be and a door to the roof that would take me to the staircase down the outside of the building if I needed to escape. With that settled, I began to make my way through the rest of the rooms, all of which were as grimy and neglected as the first one, the dust making me cough.

I wasn't sure how much time had passed before I heard the voices. The realisation that other people were in the mill came as a shock and I switched off the torch and crept to the door of the room I was in, to make sure. I thought they must be on the floor below, but it was difficult to tell because of the way sound travelled in this old building. I didn't move, and waited till my eyes and ears adjusted and whoever it was began talking again, in the hope that I could figure out how many of them there were and their location.

There was a shout which sounded like, 'Over here!'

My heart landed in my throat as I realised that the voice was getting closer. I slowly and carefully tiptoed back to the room with the door leading to the roof, climbing the short flight of stairs that led up there, with the intention of using the wrought-iron staircase on the outside to get back down again.

The cold air hit me first. The evening was settling in, and the dark sky was filled with stars glittering icily down on the now snow-covered flat roof of the mill. It might have been a beautiful sight if I wasn't so eager to get away.

I lit up the roof with my torch, seeking out the entrance to the staircase, only to discover it had been blocked off with large, hammered-in planks of wood. I sank down beside them, ignoring the wet floor and hugging my knees to me, praying that whoever was in the mill wouldn't come onto the roof. There was nowhere to hide out here, and no way down apart from the way I had come.

I was just beginning to breathe again when the door to the roof opened and a boy's head emerged, his dark, floppy hair falling into his eyes.

'She's here!' he shouted back to his companions.

It was Paul.

I slowly stood up, looking at his face, unable to find any words. He kept his eyes on me too, neither of us breaking contact until two other people appeared. Sharon and Ishtiaq. Sharon ran straight to me, holding me tight as I stood there, arms rigid to my sides at first, then melting into her embrace.

'We were worried,' she said. 'Me and Ishtiaq bumped into Paul after school and realised that you'd not told us the truth. I couldn't understand where you would've gone, but then I realised. I knew you'd be here, I knew it.' She held me even closer. 'It's the only thing left on the list,' she whispered.

'I'm so glad we've found you,' Ishtiaq said.

Paul had stepped back when Sharon ran to me, but he stepped forward now.

'I knew there was something wrong when I saw you earlier,' he said. 'Why did you lie?'

I shook my head. There was too much to say and no words with which to say it.

'We should go home,' said Sharon. 'It's getting late.'

'Can we lie here – just for a minute?' I said. 'Watch the stars?'

They all looked at each other, their faces seeming to say, *indulge her*, and we lay down together like snow angels, looking up into the sky, all four of us. Our heads were touching, damp hair intermingling in the snow, and the only sounds were of our breathing. I felt the warmth of acceptance override the cold.

After a while Sharon spoke into the silence.

'We should go back to the list,' she said firmly. 'You never know, we might catch him.'

'I'll help,' said Ishtiaq.

'And me,' added Paul. Sharon had clearly told them both what we'd been up to.

We were all sitting now, and I was about to tell them about my latest investigations when the sound of a door banging nearby silenced us.

'Shhh, did you hear that?' Paul said.

'Hear what?' Sharon and I said together, then laughed at each other.

'Jinx.'

When the door to the roof opened, we all turned towards it to see two more familiar people appear. Richard Collier and Neil Callaghan.

'What you lot up to?' Richard said. 'Some sort of weirdos' gathering?' He walked towards us with a swagger, one arm behind his back. Neil trailed behind him, a sneer on his face. Paul got to his feet, brushing down his jeans, and Ishtiaq stood too, then the rest of us.

'Fuck off,' Paul said, to my shock. I had never imagined him swearing.

Richard laughed, a low chuckle that stirred something deep inside me. The same instinct that had told me to run from Mr Andrews kicked in. In that moment I knew he was dangerous, far more than I had recognised before.

'Come on. Let's go,' I said.

'Yeah, go on, back to your sad little lives,' Richard said. 'Oh, except this one.'

He pointed to Sharon with the arm he had been holding behind him. In it was a large metal pipe. Sharon looked down at her shoes.

'She can stay here and hang out with us.'

At the sight of the weapon, we all stood stock-still, the fog of our breathing floating off into the sky.

'Yeah. Oh, on second thoughts though, have you been snogging him?' said Neil, his sneer changing to a look of distaste. He nodded his head towards Ishtiaq. 'I don't want to catch anything.'

'I bet she has. Slag,' said Richard, staring at Sharon with half-closed eyes.

'It's none of your business,' Sharon replied and took a step towards the door. Richard pushed her back using the pipe.

'Don't. You. Touch. Her!' said a voice I barely recognised as Ishtiaq's. I looked to see his hands quivering – with fear or rage, I wasn't sure. Paul stepped in front of him. Richard threw his head back and laughed.

'And what exactly do you think *you* are going to do to stop me?'

He moved forward and touched Sharon's hair with his free hand, running his fingers through it.

'You should stay with your own kind.' He spat the words at her. 'You're wasted on the likes of him.'

Sharon shook her head to remove his hand and took a step backwards. As Paul and Ishtiaq both stepped forward, Richard pushed Paul out of the way and shoved Ishtiaq hard. He stumbled, going over on his ankle, and reached out to steady himself. Paul and I went to grab him. While we did so, Richard reached for Sharon again. She jerked back as he took another step towards her, holding the pipe up, threateningly. Things seemed to move in slow motion as Ishtiaq, having regained his balance, tried to get hold of the pipe, but Richard swung it at us wildly, causing us all to step back and duck out of the way, arms over our heads.

I hadn't noticed how close we all were to the edge until Ishtiaq's strangled cry rang out, cutting through me.

'No!' he screamed, and I realised that Sharon wasn't there any more. For a moment we all stood there in shock, then I heard a voice scream, 'Sharon!' over and over again, and it took me a few seconds to realise it was mine.

*

Ishtiaq was by my side, holding on to me, as I looked over the edge of the roof. With shaking hands, my heart thumping in my chest, I shone my torch into the darkness. Nothing.

'We need to get down there,' Paul said. I moved the torch in his direction, his pale face reflecting the light back. Even Neil and Richard looked frozen in horror.

All of us headed from the roof back down the stairs inside the mill, using the torch to light the way. I almost tripped over my feet in my haste and slowly lost the feeling in both my hands and feet, from the cold, or shock, or both. The only sound was our footsteps echoing on the metal staircase and my heartbeat pounding in my ears. At the bottom, Richard and Neil ran off into the night while Ishtiaq, Paul and I paused for a moment at the entrance to the mill.

'Wait here,' said Paul, panting as he caught his breath. 'Me and Ishtiaq will go.'

'No!' I said. 'No, no, no, no, no,' and I headed out first into the dark, swinging the torch in all directions. We slowly made our way around the mill, calling Sharon's name as we went, my voice becoming hoarse in the freezing air. I sensed rather than saw her body as we came upon it, and slowed. It looked like her, but at the same time it didn't, like a mannequin or a waxwork.

Her face seemed peaceful except for the blood running out of her nose and the grey colour of her skin.

'I'm going to get help,' Paul said, and ran off into the

night, the thud of his shoes disappearing until we were left in stunned silence.

I knelt beside my friend, holding her pale hand in mine. The cold of the night seeped into my very bones and my teeth began to chatter so hard it felt like my whole body was vibrating.

'She'll catch her death,' I said. 'We should cover her up.'

I wriggled out of my coat and placed it over Sharon.

'There, there,' I said, patting her shoulder as if talking to one of the dolls we used to play with only a short while ago. 'You know how Aunty Jean always tells us to keep warm.'

I got up again, looking at her face, tracing every familiar freckle, while Ishtiaq stood beside me, shoulder to shoulder, the only sound his quiet, heartbroken sobs. I held his hand in mine.

It seemed like a lifetime before Paul came back with Hazel and DS Lister, closely followed by the sirens of an ambulance. Hazel enveloped us all in a hug, tears streaming down her face, which was stricken with shock.

DS Lister spoke on the radio in his car and drove us to the hospital behind the ambulance, putting his own blue light on the roof – something that would have been beyond exciting were it not for the horror of the situation. Within what felt like moments, I found myself sitting on a hard plastic chair in a waiting room, staring at people coming and going. I watched as Ruby ran in, closely followed by Malcolm. I watched as Mr Bashir came in and took Ish into his arms.

I only noticed I was shaking uncontrollably when a blanket was placed around my shoulders and my stunned brain registered an unexpected voice.

'Miv. My Miv. My poor Mavis. They said a girl had been hurt. And I thought it was you. I thought it was you.'

As she reached for me, the tears finally began to fall. It was my mum.

50

Helen

At the news there had been an accident at the mill and Ishtiaq was involved, but unhurt as far as the police were aware, Omar had crumpled, the rage of the previous minutes gone in an instant. Jim had immediately moved into practical mode, working out the best way to go to the hospital to manage the falling snow, while Helen held Omar's hand briefly, wanting to say so many things to him, hoping to convey multitudes through her touch, mostly the hope that his boy would be OK.

Jim had insisted that he drive Omar to the hospital, and they left almost immediately. After a few minutes of fretting anxiously together, Helen and Arthur decided to go too, and she slowly eased herself from the camp bed and let her dad dress her, like he had when she was a child, while she cried.

'They'll be all right,' said Arthur, once they were in the car, moving his hand from the gearstick to pat her knee. Her thoughts immediately went back to the children. She wondered who had been hurt, and how.

By the time they got to Casualty, Omar and Ishtiaq were sat next to each other on orange plastic chairs,

Ishtiaq's arms around his father, clinging to him. You couldn't tell where one of them started and the other began. Her body almost sagged with relief for Omar. He looked up, and they exchanged the smallest of smiles.

Jim was on one side of them and Miv was on the other. Her dad and Jean were there too, and Helen nodded at them. Jean's eyes were glassy with tears as she nodded back. Miv was sitting next to someone she didn't recognise, a pale, slight woman who looked as though she hadn't seen sunlight in a long time and would simply float away if you tried to touch her. The woman was stroking Miv's hair. She looked up and their eyes locked.

Was this Miv's mum?

There was no sign of Sharon or her mum and dad. Presumably they were all together somewhere. Helen shuddered, not wanting to imagine where. A nurse appeared briefly in the doorway, as if looking for someone, her eyes tired and her skin grey. Miv and Ishtiaq jumped straight up.

'How is she?'

'Is there news?'

The nurse looked at them both, compassion in her pained, weary expression.

'I'm so sorry, my loves.'

It was then that Miv began to scream.

The Aftermath

I

Miv

I don't remember that Christmas.

The weeks following the funeral were a blur. I was carried through it all by Mum. It was as if she were a light that had been switched back on; she handled all the practicalities of life as though she had never been away. The light dimmed every now and then, and I would sense it, my grief replaced by worry, but it never lasted long. She was back to stay.

Aunty Jean carried Ruby.

One of the few times I emerged from my own darkness was to watch the three of them make rounds and rounds of potted-meat sandwiches for after the funeral, quietly murmuring to each other as they did so, working as the most unexpected team, united in their grief and pain. As I watched Aunty Jean, it felt as if her hard edges had softened.

Mr Spencer led the service, and I was momentarily shocked to see him up there, in the pulpit. It was as though I'd forgotten him, and the fact he had been on the list, entirely. He talked about Sharon with such love and tenderness, almost as if he had been her best friend, but I wasn't cross about that. It felt like that was how it should be.

I watched him closely while he spoke. He was stood straight, his eyes clear and bright; he looked almost handsome. I remembered how he had been that day after the concert, and I realised, just for a moment, that it was possible to come back from the worst thing that had ever happened to you.

After the funeral it felt as though life had shrunk, so that I could only see the day in front of me, and sometimes only the hour. That's how I got through it. One of the things I found the hardest to reconcile was the fact that in death I could see Sharon more clearly than in life, and I wanted more than anything to tell her the things I appreciated now, which I hadn't then: her choosing to be my friend, when others didn't; her strength of character in standing up for others, like Stephen and Ish; her joining me in almost every scheme I thought up, whether she wanted to or not, just to support me.

But above all I realised that I had always thought of her as a 'type' – one of the pretty ones, one of the lucky ones – and she was so much more than that. She was like the kaleidoscope she once got for her birthday that we played with endlessly: she was full of colour, never stuck in one pattern, always moving, changing, but always landing somewhere beautiful.

The thing about having a best friend is that some-where along the line they become part of you. Like an extra limb. And if you lose them, you have to learn to do everything again without that limb. Learning to live without Sharon was like learning to walk again. Some days I couldn't get up. Some days I could take a few steps. Some days I kept losing my balance and falling, falling, falling. But before I knew it, those days had turned into weeks and then months.

And life carried on.

At school I began to observe Ish, like I had before. I watched him in class, where sometimes he would sit, reading or writing, with tears streaming down his face. And he would talk about her all the time, to anyone who would listen.

'How do you know to do that?' I asked him.

'I've done it before,' he said.

'What?'

'Had my heart broken and lived.'

I learned how to grieve from him.

Every weekend he and Paul would come and call for me, whether I was up for going out or not. Most days we would wrap ourselves in coats and scarves and gloves and just walk the streets of our town, as though we could walk away the grief. I took them to all the places the list had taken us, and told them the stories of our investigations. It helped.

I started to write some of the stories down, along with my memories of Sharon, until one day I went to Mr Bashir's new shop and bought another notebook. This one was prettier than the last one, the cover made up of swirls and patterns in a kaleidoscope of colours; it reminded me of Sharon. In my best writing I began a new list. A list of wonderful things. A list of all the things I loved about her and all the adventures we had had, and all the ways in which I could be more like her. When I got to how she'd helped Stephen Crowther with his running, my words blurred into the patterns and swirls on the cover as my tears dropped onto the page.

I put my first notebook away and kept this new one by my side.

There were days when the guilt was too much.

No one said it to me, but I knew they must be thinking it was all my fault. *I* thought it was all my fault. All that time I had been avoiding feeling the pain on my doorstep by looking for someone else, and I had ended up bringing pain to our doorstep in the worst of ways.

On those days, I took life a minute at a time and curled up in my bed, alternating between reading and sleeping. On those days, I would sometimes wake up and find Dad sat on my dressing-table chair, reading the paper or drinking a cup of tea. He was around all the time then. He'd stopped going to the pub. One day, I woke up to him sat there, and before I knew it the words came out of my mouth.

'Dad,' I said. 'Can I talk to you about something? Something important?'

He looked at me, surprised. 'Course you can. What's the matter?'

'I saw you. The night before it happened. With Ruby.'

His face turned pale, then quickly flushed a deep red.

'I don't know what you mean,' he said. 'When? What are you on about?'

I could hear a tinge of anger that almost made me stop for fear of stoking it, but then I recalled how resolute Sharon had been when tackling me about the list. I wasn't going to back down.

'Dad. There's no point pretending. I saw you. I saw you kiss her. Properly, like. Not like friends.' I could feel my voice rising with anger and tried to breathe deeply.

He looked closely at me. I could almost see him weighing up his options and deciding how to counter my accusation. I stared back, unflinching on the outside, quivering on the inside, picturing Sharon's face in my mind as I did so. He was starting to deflate like a balloon, his face crumpling. He tried again.

'I don't know what you think you saw, but you've made a mistake,' he insisted, his eyes flitting from one side of the room to the other.

'Dad. You know I'm not a kid any more,' I said wearily. 'I know about you and Ruby. I know that you used to call her in the night. I know that you didn't go to the pub when you said you did.' My voice began to quiver with the fury I was trying to hide, and I felt my face flush.

He sighed deeply and we sat in silence for a moment before he said, 'It's over. I promise you it's over, and I'm sorry.' He looked at me, eyes shining with unshed tears.

I was stunned. I wasn't sure what I had expected, but it wasn't this.

'Why?' I said, my tears flowing freely now. 'Why did you do it?'

'You're too young to understand yet,' he said. 'But one day you might. Your mum. Being like she was. It was hard. It's not an excuse.' He shook his head. 'I shouldn't be talking to you about this. But it's over. I promise you, love. It ended that night.'

'Did it end because of . . . because of what happened though?' I couldn't yet say the words *Sharon's death* out loud. Dad looked at me squarely in the eyes.

'No, Miv. That night – when you saw us – I'd gone there to say goodbye. It had nothing to do with what happened to Sharon.' He took a deep breath before he carried on. 'I don't know if you can understand, but the police had been to work, to ask about the Ripper and that. And I . . . well . . . I lied to them. I couldn't tell them where I was. And then I couldn't live with the lie. It made me no better than him.'

I wanted to say something, but the words were stuck in my throat.

'And I didn't want to be that person. That man,' he said, his glistening eyes reflecting mine. 'I wanted to be someone you, your mum and Aunty Jean could be proud of.'

And in that moment, knowing what I had done to make the same people proud of me, I understood.

*

On 20 August 1980, Marguerite Walls, a 47-year-old in the Department of Education and Science in Pudsey, Leeds, was working late. On her way home, she was hit on the back of the head with a hammer and garrotted with a rope. Her body was found by gardeners the next day.

On 17 November 1980, twenty-year-old Jacqueline Hill was murdered. She was a student who had been attending a seminar and was on her way home to her halls of residence in Leeds when she was hit on the back of the head with a hammer, dragged onto some waste ground and stabbed repeatedly with a screwdriver. Her body was discovered the next morning by a shop manager on his way to work.

She was the Ripper's thirteenth and final victim.

I didn't know. All I could think about then was Sharon. The news of their murders didn't penetrate the unrelenting waves of my grief.

2

Austin

The first time he saw Ruby on her own after the funeral was on Marian's instructions, which made it all the more excruciating. He'd resisted going round there, but she had insisted, saying, 'Go and fix Ruby's broken fridge door. She's got enough to worry about without having to sort that out too.'

'What about Malcolm?' he'd asked, to which his wife had shrugged and raised her eyes to heaven. 'OK then,' he said, rolling his eyes back at her and smiling, surprised at how quickly they had reverted to the shorthand of a long-married couple, almost as though the last few years had not happened. But not quite.

He chose to walk, treading the familiar route with an almost overwhelming sense of nostalgia, despite the last time being only months ago. His mouth grew increasingly dry and his heart pounded so loudly he wondered if the people in the street could hear it. It was almost like it had been the first time, but for very different reasons. It all felt like a lifetime ago, or another lifetime altogether.

She opened the door as he walked up the drive –

Marian must have called to say he was on his way – giving him a glimpse of her hollowed-out eyes and gaunt frame before she turned round and went back into the house, leaving it open for him to follow. He found her sat at the kitchen table, hands around an almost finished mug of tea, staring at the contents, and he sat down next to her.

'I take it Malcolm isn't at home?' He knew he was stating the obvious, but how to even begin the conversation?

'No.' Her voice was flat, without emotion. 'He's gone back to work. He thinks it's best we go back to normal.' She gave a mirthless laugh.

'How are you?' he asked, his voice cracking as he said the words. He stared at her properly for the first time. She looked as though the last few months had decimated her, and he wanted to hold her, all the while knowing that he, of all people, could offer her no comfort. She sighed.

'I don't even know how to start to answer that question.' Her eyes met his as she looked up from the long-cold tea and said, 'You know, I used to look at Marian and judge her, think she should pull herself together. I thought that justified what we did.'

There was a long pause and he held his breath.

'Now I realise she had no choice. That sometimes things happen that you can't just get over or snap out of straight away. Now I just feel admiration that she kept going, kept living until she was ready to come out of it.'

Austin felt as if he was staggering from the sickening punch of guilt that assailed him, along with the knowledge that Ruby was right.

'I'm so sorry,' he said, not knowing exactly which part of it he was apologising for. Maybe all of it.

'What for, Austin? What's done is done. And of the two of us, you did the right thing in the end.'

He went to shake his head, but she stopped him and put her hand on his arm.

'It's OK, Austin. It really is.'

She made him a cup of tea while he fixed the fridge door and she left him to it, disappearing upstairs. He could hear her faintly, moving around in Sharon's room. He had just finished when she appeared again, holding a small, scruffy ragdoll in her hands.

'It's for Miv,' she said, holding it out to him. 'I haven't been able to . . .' She stopped for a moment, as if summoning the strength for the rest of the words. 'I haven't been able to go through her things yet, but I thought Miv might like this.' He nodded, unable to speak, and reached out for the doll, but Ruby pulled it back. 'Maybe I'll hold on to it a bit longer,' she said, and so he reached out for both of them, holding her and the doll briefly in his arms. And then he left.

When he arrived home, the house was alive with the women in his life. Jean and Marian were gently arguing over something in the kitchen while Miv was reading on the settee, her face grave with concentration. He was struck by how much she was beginning to look like Marian. Tall, pale, refined features, her movements no longer awkward but graceful. As he watched her, he was overcome with the emotion he hadn't been able to access in Ruby's house. Miv sensed his presence and looked up at him, nose crinkling with concern.

'You all right, Dad?'

He wanted to go and kiss her on the forehead, as he had done for many years every night before bed, but she somehow felt too old now. She'd seen too much. Instead, he sat on the settee next to her, and was surprised when she closed her book and curled into him, tucking her legs under her. So he kissed her on the forehead anyway.

3

Miv

It was just after the first anniversary of the accident. That's what I called it in my head. To name it was too much. We had tentatively celebrated Christmas, though the guilt at having a nice time and presents still tapped me on the shoulder every now and again, reminding me of what I'd lost. In those moments I had taken to talking to Sharon, telling her all about my days and how much I missed her.

We hadn't moved away in the end. Aunty Jean lived with us all the time now, and that day in early January, Dad was in the front room, putting some shelves together for her books. I could hear the occasional curse as he hit his hand with the hammer, along with the low hum of the television. Mum was baking and Aunty Jean was out doing her 'visits' with the various people she needed to look after now she didn't have us to take care of. At least there were plenty of those in our town – Ruby, Valerie, even Arthur now that Helen and Mr Bashir were going out with each other. They tried to include Arthur in everything, they told me, but he would insist, 'You young 'uns need time on your own.' I was in my bedroom and stopped for a moment to listen, comforted by the ordinariness of the domestic sounds. It had taken a while for me to notice them again, to realise that normal life carried on, even in the face of unimaginable loss.

On the anniversary, Ruby had given me some of Sharon's things that she thought I might like, and I was now sorting through them. I had thought she might blame me for what had happened, but instead she seemed to want me to be happy. Being surrounded by Sharon's things made me feel close to her, and as I held her ageing Holly Hobbie doll to my nose – the only relic of the girl I first met – I imagined I could smell her scent, a mix of Impulse body spray and Imperial Leather soap, even though that was impossible, it had been too long. I looked at my new list too. It helped me to keep her with me, and to try to be more like she had been.

There was a triumphant shout from downstairs.

'Bloody hellfire! They've caught the bugger.'

Both Mum and I joined Dad, who was staring at the television, hammer still in his hand. Against the backdrop of a photograph of a man with dark hair, dark eyes and a moustache, the newsreader announced, '*On the second of January uniformed police constables from the South Yorkshire police force were conducting a routine traffic stop in the red-light district of Sheffield and came across a man with false number plates on his car. He was accompanied by a woman. The man in the car, Peter Sutcliffe, was arrested. During the course of his police interview he confessed and was charged with the murder of thirteen women.'*

As the words slowly sank in, I realised that Dad was still stood frozen, watching the screen closely.

'What's the matter, Dad?'

'I know him,' Dad said, his voice trembling. 'I bloody know him. He worked at our place. I saw him every single day.'

He sank into a nearby chair.

'He watched all that business with Jim Jameson, and he never gave a thing away.'

I began to cry. 'You knew him all the time and yet we still didn't catch him and now Sharon's gone and it's all my fault.'

Mum pulled me into her arms as I sobbed uncontrollably. 'Shhh, Miv. It's OK, it's OK.'

Dad turned the television off and switched the radio on as Mum stroked my hair. Her hands were shaking as she did so. Mum and I sat down on the settee and as she slowly rocked me calm, she began to hum. I realised that on the radio Johnny Cash was singing 'You Are My Sunshine'.

'I'm so sorry, Sharon,' I whispered quietly. I thought about Brian and said a little prayer for him too.

Dad watched the two of us. I saw his eyes fill up with tears as he said to Mum, 'I think it's time.'

'Yes, it's time,' Mum replied.

Dad switched the radio off and joined us on the

settee. I stayed with my head on Mum's lap, my heart thumping loudly. Dad began.

'Miv, love, we've something to tell you.'

Mum took a deep, shaky breath in and placed her free hand on his arm, the other still stroking my hair. 'No, Austin, I need to do this.' She paused, sitting up straight.

'You know how I was poorly for all that time,' she said.

'Yes,' I whispered.

'Well. Something happened to me. Something . . . something very painful.'

She took another deep breath while Dad took her hand and enveloped it in his. When the words came out, they were in a sort of staccato.

'It still feels like it were yesterday, but it's years ago now, I suppose. I'd gone out, only to the bingo with some friends. But it was the first time I'd been out for the evening without you and your dad for a long, long time. I had a drink or two. Hardly anything really, but I felt all tipsy. I'd not had a drink for a long time either. When I left to come home, I decided to walk, to clear my head, like. And. Well. I was attacked.'

We sat in silence while I took this in, listening to my mum's quiet breathing as I did so, my heart continuing to thump, in time with her own. I could feel it through her lap, her hand.

'I got away. But only after. And then when I got home – well, you know what happened the next day.'

'But why?'

'Because I felt like it was my fault. That I shouldn't have been out. That I shouldn't have had a drink. That I shouldn't have walked home on me own at night,' said Mum.

'Then, when I saw what the police were saying about the women the Ripper had attacked, and how they seemed to think it were their fault, I decided I could never report it.'

I suddenly registered the implications of this.

'Was it . . . was it him?' I asked, breathlessly.

'I don't know, love,' she said. 'All I know is that I blamed myself. And the more I blamed myself, the more I shut down. When I realised I couldn't talk about it, I stopped talking at all.' She paused, looking at me, her face seeking something that I didn't know how to give out loud. 'I don't expect you to understand properly yet, love,' she said eventually, 'but me and your dad, we thought we owed it to you to tell you. To explain. You've been through so much.'

I held on to her tightly, pressing myself into her, as if to make us one. We would be stronger as one. And inside, I understood more than she knew.

'Do you think it was my fault?' she asked quietly.

I jerked up out of her arms. '*No!*'

'Then can you see it wasn't your fault that Sharon was killed, Miv? It was the fault of the man who attacked me, just as it was the fault of the boy who attacked Sharon.'

I nodded. Understanding glimmered through the haze of grief. I thought about Sharon. About her loyalty to those she loved. About her righteous anger and her straightforwardness in expressing it. About how she helped me with the list because she loved me and wanted me to be happy. I thought about all those things, and all the things I'd written down about her on my new list, and knew I wanted to do better, to be better. Maybe Mum was right. Maybe it wasn't my fault, but maybe I could still try and be a better person anyway.

By the time the telephone rang hours later, I was back in my room.

'Miv,' I heard from downstairs, 'it's for you. It's Paul.' I ran down and picked up the phone, standing awkwardly in the hallway, suddenly shy at having a conversation with him when Mum and Dad were so close by. I pulled both cord and phone to the stairs, in an attempt at privacy, then Dad smiled, winked at me and closed the door.

'Ey up?' Paul said. He was becoming a proper Yorkshireman, all his public-school poshness disappearing.

'Ey up,' I said, while listening to bangs and crashes in the background.

'Sorry about the noise,' he continued. Paul and Ishtiaq had started a band. Many of our conversations now revolved around their ambitions of Top 40 stardom. Their friendship reminded me of the good bits of mine and Sharon's.

'Ish is practising his drum solo, though I don't think

Mr Bashir is happy and he's already cross with us that we won't just play Elton John songs.'

I laughed, imagining it. The new shop had a garage attached where the boys rehearsed, and Mr Bashir would shake his head and roll his eyes a lot, but never stopped them.

'Say hi from me.'

'I will. Anyway, I was ringing to say we need you for the vocals. After the trial is finished.'

In a macabre echo of the boys involved in the death of John Harris, Richard had eventually been charged with manslaughter. The trial would be starting soon, and we were to be witnesses. DS Lister said he would look after us. It was to take place in the same court where Uncle Raymond had been convicted, and Mr Andrews would go for his trial too. There was at least some measure of peace in the fact that although we hadn't found the Ripper, we had helped bring Mr Andrews and Uncle Raymond to justice. I wondered if it was the same court where the Ripper's trial would be.

'Are you coming on Saturday? Shall I come and call for you?' Paul said.

'Of course you can,' I said, blushing.

On the first Saturday of every month, we all went to Valerie Lockwood's house for tea. It was a group for people who had lost someone, though we never called it that, it was never named, it just sort of happened. Mr Bashir and Valerie had set it up, and between them would make a buffet. It was funny to see samosas and potted-meat sandwiches side by side on Valerie's sideboard together with Mr Bashir's tape recorder, which he would bring to play Elton John songs while everyone got their food. Although it was held at Valerie's house, it was Mr Bashir who took the lead, and we followed him. We all brought pictures and mementos of the people we'd lost, and we talked about our memories and feelings about them.

'A bunch of lost souls,' Aunty Jean called us. She never came.

That Saturday morning Paul called for me early, and we held hands as we dawdled over to Thorncliffe Road. Arthur would always nudge me when he saw us together. 'Love's young dream,' he'd say, and Paul and I would both blush; we still did that a lot. At Valerie's the door was already open, and the noise of people chattering and the clatter of cups was audible from the street. As well as Valerie and Mr Bashir, all the usual people were there: Helen – I had got used to calling her that – Ishtiaq, Ruby, Mr Ware (who never said anything but seemed different from the teacher I remembered, sadder, and softer somehow), Arthur and Jim. Sometimes there were more people than there were seats and Mr Bashir used to go and get spare deckchairs from Arthur's.

After all the 'how do's and 'ey up's were done, we all took our seats in the cramped front room. Every possible surface had someone sat on it, from the battered settee to the kitchen chairs and a crocheted pouffe which Mr Bashir perched on. Paul, Ishtiaq and I sat on the swirly-carpeted floor. Ishtiaq had two spoons he'd taken from the buffet table and was tapping out the rhythm of a song idea he'd had on his knees, when he sensed the whole room had gone silent and his dad was staring at him to be quiet. He put the spoons down and we swallowed our giggles. Then, as Mr Bashir was doing the welcomes, a face appeared in the doorway, and an 'oh' escaped out of my mouth before I could stop it.

Aunty Jean looked more buttoned up and hesitant than I had ever seen her, in her best bottle-green winter coat, clutching her stiff, brown, rectangular handbag in front of her, like the Queen. Only her eyes gave away her need to be there, swimming as they were with tears. Mr Bashir's voice faded into the background as I watched Jim get up and offer Aunty Jean his chair. She smiled at him, pink-cheeked, and sat down, putting her handbag down too, but not before she had pulled out a grainy black-and-white photograph, which she clutched in place of the bag. From where I was sat, I recognised it immediately. It was the photo of my grandad that sat next to her bed. It occurred to me then that maybe Aunty Jean knew what it felt like to lose someone too. Which meant that she could heal. Just like I could. She looked up and our eyes met. We smiled and held each other's gaze until she was distracted by Jim, now stood behind her, who reached out and squeezed her shoulder. Aunty Jean's hand sought his, and she patted it and left it there.

When my turn came, I spoke about Sharon and the things we had done together, making everyone smile and shake their heads with sad fondness. I glanced at Ruby and was momentarily silenced by the look of love in her eyes. Somehow she had become more loving and forgiving, not less. In general, I was getting much better at talking about it. The words kept Sharon alive somehow. I also wrote down everything I remembered in my new notebook, and after a while the words began to take the shape of this story, the one I am telling now, the story of the list of suspicious things, but more than that. The story of a friendship.

The next afternoon I went to Mr Bashir's shop. It was bigger than the old one, as was the living space at the back, which was helpful not only because of the frequent band rehearsals but because Helen had practically moved in – much to the horror, or more accurately the delight, of the town gossips. Helen was behind the counter serving customers as I walked in.

'Do you want to stay for your tea?' she asked, and I was tempted for a moment. Between them, Mr Bashir and Helen made the best food, and I hadn't spent time with Ishtiaq on his own for a while – he was perpetually behind his drum kit or with Paul – but I shook my head. I had a mission to complete. I was going to get copies of all the latest newspapers so I could cut out the articles about the capture of Peter Sutcliffe for the old notebook. It felt right to finally complete it.

I arrived home shortly afterwards to the sound of laughter. I followed the noise to the kitchen. Dad was sat at the yellow Formica table, chuckling and waving his hands in front of his face. 'Don't bring me into it!' he said, while Mum and Aunty Jean stood over a large bowl debating how much brandy to put in the trifle they were making to celebrate Arthur's upcoming birthday. Ingredients were spilled haphazardly on every surface, including Mum's cheeks. She was a 'creative' – meaning messy – cook, but we all knew Aunty Jean would have everything cleaned and sorted as soon as she was done, leaving no evidence that any activity had even taken place. 'We make an excellent team, Jean,' Mum would declare frequently.

To my surprise, Aunty Jean was the one arguing noisily for more brandy. 'If we've learned owt from t'last few years, it's to take our joy where we can,' she said. We all stopped for a second, letting the moment be, then Mum swept her arms around me, one hand still holding a wooden spoon filled with custard, firing yellow blobs in all directions so Dad had to duck. She kissed me on the cheek and, as she did so, Aunty Jean sneaked another spoonful of brandy into the bowl and winked at me.

My heart full, I left them to it and went up to my bedroom. It took me a while to find it, but eventually I pulled the old notebook out of the shoebox where it sat in my wardrobe. As I did so, a photograph fell from its leaves. It was the one I had taken in the park, with Ishtiaq's camera. It was of Sharon and Ishtiaq, sat on the checked blanket. Her head was thrown back as she laughed at something, her blonde curls framing her face, and Ishtiaq was laughing too, his eyes pinned on her, and only her. She looked so beautiful and happy my heart ached for her, but I felt glad she had been so loved, and knew my life was better for having known her. I put the photo on my wall and closed the note-book for the final time.

Everything had been crossed off the list.

Acknowledgements

My heart feels so full. This is a list of THE BEST people, all of whom have played a part in getting this book to where it is. I am so grateful for all of you.

I have to begin with the woman who changed my life with one email. Nelle Andrew, you are the agent of my dreams. Thank you for taking a chance on me and for your tireless work and support – especially in our year of 'writing bootcamp'. Thank you also to Charlotte Bowerman and Alexandra Cliff at RML for everything.

Then there is literary legend Venetia Butterfield ('you had me at Swarfega') who has made this whole process a dream, and whose editorial insight, along with that of the gorgeous Ailah Ahmed, took the book to the next level. You have both been incredible and I have learned so much from you.

Charlotte Bush, with whom I had my first ever 'publishing lunch' and who dispelled my nerves with her warmth and support. You've been a constant throughout, as well as a total expert in your field. Thank you.

Thank you to the wider team at Hutchinson Heinemann, especially Isabelle Ralphs, Claire Bush and Rebecca Ikin, who have shown such generosity along with their brilliance in working on *TLOST*, and Joanna Taylor for her endless patience with my 'final' versions!

I have felt surrounded by the most fantastic team of people from the very beginning. Special shout-out to Ceara Elliot for the incredible cover illustration.

Then there are the folks who cheered me on while the book was being written. You'll never know how much your support and belief in this book has meant to me:

My wonderful, generous friend Maddy Howlett, who read the first ever sentences and told me I was onto something. I am so grateful.

Cathi Unsworth, my tutor at Curtis Brown Creative, who really made me think, 'I can do this.'

Simon Ings, who wrote my first feedback report and whose words gave me the courage to keep going.

The whole team at CBC (especially Anna Davis), who do such brilliant work supporting writers, and who have helped me so much.

Hannah Luckett and Laina West, who I met on one of those CBC courses and who were my first ever writing group – two talented women whose feedback helped shape the book and whose friendship is so special.

My beta-readers Maddy Howlett, Jo Tomlinson, Sarah Lawton, Neerja Muncaster and Tiffany Sharp, who were all so fantastic with their praise and thorough with their feedback.

Phil Daoust at the *Guardian*, who commissioned my first ever published piece of writing and who told me I could be a writer, at a time when I really didn't know what on earth the future held – that meant so much to me – and the uber-talented writer Joanna Cannon, who read that first piece and said the same. You both changed my life without knowing.

I'm also so grateful to the amazing editor Phoebe Morgan, who generously offered a competition on Twitter – the prize of which was a review of the first three chapters of a book – which I won! Your feedback was invaluable.

Then there is the incredible Marian Keyes, whose work has always inspired me since *Rachel's Holiday* changed my life, but who also gave me the courage to write by saying something along the lines of, 'I think prolific readers can learn to write by osmosis' at the launch of *Grown Ups*. That struck a chord with me, and I began this book the very next day.

Thank you to Will Dean (not just for the Tuva books, of which I am a massive fan!), whose YouTube videos about the writing and querying process were so informative and generous.

There are also some very talented people whose work helped my research for this book enormously:

Liza Williams, whose BAFTA-winning documentary series *The Yorkshire Ripper Files* I have watched numerous times, and who reminded me of that time in my life so viscerally I had to write about it.

M.Y. Alam, whose book *Made in Bradford* contains transcripts of interviews with Bradford-based Pakistani men post the 2001 riots, was hugely insightful, as was *Muslim, Actually* by Tawseef Khan.

Jane Roberts, whose website 'Past to Present Genealogy' provided some invaluable information about the mills of West Yorkshire, including the story of John

Harris (the location and details of which I have slightly changed to suit my fictional ends!).

Then there are the people I've met through writing who have supported me throughout whether knowingly or not:

Sophie Hannah, whose Dream Author programme keeps me sane, and whose expert coaching helped enormously at crucial moments, and Johanna Spiers, who I met on my first Dream Author retreat and has become a lovely writing friend.

All the writers, readers and book bloggers on Twitter who share my obsession with books and who have followed my journey and allowed me to follow theirs. Special mention here to Chloe Timms (and her Thursday night writing group) and Julie Owen Moylan, who have supported me and provided advice and friendship.

Dr Jo Nadin, my PhD supervisor, friend and talented author, thank you for your wise counsel.

The team at Taunton Waterstones (especially 'DAVE!') for listening to me talk endlessly about 'my book' (and other books too).

Georgia and Karen from *My Favourite Murder* podcast, whose 'hometown' concept was what sparked this whole thing off.

Elizabeth Day, you will never know how much your *How to Fail* podcast kept me going (and still does). I will always be a super-fan.

Hattie Crissell, whose podcast *In Writing* held my hand throughout my first draft.

I also need to thank John El-Mokadem, whose

question 'Do you want to be doing this any more?' led to my leaving corporate life and writing. You changed the course of my life. And Michael Neill, who saved me when I had a wobble.

Thank you to my family, who have inspired so much of this book (including the names!), especially my dad, whose experience inspired the book, and big sister, Susan, who teaches me to live in the moment.

Thank you also to my chosen family:

The Barkers (especially Adele and Herbie), whose constant grounded 'practical' love (and house rental) meant this book got written. Get that blue plaque ordered!

Glamorous Helen Smith, whose friendship and support right from the beginning has meant SO much, and with whom I have the best weekends!

Maddy Howlett (again!), Faye Andrews and Olivia Sharp (the IC), with whom I realised I could climb mountains and run marathons. Special mention here to Faye's family, 'The Andrewses', who are the opposite of the Andrews family in the book, especially Veronica. You have always exemplified what love is.

My friends Sophi Bruce, Emma Canter, Sharpie, 'cousin' Chloe Haines, Amanda Gee and Peggy 'Pegmina' Shaw, whose love and acceptance kept me going WAY before this book was a twinkle in my eye.

And finally, this book is for Rachel, Guy, Eva and Hugo Farley, without whose love and support it would not have been written, and Sam, my oldest friend, who always, always has a room ready for me.

Remembering the Victims

Wilma McCann, 28, died 30 October 1975
Emily Jackson, 42, died 20 January 1976
Irene Richardson, 28, died 5 February 1977
Patricia Atkinson, 32, died 23 April 1977
Jayne MacDonald, 16, died 26 June 1977
Jean Jordan, 20, died 1 October 1977
Yvonne Pearson, 21, died 21 January 1978
Helen Rytka, 18, died 31 January 1978
Vera Millward, 40, died 16 May 1978
Josephine Whitaker, 19, died 4 April 1979
Barbara Leach, 20, died 2 September 1979
Marguerite Walls, 47, died 20 August 1980
Jacqueline Hill, 20, died 17 November 1980

Q&A with Jennie Godfrey

Many of the themes explored in *The List of Suspicious Things* are as relevant today as they were in the 1970s. How much do you think life has changed, and in what ways has it remained the same?

As well as wanting to reflect the societal realities of the time and place, it was really important for me that readers experienced the light and shade of 'real life' through the novel and its characters. Life isn't binary. It's a mixture of happy, sad, hilariously funny, hard work, loss, abundance, love, luck (or lack of) and more, sometimes all in the space of twenty-four hours. Humour, for me, is a really important element of life, and the thing that has saved me on so many occasions. I hope the novel feels true, and that it makes people laugh as well as cry.

Although the novel covers some serious topics, it also contains a lot of humour. How did you get the balance right?

The thing I hope people take away from the novel is hope. Terrible things can and do happen in the world, but through resilience, love and community, the human spirit continues. I wrote the book during lockdown, and I distinctly remember the feelings associated with those early days, when we didn't know what was happening, or going to happen, with Covid 19. It was scary, and (dare I say the word!) unprecedented. But I also remember coming home from a 'designated walk' and finding cake made by my neighbours in my porch. I remember teaching my godchildren over Zoom, to give their frazzled mum a break every day, and I remember shopping rotas for the elderly in my local village. There was something about that time that brought out the best in (I would argue most) people.

Would you describe *The List of Suspicious Things* as a crime novel or something else? Did you set out to write in any particular genre?

As a reader I tend towards crime. I love a good thriller, police procedural, whodunnit or true-crime story. When I started writing *The List of Suspicious Things* I thought it was going to be a crime story, but the novel had other ideas! I used to wonder what writers were talking about when they said that their characters had a life of their own, but now I understand, because the characters felt as though they had their own stories to tell, whether I liked it or not, and so I let them. I now think of the novel as 'book group fiction' – that's the label I think best describes it – but I am equally happy with however the reader experiences it!

Who was your favourite character to write and why? Do you miss any of them?

I'm not sure I am supposed to say I have a favourite character (isn't it similar to having a favourite child?!) but in truth I do; it is Omar, and I miss him very much. For me, Omar is the heart of the book, and represents authenticity and kindness, which are the values most important to me. He is probably the character I spent the most time on in terms of research (given his background and circumstances are different to mine) so I got to know him incredibly well through that process too. I also adore Aunty Jean (who is based on my own aunty), and now I feel as though I am going to list all of the characters, so I will stop there.

Reader Reviews

'An incredible story. The characters warmed my heart'

'What a brilliant book. It made me smile'

'Loved every moment of this story. It comes highly recommended'

'Jennie Godfrey is a brilliant, genius, author extraordinaire'

'A book that stays with you for a long time'

'*The List of Suspicious Things* blows my mind. It is absolutely stunning. From the first page of this book, right until the last page, I was completely obsessed'

'Blew me away with how gorgeous it was'

'Wow! This book has me hooked! I was up reading until 4am'

'Love this. So many twists and turns. It had me hooked and I loved the characters'

'So far my book of the year!'

'One of the best books I've read in a long time'

'A real page-turner with some brilliant
characters and a great plot'

'Once I got started, I kept on reading to the end –
yet another up-all-nighter'

'This is exceptional. I loved every page'

'What an incredible debut'

'I simply couldn't stop reading'

'Heartbreaking and heartwarming at the same time'

'I was in tears more than once whilst reading
this book. I loved this'

'This has to be one of the best books
I have read. The characters will stay with me.
A simply wonderful story'

'Funny, poignant, sad and clever. Brilliant'

'Will stay with me forever'

'A fabulous read. I was enthralled from start
to finish. Not to be missed'

'What a brilliant read. I was engrossed from the first page and could not put it down until I was finished'

'Godfrey's writing is nothing short of beautiful'

'An absolutely brilliant book. The characters all felt like my friends. It felt like home. It will stay with me for a long time'

'Just read it – you won't regret it'

'Such a lovely book about friendship and relationships, intriguing and thrilling too. I absolutely loved this book and have given it to many friends as a gift'

'I absolutely loved *The List of Suspicious Things*! What a heartwarming and moving tale from start to finish. The characters were brilliantly drawn, the setting and time period was rich and well-wrought, and the story was intriguing. I'll definitely recommend this'

'What a brilliant book! The nostalgia made me smile as I also grew up in the 80s, and I related to so many cultural references'

'A delightful masterpiece that deserves high praise. The book perfectly captures the perspective of its young protagonist, drawing readers into her world with remarkable authenticity'

'Absolutely loved this book. So many reasons.
It was just brilliant, I was truly absorbed
from the very first page'

'I loved every page. I'm a nostalgia junky at the
best of times, but this novel made it all the
more enjoyable. What an incredible debut.
Read it now. Not a moment to waste'

'I actually had to double check that it actually was a
debut . . . it utterly hooked me from the very start'

'Funny, sad, poignant and oh so clever'

'Heartwrenching, brave and unexpected. I'll be
recommending this to everyone I know!'

'Will stay with me forever. Emotions that
I did not even know that I had surfaced.
A brilliant well written book'

'Wow wow wow. All the rave reviews are
worth it, Jennie Godfrey has written something
so wonderfully captivating and real'

'What a beautifully written book – one that
I will not forget for a while'

'This is a really special book and I can't recommend it strongly enough'

'Wow! I absolutely loved this. I can't believe it's a debut. It's just brilliant. It's funny, sad, poignant and uplifting'